THE PRINCE'S Consort

ANTONIA AQUILANTE

DREAMSPINNER
PRESS

Published by

DREAMSPINNER PRESS

5032 Capital Circle SW, Suite 2, PMB# 279, Tallahassee, FL 32305-7886 USA
www.dreamspinnerpress.com

The Prince's Consort
© 2015 Antonia Aquilante.

Cover Art
© 2015 Anne Cain.
annecain.art@gmail.com
Cover content is for illustrative purposes only and any person depicted on the cover is a model.

ISBN: 978-1-63476-301-1
Digital ISBN: 978-1-63476-302-8
Library of Congress Control Number: 2015945181
First Edition October 2015

Printed in the United States of America
(∞)
This paper meets the requirements of
ANSI/NISO Z39.48-1992 (Permanence of Paper).

To my mother, Patricia, for everything you do and especially for believing even when I didn't. I love you.

CHAPTER 1

AMORY GIGGLED as he and Tristan practically fell through the garden gate. He slapped a hand over his mouth, but Tristan must not have heard. If he had, he would have teased without mercy, as was his right as Amory's closest friend. But Tristan just tugged him along, barely giving him a chance to latch the gate behind them so the lock spell would reengage.

All morning Amory had noticed Tristan's high spirits, which were unusual as Tristan was usually the more focused one in classes. But when Amory asked him what was going on, Tristan only shrugged. Maybe it was the weather. All of Jumelle seemed livelier now that the warmth of spring burst over the city. The walled garden was blooming, giving them plenty of dense foliage to duck behind.

He let Tristan pull him down the stone path to a secluded corner of the garden shaded by large trees. With a wicked grin, Tristan turned and pushed him back against a sturdy tree. Before Amory could say a word, Tristan sealed his mouth over Amory's in a breath-stealing kiss.

The kiss wasn't a surprise, not then. They had been kissing a lot over the past year or so. The first time had been a surprise, even for Tristan who seemed shocked at his own actions. Amory never thought his friend would want to kiss him. He hadn't thought Tristan saw him that way, saw men that way at all. Their first kiss had been tentative and awkward. They had gotten better at it quickly.

Much better.

He moaned into the kiss and pulled Tristan closer, urging him to settle his weight against Amory, relishing the feel of Tristan's firm body against his, even as it pushed him into rough tree bark. But who cared about tree bark when Tristan was kissing him as if he wanted to consume him? Deep and passionate, with tongues tangling and teeth nipping. Yes, they had definitely gotten better with all the practice.

"Tris," he gasped when Tristan pulled back. He wasn't done with that kiss. But Tristan said nothing, just began kissing along the line of Amory's jaw. The light little kisses made him shiver and stifle another moan. Though they were in a back corner, away from the house, they were still in his family's garden. He didn't want anyone finding them. They should go somewhere else, but then a nip to his earlobe made him shudder, and a nuzzling kiss under his ear drove the thought right out of his head.

He grabbed the back of Tristan's neck and pulled his lips back to Amory's own for another kiss. Tristan's slightly larger frame still pressed him into the tree, but Amory took control of the kiss, deepening it and exploring Tristan's mouth with his tongue. He nearly laughed when Tristan whimpered, loving that he could provoke such a reaction in the other man. Tristan pulled back with a gasp, and they leaned there together, panting.

"I love kissing you," Tristan gasped.

A burst of relief filled Amory's chest. Tristan hadn't said he loved Amory. Tristan was his best friend, but even with all the kissing, Amory wasn't in love with him. "Me too."

Tristan grinned and dropped a quick kiss on Amory's lips. "I want to do more."

"M-more?" His cheeks heated at the stutter.

Tristan grinned and kissed him again. "Yep. More."

Amory's nerves didn't abate at the confirmation, though he wasn't sure where they came from. In all the time since that first awkward moment, they hadn't done anything but kiss. Oh, they touched a little, but never on bare skin and never below the waist. They'd never discussed the concept of "more" before.

The idea did intrigue him. It wasn't as if he hadn't thought about what it would be like—he had. But imagining it and doing it were two separate things, and the idea of doing more with Tristan made him vaguely uncomfortable. He wasn't sure why. They were best friends, and they'd come that far. There was no reason not to go a little further.

Tristan watched him, his blue eyes intense and a little quizzical. How long had Amory stood there, not saying anything? He smiled past his nerves. "Like what?"

Tristan grinned, slow and wicked, and reached out to unfasten Amory's breeches without a word. Before Amory could protest, before he could decide whether he wanted to protest, Tristan had his hand inside Amory's breeches, gripping him and beginning a tight, slow stroke. The feel of another man's hand on him for the first time stole his breath, and when he got it back, it was only to moan.

Tristan's grin widened at the sound, and his hand sped up, working Amory faster. After a few moments standing there, struggling to breathe, he realized he wasn't doing anything for Tristan. He scrambled to unfasten Tristan's breeches with fumbling fingers as Tristan whispered encouragement. Finally, Amory wrapped his hand around Tristan's hard member, and began to stroke him in time with Tristan's strokes. It felt awkward at first, different from touching himself yet not that different, but Tristan didn't voice any objections.

"Yes, yes, yes. Amory," Tristan gasped into Amory's ear.

It didn't last long. Amory might have been embarrassed at how quickly he found his release if Tristan didn't finish just as fast, spilling over Amory's hand, and collapsing against him. He was glad of the tree at his back, rough bark and all, because his wobbly knees didn't have a chance of holding the both of them up.

He didn't know what to think about what they'd done. He'd enjoyed it, but the uncomfortable feeling still plagued him. Before he could begin to think about it, Tristan was chuckling, low at first, quiet in Amory's ear, his body shaking against Amory's chest. Tristan pulled back enough to look at him. His eyes sparkled with happiness, and Amory's laughter bubbled up to join his friend's.

The laughter eased the way as they fumbled for handkerchiefs, cleaned themselves up, and neatened their clothes again. Then they leaned against each other and the tree, still laughing a little. It was Amory who moved for another kiss. Both of them were grinning when their lips met, and they couldn't seem to stop laughing as they kissed, as they kept kissing. But the laughter was soft and light, like the kisses, and Amory relaxed into them, wrapping his arms around Tristan. Telling himself he would think about everything later.

"Good afternoon, brother."

The unexpected voice and its snide tone had Amory jerking away from the kiss, the back of his head thunking into the tree trunk behind him. Tristan jumped back, separating them much more effectively. Amory almost wished he hadn't. The short distance between them seemed like a vast gulf, and Amory felt very alone as he straightened away from the tree and turned to face his older brother.

Alban's handsome face was twisted in a sneer even more disgusted than the one he habitually wore when looking at Amory. He studied Amory and Tristan in silence while Amory struggled not to squirm. No use saying anything to Alban, he knew from bitter experience.

"Now I know why you wanted no part of that pretty little maid last week," Alban said, disdain dripping from each word. "You're more of a disappointment than I thought. Worthless. How are you my brother?"

With a shake of his head, Alban turned and strode away, likely heading directly for the house. Amory remained frozen for a long moment, not even blinking.

"He's going to tell your father." Tristan's voice was flat, so different from its usual exuberant, almost musical quality. The shock of it broke Amory's paralysis, and Amory turned to face him. Tristan was still staring at where Alban had stood.

"Yes, he is." Amory ran a shaking hand through his hair and slumped back against the tree. Alban hadn't hit him, which was a pleasant surprise, but the consequences were still going to be bad. How would his father react? With disappointment, certainly, but that was nothing new. Most likely with anger as well. However disgusted Alban was, their father would be ten times more so.

"Do you think they'll tell my father?" Tristan turned fear-filled blue eyes on Amory.

"Tris." Amory reached out. He couldn't bear seeing him so afraid, and though he couldn't say much to reassure him, he couldn't stand by while Tristan was upset either.

But he stepped out of Amory's reach. "Do you?"

Amory tried to hold back a flinch. "I don't know."

Tristan groaned and scrubbed his hands over his face. "He can't. I don't know what my father will do if he finds out I prefer men. I'm his oldest son. I'm supposed to take over for him in the business, get married. Have sons to take over the family business after me."

"You can still do that. All right, the children part would be difficult, but you can still take over the family business." He didn't bother mentioning that Tristan had four younger brothers. Surely at least one of them would have children someday who could inherit the family's business if Tristan never had any of his own and his father insisted on an heir of their blood. But Tristan took his responsibilities as first son seriously. Too seriously. He wouldn't want to hear that at the moment.

"Not if he disowns me."

"Now you're being dramatic. Preferring men is not illegal. It's not wrong. Your father loves you. He's proud of you, and you'll be the same son he's proud of after he finds out."

"You don't know that, Amory."

No, he didn't. But Tristan had a better chance of everything working out fine than Amory did. Tristan's father was proud of his accomplishments, which was more than Amory could say.

"I don't know, but I believe it will be all right. Don't borrow trouble. My father and brother might be too busy killing me to remember to tell your father."

Tristan huffed out a half laugh and whacked him on the shoulder. "Don't joke about that."

"Who's joking?" Amory smiled crookedly. "Seriously, though, I do think everything will be all right with your father." He took Tristan's hand and squeezed, letting go before Tristan could pull away.

"Maybe. I need to go."

"All right. I'll see you soon."

"See you." Tristan slipped out of their little corner of the garden and was gone before Amory could get another word out. He tried not to think about how unsure Tristan's parting words sounded. He didn't want to lose Tristan. Not when he would likely need his friend more than ever.

He didn't think his father would kill him, but he couldn't rule out his father hitting him. It was partly why he was so surprised Alban hadn't—his older brother was a perfect replica of their father in every way. But even without actual murder, his father could make Amory's life miserable, and Amory wouldn't be able to do anything until he came of age next week. A week seemed like a short time but was long enough for his father to....

He needed to think about his options. Amory's father would never accept his preferences. Once his father knew, Amory's time in his father's house was limited. He hated to leave his younger siblings, especially Adeline, but he doubted he would have much of a choice. It might be best to leave before he was thrown out.

Sighing, he pushed himself away from the tree and started for the house. He hoped he could avoid his father long enough to spend a little time with Adeline and make some plans. And to get his hands to stop shaking.

LATER THAT night, Amory was still wondering what would happen. He'd canceled plans with friends to attend a show put on by a sorcerer with a strong Talent for illusions who was creating a lot of excitement in the city because he wanted to get whatever was going to happen over with. But nothing had. His father hadn't hit him, yelled, or even spoken to him when Amory saw him. His expression was more disgusted than usual, but that was all. It didn't make sense, and with each moment, dread tied Amory into tighter knots.

Dinner progressed as it always did in their household. The entire family ate each night in the formal dining room. Its wood-paneled walls and heavy brocade hangings made the room dark and oppressive, something even the steady glow of the light globes in the glass chandelier couldn't alleviate. The magic globes took the place of candles in many of the fixtures in the house and were a costly convenience his father coveted. Amory never liked the room. Nevertheless, he had been required to eat there with the family since he was twelve years old. Before that, he'd eaten in the nursery with his younger siblings. They were seven at the table that night—his parents, Alban, Adeline, their two younger sisters, Adora and Alva, and him. His two youngest siblings could escape the grueling family meals because they were only ten and eight years old. Lucky children.

His father ordered they eat a meal of several courses, as he insisted the nobility did each night. Amory wasn't entirely certain how his father could know with such authority how the nobility ate at the palace, or why they needed to imitate the nobility at all, but it didn't matter. Amory couldn't complain. He could only endure the long, stilted nightly affair during which his father and brother discussed business, and the rest of them ate silently unless spoken to.

Which was what Amory was doing that night, though he tried to blend into the background more than usual. He wasn't even exchanging furtive, speaking glances and signals with Adeline. He felt too much trepidation to do anything but focus on his food and hope he went unnoticed.

"Amory."

Perhaps he'd cursed himself by thinking it. He looked up at his father from his position farther down the table. "Yes, Father?"

"Alban and I are meeting with the crown prince tomorrow afternoon about a piece he commissioned from us. You will come with us."

His father's blunt words made no sense. He never involved Amory in business. Amory knew the workings of their family's glassmaking business; he'd grown up learning it. But he had no role there, and he was never taken to meet customers. Let alone customers who were so important. The principality of Tournai was known for its beautiful glasswork and fine mirrors, and his father's business was at the pinnacle of the trade. The crown prince, and his father before him, ordered exclusively from Amory's family.

But Amory had never been allowed to meet him. His father was derisive of Amory's business skills and deplored his creativity. Amory hoped his two youngest brothers had better luck living up to his father's expectations. So why was Amory being taken to the palace? His father didn't know of Amory's involvement with the piece, so it couldn't be a problem Amory would be blamed for.

"O-of course, Father," he stuttered when he realized he'd been silent too long.

His father shook his head. "Dress appropriately and do not embarrass me."

As if Amory could ever be anything other than an embarrassment in his father's eyes. "Yes, Father."

His father fixed him with a hard stare, and then made a sound of disgust low in his throat. "Maybe now you'll be of some use to me."

With that, he turned back to his conversation with Alban and left the rest of the table in silence again. Amory met Adeline's quizzical stare from across the table, and shrugged. He didn't know what was going on either.

But he didn't have a good feeling about it.

PHILIP ALEXANDER Stefan Mael threw himself down into his office chair with a long sigh, forcing the weight of responsibility that came with each of those names from his body. Audiences had been long that afternoon, some of the petitions complex, others tedious and frustrating, but he'd insisted on presiding on his own. He wasn't alone with the petitioners in the audience chamber, there were any number of people with him, but he refused to have his uncle whispering in his ear. Uncle

Umber was his father's brother and had become a source of counsel and support when his father died. But Father had been gone over a year, and Uncle Umber needed to let Philip be the ruler of Tournai. He had been trained and had prepared for it his whole life, but no one would ever see him as a ruler if his uncle was perceived to be the power behind the throne.

Uncle Umber wasn't pleased, but he hadn't protested. Maybe he was coming to terms with Philip's ability to rule on his own. Or maybe Uncle Umber was waiting for him to give up and crawl back. He couldn't see a time when he didn't seek Uncle Umber's counsel, but Philip would rule his country himself, if it killed him. And it might. Not because he wasn't capable of doing it, but because ruling was all he did. He looked at the stack of papers on his desk and sank farther into his chair.

A rap on the door forced him to sit up straight. "Enter."

Cathal opened the door and bowed. "Your Highness."

"Cathal, you realize you don't need to bow or to call me that when we're alone."

"You're the crown prince." Obviously that explained everything for his stickler-for-protocol cousin. "The glassmaker is here, Your Highness."

Philip rubbed a hand over his face. He didn't feel like dealing with Arnau at the moment. Owning the finest glassmaking business in Tournai did not make the man less irritating. But it needed to be done. "Where is he?"

"The red receiving room." Though small, it was the most formal and intimidating of the receiving rooms. The sweeping view from its large window was the one good thing about it to Philip's mind. The rest... all the red velvet and gilt and ornate furniture were too much for his personal tastes, but they made it the perfect room in which to meet a man like Arnau.

"Fine. Let's get this over with." He strode from the office, Cathal on his heels. Cathal moved ahead only when they reached the red room, pulling the door open and stepping back so Philip could precede Cathal inside.

Arnau was already there, and he'd brought his son with him. Alban was more insufferable than his father at times. Philip bit back a groan as he walked past the two men, who had all bent into bows as soon as he stepped through the door. He sat in the chair on the small dais at the other side of the room. Cathal took up a position standing on his left as the three men straightened.

His gaze slid over Arnau and Alban. They'd met with him more than once in the past, but the man with them was a stranger. He looked young, younger even than Philip, and—

Philip's mouth dried, his breath caught in his throat, and he stared. At the curling auburn hair and the slender, lithe body dressed in well-cut, well-made clothes. At the rich brown eyes staring back at him. They went almost comically wide and startled, but the young man didn't look away, and Philip couldn't bring himself to either. A delightful blush stained the man's cheeks, and Philip wanted to grin. Who was this man?

A soft noise—Cathal clearing his throat—brought his attention back to where it should be. Arnau stood in front of the dais, flanked by the two other men and slightly in front of them, a supercilious expression on his face. Philip reminded himself again that Arnau owned the foremost glassmaking operation in Tournai.

"Master Arnau."

"Good afternoon, Your Highness. I am always honored to receive an invitation to the palace." Arnau gave him another half bow, his tone an odd mix of self-important and ingratiating. As if he had been invited to the palace for a social engagement, not to give an accounting of himself. "You have met my son, Alban, previously. This is my second son, Amory."

Arnau gestured at the beautiful mystery man. He was Arnau's son? Philip never would have guessed. Amory looked nothing like his father and brother. They were bulkier in build and darker in coloring. And there was something else, something less definable separating Amory from his family.

"It is an honor to meet you, Your Highness," Amory said. His voice sent a shiver down Philip's spine, even as he noted the sincerity in the words. Another difference between Amory and his father. Arnau never seemed sincere.

"And you, Master Amory," he said before turning quickly to Arnau. He couldn't get lost watching a beautiful man. "Master Arnau, I assume you have a good reason why the chandelier I ordered from you is now a week late."

Amory's eyes widened, shock and annoyance swirling in their depths, as Arnau began to bluster. "Your Highness, the chandelier is a complex design and, as such, will take much delicate, time-consuming work to finish."

"A design you submitted to me, and that you assured me could be completed on the timetable you set." Philip focused on Arnau as he spoke but kept watch on Amory out of the corner of his eye.

"The men who work for me are artists who produce the finest glass in the world, Your Highness. A product of quality takes time." Amory's face was incredulous at his father's words, but he immediately tried to hide it. Interesting.

"I am aware of what a product of quality takes, Master Arnau. I am also aware of the quality of your workers. None of which tells me why you and your craftsmen were unable to meet a delivery date you set." Philip held up a hand to forestall whatever excuses were going to come forth. "As you were aware when I gave you this commission, the chandelier is a gift for the king and queen of Amaranta on the birth of their first child. For the honor of Tournai and for our continued good relationship with a neighboring kingdom, the gift I commissioned from you, that I trusted you and your craftsman to complete on time, must be delivered to them before their child reaches adulthood."

Perhaps that last was a bit much. It had only been a week's delay. Regardless, sending a gift late, and the delay would be more than a week by the time the chandelier was finished, would not make Tournai look good to its neighbors. They were a small principality, but their size only meant they needed to build stronger ties to their larger neighbors.

"I do apologize, Your Highness." Arnau's voice was at its most ingratiating, his face an insincere mask of contrition. "We never intended to delay delivery of your gift. We are working to complete it with all due speed."

Philip allowed more of his annoyance to show. "If you had done that from the beginning, we wouldn't be having this conversation, Master Arnau."

"Of course, Your Highness. One more week, and the chandelier will be completed to perfection. It will be the most impressive gift the king and queen of Amaranta receive. The envy of all others." Arnau seemed to clue in to his impatience and cut short his words. The man's face didn't change, but a calculating gleam came to his eyes. "In the meantime, perhaps I can do something to apologize for the inconvenience we have caused you."

He raised an eyebrow. He couldn't wait to hear what Arnau thought would appease him. A discount? If Philip hadn't needed the highest-quality glasswork for the gift, he would never have done business with Arnau again.

"As you see, I brought my son Amory with me today." Amory turned a puzzled gaze on his father, who was almost... smug. "I thought you might like to spend an evening together, Your Highness. Get to know each other."

Complete silence fell. Arnau couldn't be saying what it sounded like, could he?

"I don't understand, Master Arnau. What are you offering?"

Oh, yes, his expression was definitely smug. "I only hoped you might like to get to know Amory better, Your Highness. You are both like-minded men, and Amory hasn't known any others. I thought you might get along well, if you spent an evening, or a night, getting acquainted."

Was Arnau really...? Arnau's expression wasn't just smug, it was knowing, somehow, slimy. He was. Arnau was offering his son's virginity, or at least a night with Amory in Philip's bed, in exchange for his allowing them extra time to work on the commission. His stomach churned with a sick mixture of horror and disgust. How could a father do that to his child? For all intents selling his child for his own gain.

One glance at Amory's stricken expression told him Amory had no part in Arnau's plan. The horror and embarrassment in those big eyes caused a fire to ignite inside Philip. He opened his mouth to yell, to give Arnau the scare of his life before sending him on his way. After canceling the order that brought them there and assuring Arnau the royal family would never come to him for glasswork again.

But then he looked at Amory again. He didn't know the man at all, but there was something about him... and he didn't think it was only that Amory was beautiful. There was something there, something that told him maybe Amory could be a friend at least, if not a lover. He wanted to trust that feeling, ached to be right. But even if he imagined whatever potential he thought was there, no one deserved to be treated the way Arnau was treating Amory.

He couldn't yell and send them away. Couldn't send Amory away with them.

He turned the full force of his most regal stare on Arnau and waited. Waited. *There.* The first hints of uncertainty in that insufferable expression. Just because he found out somehow that Philip preferred to spend his time with men, and that presumably Amory did as well, didn't mean his little plan should succeed.

"I think whether Master Amory and I would like to further our acquaintance is not solely a question for me, but for Master Amory as well," he said after a pause he judged long enough.

"He does, of course," Arnau said. "He would be honored to further an acquaintance with you, Your Highness, and do anything you wish for him to do."

Philip fought to keep his voice even. "I would much rather hear that from Master Amory."

Arnau none-too-gently nudged his younger son, who remained frozen at his side. "Tell the prince, Amory. Now."

"No," Philip interrupted. "I will speak with Master Amory alone."

Amory's mouth dropped open, and Arnau flushed and turned back to Philip. "I must protest, Your Highness—"

"Must you? I don't think you're in the position to protest anything, Master Arnau." Philip was beyond tired of hearing the man talk, and even after making his decision, he was having a hard time keeping his temper in check. The meeting had turned out to be more infuriating than he'd anticipated. "Master Amory? Would you come with me, please?"

Amory's dark eyes found him as the young man's mouth snapped shut. He nodded. "Yes, Your Highness."

Philip rose from the hideous, uncomfortable chair and gestured for Amory to follow while he turned to Cathal. "Stay here."

Cathal was doing a good job of holding back his own surprise and dismay, but Philip saw it. Still, Cathal nodded and seemed to settle more comfortably where he stood. "Yes, Your Highness."

Arnau gripped Amory's arm as he whispered furiously in Amory's ear. Philip barely stopped himself from rolling his eyes. "Master Amory?"

Amory looked up at him and stepped away from his father, forcing his father to release him. "Yes, Your Highness."

He led Amory out into the corridor and then gestured for him to fall in beside him. For some reason, he wanted Amory next to him, not following behind. It would be a few minutes' walk back to his suite. He wasn't positive Amory would make it that far before he needed to sit—the poor man was white as a sheet—but hopefully Amory wasn't as unsteady as he looked. Philip wanted privacy for their conversation, and his suite was the best place to find it.

He glanced at the man walking beside him. Amory was slightly shorter than he was, so Philip was eye level with thick auburn hair. His fingers itched to find out if those curls were as soft as they looked. They would be, and then he would want to nuzzle into them, rub his cheek over them. Probably not a good way to set Amory at ease.

Shaking off temptation, he forced himself to look forward, continuing to walk through the quiet back corridors. Finally, he ushered Amory into his small sitting room and closed the door behind them, hoping to forestall any interruptions. When he turned from the door, Amory stood in the middle of the room, looking lost and more than a little mortified.

"Sit, please." He tried to make his smile as warm and reassuring as he could, and took Amory's arm in a gentle grasp to lead him to a chair. Amory's eyes went wide and startled, but his gaze never left Philip's as Amory lowered himself gracefully into the chair.

CHAPTER 2

AMORY'S LIFE had been in some sort of a spin since the afternoon
before. He'd gone through his normal routine that morning, but nothing
seemed normal. The university's spring term classes ended that day, but
he couldn't go with his friends for a celebratory lunch because he needed
to make sure he was home in time to change and leave for the palace
with his father and brother. Tristan barely spoke to him all morning, so
perhaps not going to lunch was for the best.

He trudged home to find Adeline supervising one of the maids in
pressing and laying out his clothes, something he hadn't given much
thought. Though she was puzzled at their father's actions, Adeline was
almost vibrating with excitement for him. At sixteen, she was fascinated
by the idea of the nobility and the palace. Or perhaps by the idea of
beautiful gowns and handsome noblemen. Either way, she admonished
him numerous times to tell her everything when he returned.

The green silk and velvet he wore was too heavy for the warm day,
but he was glad of it when they arrived at the palace. Not for warmth,
but for armor.

Riding through the palace gates with his father and brother, he was
swamped by a wave of nervous excitement, both for the trip to the palace
and for a potential role in the family business. Even if he couldn't quite
understand how that would happen after yesterday's revelation. Focusing
on the palace itself was far less confusing.

He grew up in the shadow of the palace. Tournai's capital was
not so large, and the district where his family lived not so far from the
palace, that he could avoid seeing it every day. The palace was built at
Jumelle's highest elevation and separated from the city by a thick, high
wall, but the main gates opened onto the city's largest square. Many
of the city's major celebrations were centered there, swirling around an
elaborate fountain. The square was as close to the palace as he'd been.

They dismounted in a large courtyard paved in an intricate pattern
of red and gray stone, and he had a moment to look up at the building
itself while his father spoke to the servant who met them. Seeing it from a

distance didn't do its grandeur justice. The stone was so white it sparkled in the bright afternoon sun, almost blinding him. He got the impression of towers reaching upward toward the sky and large, arched windows set with stained glass. Some of that glass had probably been made by his own ancestors.

The servant led them up wide steps, through a thick door crowned with the royal family's coat of arms with its rearing cat, a reference to the legends of large, magical cats that came to Tournai's defense in battle hundreds of years ago, and inside to an entrance hall floored in red, ivory, and gray marble. The quick pace the servant set kept him from dawdling to gawk at everything they passed. His father strode behind the servant with his chin up, not looking around him, as if he belonged in the halls of the palace. Alban emulated their father perfectly.

Amory didn't think he could feign that sense of entitlement if he tried, so he concentrated on not staring at the people and the rich interior of the building while committing it to memory. Adeline wanted a report, and he wanted to see as much of the art and architecture of the palace as he could.

The servant led them to a receiving room and left them there to wait for the prince. Amory glanced around. Everything that could be decorated in the small room seemed to be, most of it in heavy red silk and velvet, and gold. His father and brother approved quite vocally of the choice of room, admiring the decor as they settled in to wait. They went to the refreshments on the sideboard, pouring glasses of wine and sampling what looked to be savory tarts of some kind.

Amory didn't join them. While the food and drink were most likely meant for them, no one had invited them to eat, and he felt wrong presuming. Instead, he stood there, in the too-fancy room, listening to his father and brother comment about the food and complain about the wait, as if their time was more valuable than a prince's.

His father and Alban put down their glasses quickly enough when the prince entered the room several moments later. As Amory took up a position slightly behind and to the side of his father, as he bowed, all of his focus was on the prince.

He had only ever seen Crown Prince Philip Alexander Stefan Mael at a distance. The representations of him, the drawings, his face on the coins, didn't come close to showing how handsome the prince was. Tall, broad shouldered, and narrow hipped, the prince was well built, his physique obvious in his well-tailored clothes. His dark hair was perhaps slightly too long for fashion, but somehow that endeared him to Amory. The prince was only a couple of years older than Amory, but he looked more mature than that, probably owing to his ascension to the throne at such a young age. Amory let his gaze roam over the prince's form while the man's attention was on his father and Alban.

Then, with a shock that took his breath, he found his gaze caught by the prince's. Embarrassment at being caught staring spread heat over his face, but he couldn't look away. Those eyes drew him in, staring into his as if they were trying to discern everything about him. Outlined in a thick fringe of lashes, the mix of green, amber, and gold all swirled together reminded him of cat's eyes. He supposed he was romanticizing plain hazel. Still, they captivated him, and it was a blow when the prince finally looked away.

Amory worked on gathering his scattered thoughts and controlling his wayward, sudden attraction to the prince of all people while the prince spoke with his father. He wasn't having much success, only barely managing a polite response to his introduction to the prince, until he heard the reason for their visit.

The chandelier was late. He didn't understand how it could happen. However much his father posed and postured, his business was well-run. Commissions were never late, especially important ones. And a commission from the prince for a gift to the reigning monarch of a neighboring kingdom was important. He couldn't fathom why his father would think he could get away with insulting the prince of Tournai so blatantly.

Saying the chandelier showcased the best of Tournai's glasswork tradition was not a lie. It had been designed for just such a purpose. The craftsmanship would be impeccable—once the chandelier was crafted. And the design itself was both traditional and innovative. Its sinuous curves were elegant and refined, yet intricate as well. The bold blue shades of the glass did nothing to take away from that elegance, while making the piece more special. He loved it, and not only because the bulk of the design was his. He was proud of it, even if no one else would ever know. It would be given as an important gift, and people would appreciate its beauty.

But his father had ruined everything. Any idiot could see the prince—ridiculously handsome though he was—was furious.

Amory frantically tried to think of anything they could do to appease the prince, even though he could promise nothing were he to think of something. His father gave him no authority in the business. His father and Alban would have to find a solution.

But he couldn't believe his father's proposed solution, or really, the way his father was trying to bribe the prince for more time. His father was... whoring him out to the crown prince of Tournai, telling the prince he could be the first to have Amory.

What his father said about getting some use out of him suddenly made sense.

Shock and horror churned in his stomach and made ice of his veins. His thoughts whirled in dizzying circles. Struggling to keep up with the prince as they walked, he no longer saw the beauty of the palace, and hardly realized how close he was to the handsome prince. The only thought he could hold on to was the hope that he wasn't going to be sick right there. He was embarrassed enough—he could not be sick in front of the prince. Concentrating on the sound of their footsteps, curiously in step, he forced himself to breathe.

He was so focused he was almost startled when the prince stopped and opened a door, ushering him into the room beyond. Once inside, Amory had no idea what to do.

A quick glance showed him a sitting room that was nowhere near as ostentatious as the room they'd left. Amory's family was quite wealthy, and his father's house reflected their wealth, but the palace was on an entirely different scale. The sitting room didn't make him uncomfortable, though. He couldn't say it reminded him of home, because his father's tastes ran toward keeping up appearances, which always meant something more formal and fashionable than Amory would have chosen. The room was luxurious but comfortable too. Rich fabrics in warm colors covered plush chairs, couches, and pillows, almost inviting a person to curl up there. A thick carpet covered the floor in front of a massive fireplace, and drapes were drawn back from wide windows. Yes, it was a comfortable room, the first room in the palace where he felt that way, and he calmed a little more because of it.

"Sit, please."

He jumped at the unexpected voice. Then something more unexpected—the prince's hand, gently taking his arm. Amory's gaze flew up to meet the prince's, and he found concern and even compassion filling the prince's eyes, not pity or something more disturbing as he half feared. Those green-gold eyes caught his again, as they had earlier, and he couldn't seem to look away from them as the prince guided him to a chair. The care was so nice, the hand on his arm so warm, he couldn't bring himself to complain about being treated like he was made of glass.

"Can I get you something to drink? Water? Though you could probably use something stronger."

The prince's words were kind, but Amory felt a flash of insult. At least the heat of it burned away more of the shock. "I'm not weak. Your Highness."

The prince didn't seem to take offense to the sharp words. "I never said you were, but you did have a shock." His expression turned wry around the edges. "We both have."

"I suppose we have."

Without waiting for more of a reply than that, the prince went to a sideboard and poured two glasses from the decanter sitting there, the distinctive gold color of the liquid marking it as plaire, a liquor unique to Tournai.

As he sipped from his glass, the liquor smooth and warm and subtly spicy on his tongue, Amory watched the prince. The prince sipped his drink as well and let out a slow breath. Perhaps he was more frazzled than he looked.

That was reassuring. Knowing the prince had been shocked at his father's offer made Amory a little less nervous. Not that he wasn't still worried. His father was trying to sell him to the prince, and Amory didn't know what the prince would do. He told Amory's father he wanted to hear Amory's agreement from him. Did that mean the prince intended to accept his father's proposal?

Amory took a large gulp of his drink. Prince Philip was gorgeous with all that thick, dark hair, and the fluid grace of his movements, and those eyes—really amazing eyes. But that didn't mean Amory wanted to be ordered to share his bed.

"Do you work with your father and brother?" The prince's voice broke the silence and Amory jumped again. The prince smiled another of those warm, almost intimate smiles. "I only ask because I haven't met you before today, but I have met your brother."

"No, I don't work with them. I've learned the business, of course, but my father hasn't asked me to be a part of it. My brother has helped him for years."

The prince's face turned almost sympathetic. Did he realize Amory's father had never wanted Amory to be a part of the business because Amory was a disappointment to him? But what he said was, "And you thought maybe he finally was by bringing you with him today."

It wasn't a question, but Amory answered anyway. "I did. I didn't expect...."

The prince laughed shortly and shook his head. "I didn't either, though I wasn't looking forward to meeting with your father. What do you do, then?"

Amory could imagine why the prince hadn't wanted to meet with his father. He knew how difficult a man his father could be. "I was taking some classes at the university, but they finished today. And I like to spend time with the craftsmen at the glassworks."

The prince grinned. "Have you seen my chandelier, then? Does it exist?"

That lightning-fast grin made Amory's insides flip around in strange, but not unpleasant, ways. He managed to smile back. "It exists, Your Highness."

"How far behind are they really? Can it be finished in the time your father is asking for?"

"I don't know, Your Highness." But he would have told the prince if he did. "I wasn't aware they'd fallen behind. With classes ending, I haven't been there to see it lately. But I'm familiar with the design, of course, and the chandelier was coming along beautifully."

The prince's eyes sharpened. "Are you? How familiar?"

"Well, Your Highness, I...." Amory had always been miserable at dissembling, and was apparently worse when seated next to a wildly attractive prince. It would have to be the truth then. "The design was my idea."

"The design was yours? I thought you said you have no part in the business?"

"I don't. My father doesn't know. I was visiting with the most senior of the glassworkers one day, and he described the commission to me. I sketched out some ideas he ended up liking."

"I liked them too."

Amory felt his cheeks heat at the praise. "Thank you, Your Highness."

"Do you work with the glass too, or only the designs?"

Amazing that the prince came to the correct conclusion from so little. "Only the designs, Your Highness, and only sometimes. I tried working with glass, but I don't have the skill for it." He had wanted to be good at it, despite knowing his father would never allow him to work in the business as a craftsman. Still, he would have liked to be good at it.

"From what I've seen, your creativity with the designs makes up for that. Did you want to work in your family's business?"

"It's what I always expected I would do, what we're raised to do. But I don't think it's ever going to happen, especially not now." Amory doubted he wanted it to happen after the events of that afternoon, even if it could. His father hadn't shown himself in a good light, and Amory didn't think he could go back to the way everything had been before.

"I suppose not." The prince's gaze was keen. "So what is it you do want?"

"Your Highness?" Amory blinked in confusion.

"What do you want to do, Amory?" the prince asked again, his eyes earnest. "You could stay here, with me."

"I don't understand, Your Highness."

"I told your father I wanted to speak with you alone, that I wanted to hear from you. I wanted to ask you if you might like to stay with me, but not just for tonight."

"For how long, then?" Amory was having a difficult time keeping up. Too many strange things were happening that day.

"A long time, if we're lucky and we both want. I don't just want a tumble tonight, Amory."

"What do you want, Your Highness?" he asked, suddenly bold.

"A friend, a lover," the prince said, his words simple but stunning, his gaze never wavering from Amory.

He struggled to find his voice. "And you want that to be me? After what my father did?"

"Your father's actions are reprehensible. No one should treat his son the way he's treating you. But that's your father, not you."

"How do you know I wasn't a part of his plan?"

"You weren't. Everything you felt was written all across your face. Horror was predominant."

Amory flushed, again. "I can't believe he would do this, Your Highness. I have sisters at home—would he do this to one of them? Whore us out for his own gain?" He could hear the bitterness in his own voice, and the anger, the choking worry for his sisters. Then weariness swept through him. "I don't know how he even knows whether I've...."

"Have you?"

"Does it matter?"

"Not to me."

The sincerity in the prince's expression reassured Amory, but it didn't stop the sudden rush of insecurity. His father was correct. Amory was a virgin with almost no experience to speak of with other men. He had no idea what the prince would expect of him. And right then the prince was watching him, expecting him to say something. "No. I mean, some kissing, but hardly anything beyond that."

"I've only had one lover."

"Really?" That couldn't be true. He was the prince. He could have anyone he wanted, surely.

"Yes." The prince smiled, but it had a self-deprecating quality to it Amory found charming and unexpected. "I don't want meaningless affairs. For any number of reasons, they don't appeal to me. So it's only been the one man. We can take things slowly, get to know each other, see if we suit."

"And if we don't suit, Your Highness? My father is giving me to you. Well, selling me." If they didn't suit, what would that mean for Amory? He could be back where he started with the addition of his father's anger.

"No, he isn't. This is between us. He has nothing to do with it. If you decide to stay, it's your choice alone. And if we find we don't get on with each other, it will be your choice what you do next."

"He's not going to like that." An incredible understatement.

"I don't find I care what he thinks, though I don't mean to offend you since he is your father. How old are you?"

Amory blinked, surprised by the sudden subject change. "Seventeen. Eighteen next week."

"Well, then. Next week, you're of age, and he can't ever tell you what to do. Until then, I can make sure he doesn't. So it truly is your choice."

He hadn't thought about it that way. "And you? What would you choose?"

"I'm asking you to stay," the prince said. "I think, I hope, there could be something good between us. I'd like to find out. Now, what do you want?"

The question was devastating because Amory had heard it so rarely in his life.

The prince seemed honest, and rather endearingly hopeful. As if he hoped Amory would stay but wasn't sure he would. Amory would have thought a prince would be more confident than Prince Philip appeared, more arrogant. More demanding. But Prince Philip was asking him if he wanted to stay, and giving him choices if he wanted to leave. It was... sweet, if a bit disconcerting.

What confused him more was that the prince wanted him to stay in the first place. Amory's father offered the prince a night with Amory, to take his innocence. The prince, who admitted he didn't have any desire for meaningless affairs, wanted more. With him, Amory.

And Amory wanted to stay. Not only because he wanted to get away from a father who would barter using his son, but also because he saw something too. Something genuine and good in Prince Philip, and the possibility for something good between them. He didn't know why, or where the belief came from, but he wanted to see if it could be true. It scared him a little how certain he was of the possibility. He didn't know the prince at all. As much as Amory's instincts told him Prince Philip was a good person, he didn't know it. He couldn't be sure of the prince from so short a time with him.

Amory stared into the prince's eyes while he turned it all over in his mind, but he'd already decided. He wanted to find out if he was right about the prince. He would regret it if he didn't, would regret not finding out what it could be like between them. He had to know what it felt like to touch the prince, to be touched by him. He wanted to know that very much, too much perhaps.

"I would like to stay, Your Highness," Amory began tentatively, "But, will it be all right? What will people say about your keeping a male... I don't know what word to use."

The prince's eyes softened. "Right now, we'll say friend, but I'm hoping soon, we can call each other lover. Unmarried princes in the past have had lovers living with them in the palace. It shouldn't matter that you're a man. I won't let it."

Amory had his doubts, but the prince would know better than he. "Then I'll stay, Your Highness."

The prince's smile lit the room, like the sun appearing, and Amory was dazzled looking at him. When he stood and held out a hand, Amory didn't hesitate to take it and let the prince draw him to his feet. They were close together, so close Amory could feel the heat of the prince's body. The prince leaned down the few inches separating them and brushed his lips over Amory's.

The kiss was light and quick, but utterly stunning. Amory knew his eyes were wide as he stared at the prince, his breath coming faster, a tingle of warmth shimmering over his entire body. All from one chaste kiss. He wondered what would happen when they really kissed.

The prince's eyes were wide as well as he watched Amory. Had it felt the same to him? It had barely been a kiss, but it felt like a start. Maybe even a promise. As the prince bent to kiss him again, it definitely felt like a promise.

THE SECOND kiss still wasn't more than the tender slide of lips over lips, but it wasn't as brief, nor as innocent as the first. Amory's lips were soft against his, his body warm and fitting just right against Philip's as he pulled Amory closer. The kiss was perfect, as the first had been. It felt as if he'd been waiting for the kiss, for the man, for years, and at that moment everything had fallen into place. It felt as if they were the only two people in the world for those moments, and the feeling was wonderful.

He shivered when Amory's hands came up to caress over his biceps and settle on his shoulders. He didn't try to deepen the kiss, just held Amory's trim waist and let the kiss spin out between them, despite wanting to take it further, to devour Amory's sweet mouth. He wanted to do more than that, to urge Amory down to the couch or to carry him off to bed. His fevered imagination gave him many ideas for what they could do there.

But he needed to take his time with Amory. Amory was inexperienced and plainly shaken by what his father had done. He needed the time to settle in, to become calm and comfortable again. And it wasn't only for Amory that they should go slow. He wanted it for himself too. He wanted time to get to know Amory, to find out if he was right about the man. Despite wanting to carry him off to bed right then.

He broke the kiss with some difficulty but couldn't bring himself to step back from Amory. It had been a long time since his affair with Vasco ended, and Amory felt so good against him, better than Vasco had. But he didn't want to think about his old lover then. He nuzzled into Amory's hair and breathed him in for a moment as Amory shuddered against him.

He looked into Amory's eyes. They were wide and dark, somehow both surprised and filled with desire. Philip bit back a groan and forced himself not to dive back in for another kiss.

"So you're staying?"

Amory smiled, a slow, sweet smile that hit Philip right in the stomach. "Yes, I'm staying."

"Good." He made himself step back. "We should get back before they start to wonder what we're doing."

Amory laughed. "I'm sure my father is already wondering, Your Highness."

"All the more reason."

The walk back a few moments later was much more relaxed than their earlier walk had been.

"When we go back into that room," he said into the silence as they walked, "stand near me."

Amory turned to look at him, his brows pulled together in a frown. "I doubt he could grab me and make me go."

"That's not why." He wasn't sure how to explain why he wanted Amory at his side and not at Amory's father's without sounding either pathetic or domineering. Neither was a way he wanted Amory to see him.

Amory looked at him for another moment and then nodded. The dawning understanding in his eyes telling Philip that Amory knew somehow. "All right."

Amazing.

The scene in the red receiving room was almost amusing. Cathal didn't seem to have moved an inch since Philip and Amory left. Arnau glared at Cathal, his face red, a vein visibly throbbing in his forehead. Alban was still at his father's shoulder, less than calm himself. Though Cathal's expression would tell most people nothing, Philip knew his cousin well enough to see the signs. Cathal was about to lose his considerable patience. He suddenly wished he were back in the sitting room, alone with Amory.

"Gentlemen." As the three men in the room turned to face them, he took Amory's arm, and walked to his chair. Amory let himself be guided to stand at Philip's right, mirroring the position Cathal still occupied on the other side, but Amory stood a step closer. Philip liked that he did.

"Your Highness—"

"Yes, Master Arnau." He cut the blustering man off before Arnau could get started. His own patience with the man had run out about the time he made his disgusting offer. "You protest. Yet I fail to see why. You were the one to suggest that I might enjoy spending some time with your son."

"I did, Your Highness." Master Arnau's voice became almost conciliatory. Did he see how close he was to angering Philip? "And I still do. However, I did not think you and my son would spend time alone together so soon, and before we discussed anything. He is my son, Your Highness, and quite young."

Philip resisted the urge to roll his eyes. Was Arnau really playing the concerned father trying to protect his son's virtue after offering it to Philip? Or just upset Philip hadn't agreed to an extension on the delivery date before spiriting Amory away? "It seemed you'd said everything you needed to say, Master Arnau. I wished to speak with Amory. As you said, Amory and I seem to have much in common. We have agreed to see if a friendship might grow between us. As such, Amory will be staying here at the palace for the foreseeable future."

"Your Highness!" Arnau exclaimed. Alban's mouth dropped open, making him look like a landed fish.

Philip hoped Amory could find some amusement in his brother's reaction at least. "I think Amory and I will get on quite well."

"Your Highness—"

"There are two men in the corridor who will accompany you home, and return with Amory's things." They also carried a note Amory dashed off to his sister, giving an explanation and asking her to pack his possessions. Philip wasn't sure what his servants would return with if Amory's father was left to supervise the packing. "I will give you an additional week to deliver the chandelier. One week, Master Arnau, and I will expect the completed chandelier."

"Of course, Your Highness." Arnau bowed, and though he did not look happy, he allowed Cathal to usher them from the room.

Philip turned to Amory as soon as they were alone. "Are you all right?"

Amory blinked large, dark eyes at him. "Yes, Your Highness."

He wasn't convinced despite Amory's assurance. Amory looked a little dazed, but a lot had changed for him that afternoon. Philip reaffirmed his decision to take everything slowly. "Let's get you settled, or as settled as you can be until your things get here."

"Thank you, Your Highness."

"You're welcome." Impulsively, he took Amory's hand and brought it to his lips. Surprised pleasure lit Amory's expression. "Your sister won't have any trouble supervising the packing?"

Amory's expression softened further. "Thank you for your concern. Adeline should be fine, Your Highness. I'm glad for the chance to explain what happened to her, even briefly. She would have been worried otherwise."

"You and she are close."

"Yes, very close." Amory's expression turned fond. "I'm sure she won't be satisfied with the note for long. Hopefully, I can see her."

He frowned at Amory's tentative tone. "You can see her whenever you want. I'm not keeping you prisoner, Amory. You're living here now, but I'm not going to keep you from seeing your family or friends."

He gave the hand he held a comforting squeeze, and Amory smiled at him again. He liked that smile already, wanted to see it all the time. Wanted to kiss those smiling lips again.

"Your Highness."

Cathal's quiet voice drew him back from Amory. When had he gotten so close? He didn't remember sliding to the edge of his seat and leaning toward the other man. Nor had he realized Amory had leaned closer to him. It seemed Amory hadn't either. A slight flush stained Amory's cheeks as he stepped back.

Keeping hold of Amory's hand, Philip turned to face his cousin. He didn't want Amory going far. "Yes, Cathal?"

"Master Arnau and Master Alban have left the palace with the men you sent to retrieve Master Amory's things."

He wasn't sure he cared for Cathal's carefully blank expression. As proper as his cousin was, Cathal usually allowed himself to show some emotion when they were alone. "Thank you, Cathal."

His cousin stared at him. "May I speak with you in private?"

Philip could guess what was coming. He turned to Amory. "Please give us a moment alone."

"Of course," Amory said. "Should I go out into the corridor?"

"No, stay. Over by the door is fine. Thank you."

Cathal waited until Amory stepped away and spoke in a low voice. "You can't move a lover into the palace."

"I don't see why not." He glanced at Amory to make sure he wasn't listening. Amory seemed the type to worry about how his presence would affect Philip as prince, but he didn't want Amory to carry that concern. "You think I don't know that the reason you lobbied for Lady Celeste to receive a position as one of Elodie's ladies is she's your mistress and you want her conveniently close?"

Cathal's mouth fell open in a less-than-flattering manner. Obviously, he hadn't realized Philip knew. Cathal pulled himself together. "That's different."

"It is." Philip was the prince, but it wasn't unheard of for a prince to have a lover live in the palace with him. It wouldn't even be the first time a prince openly had a male lover living in the palace, though neither had occurred recently. The true difference was Cathal never kept his lovers for more than a few months at a time. He'd lay money on Amory being there longer than Celeste, and Philip had just met the man. "But not in the way you're thinking. Not because Amory is a man."

Hurt flashed in Cathal's eyes. "You know I've never had a problem with your preference for men."

True, Cathal hadn't. "I know."

"I worry about the implications of your decision." Cathal flicked his eyes to Amory and back to him. "But I don't care who you sleep with."

"Let me worry about implications. Don't think about who I sleep with. As I try my hardest not to think of you with any of the women you've slept with." He gave an exaggerated shudder and got the reaction he wanted, Cathal laughing. "Just keep accepting it, the way you always have."

"Yes, Your Highness."

"Amory is staying. Hopefully for a long time."

Cathal considered for a moment, something like comprehension dawning in his eyes. He nodded to Amory and raised his voice enough for him to hear. "A pleasure to meet you, Master Amory. Welcome to the palace."

Faint surprise flitted over Amory's face, but when he spoke his tone was gracious and sincere. "Thank you, Lord Cathal."

Cathal turned back to Philip. "You don't have any other meetings this afternoon, Your Highness."

"Good. I'm going to get Amory settled."

"Let me know if there's anything you need. I'm going to deal with some correspondence." With a polite bow, Cathal left the room, leaving Philip alone with Amory.

He turned to Amory. "Shall I show you your room? It will probably be a while until your things get here, but I can show you around a little until then."

"I'd like that, Your Highness, if I'm not taking you away from anything." Amory's expression had a hint of uncertainty to it, and his dark eyes were thoughtful.

"Not at all. You're saving me from paperwork. I'm grateful." He grinned and stood, offering Amory his arm.

Amory hesitated. "I'm not a girl, Your Highness."

"I am well aware of that."

Amory laughed and shook his head, but he looped his arm through Philip's. They garnered a few looks as they walked through the corridors, but he didn't see any reason to hide Amory. That he asked Amory to live there would be all over the palace by nightfall, all over the city by tomorrow. Servants talked, and for all his propriety, so did Cathal.

"May I ask you something, Your Highness?" Amory asked when they were away from the more populated corridors.

"Of course."

"Your cousin seemed upset. Was it about me? You said it would be all right for me to stay here with you." Amory's voice was quiet with a thread of concern underlying it, and he couldn't help but be pleased yet again that Amory would be concerned for him already.

"Cathal worries, but it is all right. It's rather traditional for princes to keep lovers. Going back generations, princes have moved their lovers, male and female, into the palace. Sometimes more than one at a time if you go back far enough. Sometimes they kept their lovers after they married, sometimes not. A couple never married, but kept concubines in the palace during their reigns." His own father kept a lover in the palace for several years—of course, then he married her, so many people had forgotten how they started. Philip had never given thought to keeping a lover, but there was something about Amory. "There are people who will be surprised or upset you're a man. I've kept my preferences private by choice. But that really is all. I've learned I can't please everyone as prince."

Amory was quiet, his face thoughtful before he finally nodded. "All right, then."

"No second thoughts?" He hoped not. He would let Amory go, but he didn't want to, not yet.

"No, Your Highness."

The relief washing through him was out of proportion considering he'd known Amory less than a day. He pushed it aside. "Good. Here we are."

Amory looked around as Philip ushered him through the door and back into his sitting room. "We're back in your suite, aren't we, Your Highness?"

"Yes."

"You want me to share your suite?"

He tried to put as much reassurance into his expression as he could. "Yes. But you have your own bedchamber. Is this all right?"

Amory still looked nervous, but he nodded. "Fine."

"Then let me show you your bedchamber and the rest of the suite."

He had lived in the suite for several years and redecorated it to suit his tastes two years ago. After his parents' deaths, everyone assumed he would move into their suite, which traditionally belonged to the crown prince, but he liked where he was, and he didn't like the idea of living in his parents' rooms so soon after their deaths. So despite tradition and the urging of his uncle, those rooms remained vacant, and he remained in his old suite. He was glad of that decision. He liked bringing Amory to a place that was his.

CHAPTER 3

KNOWING HE was living in the prince's suite, in a bedchamber separated from the prince's only by that comfortable sitting room, brought Amory's new situation into stark clarity. He was officially the prince's lover, or the prince's official lover, if such a thing existed, and it seemed it did. Regardless, he was Prince Philip's lover, and it didn't seem to matter that the prince hadn't done more than kiss him. Yet.

Odd, considering a day ago he hadn't known the prince and had been kissing another man. Tristan was his oldest friend, his best friend, and the kissing had been nice, but Amory didn't want anything more with Tristan. He wanted more with a man he just met, and that realization made him nervous.

And confused, to tell the truth, but there was no denying his attraction to the prince. The little flutters in his stomach every time the prince smiled at him made it more than evident. Then there was the urge to be closer, to kiss more, to touch. Even though he didn't know the prince at all.

His new bedchamber was a large room with wide windows that looked out over the same beautiful view of city and coast as the sitting room windows. Also like the sitting room, it was decorated in an elegant but comfortable style—lots of overstuffed cushions and soft fabrics all in warm colors. The whole suite was the same he found as the prince showed him the rest. Not overly ornate or fussy, but cozy, almost hedonistic in its luxury. He didn't find it difficult to picture himself curled up in one of those chairs with a book or a sketchbook, or snuggling into the large, soft bed to sleep.

He found it disconcertingly easy to imagine the prince snuggled up with him too. A strange, but curiously exciting, thought.

The prince stayed close to him as he showed Amory the suite, inciting a prickly awareness all through Amory. He tried to ignore it and concentrate on the tour. The suite had two bedchambers: the one given to Amory and the prince's on the other side of the sitting room. The prince's was decorated similarly to Amory's but was larger and had walls painted a deep red instead of the pale gold of Amory's bedchamber. The prince showed him the room quickly and then guided him back out with a gentle hand on his back. Amory didn't think the prince did so because he wanted Amory out of the room. It felt more as if he hurried them out to keep Amory from feeling pressured, or perhaps to avoid temptation. Amory shivered. Probably a good idea.

Each bedchamber had its own bathing room. There was also a small dining room, a library with floor to ceiling bookshelves and more comfortable-looking chairs, and the prince's personal study. He wanted to spend days studying the paintings scattered around the suite and the frescoes painted on the ceilings. He supposed he would have the time.

"That's all there is of the suite," the prince told him as they returned to the sitting room.

"I like it." The sitting room was the first place in the palace he had felt somewhat at home, and the rest of the suite provoked the same feeling.

"I'm glad. I want you to be happy here. I'll show you around the rest of the palace as well."

"I don't want to keep you if you have obligations, Your Highness." Though he hated to part ways so soon.

"No obligations that would keep me from giving you at least a quick tour." The prince smiled, warm and slow, and Amory felt those flutters in his stomach again.

He hoped he wasn't blushing. "Thank you, Your Highness."

When the prince offered his arm, Amory didn't hesitate to take it. He liked the connection, and the care the prince took with him. He hadn't felt anything like it before.

The palace was emptier than it had been when Amory arrived with his father and Alban. Most of the people involved in the running of the government left the palace at the end of the day, the prince explained, and the army of servants was supposed to be invisible. Without a social function scheduled, the palace would be quieter in the evenings. It made him wonder about the prince living mostly alone in the echoing building since his parents died.

They walked through the corridors, the prince showing him the different rooms. There were receiving rooms, ballrooms, offices, and parlors. Formal dining rooms of different sizes, a larger palace library, an audience chamber, and the prince's more public office. A dizzying array of rooms large and small, all decorated far more richly than anything he'd ever seen. There was also more art than he'd ever seen in one place, each room decorated with master sculptures and paintings, frescoes and tapestries. He could have stood for hours in front of so many of the paintings, but there was no time for that on the brief tour.

The views were as beautiful as the art. When the prince saw how enthralled Amory was by the scene outside the large windows, he tugged Amory up the spiraling stairs to the top of the highest tower. They were breathless and laughing by the time they reached the top, but as the prince led him outside to a windswept parapet, Amory's laughter died away. The world spread out at his feet in the golden glow of the late afternoon sun. He had never been up so high, had never seen Jumelle from that perspective, and he didn't think it ever looked so beautiful. The stone buildings with their tile roofs, some with peaks, some towers or turrets, all warm in the sunlight.

Outside the city walls spread a green countryside of farms, meadows, and woods along the sparkling ribbon of the river. Jumelle's harbor bustled with activity, ships large and small gliding through water glistening in the sunlight. He itched to capture the glorious sight on paper or canvas, but he doubted he could do it justice. And really, he didn't want to move from that spot with the prince quiet at his side, his hand over Amory's on the stone rail.

They were outside on a terrace overlooking the garden when a servant informed them that Amory's things had arrived. The prince had brought him outside to see the garden after they came down from the tower, but they made it only as far as the terrace before stopping to watch the beginning of the sunset together. The prince stood beside him, the warmth of his body making Amory aware of how close they were, of everywhere they almost touched.

They weren't talking about anything in particular, and then they weren't talking at all, just watching the sunset paint the sky in rose and gold, standing close together. Amory's mind spun with the sensation of having the prince so close, with the anticipation of what might happen. His breath came quicker.

Feeling somehow compelled, he looked up, finding the prince's eyes on him as well. There was a smoldering heat in the prince's gaze that mesmerized Amory. He swayed forward, and the prince smiled, a devastating, wicked smile, as he leaned forward too.

Of course, that was when they were interrupted.

The prince's face turned rueful as the servant bowed his way off the terrace. "I guess we should go and make sure all of your things arrived."

"I suppose." His disappointment colored his voice, and Amory's cheeks heated.

On the walk back through the quiet halls, the disappointment faded a little. They would have time, there together. He began thinking again about the prince so alone in the palace, except perhaps for the servants. Which seemed both lonely and lacking in privacy, as shown by that ill-timed interruption.

"Who else lives in the palace, Your Highness?"

"Other than me and the army of servants? My sister, Elodie, and her ladies. She has four now. They're good company for her, including Lady Celeste." The prince shook his head in what looked like good-natured amusement. "Cathal sometimes, though he spends as much time at his family's house in the city as he does here."

"And with Lady Celeste when he is here?" he asked, his voice purposely light and amused, but inside he was hit again with the sense that the prince was so alone, so apart in his palace. And Amory hurt for him. He resolved right there, so quickly it terrified him, that he would make a relationship work with the prince. He had to so he could be there for the prince and care for him, so the prince wouldn't be alone anymore.

Back in his new bedchamber, they found two maids already unpacking Amory's clothing into the wardrobe. Both young women paused in their tasks to curtsy as he and the prince entered the room. One of them, a petite, dark-haired girl, spoke, "Everything was delivered here, Your Highness, sir. We've begun unpacking. Also, Your Highness, the princess is asking for you."

"Thank you, Trina." The prince turned to Amory with a long-suffering look in his amazing eyes. "I better go see what Elodie wants, though I can guess."

Amory could guess too. Certainly what the prince did that afternoon had made it all over the palace by then. "Of course."

"I'll leave you here to get settled. Trina and Clea are the maids who take care of the suite. They'll be able to get you anything you need."

"All right."

"After I get back from speaking with Elodie, I thought we could dine together, here in the suite."

How tentative the prince sounded was sweet and made Amory melt a little. "I'd like that, Your Highness."

Heedless of their audience, the prince lifted a hand to gently brush the backs of his fingers over Amory's cheek. Amory couldn't help a little shiver as the brief, light touch sent ripples through his body. Amory took a moment to breathe after the prince disappeared out the bedchamber door and then turned back to the room. Both maids were studiously not looking at him as they unpacked his trunk. He fought back embarrassment and went to supervise the unpacking.

PHILIP COULD have summoned Elodie to him, but he decided exposing Amory to Elodie on his first night in the palace might be too much. He was being too hard on his sister, but she could be a bit… enthusiastic sometimes. Best to let Amory settle in first. He didn't want Amory to run.

Instead he strode through the corridors to his sister's suite in the east wing. Lady Celeste greeted him, and settled him in the sitting room while she went to announce him to Elodie. The room, the whole suite, was quintessentially Elodie. The delicate furniture in pale gold wood, the light, gauzy fabrics in pale blues and white… just right for her, and indeed she and their mother decorated the suite for Elodie before their parents died. They'd enjoyed themselves doing it as well. He was glad Elodie had those memories of their mother.

He wandered to the window and pushed aside the gold-embroidered sheer white curtains. The garden spread below him, just visible in the twilight. If only he and Amory hadn't been interrupted out on the terrace.

"There you are!"

Elodie exploded into the room like a whirlwind. She was so tiny, so delicate, with her slender limbs and the top of her head barely coming to his shoulder, he was always surprised at the sheer amount of commotion she could make.

"Elodie, you look lovely this evening." She was dressed to go out in an aqua silk gown and delicate pearl jewelry, her dark hair arranged in a complicated, braided style that made her look far too old for his comfort. He liked to think of his younger sister as still being a child, but she wasn't.

"Thank you. But don't change the subject."

"What subject was that?"

"Don't play dumb." She fixed her golden-brown eyes on him. "Is it true? Did you really move a male lover into the palace?"

"Who told you that?" Though he could guess.

"Cathal. Is it true?" She was bouncing in front of him, her impatience making her practically vibrate.

And he had guessed correctly. Forget the servants, because of Cathal the whole city would probably know by midnight. "Cathal is such a gossip."

"It is true," Elodie exclaimed, giving a little hop and clapping her hands together. "I couldn't believe it when he told me."

"I wish he hadn't. I was going to tell you myself." He studied her. She didn't look upset. He wasn't sure how she did look… a little gleeful, but that could be the result of good gossip. Elodie liked it as much as Cathal did.

"I wish you'd told me yourself. I didn't know you were interested in anyone that way. You're so quiet about these things."

Yes, he was. He preferred to keep his private life as private as possible, which wasn't always very private considering his position. That was another reason why he'd had only the one lover. If there wasn't anything there, then no one could talk about it. Of course, then people made things up.

"But I'm all right with it," Elodie continued. "I'm shocked. You've never talked about taking a lover. I guess I never thought you would. But I want you to be happy. If he makes you happy, I'm happy for you."

He was touched. "Thank you."

Her innocent, sunny smile suddenly turned mischievous. "So what is he like? Is he handsome?"

"Elodie." He made his tone as forbidding as possible. He had to stop her before she got started.

"I mean, he must be if you're taking him as a lover. Not that looks are all that matter to you, but he had to have caught your eye somehow. So he's handsome, right? What else? Cathal said he's Master Arnau's son?"

He waited for the rush of words to stop, wondering how he could put an end to the conversation. "Yes, he's Master Arnau's son."

"I thought you didn't like him. You said he was like his father, and his father makes you crazy."

"That's the oldest son. Amory is the second son, and he is not like his father." Amory also didn't make him crazy—well, not in that way.

Something told Philip not going to bed with Amory was going to make him more than a little crazy as time went on. But he would do it, to make Amory more comfortable and to see if they could really build something.

"All right, good. His name is Amory, and he's the second son of a successful glass merchant. That's good information. What else?" Her eyes were bright and eager, her gaze fixed on his face. "Oh, never mind. I'll meet him myself. You can introduce me now."

Oh, that was a bad idea. Elodie, though he loved her dearly, could be overwhelming, and even if she did manage to calm down and turn herself into the proper young lady she was supposed to be, it still wasn't a good idea. Amory had a trying day to say the least, dealing with what his father tried to do and his sudden move to the palace and change in circumstances.

Best to let Amory settle in that night, to begin to adjust to his new situation before Philip unleashed Elodie on him. He couldn't keep Elodie away from Amory for long, but giving him one night of calm before the reality of court life caught up with Amory seemed like the least he could do for the man.

"Not tonight, Elodie."

She stopped abruptly in her walk to the door, and whirled to look at him with wide eyes. "Why not?"

"I think it's best to let Amory get settled in tonight. And aren't you on your way out?"

"Oh, yes." She looked as if she'd forgotten her own plans in the excitement, and perhaps she had. "I'm going to a dinner party at Lilliale's family home."

Lilliale was Elodie's closest friend, and a daughter of one of the noblest families in Tournai. Lilliale's oldest brother inherited the title and married a couple of years earlier. Right after he and Philip ended their affair. Not that Elodie knew there had ever been an affair. The friendship their sisters began practically in the cradle was only one reason they'd been so discreet. It didn't matter anymore. Vasco was married, and Philip had Amory, or he hoped to.

Lilliale's whole family lived in a large house in the city and entertained frequently, often with lavish dinner parties and balls. He had turned down the invitation to the small party that night. He turned down all the invitations, unless they were to large events. But Elodie often attended or spent time at their home, just as Lilliale spent copious amounts of time at the palace with Elodie, and he was glad his sister possessed such a close friend. Even if his own past choices made it uncomfortable for him.

"That's nice. Please give my regards to her and her family."

Elodie grinned. "I always do. I better be leaving." She hesitated. "You promise you'll introduce me to Amory tomorrow?"

He stifled a sigh, but he couldn't keep Amory hidden away forever. "I promise."

He saw Elodie off for her evening and returned to his suite. Nothing urgent needed his attention in his study, so he moved on to his bedchamber. Dinner had been arranged for him and Amory in the suite's dining room, but he took time to clean up and change his clothes. He wanted his first night with Amory to be perfect, and as Amory's presence was sudden and unexpected, he hadn't had time to plan. If he had, the meal would have been something special and he wouldn't have so much trouble deciding on clothing. The giddy, jittery feeling in his chest surprised him. He wanted that night to be the beginning of something good, something real.

Amory was already in the dining room when he arrived, studying a large painting on the wall opposite the fireplace, but he turned when Philip walked in and smiled. He answered with a warm one of his own. Impossible not to, even as his mind stalled again on how beautiful Amory was. Amory had changed his clothes as well, into a rich green tunic and an ivory shirt, both well-tailored to his frame. The soft candlelight teased out red and gold in Amory's auburn hair and made his features look finer.

Philip was across the room and at Amory's side before he thought about moving, but once there, he hesitated. He didn't pull Amory into his arms the way he wanted, but he did take his hand, needing contact. Amory's smile widened, and his slender fingers wound through Philip's. A warm glow spread through him, as pleasing as it was surprising.

"I was admiring this painting, Your Highness. It's beautiful."

He reluctantly tore his gaze from Amory and focused on the painting. The landscape depicted a lush field of green and deep purple spreading back to thick trees. They almost hid a stone house, which seemed to glow under a flawless blue sky. "Yes. It's a favorite of mine."

"Where is it?"

"Not far. It's north of the city, an estate of mine called Alzata." Alzata was his favorite place, but he hadn't gotten to spend much time there since his father died. Before his father's death, he had escaped there whenever he could.

"It looks peaceful."

"We'll have to visit soon. We can ride, swim, ramble around with no one to bother us." He suddenly liked the idea of sharing the place with Amory. "You'll like it there, I think."

"I think so too, Your Highness. Will you tell me more about it?"

"Of course. While we eat, though." He tugged on Amory's hand and led him to the table.

The meal was everything he wanted it to be that night. The food was exceptional, and he wondered if the cook had wanted to do something special as well. The servants were unobtrusive, serving each course, then disappearing, leaving him and Amory to their conversation.

They talked about the estate for a while, and then bounced from topic to topic, none of them serious but all of them allowing him to know Amory more. The conversation was easy, and he felt almost giddy throughout it, knowing that. Amory didn't seem to have any pretenses. He showed Philip who he was with each gesture and word. In return, Philip found himself relaxing as well, foregoing his usual masks; his laughter and smiles were freer because of it.

But for all the laughter and light conversation, a simmering tension lurked beneath the surface. He couldn't stop looking at Amory across the table, and neither of them could seem to go more than a moment or two without touching. Little brushes of fingertips while they told stories of their childhoods, hands clasped as they sipped wine between courses. He hardly looked down at his plate, so loathe to break eye contact with Amory was he, but he took special notice of what they ate for dessert, a buttery pastry filled with berries and cream, only because of how much Amory enjoyed it. It was a pleasure to watch him eat it, to see him close his eyes at the first bite and let out a little hum of pleasure. He wondered if Amory would sound the same way in bed. When Amory licked some cream from his full lips, Philip doubted he would survive until he found out.

Once they finished dessert, he stood and held out a hand to Amory. They took their refilled wineglasses and went back to the sitting room, fingers twined together. A fire crackled in the hearth, banishing the evening's slight chill. Without speaking, they settled close together on the couch in front of the fire, the amber cushions soft around them. They were quiet for a while, the first silence between them since dinner began, but the silence wasn't uncomfortable, though that tension was still there. They had talked and would talk more, but Philip didn't feel the need to fill the quiet. So they sipped wine out of goblets made by Amory's family business and watched the flames dance in the hearth.

He looked at Amory often. He liked looking at him, liked that each time he did, he discovered something else. The glow of Amory's skin in firelight. The thick sweep of Amory's lashes as he blinked. Amory's gaze met his and held, as a faint blush colored Amory's cheeks. Slowly, he reached out, took Amory's glass, and set it down on the table with his own. Then he turned back to Amory and gently cupped his face. Amory's tongue darted out to moisten his lips, and Philip had to bite back a groan. He leaned forward and pressed his mouth to Amory's.

At the first touch of their lips, Amory moaned and pushed forward, hands coming up to clutch at Philip's shoulders. Philip gave in to temptation and deepened the kiss, sweeping his tongue into Amory's mouth to explore and taste. Amory tasted sweet, of red wine and the cream from dessert and something that had to be Amory himself and was utterly delicious.

Philip couldn't get enough of the taste, of that sweet mouth under his, so responsive and giving. He gathered Amory close. Philip told himself they would only kiss, but that didn't mean he couldn't touch a little, couldn't see what Amory's body felt like against his own. Amory came to him eagerly, pressing so close he was almost in Philip's lap, wine and kisses overcoming any reticence Amory might have had. That eagerness was thrilling, heady.

He moaned, feeling Amory's lithe body pressed up against his. Even through their clothes the sensation was incredible. He wanted skin on skin, but they couldn't that night. He pulled back for a breath, to slow them down, to keep himself from devouring Amory. One look at Amory's passion-glazed eyes and swollen lips, and his resolve was tested to the limit. Drawn back to Amory, he brushed light kisses along the line of Amory's jaw, down his neck. Amory gasped when he reached one spot, so he lingered, kissing, licking.

Amory's hands cupped Philip's face and pulled him up into another kiss. Amory took control, and oh, could he kiss. Philip felt a bolt of jealousy for whoever had been kissing Amory for him to be so skilled, even as he pressed closer to Amory.

Didn't matter. Amory was kissing him.

They lingered over kisses for a long while, separating only briefly for breath before coming together again. Finally, the kisses slowed, and Amory pulled away, but he snuggled back an instant later, nuzzling his face into Philip's neck. Philip brushed a kiss over Amory's soft hair. Heat still thrummed through his body, urging him on to more, but sitting curled around Amory was nice. Perfect even, to have Amory in his arms, with Amory's arms wrapped around him too. He'd never had that before. He sank into the sensation, savoring it, holding Amory close. He looked forward to many more nights of doing the same.

But for the moment, they should go to bed. Sadly separate beds.

"Probably time for sleep," he murmured, hating to disturb Amory and end their time together, but knowing they both did need sleep after the day it had been.

Amory shifted a little but didn't move away from Philip. If anything, his arms tightened. "I suppose you're right, Your Highness."

"I don't want you to call me that." It came out of nowhere, but when he examined the statement, he found he meant it.

Amory moved then, but only enough to be able to see him. "But then what should I call you? I can't call you by your name."

He almost laughed at the dismay in Amory's voice. "Why not?"

"Because I'm just—I'm not—I can't—"

He took pity and interrupted Amory's stuttering. "I don't want you to call me by a title. I don't want to be that to you. I want you to use my name."

He hoped Amory understood what he was trying to say, because he was having a difficult time articulating his own reasons. But he couldn't have Amory calling him Highness.

A dawning comprehension lit Amory's eyes, followed by other things... warmth, maybe a bit of hope, perhaps the beginning of affection. "So should I call you Philip Alexander Stefan Mael?"

He laughed a little at the tone of Amory's voice. "It's long."

"I've always wondered why you use so many names."

"I don't like all the names, but I was named to honor many people."

"They're nice names."

"Yes." He sighed. "Take Alexander. The name honors a relative whom my father was close to, but he turned out to never like me very much. Never treated me well. He wasn't a very good person really. I'm not sure why my father never saw it."

"I'm sorry."

He shook himself out of the mood. "It's done now, but I've never cared for the name because of the association. I still have to use them all."

Amory seemed to understand he didn't want to discuss it any further. "What should I call you, then?"

"You can call me Philip. My sister does and a few others."

"All right, if you want me to. I guess we should go to sleep." Amory stood and held out a hand to help him to his feet. Then Amory stretched up and kissed him lightly. "Good night, Philip."

"Good night, Amory. Sleep well." Philip couldn't resist one last kiss, a quick one before they parted and walked to their bedchambers on opposite sides of the sitting room. Neither could he stop himself when he reached the door to his bedchamber from taking one last look at Amory, and found Amory doing the same. They both laughed.

Behind his closed door, he laughed again at his own silliness. He was behaving more like a boy than a grown man, let alone a prince, but he couldn't care. He felt a little like he was floating instead of walking, and the giddiness was all due to the promise of what was to come with Amory.

CHAPTER 4

AMORY EMERGED from his bedchamber the next morning not entirely
sure what he would find. To his surprise, he slept well. He'd been sure
anxiety and excitement, not to mention the memory of the prince's kisses,
would keep him awake all night, but he was asleep almost as soon as he
climbed into the large bed. In fact, it had been difficult to climb out
of it that morning. The mattress was comfortable, the pillows plentiful,
and the bedding soft and luxurious. The bed was too decadent to resist
wallowing in it for a while.

Sunlight streamed through the sitting room windows and over
Prince Philip, still clad in his dressing gown, sitting at a small table set
with breakfast for two. The prince looked gorgeous in the morning light.
The urge to drag him off to bed and see what was under the dressing
gown shocked Amory breathless.

He was still staring when the prince looked up at him. The welcome
in his eyes made Amory feel warm inside. The prince really did want him
there. And Amory was supposed to stop calling him by his title.

"Good morning, Amory."

"Good morning, Pip," he replied, taking the chair opposite the
prince—Philip, Pip—and watching for the other man's reaction. He
didn't think Philip would be upset, but he wasn't certain.

Philip's mouth dropped open slightly, and he froze, a pastry held
in midair. "Pip?"

"Yes."

"You're calling me Pip?"

"Yes." The platters on the table were piled with delicious-looking
pastries, fruit, and cheese. He looked over the selections while watching
Philip from under his lashes.

"I thought you were going to call me Philip." Philip lowered the
pastry back to his plate.

Amory gave up all pretense of deciding what to eat for breakfast
and looked up at Philip. He'd known giving Philip a nickname was a
risk. He'd been given leave to call Philip by name, but he found himself

wanting something more, something special between them. Something only for them. "Yes, and I will, but I decided I like Pip better for you. For me to call you in private."

Something changed in Philip's eyes. Was it a hint of pleasure? Then he grinned. "And you decided to call me Pip and see what happened?"

"I did, yes." Amory wasn't sure where the mischievous impulse came from. He should have been worried about whether the prince would be angry, but in fact, he'd hoped to get a smile out of Philip with it. "Do you mind?"

"That you have your own name for me? No, I don't mind." Philip's gaze softened, became more intimate, and Amory found himself captivated by it, by the promise in Philip's eyes, and sat there staring back at him.

A bird's call outside the window startled them both, breaking their trance. They laughed, but then Philip took Amory's hand and lifted it, brushing a light kiss over his knuckles before returning his hand to the table.

"Have some breakfast," Philip said. "The almond pastries are especially good. They've always been my favorite."

They were delicious, Amory found, once the butterflies in his stomach calmed enough for him to eat, but he decided he liked the sticky apricot ones better. Everything was good, which wasn't a surprise. The palace would have the best cooks and bakers. He and Philip ate almost all the food laid out for them while talking about nothing in particular. He enjoyed talking with Philip. Conversation with the prince was far easier than he ever would have imagined.

They had finished eating and were sipping the last of the chocolate poured from the little silver pot when a knock at the sitting room door interrupted them. Philip sighed. "I'm sorry."

"It's all right." Philip was an important man. It was probably unusual they'd had so much uninterrupted time so far.

"You're far more patient than I am." Philip raised his voice. "Enter."

A thin blond man, dressed soberly, came into the sitting room and bowed, displaying no reaction to Amory's presence. "Good morning, Your Highness, sir."

While Amory tried to control his surprise at the man's courtesy toward him, Philip greeted him. "Good morning. Amory, this is my secretary, Donatien. He keeps me properly organized. Donatien, this is Amory."

Was Amory deluding himself thinking there might be some fondness in Philip's voice already? Probably.

"An honor to meet you, sir." Donatien bent in another bow, this one for Amory.

"And you, Donatien."

"What can we do for you, Donatien?" Philip asked.

"I'm sorry to disturb you, Your Highness. Your uncle has sent word that he would like to speak with you this morning at your earliest convenience."

"And I'm sure you've phrased his request more politely than he did." Philip's voice was light, but there was an edge of something in his eyes that Amory didn't like to see. Philip's face settled into resigned lines. "I'll see him first thing, after I finish breakfast and dress."

"Yes, Your Highness."

"Do I have anything scheduled at lunch?" Philip asked.

"No, Your Highness."

"Please keep lunch free today." Philip looked at Amory. "My sister wants to meet you, and I thought lunch might be a good time. She won't be awake and around until almost then anyway if she stayed at her friend's home too late last night."

Even though the thought of meeting Philip's sister was enough to make his stomach flip unpleasantly, Amory nodded. "I'd like to meet her."

"Thank you." Philip turned back to Donatien. "Any other changes I should know about?"

"No, Your Highness. I'll leave you to your breakfast. Your Highness, sir." Donatien bowed again, and left the room.

Philip faced Amory. "I'm sorry about that."

"It's all right."

"He comes to see me during breakfast to go over my schedule sometimes. It never really mattered. I was always alone."

Amory felt a little glow of pleasure at the implication that it did matter then, that Philip might consider their time together important enough to not want anyone intruding on it. "It really is all right. I understand."

"Thank you. But still."

They were quiet for a few moments. Philip didn't seem to feel any inclination to rush to dress and see his uncle. He supposed Philip was the prince and could do as he pleased, but Amory still found it somewhat strange. Maybe because he was so used to having to jump when his father called for him. He wasn't going to complain about extra time with Philip, though, especially when he wasn't sure what his own day would hold.

"Pip?"

"Yes?" Philip smiled at him warmly, but there were shadows in his eyes.

"I was wondering… your secretary. He was so respectful, deferential even, to me."

"As he should be."

"I just… didn't expect it."

"Why not?" Philip's dark brows pulled together in a confused frown.

He shrugged. "I'm not a nobleman, I'm not anything. And I came here so suddenly yesterday as your…"

"As my lover?" Philip's gaze was gentle.

"Yes. And even though we aren't yet, everyone thinks we are, and I didn't expect to be treated the way he did."

"You didn't expect to be treated with respect." Philip waited for Amory's nod. "I wouldn't let anyone treat you poorly, but they won't. I told you yesterday that princes have taken lovers in the past?"

He nodded again.

"For a long time, it was tradition for the ruler to take a lover before he married, and move the person into the palace. Sometimes, the lover stayed after the prince married, most often if the marriage was an arranged one and if he and his lover had some affection between them. Both of which were common. Some of my ancestors probably took other, more casual lovers, but the one who lived here with the prince was someone special. It hasn't happened as much in the last few generations, but it's still done. Long ago, they were called concubines, and they had a special status of their own. Close to that of the prince's spouse." Philip took his hand. "So you don't have to worry. No one is going to look down on you for this, and if they do, I'll put a stop to it."

He wasn't sure what to say. Not to Philip's promise really, more to his explanation of what his status was. Almost like being the prince's spouse? He couldn't believe that. "Thank you. But I can take care of myself, you know."

Philip grinned. "I'm sure you can, but... I think I'd like it if you'd let me take care of you sometimes."

Warmth washed through him. "Only if you let me do the same for you."

"I think I'd like that too." Philip sighed. "I suppose I have to dress and deal with my uncle."

"Probably." Amory hesitated. "What should I do?"

"What do you mean?"

"Well, I don't know what I should do here. I'm feeling a little at loose ends." He shrugged, hoping Philip wouldn't be insulted by his questions.

"Well, today, my sister wants to meet you, so we'll be having what will probably turn into a long lunch with her. Otherwise, you can do whatever you like."

"Oh." That wasn't very helpful, actually. He didn't think there had ever been a time when he had complete freedom.

Philip looked as if he understood. "What do you like to do?"

"Ride, swim, sketch." What else did he enjoy? Spending time with his friends, of course. He should let Tristan know what happened to him.

"You can do all of those things here, and we really are going to have to go out to Alzata. There's a lot more private space outside to do those things. Do you have a horse?"

"Yes." He hadn't thought about her since he arrived at the palace with his father and Alban yesterday.

"You rode here yesterday? Then your horse should be in the stables. You can check on her if you like." It was almost as if Philip was reading his mind.

He nodded. "Thanks. But that isn't enough, is it?"

"You said you were taking classes at the university. Do you want to continue with them?"

Having a choice about his studies was strange too. "I don't know. I never really cared for it."

"Because of what you were studying?"

"Maybe. My father chose my course of study. Alban's as well. I never found it particularly interesting."

"Well, if you want to continue your studies, you can, and you can choose what you study this time. And if you don't, you don't have to." Philip shrugged. "You have plenty of time to decide."

"I suppose so."

"Yesterday was a long day. Settle in for a little while, and think about what you want."

"All right."

"Good." Philip was still holding his hand, and he gave it a squeeze. "Meeting my sister is enough to deal with today."

Philip's words startled a laugh out of him, which was probably what Philip intended. "Is she so fearsome?"

"No, just enthusiastic. Elodie is looking forward to meeting you. She wanted to run right in here last night, but I restrained her. All right, now I do need to dress and see my uncle."

"Yes, you do." He paused. "I'm sure you're busy today."

Philip tilted his head to the side as he studied Amory. "No more busy than usual. Why?"

"Well, I don't really know what you do each day. Could I spend some of the day with you and see? If I wouldn't bother you."

Philip looked startled then pleased. "Certainly. You wouldn't bother me, but you might end up bored. I'll be in my office all morning. You can come in whenever you like."

"Thank you."

Philip squeezed his hand again before releasing it. Amory felt the loss of contact immediately, but as soon as Philip stood, he stepped around the table and bent to kiss Amory briefly. Too briefly. He wanted more of those lips on his, but Philip was backing away already. "I'll see you soon."

PHILIP COULD get used to sitting across the breakfast table from Amory. His warm presence made starting the day easier. Amory didn't even need to talk, but they had. He could even get used to being called Pip. It seemed like such a silly little name, but somehow, when Amory called him that, it felt special, something unique to Amory and their developing relationship. He could be Pip to Amory.

Such a simple thing, their shared breakfast, yet it left him feeling so light. He almost didn't mind the upcoming discussion with his uncle. He settled in his study, looking over some documents while he waited. Uncle Umber would have concerns about Philip openly taking a male lover and would likely not express them tactfully, but he was a good man at heart, one who cared about Tournai. Still, governing the country was Philip's duty and responsibility, not Uncle Umber's.

His uncle arrived in his usual fashion a few moments later, walking into the study without knocking or waiting to be announced. "Is it true?"

"Good morning, Uncle."

"Good morning. Is it true," he repeated, less a question than a demand.

Philip sighed. He knew the discussion was going to be unpleasant, but for once, he didn't feel like mollifying his uncle. "Is what true?"

"Don't be coy with me, Philip Alexander."

Uncle Umber must be more upset than Philip had anticipated if he forgot the proprieties he adhered to so closely. In that way, his son Cathal was quite like him.

"Is it true you named a male concubine yesterday?"

"I did. Amory moved into the palace last night."

"What were you thinking?" Uncle Umber threw up his hands in a rare display of exasperation. "You need an heir. Don't you see? If you openly take a male lover, who will ever want to marry you?"

Philip bit back an exasperated noise. "The same people who have always wanted to marry me—those who want the power and status that come with marrying into a royal family, alliance-seekers who want the connection to such a strategic trading country, starry-eyed young noblewomen."

All the people he wouldn't want anyway. He wanted his future marriage to include love, naïve as that sounded even to himself. He didn't want it to be solely about producing an heir and gaining an alliance. He wanted something, someone, for himself, which was why he'd acted on the connection he felt with Amory, despite its suddenness.

"None of that changes, Uncle Umber."

"You don't know that. Don't think you know everything after a year on the throne." The tone gave the impression of an admonishing finger shaking in his direction, but thankfully Uncle Umber didn't go so far as the actual gesture.

"I would never presume to believe I know everything, but I think we can both agree there will always be people who want to marry into royalty." Though the idea of it disgusted him. "It's fine. Even if it weren't, Elodie is my heir. She'll marry and have children someday. And if, for some reason, she doesn't, I have you and all of your children and their future children. The succession is not in jeopardy."

"Don't tell me you're thinking of not marrying." Uncle Umber's face went an alarming shade of purple.

"I didn't say that. I said the succession is not in danger should I not produce an heir. You have nothing to worry about."

"You can't make light of this. Producing an heir is vital, and it is your duty. If you had to have a male lover, you could have at least been discreet about it." Uncle Umber planted his hands on his hips and glared down at Philip, his whole demeanor one of intimidation, and suddenly Philip was finished with the discussion.

"This is not up for debate, Uncle. Amory is here, and he is going to stay as long as he wants. I'm hoping that turns into a long time, because I want him here. Are we clear?"

His uncle flinched, but nodded sharply. "Yes. But I believe you're going to regret this decision."

"As is your right, but I disagree."

They were interrupted then by a knock on the door.

"Enter," Philip called.

Despite his worry about what his uncle might say, Philip was happy to see Amory standing there when the door opened.

"I'm sorry. Am I interrupting?"

"Not at all." Philip rose from his seat behind the desk, and held out a hand to Amory. Amory glanced at Uncle Umber, but came to Philip without hesitation. He gave Amory's slender fingers a squeeze. "Amory, this is my uncle Umber, my father's brother. Uncle Umber, this is Amory."

"It's an honor to meet you, Your Grace." Amory bent in a half bow, probably as much as he could manage with his hand in Philip's. Nevertheless, the bow was executed gracefully.

Uncle Umber glared at Philip before turning to Amory. His tone was icy when he spoke. "Master Amory."

Philip felt Amory tense beside him, but Amory said nothing. Uncle Umber faced Philip again. "You're making a mistake. This was my brother's country, my brother's throne, and I refuse to stand by and watch you harm it."

Anger ignited within Philip. He was grateful to his uncle for all he had done since Philip's father died, but he wasn't going to let his uncle say those things to him, to think those things about him. Tournai was his country, he'd given his life to it long before his father died, but Amory was rapidly becoming his too, and Philip needed that. "Yes. Tournai was my father's country. My father's throne, and now it's mine. I would never harm it."

"You will if you proceed on this course."

"Enough," Philip interrupted. "This discussion is over. I've heard your opinion, though it was unsolicited, and I don't agree. Even if it turns out to be the mistake you think it is, it's my mistake to make. It's my throne."

Uncle Umber stared at him before giving him a curt nod. "Yes, Your Highness. If you'll excuse me?"

After the door closed firmly behind Uncle Umber, Amory turned to Philip, his eyes troubled. "Is everything all right?"

Philip blew out a breath and forced himself to relax. Uncle Umber might have more years and experience in governance and diplomacy than he did, but Philip was Tournai's crown prince, a role he had prepared for his entire life. He preferred not to argue with his uncle, but he couldn't back down. He needed someone of his own, and he didn't want secrecy to enter into it.

He realized he hadn't answered Amory's question, and Amory looked even more concerned.

"It's fine. Everything is fine." He tried to make his voice as reassuring as possible.

"Everything doesn't look fine. Was that about me?"

Philip sank down into his chair, but he kept hold of Amory's hand, and the other man settled against the edge of the desk near Philip. "Yes, I suppose. Or rather it's about my openly taking a male lover. My uncle feels it could adversely affect my marital prospects."

"Will it?" Amory's large, dark eyes held something indefinable in addition to the concern that hadn't faded. "I didn't realize you were looking for a wife. But that's silly. Of course, you would be. You need an heir."

"It's an obligation I'm reminded of often enough, but I'm not looking for a wife, Amory. I'm young, and I have plenty of family. The throne will be fine."

"I don't want my being here to hurt you."

He couldn't let Amory start thinking that and pulling away, maybe leaving. He had too good a feeling about what could be between them for it to end before it had a chance to begin.

"It won't." He tugged on Amory's hand until he tumbled onto Philip's lap with a startled exclamation. He wrapped his arms around Amory and nuzzled into his neck. "I like having you here already. I was happy this morning before my uncle irritated me."

Amory's tense muscles relaxed at his words, almost melting into Philip. "I like being here with you too."

"Good."

AMORY DID like being with Philip, and he already knew he didn't want to leave, but he worried his presence would harm Philip in some way. Especially after walking into that scene with Philip's uncle. He didn't want to come between Philip and his family or his responsibilities. Philip seemed more angry at his uncle than anything. Amory wondered if the apparent animosity was all because of him, or if something else was involved as well.

He spent the morning in Philip's study with him. He didn't know anything about governing a country, but he was curious, and since Philip said Amory wasn't bothering him, Amory stayed. Philip talked to him while he worked. Donatien was in and out of the study with paperwork and correspondence throughout the morning.

Cathal came in while Amory was using a small table and some borrowed stationary to write a letter to Adeline. He hadn't had much time yesterday to write anything other than a plea for her to help pack his things. She would worry if she only received the short note, but he wasn't sure what to say to her, and he worried about putting too much in a note someone else might see. It took him far longer than it should have to write.

He signed it and hesitated before pulling a blank piece of paper in front of himself. There was someone else who deserved a letter. Tristan. He needed to tell Tristan what happened, that everything had changed, but he wasn't sure what to say. He didn't love Tristan, not as anything more than a friend, but he wasn't sure how Tristan felt about him, and Amory didn't want to hurt him.

When he finally finished, it seemed Philip and Cathal were finishing their conversation too.

"You haven't forgotten our game later, have you?" Cathal asked Philip.

"Of course not. The new ambassador from Kavalas is arriving this afternoon, but we'll play after."

"Good." Cathal's attention turned to Amory. "Do you play tino?"

Amory jumped a bit. It was the first time Cathal spoke to him since his brief greeting when Cathal arrived. "No, I'm afraid I don't."

"I think you would enjoy it," Philip told him, grinning. "Come watch us play later, and then I can teach you."

"Thank you. I'd like that."

"That's settled, then. I'll be in my office if you need me," Cathal said. "See you both this afternoon."

After Cathal left, Philip turned back to Amory. "I think you and Cathal are going to get along well."

"I hope so." He really did, for Philip's sake. Philip was obviously close to his cousin, and Amory wanted to like Cathal, and for Cathal to like him, for Philip. He wasn't sure how Cathal felt about him despite Cathal's politeness.

Philip stood and walked over to Amory, perching on the table in front of him. "You will."

Philip leaned down and pressed his lips to Amory's. Amory sighed and leaned up into the kiss, enjoying the rub of Philip's soft lips against his. It had only been a day and he was already addicted to the kisses. Philip groaned and deepened the kiss, trapping Amory's moan between them. Amory clutched at Philip when Philip ended the kiss and sat back. He was embarrassed to realize the sound he made was something like a whimper.

Philip cupped his cheek, brushing his thumb back and forth over Amory's lips. Amory shivered. "I know. I'd like to keep kissing you too, but we have to go have lunch with my sister."

That was enough to clear Amory's head of the fog Philip's kisses provoked. He wanted Princess Elodie to like him even more than he wanted Cathal to like him. He was so close to his own sister that he was already anticipating introducing Adeline to Philip, but he didn't know how he would feel if Adeline hated Philip. He needed to make sure Philip's sister liked him. All things considered, he'd rather keep kissing Philip.

Well, he'd probably rather keep kissing Philip no matter what the alternative was.

Philip had a knowing look in his eyes. "Continue this later?"

He nodded. "Definitely."

"Let's go see Elodie." Philip stood and held out a hand to Amory, pulling him to his feet. Philip drew Amory's hand through his arm, connecting them as they walked to Elodie's suite. Amory tried not to feel self-conscious. He wasn't used to walking around on someone's arm, but he liked walking close to Philip, liked the feel of Philip's strong arm under his fingers.

Lady Celeste, who Philip had mentioned was Cathal's lover, greeted them and showed them into a sitting room to wait. Curious, Amory took a moment to study her surreptitiously. Celeste had golden-brown hair, large green eyes, and a curvy figure in her demure gown. He could see the appeal she would have to Cathal. She left them with a graceful curtsy.

"She's just the type of woman Cathal likes, and he was so obvious about getting her here. I have no idea how he thought I didn't know," Philip said, his low voice vibrating with good-natured amusement.

Amory laughed quietly.

"By the way, Elodie is almost always late. So we may be waiting." Philip wandered farther into the room, and Amory followed. It was a pretty little sitting room, cool and delicate and feminine, very different from Philip's. The way Philip propped himself against the window frame spoke of long habit.

Amory joined him, and they stared out the window together, Philip pointing out things in the garden they could see from their vantage point, until Amory heard the door open behind them. He turned as a young woman rushed headlong into the room, followed by another young lady at a much more sedate pace.

Philip stepped up next to him as the first lady came to a halt not far from them. She was obviously Philip's sister, but they had only dark hair and a pale golden cast to the skin in common. She was much tinier than her brother, her form and features delicate, almost fragile. She fit in the feminine jewel box of a room. The only thing at odds with the image was her energy. She seemed to vibrate with it, even standing still. Her dangling earrings were swinging from her rush into the room.

The woman beside her was more what Amory imagined of a young noblewoman. Calm and elegant, her posture perfect, her hands neatly folded. She was taller than the princess, her hair dressed in thick golden curls, her eyes so blue as to be nearly violet. Her gown seemed formal for a lunch, but perhaps more formality was appropriate for a meal at the palace.

"Elodie—"

"I know! I know I'm a bit late, but Lil was helping me dress and time got away from us." Princess Elodie smiled at him and Philip. "I really am sorry."

"It's all right. Elodie, this is Amory. Amory, my sister Elodie."

Amory bowed. "I'm honored to meet you, Your Highness."

"And I you, Master Amory. I'm still vexed with my brother for not letting me meet you last night. Oh, this is my dearest friend, Lady Lilliale."

Amory bowed to the blond woman at Princess Elodie's side. Lady Lilliale dipped into a brief curtsy. The princess looped her arm through Lady Lilliale's as she straightened.

"I didn't know you would be joining us today, Lilliale," Philip said. Amory was surprised at his use of her given name.

"I came back with Elodie last night, Philip. I was going to come and watch your match with Lord Cathal later anyway."

Amory's surprise ratcheted up further. Philip must have a close relationship with his sister's friend.

"I'm surprised you would bother. It's only a casual game between cousins. We do it often enough."

"Of course I'll be there, Philip. You know I enjoy watching your games. Elodie and I are both going to be there, and a few more of our friends. I'm sure there will be many people there." Lady Lilliale smiled at Philip.

"Yes, and most of them will only be there to try to curry favor." Philip rolled his eyes, and flashed a grin at Amory, but there was a trace of annoyance in Philip's eyes. "Very few people would choose to watch a match that is only for my and Cathal's enjoyment otherwise."

He flushed, enjoying the feeling that they were sharing some sort of private joke. "Well, I'll be there."

"Yes, but you have reason to." Philip's gaze, suddenly more intense, caught Amory's and held, making Amory think of their kisses.

Lady Lilliale's voice interrupted before he could get lost in daydreams. "Elodie and I have reason to be there as well. It's going to be great fun."

"Yes, it will be a lovely afternoon," the princess added. "Shall we go in to lunch?"

They ate at a round table covered in a lace cloth, set with porcelain and delicate glassware, in the small dining room in Princess Elodie's suite. The dining room was another feminine room, the furniture almost dainty, making Amory fear he might break something. To his practiced eye, the glassware looked like something his family had made. Philip kept him by his side, seating Amory at his right. Lady Lilliale claimed the chair to Philip's left, which left Princess Elodie between Amory and Lady Lilliale.

As they ate, Princess Elodie peppered him with questions about himself and his family. In the brief silences she allowed, Lady Lilliale asked Philip questions and interjected comments about her family and court gossip and news. It had the effect of creating two separate and rather disjointed conversations at the table, but Philip juggled both with ease. Amory wasn't so proficient, but he did his best and was grateful for Philip's explanatory comments to him, or he would have been unable to follow Lady Lilliale's stories. All in all it went well enough.

They finished the meal with a custardy fruit tart. Princess Elodie and Lady Lilliale both reminded Philip they would see him later that afternoon, and Philip and he escaped into the corridor. Philip looked pensive as they walked for a few moments, but finally he sighed.

"So that was Elodie," Philip said with a rueful look.

"Yes." He wasn't sure what to say about her. The reality of Princess Elodie was not what he expected. "Is she always so, um, exuberant?"

"That's one way of putting it." Philip laughed. "Yes, though she can pretend to calm."

"I suppose she would have to."

"She manages to play the proper princess when people other than family are present." Philip took Amory's hand and brought it up to his lips for a quick kiss before placing it back on his arm. "She didn't do that today. I'm glad. It means she's going to consider you family."

"You think so?" Hope rose inside him.

"Yes, I do." Philip sobered, his eyes becoming troubled. "I didn't know Lilliale would be there. I'm sorry."

"It's all right."

"No, it isn't. Not really. I wanted you to meet Elodie and get to know her, but instead, Lilliale was there pulling away El's attention and talking about people you haven't met, some of whom I don't even like and some who...." Philip shook his head. "I wanted it to be the three of us this first time."

At lunch, Amory hadn't been able to tell what Philip thought of the conversation. He was surprised to hear the strength of Philip's dismay. "It's fine. I did like your sister, and I'll have time to get to know her."

"Yes. Good."

"Your sister and Lady Lilliale are close."

"Yes, for all their lives. She and Elodie were born only a month apart. They grew up together since our families have always been close. Elodie considers her the sister she never had. She's a little like another sister to me too."

For some reason, something inside of him loosened at Philip's words.

"You'll see a lot of her, I'm sure. Sometimes I wonder that she doesn't actually live in the palace with Elodie."

He glanced at Philip. "Is something wrong?"

"No, not really." But Philip still looked uncomfortable, and Amory became concerned.

"What is it?"

Philip looked at him. "Lilliale was talking about her family. Her oldest brother, quite a bit."

"Yes, I remember." He could feel the tension in Philip's body from the hold he had on Philip's arm, but he was puzzled as to why Philip was so tense, and why Philip was bringing up Lady Lilliale's brother.

"Her brother, that brother, was the man I...."

It took Amory only an instant to realize what Philip was reluctant to say. Lady Lilliale's oldest brother was Philip's one former lover. "Oh. Does she know?"

"No one knew. We were extremely discreet."

"You're not being discreet now."

"No, I'm not. I don't want to be anymore."

A warm feeling moved through Amory despite his worry at Philip's stubborn insistence. There was just something in Philip's eyes. "All right."

"Are you? All right, I mean?"

"Yes, fine." Then Amory's stomach sank. "You aren't—you don't have feelings for him still, do you?"

"No, no." Philip's voice was firm, and his gaze never wavered from Amory's. "I felt awkward with her talking about him, and you didn't know. I felt you should know. Especially since you'll meet him sooner or later. His family is prominent among the nobility."

He hadn't given much thought to the identity of Philip's former lover before. He probably would have at some point, but everything had happened so quickly over the last day that he hadn't gotten there. He could hardly believe it had only been a day. He wasn't sure how he would feel seeing Philip's former lover. He supposed he would find out then.

He looked into Philip's eyes and saw worry. "Thank you for telling me. I'll be fine. Promise."

And he would keep that promise. He wouldn't do anything to upset or embarrass Philip if he could help it.

"I had to tell you." Some of the worry faded from Philip's eyes.

"Will you tell me what happened? Why it ended?" he asked carefully.

Philip nodded. "But not here. Later, when we're alone, all right?"

"Of course." He had almost forgotten they were in public, walking through the palace corridors. The residential corridors were quiet and mostly empty, but they might still be overheard. Amory wouldn't be the cause of Philip's secrets being exposed.

But he couldn't stop thinking about it. Philip had been so uncomfortable talking about his former lover. Because of how Philip thought Amory might feel? Or because there were still feelings left on Philip's part? Philip denied it, and he hated to think of Philip lying to him, but that didn't mean Philip wouldn't. If Philip did have feelings for his former lover, what did it mean for them?

It shouldn't matter. He was going to be Philip's friend and lover, his concubine if they still called it that, but nothing more. He could never be more. They hadn't spoken of the possibility of feelings developing between them, and it was too soon to be feeling anything anyway. So why was Amory dejected at the thought of Philip loving someone else?

CHAPTER 5

THE NEW ambassador from Kavalas was being presented to Philip that afternoon, and that, in conjunction with the tino match he'd promised Cathal, meant Philip had to put off telling Amory about Vasco. He didn't mind the delay. He'd never spoken about Vasco to anyone—it would have been difficult to do so and keep the affair a secret—and he wasn't especially looking forward to it. But Amory deserved to know, especially since Amory would meet Vasco sooner or later. Probably sooner.

He asked Amory to accompany him to the ambassador's presentation, eager to keep Amory at his side. He was amused to see astonishment wash over Amory's face when Philip led him into the throne room, to the chair placed for him beside Philip's throne. His Amory would have to cultivate a less expressive face to survive among the nobility. Selfishly, he didn't want Amory to change. He liked how expressive Amory's beautiful face was. He didn't want to lose that to the jaded attitude so prevalent at court.

Despite his surprise, Amory smiled at him once they were seated, even if the smile looked a trifle forced. Philip leaned toward Amory and spoke so the words only reached Amory's ears. "Are you all right?"

"Fine." Amory's lips quirked. "I didn't expect to be up here in front of everyone."

A fair-sized crowd filled the throne room that afternoon. People wanted to get a look at the new ambassador. Many of them probably wanted to get a look at the prince's new lover as well.

"I'm sorry. I should have warned you."

"I know you said I would have some sort of status, but I never believed it would be all right for me to sit here with you in front of everyone."

He took Amory's hand, hoping to reassure him. "It is, and what's more, I want you sitting here with me. All right?"

Some of Amory's tension eased. "All right."

"Good." He gave Amory's hand one last squeeze before letting go and settled back on his throne. He gave the signal that they should begin.

The new ambassador strode into the room as soon as the doors were opened. He made his bows to Philip, presented his credentials, gave a flowery speech that included the greetings and well wishes of the King and Queen of Kavalas, and also bestowed gifts from them on Philip. Philip then introduced his own advisors and his Minister of Foreign Affairs to the new ambassador. Through the pomp and protocol of the ceremony, Philip kept a watch on Amory. Amory wasn't used to functions of this kind, let alone being on display during them.

Amory sat in the chair next to Philip's throne, his expression one of interest. His posture was tense, but Amory managed to mostly hide whatever nerves he felt. Amory's interest in the proceedings probably helped. While Philip had grown up participating in ceremonies like this, Amory had never attended one. Whatever Amory said about not caring for his university classes, Philip could see already that Amory enjoyed new experiences and the learning that went along with them. He would be interested to hear Amory's impressions later.

A short reception was held afterward. Philip kept Amory at his side, hoping to ease him into court social situations, but Amory did well, leaving Philip flushed with pride. Amory was polite and gracious to everyone he was introduced to, even when it was blatantly obvious they were fishing for information about the prince's lover. He should have warned Amory about those types of people. His life was filled with gawkers and hangers-on, but Amory's hadn't been. He would have to talk with Amory about people trying to get close to Amory to curry favor with Philip.

However, there wasn't any time to talk about it after the reception. He and Amory hurried to change into less formal clothing and then strode out toward the gardens where the tino court was located.

"Should you be hurrying? You're the prince. Don't they have to wait for you?" Amory teased.

"Ha." True. But it didn't mean he liked keeping people waiting for no good reason.

More people milled around the small court in the far corner of the garden than he expected. The game was only a friendly match with Cathal, something they did often, sometimes with one or two of the other cousins. The matches attracted more attention than they deserved, mostly from tittering young ladies and politicking courtiers. It exhausted him beyond belief. Philip should have realized there might be more people that day. Amory was big news.

The usual group of ladies was there, but some were pouting a bit. They clustered around Elodie and Lilliale in a tight group on one side of the grass court. Other courtiers mingled at the edges. Philip led Amory through the crowd to where Cathal and two of his brothers stood.

Philip had several cousins, but he was the closest to Cathal, Vrai, and Etan, and he hoped they would accept Amory. He didn't think Vrai and Etan would be a problem. A couple of his other cousins, maybe, but not those two.

Both men greeted Amory warmly and waved away any attempt to call them anything but their names. Etan was perhaps too warm and looked at Amory for a little too long in a way that made Philip bristle. He put a hand to Amory's waist without thinking, needing, for some reason, to show his claim on Amory. He hadn't realized Etan was interested in men that way. He would have to think about it when he wasn't so annoyed.

Annoyed with him looking at Amory. Obviously, he was going crazy if he was upset at Etan for looking at Amory.

Amory turned to look at him, surprise flooding his dark eyes. There was pleasure there too, and Amory leaned into him a little before turning back to Vrai and Etan.

"Do you play, Amory?" Etan asked.

"No, but Philip said he would teach me."

"We'll have to play once you've learned," Vrai said.

"I'd like that."

"But perhaps in a setting a little less public," Philip said. He brushed his fingers over Amory's, a light, fleeting touch, before turning back to his cousins. "Time to play."

He accepted the small wood-framed racquet from one of the servants and joined Cathal out on the court, which was put in when Philip was a child and the game came into fashion. He used to watch his father and his friends hit the small, leather ball back and forth across the net when he was young and wanted so much to play too. When no one was around, he and his cousins used to go out on the court and wildly whack the ball back and forth, until Uncle Umber told them if they were going to play, they should learn to play properly. Lessons soon followed.

That day, he and Cathal played as they always did, throwing themselves into the game and the competition, friendly though it was. Philip had to admit he played a little harder than he usually did, and he was embarrassed to realize he was trying to impress Amory.

Embarrassment didn't stop him from doing it.

And Cathal, that bastard, knew it. He smirked through the whole match and played his absolute hardest. He wasn't going to make it the slightest bit easier for Philip to win. Usually they didn't care much who won. It was only a game, despite their competitiveness, but he needed to win the first time Amory watched. He cursed himself for it. As if Amory would be impressed.

Philip did eventually win, but Cathal made him work for it. Both he and Cathal were dripping sweat by the end, but that didn't stop Elodie, Lilliale, Celeste, and several other young ladies from waylaying them before they were off the court. Servants insinuated themselves deftly around the ladies in their pretty spring gowns to hand him and Cathal towels.

He blotted his face with the soft towel while listening to the ladies chatter about the match, gushing over his and Cathal's playing. Mostly his. Lady Celeste positioned herself closest to Cathal, but the others vied for Philip's attention. No matter what Uncle Umber thought, Philip was a prime catch, even with a male lover. Well, not a lover yet, but no one else knew that. He half listened to the ladies while peering over their heads to search through the encroaching crowd for Amory.

Amory still stood with Vrai and Etan where they had been since the beginning of the match, but each of them had refreshments in hand. Vrai and Etan were carrying on an animated conversation, but Amory looked toward Philip and the women surrounding him. Philip frowned, concerned by his pensive expression, but Amory snapped free of whatever he was thinking and smiled over at Philip. He managed a discreet eye roll so Amory would know what he thought of the crowd, and was rewarded with Amory stifling a laugh before Vrai and Etan drew him back into conversation. Philip focused again on his sister and the other ladies, suddenly much lighter.

He and Amory ate dinner alone again that night. It wouldn't happen every night—he had obligations that often meant dining with nobles, ambassadors, and other dignitaries, and sometimes he liked to eat with

Elodie or his cousins and friends. But he enjoyed having the time alone with Amory while he could.

Conversation was easy and enjoyable again, despite the knowledge that soon he would have to tell Amory about Vasco. Easy to put it off for a little while longer, to let the conversation stay light, to talk about the match earlier and explain the rules of the game, clarifying what his cousins told Amory.

After dinner, they drifted into the sitting room as they had the night before. He liked the idea that it might turn into something they did many nights, a habit for them. Dinner and relaxing, perhaps curling up together and reading or talking before going to bed, again together. It sounded nice, better than nice. Surprising how much he wanted it, not just for that night but for the rest of his life, and how he hoped Amory would be the one he did all of those things with.

They settled again on the couch. He considered putting some distance between them while he told Amory about his former lover, but Amory seemed to be getting bolder. He twined his fingers through Philip's, keeping him close by Amory's side. Philip gave in without even a token protest. He wanted to be close to Amory.

They sipped the slightly spicy, deep-red wine in silence. He wondered if he was making too much of it, but he had never spoken of his affair with Vasco with anyone. He'd never imagined doing so, let alone with someone who was going to be his lover. He wasn't sure how he was going to feel telling the story.

"Do you want to tell me?" Amory finally asked. His gaze was soft, understanding. "You don't have to. I understand how it could be difficult."

"Yes, but not the way you think. I do want to tell you." He brushed Amory's curls off his forehead and smiled when they fell right back. "I told you our families, mine and Vasco's, were very close. That's why Elodie and Lilliale are so close. Lilliale has brothers, both older and younger. She's the only girl."

"She must be doted upon."

"Oh, yes. I was friends with her older brothers growing up. Vasco is the oldest, older than me by five years, and I found him very attractive as I grew up. It took me a while to figure out he found me attractive too. We were friends, and we kind of fell into an affair.

"We kept it a secret—no one knew. I didn't want the rumors, the talk, and neither did he. Which was one of the reasons I hadn't done anything like it before. That, and I guess I didn't want a series of meaningless tumbles." He shrugged, more self-conscious than he imagined he would be.

"I understand that." Amory tentatively stroked a hand over Philip's hair. Philip leaned into the caress, nearly purring at the pleasure of it. He wanted to close his eyes and revel in the gentle petting, but he needed to finish his story.

He sighed. "It really isn't much of a story after that. We slept together whenever we could for about a year. Then he ended it. His father was ill, and he wanted Vasco to marry. Vasco didn't seem all that upset about his father's wishes. I don't know. However he felt, our affair was over, and he married six months later. His father passed away not long after."

"I'm sorry."

"I wasn't in love with him." It seemed important for Amory to know that. "He was my friend, and we had plenty of lust between us, but that was it. The worst of it is that after he ended our affair, he ended our friendship too." Vasco had disappeared from Philip's life. Some of his absence was caused by his marriage and his increased responsibilities, but not all of it. "I miss his friendship sometimes."

"I'm sorry for that, then." Amory's hand was still in his hair, and Philip didn't want him to remove it. It felt so good there. His whole body was starting to hum from that one contact, despite the awkward subject of their discussion. "I may have lost my closest friend, so I understand."

"How? Will you tell me?" A fierce need to make everything better for Amory washed through him. He had no idea where it came from.

"Sort of like you and Vasco, Tristan and I have known each other our whole lives. We played as children, went to school together, and then... well, we started kissing." Amory shifted in his seat, his expression screaming that he wished he'd never brought it up. "He's the only person I'd ever kissed, before you."

"What happened?"

"We got careless and my brother saw us. I knew my father wouldn't be pleased. Tristan was terrified of what his father would do if Alban or my father told him. I don't blame him, but I don't want to lose my friend."

"Of course you don't."

"Maybe when he calms down, everything will be all right." Amory gave a small shrug.

"I hope so." Then Amory's words struck him. "When did this happen?"

"The day before I met you."

Philip drew back, away from Amory. "You were kissing someone else the day before you met me and I asked you to stay here?"

Amory's brow furrowed and his hand, the one that had been stroking through Philip's hair, fell to the back of the couch. "Yes."

"And you agreed to stay here with me? To become my lover when you had someone already?" Shock and betrayal coursed through him, leaving him nearly shaking. Had he misjudged Amory? Was it all part of Arnau's plan?

"What?" Wide-eyed bewilderment gave way to comprehension and almost panic on Amory's expressive face. "No. It's not like that. It's not like that at all."

"Then what is it? You were kissing someone else two days ago. Maybe more than kissing for all I know." Amory's swiftly indrawn breath came like a slap to Philip. "There was something more."

Amory was shaking his head before Philip finished speaking. "Not really, not much. It was just the last time, and we only touched each other. It wasn't... I didn't...."

Anger made his stomach roil when he thought of someone else touching Amory, of Amory touching someone else. He wanted to hunt down this Tristan and tear him apart. But Amory's dismay pulled at him too. "You didn't what?"

Amory took a breath. "We'd only kissed until then, but Tristan wanted to do more. I wasn't sure, but before I could decide, his hand was in my breeches, and it felt good, so why not? We touched each other, that's all. Then it was over, and then my brother was there."

Philip wasn't sure what to say. He hated the thought of Amory with anyone else, especially mere days ago, with a fury that shocked him. He had known he wasn't the first man Amory kissed, but he never imagined the other man had been a few days ago. He couldn't help the suspicion and the... was it jealousy?

Amory spoke again when he remained silent. "I didn't even know what to feel about it afterward. I enjoyed it, but I think I didn't want to do anything more than kiss Tristan because I wanted anything else to mean something more. And Tristan and I… we're friends, nothing more than that. Never anything more than that for me."

Amory reached forward and took Philip's hand, holding it when he would have pulled away. "It's over now, and that's fine with me. The kissing was nice, but the time had come for it to end. I don't want Tristan as a lover. I only want him to be my friend."

Philip looked at him for a long moment. He wanted to believe Amory, wanted to believe everything he thought about Amory and what they might be able to have was real and not wishful thinking. But so many people would take advantage to try to get close to him—Amory's father was only one.

But Amory wasn't his father. Philip knew that already. His instincts had told him to trust Amory from the first moment. "I believe you."

Amory let out a long breath, his whole body sagging into the cushions. "Thank you."

"I… the way it sounded. For a moment, I wondered why you were here." He squeezed Amory's hand, almost embarrassed for his reaction. "If this was a lie."

"If I was a part of some plot of my father's." Amory nodded, despite the hurt in his eyes. "I understand, but I'm not. I haven't lied. I want to be here with you."

"Me too."

Amory smiled that sweet smile of his, and then spoke, his voice hesitant, halting. "I already believe… whatever we do together, it would mean something more."

He wasn't wrong about Amory. "I think so too."

They looked at each other, and then Amory leaned forward, capturing his lips in a gentle kiss. When Amory pulled back, Philip followed, chasing another kiss and pressing Amory back into the soft cushions while he took it deeper. Amory pulled him closer, wrapping surprisingly strong arms around Philip's back and holding their bodies together. He already loved the feel of Amory's body against his, even through the layers of their clothes. He wanted to feel it with nothing between them.

But not yet, not that night. As much as the thought of waiting pained him, they needed time to get to know each other, to trust, before they fell into bed.

But he wasn't going to be able to keep from kissing Amory. Amory moaned into the kiss and swept his hands up to thread his fingers into

Philip's hair. He didn't think Amory would let him stop if he tried. Philip pushed closer. No, they would definitely keep kissing.

AMORY'S FIRST few weeks at the palace were a period of anxiety and adjustment, but he never once regretted his decision to stay with Philip. As impulsive as the choice was, it never seemed less than right, and it felt more and more like the only choice he could have made the better he got to know Philip. Despite the struggle of figuring out how he fit into palace life.

"What do you mean?" Adeline asked when he mentioned it to her. They'd managed to meet in the large city park near the palace almost a week after Amory's move.

He took a moment to think about how to phrase his answer as they strolled arm in arm along a shady path. The path was deserted except for them and the royal guardsman who followed at a discreet distance. "I don't really know how I should spend my days there. I can't do nothing— well, I suppose I could, but I would go crazy."

"Yes, I can see that. What have you been doing with your days so far?"

"Settling in, learning the palace. I've mostly been spending time with Pip when I can."

Adeline grinned. "Only you would call the prince of Tournai Pip."

And he shouldn't have done so in front of his sister, but he trusted Adeline and it slipped out. "I suppose it is a bit incongruous."

"Just a bit."

"But it fits him somehow, at least to me."

Her expression softened. "I'm sure it does. So what do you two do when you spend time together? But don't tell me any of the bedchamber things!"

He laughed at the horror on his sister's pretty face at the thought of hearing anything so personal in connection with her brother. "I wouldn't. We talk a lot. We've gone riding, and he's teaching me how to play tino. Also archery, and I'm brushing up on my fencing. Philip and his cousins practice together most days.

"I've also been going to all the court ceremonies and events with him, and his social obligations as well." And the social events were a whole other issue he would have to deal with. "I've been spending a lot of time in his office with him while he's working. Obviously, there are some things I can't be privy to, but otherwise he doesn't mind. He's very patient when I ask questions. I want to know what he does, Adeline."

She nodded. "You want to understand so you can know him, so you can make his life easier whenever possible. That's what you do for the people you love."

He stopped walking and gaped at her. "I didn't say I love Philip. I haven't known him long enough for love."

She tilted her head and looked at him in that knowing way that was so irritating. "Fine, because that's what you do for the people you care about."

"Fine." He accepted her correction and pushed all thoughts of love aside.

"I think it's a lovely thing, Amory, and I think it's sweet you want that with the prince." She squeezed his arm, and they began walking again. "Do you know what goes into ruling Tournai now?"

"Some. I don't know enough. The courses I took at university didn't teach me about governance and diplomacy, or any number of things. There's so much he knows that I don't have any understanding of."

"So learn. Read or get tutors or take more classes at the university. Would the prince let you do that?"

"Yes. He's already said I can continue if I want. He wants me to be happy." He knew that beyond any doubt. Philip wanted him to be happy in his life at the palace—Philip wanted Amory to make a life at the palace with him.

"Then perhaps you should think about it."

"I will."

"Good." She smiled at him. "I'm glad to hear he wants you to be happy. It makes me far less worried about you."

He pulled her closer. "You don't need to worry about me. I am happy there."

"In spite of Father's manipulation?"

"Father wouldn't have been able to manipulate Philip into anything Philip didn't want, that much I can tell you. He asked me to stay in spite of Father." What his father tried to do was too reprehensible. Amory wasn't sure he would ever manage to forgive him for it, nor would he stop worrying for his siblings, especially Adeline. "How are things at home?"

"Same as always," she said in a tone he was sure was meant to be reassuring. "Father was angry, but he's calmed down. Well, he's scheming something. You can see that look in his eye, but it's been quiet."

"It's the scheming I worry about, Adeline."

"I know. I think he's scheming something to do with you. From the little I've managed to overhear, I think he's trying to find a way to use your position with the prince for his own gain."

"Sounds like him."

"It's why I asked we meet somewhere other than the palace. I do want to meet the prince, Amory." She stopped walking and turned to look up at him with dark eyes that were the mirror of his. "Not because he's the prince, not anymore, but because he's yours. But if I said I was going there, then Father would have found a way to come with me."

He sighed. She was right. "We'll figure something out, because I do want you to meet him, and he wants to meet you too."

"He does?" Delight pinked her cheeks and infused her voice.

"Of course. I've told him about you." He would like her to meet Elodie as well, but he wouldn't overwhelm Adeline with that yet.

"Oh. I hope he'll like me." She grabbed his hand. "I want him to like me for you."

"He'll love you. Don't worry." He gave her a quick hug. "We'll figure out a way for you to meet. For now, let's get something to eat. A pastry from the bakery you like?"

Adeline agreed, and they finished their visit sitting on a bench in the park, eating sticky fruit pastry, watching ducks swimming in the pond and children playing in the grass, and talking about their younger siblings.

Amory's birthday came a few days later. He received notes and small tokens from his sisters and brothers, and an elegant pair of leather riding gloves from his parents. The gift surprised him somewhat in its extravagance. The quality of the materials and workmanship marked them as quite expensive. He was probably unkind to wonder if his father would have sent so costly a gift if Amory hadn't been living with the prince. But unkind didn't mean untrue.

Philip surprised Amory by clearing his calendar for the day so they could spend it together. He protested, not wanting Philip to upend his schedule for an entire day, but Philip waved his concerns away as if they were nothing. They spent the day together, and though they didn't do anything all that exciting, it was special. He didn't think he would ever get tired of spending time with Philip.

He was surprised again that evening with a small dinner party in his honor. Just Elodie and some of Philip's cousins, but the party was enjoyable, and it was kind of Philip and his guests to come and celebrate with him. There was a lot of laughter, Elodie talked almost non-stop, and Etan even flirted with Amory. Philip bristled each time Etan directed a comment in Amory's direction, so Amory took Philip's hand under the table. Etan was handsome and charming, but he wasn't Philip. The mischievous sparkle in Etan's eyes belied any thought of Amory's taking him seriously. Perhaps he just wanted to get a rise out of his cousin.

The hour was late when their guests finally left. Amory was tired but not sleepy, his body humming with happiness and anticipation. He settled in what had become their usual place in the sitting room. Philip handed him another glass of wine and sat close beside him. Amory sipped the wine, a crisp white that night, and watched the play of firelight over Philip's face and glossy dark hair. So beautiful. He gave in to overwhelming temptation and stroked his fingers through all that silky hair. Philip's eyes closed, and he made a sound close to a purr.

Philip always did that, and Amory was secretly delighted by it. Philip nuzzled into his hand and pressed a kiss to his palm before leaning forward to press another to his lips. He slid his arms around Philip and sank into the kiss, opening to Philip, letting him explore. They fell back on the couch, and he thrilled to feel Philip's weight pressing him into the cushions. The hard planes of Philip's muscles seemed to fit perfectly against Amory's slightly slimmer body. He wanted to feel it without the layers of silk and velvet in the way.

But Philip seemed in no hurry. His hands stroked over Amory's body, sliding on top of clothing, slowly. Their kisses were deep and sensual, exploring and savoring, and Amory was unable to do anything but let go and enjoy each soul-stealing kiss.

They didn't go to bed together that night, as Amory half expected. But, they didn't go to bed separately either. Eventually, their kisses slowed and stopped, and they fell asleep, fully dressed except for their shoes, snuggled up together on the soft cushions of the couch. And despite the twinge in his back from sleeping on a piece of furniture not quite large enough for two full-grown men, Amory thought it amazing to wake tangled up in Philip's arms.

He couldn't really be disappointed they didn't go to bed together that night. He liked that they hadn't yet, that Philip was happy for them to take things slowly. And he liked what they were doing, the talking and laughing and the little touches. He loved all the kissing. Craved it, whether the kisses were sweet and gentle, or long and lazy, or passionate and frantic, or a hundred other ways. He couldn't begin to describe those kisses, and he wondered what he'd been doing before, because kissing Tristan had never felt like kissing Philip did. Maybe who he was kissing made the difference. He thought he could keep kissing Philip forever.

Not that he didn't want to see what more felt like with Philip. He did. It was strange how right the idea seemed with Philip, someone he'd known for so short a time, and how wrong it had felt in relation to Tristan, someone he'd known practically his whole life.

He was pondering why that could be as he sat one morning in the cozy chair in his bedchamber, idly sketching the view outside the window. The city spread out below him, tiled roofs warmed in the light of the sun, the sparkle of river and harbor, the sweep of green countryside beyond. Normally, he spent more time appreciating it, but at that moment he only thought of Philip. He should worry about how quickly he was coming to care for Philip, because that must be what was happening, and it couldn't turn out well for him.

"That's amazing."

He jumped, just managing to keep from jerking his hand and ruining the sketch with a line of charcoal. He turned in his chair to find Philip right behind him, looking down at the sketch in his lap. Sunk in his thoughts and his drawing, he hadn't heard Philip enter the room. "You startled me. How was your meeting?"

He only knew the most general idea of what Philip's meeting had been about, since the discussion was confidential.

"Long. I'm sorry I startled you." Philip leaned down to kiss him quickly, but Amory pulled him back for a longer, more leisurely kiss. Oh, yes, he did love kissing Philip.

"I didn't know you could draw like that," Philip said when they drew back. Though he didn't go far. Philip stayed bent over the back of the chair, his cheek brushing Amory's as he stared down at the charcoal sketch.

Amory shivered. "It isn't anything much."

"Yes, it is. It's beautiful." Philip reached out a hand to angle the sketchbook toward himself. "You sat here and drew it right now. Amazing. Do you have any others I can see?"

Amory nodded and flipped to the beginning of the book before offering it to Philip. Philip took it but stayed draped over Amory while he looked through the sketches. Amory felt his face heat. He had never shared his sketches with anyone, except for the designs he showed the glassmakers, and it was an uncomfortable feeling to sit there while Philip studied his work.

Philip examined each sketch before moving on to the next, and Amory was forced to do the same, seeing each landscape and cityscape, each glass design, again. And to wonder what Philip thought of them. Finally, Philip came back to that day's drawing and stared at it for a moment more before closing the sketchbook.

"These are wonderful, Amory. You said you did some glass designs, but I didn't know you drew like this."

He shrugged a little, his flush at least partly pleasure. "It's just something I like to do if I have a free moment. They're not that good."

"Yes, they are," Philip told, his voice firm, and pressed a short kiss to his lips. "I like them."

"Thank you."

"Have you ever had lessons?"

"No. One of the glass designers gave me some advice when I showed him some sketches years ago, but that's all."

"Then it's even more amazing. Do you do anything else? Paint? Or portraits? I didn't see any here."

He shook his head. "I've never been good at portraits, and I don't know how to paint."

"You could learn if you want. We could find someone to teach you. And you could practice drawing me any time you like." Philip's grin was a bit wicked at the edges.

Amory laughed, but he was intrigued by the idea, both of lessons in something he already enjoyed and in the idea of drawing Philip. Especially the latter. "Maybe."

"Think about it."

He nodded, touched again that Philip was so concerned for his happiness. "I will." He was already scheduled to take two classes when the university's summer term started the next month, but somehow the thought of adding drawing and painting lessons didn't seem like a hardship.

"Always full of surprises." Philip cupped Amory's face and brushed his thumb back and forth over Amory's lips. "What else do you have hidden?"

Amory managed a laugh despite the distraction of Philip's touch making him warm and tingly. "Nothing. I'm not that interesting."

"You are to me. Tell me something I don't know about you."

He stared at Philip. It was so difficult to think with Philip close and touching him. "Like what?"

"I don't know." Philip grinned, and Amory loved the playful light in his eyes. "You're artistic. Tell me something else you can do."

"Um. I have a minor healing Talent." It was a random thing to tell Philip, especially since Amory forgot he had it half the time. Remembering anything with Philip's fingertips whispering over his face was impressive.

"You do? Were you trained?"

He shook his head, but not enough to dislodge Philip. Amory only knew about it because he'd been tested for magical Talents as a child, as most children were. "It's not strong so Father didn't think it would be worth it. He's hoping to find a Talent to help with the glassmaking. The ancestor who started the business apparently had a magical Talent involving glass. There have been a few after, but none recently."

"A healing Talent is useful," Philip insisted.

"Not one that's so minor."

"You don't know that. If you've never had any training, you don't know what you could do."

"I know I don't have enough power to be a healer." He'd been told that much when he was tested.

"That doesn't mean the Talent isn't useful. Even if all you can do is heal the paper cuts you get from your sketchbook."

Amory laughed and was rewarded with Philip's grin. "I suppose."

"Do you want to learn to use it? I'm sure the royal healers can teach you what you can do with it," Philip asked, becoming serious again.

"I don't know. It's a lot of lessons I'd be having." Was that his hesitation? Too many lessons when school had always bored him? Or was it something else, like taking advantage of Philip's generosity?

"But if it's things you enjoy learning?" Philip's eyes were shrewd, and Amory wondered if Philip could tell what he was thinking.

"Maybe." The idea of finding out if his Talent was worth anything did have appeal. "I guess it wouldn't be a bad idea to talk to someone, see what I might be able to do with some training."

Philip smiled in such a sweet, brilliant way that Amory's stomach fluttered. "I'll set up a meeting with the chief healer."

"Thank you." He leaned forward and kissed Philip gently.

"You're welcome."

He grinned, feeling mischievous. "Now you tell me something."

"Like what?"

"I don't know. Do you have a magical Talent?"

The playful look fell away from Philip's face, and he looked away, everything in his posture screaming uncomfortable. He hesitated so long Amory was about to take the question back when Philip spoke. "Yes."

Amory hesitated. "Will—will you tell me what it is?"

Philip nodded slowly. "It's a strange Talent and not at all useful, or at least not anymore. There are family legends… but that doesn't matter."

"Pip?" he prompted, keeping his voice gentle.

"Sorry. It's a family Talent, and we don't tell many people."

Amory frowned as he thought. "I've never heard of a Talent running in the royal family."

"Like I said. It's kept very quiet. It doesn't show up all the time. It tends to skip generations and skip around within generations." Philip was quiet for a moment. "I've never told anyone."

Not anyone? Even Vasco? And why did that make Amory feel so special? But Philip still looked worried. Amory stroked a hand over Philip's hair the way Philip liked. "You don't have to tell me."

"I want to, but I'm not sure how you'll react."

Why would he react badly to magical Talent? "It's fine. You can tell me."

Philip took a deep breath. "I can turn myself into a cat."

Well, he hadn't expected that. "A cat?"

"Yes." Philip seemed to be waiting, and hardly breathing while he did. He was really that worried about Amory's reaction.

"That's incredible. I've never heard of anything like it." Amory hadn't made a study of magic, so he supposed he wouldn't have. He'd heard of the well-known Talents, the ones everyone encountered like healing and Talents for creating fire and light and the less commonly occurring but still important ones like weather working. But there were stories, old stories, of man-sized cats who had defended Tournai against invasion long ago. The legends were vague, but they persisted, that there was some sort of magical protection surrounding Tournai, and that the cats would always return to defend the country. All to the good, he supposed, since Tournai was a small country, but an important and strategic trading center. Many countries might like to control such a place. But he never thought there was any truth to them. Could the royal family's Talent be the origin of those stories?

"It's rare," Philip was saying. "And useless to me."

Amory bit his lip. "Can you show me?"

Philip hesitated. "If you like."

"Please. I want to know all about you, Pip." He ran his hand through Philip's hair again, hoping to soothe. "But only if you're comfortable showing me."

"I want you to see and to know that part of me too."

Philip backed away from Amory's chair. Amory rose to face him.

"Don't be scared, all right? I turn into a pretty big cat."

"I won't." He hoped he could keep his promise. Philip looked so worried, and those legends were about man-sized cats.

"Elodie hates it. She doesn't use her Talent much because she turns into a little ball-of-fluff kitten." Philip was obviously stalling because he was nervous. A rush of protectiveness moved through Amory, and he wanted to soothe away Philip's worry.

"I can see Elodie as an active kitten." He grinned. But then his curiosity got the better of him. "So you can't control the type of cat, and you don't all turn into the same type?"

"No, and not all of us do. There's Elodie. My grandfather turned into a big cat according to my father. Some of the cousins have the Talent, but not all of them." Philip took a deep breath, like he was bracing himself. "Ready?"

"When you are."

Philip nodded and closed his eyes. The air around him shimmered with an almost amber light, obscuring Philip for an instant. And then sitting where Philip stood a second before was a huge cat.

CHAPTER 6

AMORY GASPED. Philip hadn't lied when he said he turned into a big cat, and he was like no cat Amory had seen before. His head would probably come up to Amory's waist. His body was sleek and looked powerful too, his fur a shimmering blue-black. But Amory wasn't afraid. Philip's unique eyes looked at him out of the cat's face, and they still were brimming with worry.

"Is that you in there?"

The cat nodded.

Amory let out a long breath. "You're gorgeous."

Philip hesitated and then walked slowly toward Amory. When Amory didn't move, Philip came right up to him and rubbed his head against Amory's stomach. Amory let out a half laugh, and lifted a hand to Philip's head. His fur was silky soft, like Philip's hair. Amory stroked both hands over Philip's head and neck. The rumbled purr was similar to the sound Philip made when Amory stroked his hair, only louder.

He froze at the thought and then laughed. Philip looked up at him, eyes questioning, but Amory shook his head. He sank to the ground and put his arms around Philip, stroking his hands over soft fur and enjoying how the purring got louder and louder. Philip kept trying to get closer, until Amory had a lap full of sleek black cat. Contented cat too, if the purring and the slitted eyes were any indication.

It should have been strange. His almost-lover turned into a cat and sprawled over his legs while Amory petted him. It should have been strange, but somehow it wasn't. It was Philip, and Philip really was beautiful, as a cat and as a man.

After a long while curled up together on the floor, Amory asked, "Can you talk when you're like this?"

Philip nuzzled into him for another moment before raising his head and looking at Amory. He seemed to deliberate or maybe struggle for a moment, but then he said, "Yes."

The cat's voice was deeper than Philip's normal voice, and sort of rumbly. The word slurred a little, but Amory understood, and he realized

Philip was probably insecure about speaking as a cat, that maybe talking was difficult for him.

"I'm glad you can talk to me, but it isn't easy for you, is it?"

Philip shook his head and then rubbed it against Amory again. Philip really was very catlike when he was a... well, a cat. And he hadn't realized it before but Philip possessed some catlike characteristics when he wasn't a cat as well.

"Then we don't need to have long conversations." He stroked his fingers through Philip's fur again. It was like some sort of compulsion. He couldn't seem to stop doing it, a lot like how he could hardly stop himself from running his fingers through Philip's hair. Philip seemed to love it either way. He leaned into Amory's hand. "You like using your Talent, don't you?"

Philip nodded and pushed farther into Amory's arms. He wondered if Philip felt freer to express his desire for touch. Or maybe it was the novelty of being touched as a cat. If no one knew about his Talent, then he probably hadn't spent any time as a cat around anyone else. Vasco couldn't have sat with Philip like this if the man didn't know. Amory could hardly express, even to himself, how honored he was Philip trusted him with his secret. But he also wondered what it meant to Philip. Did sharing his Talent with Amory mean Philip felt something for him? Probably best not to think about it right then.

He would focus on Philip being utterly adorable. It seemed like a better idea to enjoy the experience.

"The floor is getting a little uncomfortable to sit on even with this rug." Like everything else in the suite, the rug was plush and luxurious, but after a while, he could feel the wooden floor beneath. "Why don't we move?"

"All right," Philip rumbled and gracefully stood. Amory got lost for a moment watching him. He was amazed again that the cat was Philip, that his magic could turn him into that beautiful creature.

He realized he'd been staring without moving for too long when Philip leaned forward and rubbed his head against Amory's cheek. Amory laughed as he flushed at being caught. He pressed a quick kiss to the top of Philip's head and rose, shaking the stiffness out of his legs.

But where should they go? He wasn't going to sit in a chair and leave Philip on the floor. Half the fun was being close to Philip. The couch in the sitting room could hold them both, but he didn't want to go out there. Which left the bed. For all the kissing and touching he and Philip had done, they hadn't gone near a bed together. He wondered why.

He went to the bed and sat on the velvet coverlet. He pulled off his shoes and swung his legs up, lying down and sinking into the soft mattress. Philip continued to stare at him from where he stood near the window. "Aren't you going to come lie down? Much more comfortable over here."

Philip hesitated but walked to the bed and jumped onto the mattress in one fluid movement. Amory stared, enthralled by the inherent grace and power displayed. It made him appreciate Philip's grace all the time.

Philip stretched out against Amory's body and rested his head on Amory's chest. Amory stroked his hand over the fur on Philip's back and smiled fondly when the purring started up again. With Philip lying all but over him, he could feel it too, vibrating in his body.

"This is nice." Philip's voice was low, almost a purr itself.

"Yes, it is." Unreal, but incredibly nice.

AT SOME point, they must have fallen asleep, because Amory woke suddenly to knocking at the bedchamber door. Philip mumbled something that might have been a curse, but Amory couldn't make it out in Philip's cat voice. The air around Philip shimmered again. It felt warm, like little sparks wherever it touched Amory, but the shimmer and the warmth disappeared in an instant, and Philip the man lay against his side. He looked sleepy and rumpled, but otherwise just as he had before he used his Talent, from his clothes down to the shoes on his feet.

"Hello again."

Philip said in his normal, smooth voice, "Hello."

He lifted a hand and smoothed back Philip's silky dark hair. Definitely some sort of compulsion. "Thank you for telling me. For sharing that with me."

Philip's gaze softened. "You're welcome."

Another knock made them jump as Philip was leaning forward for what Amory hoped would be a long, slow kiss. He sighed and called out, "Yes?"

"Master Amory, I'm sorry to bother you, but I'm searching for the prince. Do you know where he is?" Donatien called through the thick door.

It was Philip's turn to sigh. He dropped his head, resting his forehead on Amory's shoulder. "What is it, Donatien?"

Amory felt his cheeks heat as Donatien explained some issue that had arisen. Donatien could only think one thing finding Philip in Amory's bedchamber with the door shut, especially since they did not invite Donatien into the room. Amory knew he was Philip's lover in name if nothing else, and everyone at court expected them to be doing just that. He wondered if he would be less or more embarrassed if they had been together that way.

"I will be there shortly," Philip called out, ending the conversation. He looked back down at Amory, where he lay half-under Philip. "Unfortunately, I have to go."

"It's all right."

"I wish I could stay here." Philip cupped his cheek, brushing his thumb across Amory's lips. He shivered, and Philip kissed him lightly. "I enjoyed being here with you so much, and waking up next to you."

"Yes. Me too."

Philip leaned down and kissed him. Far too quick a kiss for Amory's liking, but Philip did have responsibilities. "I'll see you later?"

"Yes." He sat up and watched Philip stand and straighten his clothing. "Maybe we could do it again."

"Do what?"

"Fall asleep together, wake up together."

The look in Philip's eyes, so delighted, made Amory's breath catch. "I would like that very much."

With one more quick kiss, Philip strode from the room. As soon as the door closed behind him, Amory flopped back on the bed and stared at the ceiling. Oh, yes, he very much wanted to wake up next to Philip again.

Apparently Philip wanted the same. That night, when they would usually part after a drink and a lot of kissing on the couch, Philip asked if he could sleep in Amory's bed. Surprise made him agree without thinking. But as he changed from his dinner clothes to his sleep shirt and pants, his nerves asserted themselves. Would Philip finally do more than kiss him? What would it be like to have Philip touch his skin, put his mouth on him, fill him? He was suffused with nervous anticipation at the thought.

He called out an invitation to enter in response to Philip's soft knock a moment later. Philip slipped into the room with an uncertain expression on his handsome face. Somehow seeing it calmed Amory's nerves, and he held out a hand to Philip. Some of the uncertainty drained away, and Philip padded barefoot across the carpet to take his hand, raising it to his lips.

Amory shivered, feeling the light brush of lips everywhere, and Philip chuckled low. Amory gasped when Philip's arms wrapped around him. Philip had held him before, but never with so little between them. The thin material of their sleep clothes did nothing to conceal the firm planes of Philip's chest or the heat of his body or the increasing hardness of his arousal against Amory's hip. It was almost frightening how good it felt to be held that way.

Philip kissed him, a soft, sweet kiss, not the passionate one Amory expected, and then looked into his eyes. "Bed?"

He responded to the whisper with a nod. Taking Philip's hand, Amory led him to the bed. He was shaking slightly as he climbed into the soft bedding and slid over. Philip followed him under the covers, and pulled Amory into his arms. "All right?"

"Yes." He didn't know why they were whispering but it somehow seemed appropriate.

"Good." Philip closed the small distance between them and kissed him, deeper and longer, but no less gentle. Amory threw himself into it, losing himself, letting all his nerves fall away in the slide of Philip's lips against his own, in the sweep of Philip's tongue into his mouth. Exploring, teasing out unexpected bursts of pleasure that tore moans and whimpers from Amory.

Philip pulled him closer, hands splayed on his back, until their bodies were flush against each other. Amory moaned again and clutched at Philip as he felt their arousals press together. Philip swept a hand down Amory's back to his backside where he stroked and kneaded. Amory couldn't control the sounds he made as the kiss grew more heated and they rocked together. He had never felt anything like this.

He gasped when Philip rolled them to put himself on top of Amory, his body pressing Amory's into the soft mattress below them. He slid his arms around Philip's back and held on tight as Philip dropped kisses over his face and neck, kissing, licking, nibbling. Amory's moans became louder as liquid heat spread through his whole body from the spot where Philip's mouth played.

Amory sucked in deep breaths when Philip left off his pleasurable torture, even as he ached for more. Philip's face was flushed, his eyes dark with desire. Beautiful. Amory threaded his fingers through Philip's hair, massaging his scalp, and was rewarded with Philip's eyes fluttering half closed as he nearly purred.

Philip kissed him again, deeply enough to make Amory's head swim. "So sweet."

Philip slid down, moving Amory's shirt out of the way so he could kiss down Amory's chest. Amory wantonly arched and writhed as Philip licked and sucked at each of his nipples. "So sweet," Philip repeated, his voice low and husky. "So beautiful. Let me."

He slid farther down Amory's body, and before Amory had any idea what Philip was going to do, he pulled down Amory's sleep pants and was running a hand over Amory's member. Amory dropped back to the pillow with a moan. He never wanted Philip to stop touching him. When Philip bent and took him in his mouth, Amory practically came off the bed. Philip grinned around his mouthful and held Amory's hips down with gentle hands. Then Philip began using lips and tongue and hand to make Amory wild. Had he thought it was good before? It was incredible. He moaned and gasped and thrashed on the bed. Far too soon, pleasure broke over him like a wave, and he spilled his release down Philip's throat.

Amory floated there, limp, as Philip crawled up the bed, looking ridiculously pleased with himself and Amory both. Philip kissed him sweetly and then lay down at his side, gathering him close.

"Good?" Philip asked.

"Better," he said, his breathing still too fast.

"For me too." Philip kissed him again.

"But you didn't… what can I…." He hadn't quite managed to pull his scattered wits together. Embarrassing.

But Philip smiled. "You don't have to do anything."

He did—as the prince's lover, he should see to the prince's pleasure—but that wasn't the relationship Philip wanted. "I want to."

"Then touch me." Philip guided Amory's hand down. Philip was hard, thick, and long in Amory's hand. He thrilled at Philip's moan, and nearly moaned himself. Philip pulled him in for a kiss as Amory set a rhythm, loving the sounds he pulled out of Philip, loving that he could give Philip that kind of pleasure. Philip found his own release not long after, gasping out Amory's name as he did.

Their kisses gentled and slowed to something lazy and languid. Finally, Philip broke away and pulled off his shirt. He used it to clean them both up and then drew Amory close while pulling the blankets higher over both of them. With a sigh of pure contentment, Amory snuggled closer, burying his head in the curve of Philip's neck. The last thing he felt before sleep claimed him was the brush of Philip's lips over his hair.

PHILIP WOKE to the delicious realization that he wasn't alone. Amory was pressed against his side, warm and flushed with sleep, his auburn curls mussed around his face. Philip wanted to wake up next to him every day forever. He wouldn't mind more of what they did the night before either.

As he watched, Amory's eyes fluttered open. Surprise, memory, and pleasure washed through their warm chocolate-brown depths when Amory focused on Philip lying beside him. A sweet, sleepy smile spread across Amory's face, and Philip had to kiss him. Amory hummed into the kiss and cuddled in closer, and they exchanged lazy kisses as sunlight slowly brightened the room. Oh, yes, he could get used to beginning his days in bed with Amory, and he very much wanted to.

He'd set up a meeting with the chief royal healer, Jadis, for later that day so Jadis could talk with Amory about his healing Talent. Whatever Amory said about his Talent, Philip had seen the sparks of interest in Amory's eyes when they'd talked about it. Amory wanted to know, and Philip wanted Amory to have everything he wanted. Which was why he was also looking for someone to give Amory drawing and painting lessons.

He thought he would do anything in his power to make Amory happy.

Scary thought. After so little time, to what lengths would he go for Amory? And as time passed and he knew Amory better, cared more for him, what would he do then to ensure Amory kept smiling?

Relieved to find that neither Philip nor Amory needed his professional services when he arrived in their sitting room that afternoon, Jadis was pleased to meet Amory and happy to help. Jadis spent a few moments with his eyes closed, Amory's hands in his, as he did whatever he needed to do to measure Amory's Talent.

Finally, Jadis opened his eyes and sat back, letting go of Amory's hands. Amory sat back as well, and Philip put a hand on Amory's back, urging him closer. Amory glanced at him but slid a fraction closer.

"What can you tell us, Master Jadis?" Philip asked.

"Your Highness, I can confirm that Master Amory's healing Talent is not a strong one." He looked at Amory. "You could never be a master healer with your Talent."

Amory nodded. "I was already told there wasn't much I could do with it."

"It is true, sir, you don't have a lot of power at your disposal, but that doesn't mean you couldn't do something with what you have." Jadis's face was earnest. "With some training, you could do some things—ease pain, for instance, and perhaps heal minor illness or injury."

"Really?" Amory asked, and Philip could feel the change in his body as Amory's interest perked up again.

"Yes, certainly." Jadis's face became thoughtful. "Tell me, sir, have you been ill much in your life?"

"No, hardly at all."

Philip looked at Amory. "I would think with all of your brothers and sisters you would all be catching things right and left."

Amory shrugged. "They all did get sick when we were children, but I've always been healthy."

"That's due to your Talent, I think," Jadis said.

"What do you mean?"

"The biggest thing your Talent could be used for is self-healing, which is rare among healers. Most healing gifts are primarily turned outward, so while a healer might be able to ease his own minor headache, for instance, he wouldn't be able to keep himself from becoming ill. I think you've been healing yourself without knowing for most of your life."

Amory seemed stunned. Philip was surprised himself. He'd never heard of such a thing. "That's possible?"

"Yes, Your Highness," Jadis said. "Master Amory's Talent has probably been keeping him healthy. He could also use it to heal or speed up healing any injuries he sustains or illnesses he does succumb to."

"I could?" Amory's voice held all of his surprise at being told his Talent was worth something. Philip rubbed his back in support, a small movement but one he hoped would soothe.

"I don't see any reason why not," Jadis said. "I would be happy to teach you how if you like."

"I—I would appreciate it very much, Master Jadis," Amory stuttered.

"We both appreciate it," Philip added. "Thank you, Master Jadis."

"You're welcome, Your Highness. I'm looking forward to working with Master Amory."

After Jadis left, Philip turned to Amory. "You're excited."

Amory smiled in the way Philip loved, the one that seemed to light up the air around them. "I am. I wasn't expecting to hear any of that. I'm excited to see what I can do with it, even if it doesn't end up being much."

"From what Master Jadis said, it seems like there will be plenty you can do once you learn how."

"Yes. But I won't be performing any amazing healing feats." Amory laughed, but Philip wasn't sure if he was disappointed.

"Would you want to be a healer if you could?"

Amory shook his head. "No, not really. If I could have, it would have given me a place, somewhere to belong. I never had that in my family's business."

"You have it now. You belong right here with me." He pulled Amory close and kissed him before either of them could think too much about that statement.

Later that night, Amory asked Philip to sleep with him again. Amory's cheeks flushed when he made the quiet, almost shy, invitation, but his gaze was steady on Philip. "I want to wake up next to you again. Do you...."

"Yes, I want that too."

Part of Philip wanted to grab Amory up and tumble him into bed, but he thought it best to be careful. So he let them separate to prepare for bed. Last night had been wonderful, and he wanted more like it, but Amory wasn't experienced. He blushed just asking Philip to spend the night in his bed. Philip needed Amory to be comfortable with him and what they did together. He couldn't go too fast. He didn't want to go too fast for himself either. He hadn't planned to do anything but sleep beside Amory last night, but he didn't regret what happened. To Philip's relief, Amory didn't regret it either.

He knocked softly on Amory's bedchamber door and walked in to see Amory coming back into the room from his bathing room. Philip swept his gaze up Amory's body from the bare feet sinking into the thick carpet, to the lithe body attired in the thin white sleep pants and shirt, to the beautiful face and tousled auburn curls. Amory flushed at Philip's scrutiny, but there was a gleam in his eyes, an almost wicked one, as he looked at Philip in turn.

"Come to bed."

Philip's bed was bigger, but Amory's was comfortable as well. Once they were truly lovers, he would ask Amory to share his bedchamber so they could wake up together every morning. They settled under the covers, Amory rolling naturally into Philip's arms and pressing against him. Amory lifted his face for a kiss, and Philip obliged him. They kissed lazily for long moments. Philip wouldn't press for more.

But apparently Amory wasn't as content with only kisses. He moved restlessly against Philip, his hands caressing Philip's chest and sides over Philip's shirt. Philip moaned at the feel of those hands through the thin fabric. He ached, wondering what it would feel like to have those hands all over his skin, to feel Amory's naked body pressed against his own. He wanted to know, so much. But not that night. He would follow Amory's lead. Even if Amory's hesitant caresses killed him.

He groaned as Amory slid down his body and loosened his pants, freeing his hard flesh. Amory studied it for a moment. His hungry gaze felt almost like a touch itself, but Philip needed more, and he barely stopped himself from begging for it. Finally, Amory took him in hand giving him one smooth stroke that had Philip gasping and arching.

Amory bent his head and pressed a kiss to Philip's member. Philip moaned. Amory looked up at him again. "May I?"

He realized what Amory was asking and bit back a groan. "Oh, yes, please."

Amory's expressive eyes held a shadow of insecurity. "I've never done this before."

He stroked his hand through Amory's hair, trying to soothe. "You don't have to."

"I want to. I just don't know how."

"You'll be fine." He continued to stroke Amory's hair, loving the feel of the thick, soft locks between his fingers and how Amory leaned into his hand. He grinned. "Go slow. And watch your teeth."

"I think I could've figured that much out on my own, thanks." Despite the tart words, Amory smiled and turned his head, nuzzling into Philip's palm before turning back to his task.

That Amory had never done it before was obvious, but he was diligent and enthusiastic, and he was Amory. Philip thought that last might have quite a bit to do with why it felt so very good.

A WEEK later, Amory rode his horse at Philip's side. He'd half expected his father to demand the horse back, but he hadn't, not yet. Amory hadn't heard much from his father since he came to live at the palace. He'd only seen him once—the day the completed chandelier was delivered, executed perfectly and within the extra time Philip had granted them. Amory didn't want to think what Philip would have done if it hadn't been. Philip hadn't forgiven what Amory's father tried to do to Amory, and truthfully, neither had Amory, but they rarely spoke of it.

But he wasn't going to think about his father at the moment. A few nights ago, while they'd been lying in bed together, his head pillowed on Philip's chest, Philip asked Amory to accompany him to Alzata. Philip had told him a lot about the estate, but they hadn't had the opportunity to make the trip before. Philip's calendar was light the next couple of days so they could stay over at Alzata and return to the palace before Amory's classes at the university began.

Alzata was only a few hours ride from the palace so Philip would not be out of touch, but Philip still seemed excited to go. Amory knew Philip wanted to show him his much-loved estate, but he thought Philip also wanted to get away. The last week had been a difficult one for Philip, involving complex trade negotiations with Kavalas that Amory didn't entirely understand the nuances of. And he knew the high-ranking nobles of Tournai were vehemently split on those issues. All of them wanted Philip's time and Philip's agreement, and Philip's uncle Umber was constantly there as well, pressuring Philip to agree with him on what was to be done. Amory could see the toll it took on Philip. His face and body were tight with tension, and he was exhausted by the end of each day but had trouble sleeping. Amory knew, because they spent every night together, though Philip had been too tired to do more than kiss since the negotiations began in earnest.

Amory wanted to help Philip and was frustrated that he didn't know how. It made him more determined to learn as much as he could so he could at least listen to Philip intelligently. Until he could, he tried to be there as an ear to listen, a distraction, a quiet presence. He took to rubbing Philip's shoulders and temples to ease the tension and pain gathered in those places, and he held Philip close at night. Amory only hoped some of what he did lightened the burden weighing on Philip.

Alzata was the obvious choice to get away during the short break in the negotiations. From everything Philip told him, Amory knew Alzata was Philip's favorite place, where he went to escape from the world. He was honored Philip asked him to accompany him. But when Philip said it would be just the two of them without Elodie or Cathal or anyone else, he began to wonder if Philip's only motivation was to get away. Did Philip also want time alone with him?

Whatever it meant, Amory liked the idea of uninterrupted time with Philip. Away from secretaries who came in during breakfast and uncles who provoked frustration and the all-seeing eyes of the nobles of Tournai, some of whom were clearly less than approving of Amory. He could only hope Philip's decision to bring him meant he helped ease Philip's burdens in some way.

"Almost there," Philip said, breaking into his thoughts.

Since Alzata was so close, they'd chosen to go on horseback instead of by carriage. A cart had traveled ahead with their bags, so it was just them riding through the countryside. Well, and the royal guards, but they were fairly unobtrusive. The guards' presence didn't spoil a ride with Philip on a clear, sunny day.

To Amory's relief, Philip relaxed more and more the farther they traveled from the palace, his whole body far less rigid than when they left. Philip smiled as he talked and pointed out various landmarks they passed. Amory hadn't spent much time outside Jumelle, so he eagerly listened to all Philip said and soaked up the sight of the beautiful countryside. Summer was beginning, and everything was lush, green, and blooming. A huge field of deep purple flowers nearly took his breath away. Under the vibrant blue sky, they were especially striking. He had to stop and stare, noticing then the sun shimmering on the river and the rolling green hills beyond. When he realized Philip and the guards were waiting for him, he turned to Philip to apologize, but Philip had a soft, affectionate look in his eyes, and the apology died on Amory's lips.

They turned off the main road onto a smaller, though still paved, lane. Large old trees formed a canopy overhead, letting dappled sunlight fall on them as they rode under the lattice of arching branches. The lane led them to a tall stone wall with wide gates of iron worked in a lacy design with the royal crest in the center. After Philip's revelations, the cats in the crest had taken on new meaning for Amory. The guards at the gate jumped to swing them open in welcome.

Philip flashed a wide grin at Amory, eagerness written all over his face, and urged his horse forward into a brisk trot. Amory nearly laughed. Philip's excitement to be there and to show him the place he loved was endearing.

The road, paved in intricate patterns of many-colored stones, wound through dense stands of large, shady trees. The trees were old, their trunks wide, their roots prominent. The pattern of light and shadow under those limbs made Amory itch to grab up his sketchbook. Perhaps he would have time to sketch in the small wood, if not on that visit, then someday. If he was fortunate enough to come back again.

Suddenly, the trees ended, and everything opened up on a vista of sweeping lawns that spread in lush, vivid green down to the house. The house. He couldn't hold back a gasp when he saw it. It was large, but not obscenely so, and graceful in design with its turrets and interesting roofline. It seemed to sparkle a rosy gold in the midday sun. He stopped to look at it, aware of Philip grinning a bit smugly beside him.

"It's beautiful, Pip, but what is doing that?"

"It's a local stone and very rare now. No one has been able to find more of it to mine in two generations at least. This was one of the last buildings constructed of it."

"How does it do it?"

"No one knows. It's a deep shade of gray when the sun isn't shining on it, but when the sun does shine, it comes alive. Sparkles or shimmers, and in the moonlight it glows."

"Maybe it's magic." It felt a bit like magic.

"Maybe. Come. I'll show you the inside."

Alzata's servants took the horses, and he entered the house at Philip's side. The entry hall was impressive with high ceilings, inlaid marble floors, and a sweeping staircase leading up to the second floor. Corridors branched off the entry in three directions, but Philip started for the stairs.

"Why don't we get cleaned up, and then I'll show you around?" Philip asked.

"All right." They climbed the stairs together to the second floor corridor. The floors there were wood, polished to a gleam, and the walls were adorned with tapestries and paintings, mostly landscapes and seascapes. Philip led the way to the left at the top of the stairs. Amory kept pace with him as he looked around with interest.

Philip stopped at a door near the end of a corridor. He turned and looked at Amory, his expression hesitant. "This is my bedchamber. Our chambers adjoin each other. They connect through the shared bathing room."

Amory nodded. They shared a suite at the palace. Using adjoining rooms here wouldn't be strange for them. That couldn't be what Philip was worried about.

"The servants have probably already unpacked our things into the two rooms. But I was hoping you would share my room while we're here. Only if you want to."

"I want to," he said without thought. Then he did think about it, and he knew why Philip seemed hesitant. They had been sharing a bed for the last several nights, but that was different from officially sharing a bedchamber, even for a short while. Sharing a bedchamber was a step, a step toward something more. Something more intimate. Some long-married couples among the upper classes and nobility didn't share a bedchamber.

They were sharing a bed already. He liked that they were, and he wanted to keep doing so. Maybe that was all he should worry about.

He smiled at Philip, who still looked a little unsure. "I want to."

"I'm glad."

He opened the door and ushered Amory into the bedchamber. His feet sank into the dark green carpet with his first step. The room wasn't as large as either of their bedchambers back at the palace, but it looked comfortable, cozy even. Two plush chairs faced the fireplace in a small sitting area, and a large bed dominated one wall. He tried not to think about what they might do in that bed—the fleeting images his imagination conjured before he pushed them away were enough to wash heat through his body.

He resolutely focused on the rest of the room. Comfortable furniture and luxurious fabrics, none of it overly formal or ostentatious, quite like their suite at the palace. He was coming to expect the style from Philip.

"The bathing room and dressing room are through here," Philip told him, leading the way through another door. "And the other bedchamber is beyond them."

Amory followed Philip into the bathing room, which he saw was even larger than his bathing room back at the palace. Probably to accommodate the massive sunken tub. Tiled in an intricate pattern of different greens and located in front of a large window, it looked as though it could fit three people without a problem. He had never seen anything like it.

Philip walked into the adjacent dressing room. "I'm going to change."

"Me too." But before he followed Philip to see what had been done with his clothes, he opened the door to the bedchamber that would have been his. The room was similar to Philip's but decorated in a sage green instead of the darker shade. A nice room, but he didn't regret his choice. Closing the door, he followed Philip into the dressing room.

They changed into fresh clothes and washed their hands and faces to get rid of the dust of the road. They didn't bother taking the time to bathe then, though Amory was intrigued by the large tub. He supposed he would have a chance to try it out soon enough.

Philip took his hand as they walked out of the bedchamber together. Philip showed him the house first. It was much larger than the house where Amory had grown up in the city but far less formal than he expected a royal residence to be. Decorated in rich, warm colors and filled with interesting art and excellent examples of Tournai's traditional glasswork, some new, some much older, the house was exquisite. For all that, it obviously wasn't meant as a showpiece, as a place for lavish parties and social posturing, but as a place of comfort and coziness and home. It also became obvious that Philip truly did love being at Alzata.

Philip walked Amory through the whole house, not only showing him the rooms but telling him stories. Some of the stories from Philip's childhood had him laughing out loud. Others made him feel a glow of affection for the child Philip. He loved hearing all of them, and the feeling of closeness with Philip that knowing those pieces of his childhood created. After walking through the house, Philip led him outside onto a large terrace at the back of the house. Awnings shaded half of it from the sun, and comfortable lounging furniture was placed in both sun and shade, creating a pleasant place to while away an afternoon. One of the chaises looked large enough to hold him and Philip together. He was interested to see if he was right about that.

But Philip seemed intent on the tour, so Amory followed him down the steps and into a small formal garden. Bright flowers bloomed, nearly overflowing their beds. Statues peeked out from behind ornamental trees and bushes, and a fountain burbled in the center. The garden was a fraction of the size of the palace gardens, but Amory thought he liked it better. It felt more intimate, and again less pretentious.

The garden ended in a lawn dotted with wildflowers sweeping down to a lake. More trees surrounded the lake on its other sides, blocking his view of whatever was beyond that. They wandered down to the near side of the lake, and stopped there. Amory breathed deep, taking in the rich scents of grass, flowers, and earth.

"The land continues out from here. There are some good trails through the wood and around the lake for walking and some for riding," Philip said. "Maybe tomorrow we can go for a ride and I can show you more. I've always enjoyed riding here. There's plenty of space."

"I'd like that." He liked the pure pleasure and calm on Philip's face, as if being at Alzata soothed him. If he could, he would bring Philip there all the time, just for that.

"So?" Philip grinned. "What do you think of Alzata?"

"It's beautiful. I can see why you love it. I think I'm going to love it here too." Not because of Alzata's beauty, but because Alzata was Philip's refuge, the place Philip felt most comfortable and himself. He could feel some of it already.

"I'm glad." Philip was still smiling as he reached out for Amory's waist, pulling him close against Philip's chest. Philip brushed his lips over Amory's lightly. "I want you to like it here."

Amory kissed Philip, a light little kiss like the ones Philip had been giving him. "I do. I can't wait to see more."

Philip leaned in for a longer, deeper kiss as they stood in the sunshine.

CHAPTER 7

THE EVENING was warm, so Philip instructed the servants to serve
dinner at a small table on the terrace. The sun was setting when they sat
down to eat, turning the sky to pink and orange over the trees and the
lake to shimmering gold. The food was delicious, if simpler than that
served at the palace. Servants brought each course and then disappeared
into the house, as Philip preferred whenever possible. It was Philip who
refilled their wine glasses as they ate and talked.

The sun sank farther, and the pink and orange of the sky gave
way to purples and dark blue. Servants returned to light candles placed
around the terrace, on the stone rails, on the tables, even some on the
stone floor. They disappeared without a word, leaving the terrace lit with
a soft, flickering glow. He and Philip finished their dessert, a sweet berry
tart, but didn't leave the table. Amory was content to sit and watch Philip
in the golden light, to listen to him tell more stories and to answer his
questions about Amory's own childhood favorite places.

After a while, Philip picked up his wine glass and stood. He held
a hand out to Amory, and pulled him up by it, dropping a quick kiss on
Amory's lips once he was standing. Amory picked up his wine glass as
well, but to his surprise, Philip didn't lead him inside the house but to
the chaise he'd noticed earlier. Philip reclined on the chaise, and tugged
Amory's hand until he settled there as well. They did both fit. He was
half on top of Philip, but that only made it better.

For a while, they lay there, listening to the quiet sounds of the
night around them. Amory finished his wine and set the glass to the
side. Refilling his glass would have involved getting up, and he much
preferred staying where he was. He nestled his head against Philip's
shoulder. Philip made a little sound of contentment and set his own glass
aside, tightening his arms around Amory. He wasn't surprised when
Philip turned to him and pulled him into a gentle kiss, but he more than
welcomed it. He surrendered to it gladly, letting the kisses turn slow and
deep. Continuing and spinning out as they lay tangled together under a
sky filled with stars.

They slept later than usual the next morning, not only because it had been late when they took themselves to bed after dozing on the terrace, but also because they had no obligations. There were no meetings for Philip or lessons for Amory at Alzata, so there was no reason to leave the comfort of the big bed and its soft mattress and blankets. And Philip told him so in a sleepy mumble as he pulled Amory back into his arms that morning, snuggling them both under the covers for a little more sleep. Amory chuckled as he settled against Philip's chest. Philip truly was a hedonist. Not that he didn't like the idea of lying around in Philip's arms. He really did.

When they finally got out of bed, they ate a late breakfast, and went for a long ride around Alzata. They returned in high spirits to find a light lunch prepared for them and a messenger just arrived from the palace with some papers for Philip to review. Amory supposed it would be impossible for Philip to be out of touch, nor did he think Philip would want to be. It would cede too much control to others when he knew Philip wanted to be a strong ruler in his own right.

Philip insisted they eat before he looked at the papers. So they ate their lunch at a small table in a sunny room overlooking the garden and the lake. They didn't rush, but they didn't linger. Philip had responsibilities despite what either of them might want.

"Go and get it over with," Amory told him as they walked out into the corridor. "I'm going to get my sketchbook and sit out on the terrace. I'll be there when you're finished."

Philip nodded. "All right."

Philip leaned forward and kissed him, slow and lingering, before striding off to the study. Amory went in the opposite direction and retrieved his sketchbook from the table near the fireplace in their bedchamber. Tucking the book under his arm, he returned downstairs. He settled into a chair out on the terrace and opened his sketchbook to a blank page, but he didn't start drawing. He relaxed into the embrace of the deep cushions and tilted his head back to the warmth of the sun.

He had never been anywhere like Alzata. He liked it there, liked how he felt there, liked more how Philip was there. Not that he didn't like how Philip was at the palace, but he was different at Alzata, almost shockingly. At the palace, Philip's gestures of affection were muted outside their suite. Philip took his arm, kissed his cheek, maybe a gentle chaste touch, but nothing more. At Alzata Philip kissed him in corridors and curled up with him on the terrace. And really kissed him on the terrace, so many kisses on the terrace last night. All of it without any hesitation.

Their relationship wasn't a secret by any means, but Philip was always careful to observe the proper decorum back in the palace and city. Amory couldn't fault his behavior—Philip was the ruling prince. He had duties and responsibilities and a certain image to maintain, and Amory understood that, as much as he could. But, Philip seemed to shed the cloak of his title at his estate. No one else was there except for the servants, and the staff had been handpicked by Philip's mother and Philip for their loyalty and discretion above all. Amory could see how freeing that was in so many ways, to be out from the watchful eyes of his courtiers, and he loved it for Philip. He kind of loved it for himself too. Maybe they could visit more often.

He opened his eyes and turned to his sketchbook. He would pass the time for however long Philip needed to work trying to capture the view down toward the lake on paper. The view was striking enough that he wanted to try, and beautiful enough that he wanted to remember it if he never made it back to Alzata. He would happily stay with Philip if he had any choice in the matter, but Philip was the prince, and Amory had already learned that sometimes there wasn't such a thing as choice.

He didn't want to think about the chance he would have to leave. Instead, he started drawing, sketching and shading, trying to capture the arching trees and the light on the water. He absorbed himself in the drawing, letting it consume his focus and lull him into calm.

Some time later, the sketch was taking shape, and he realized he wasn't alone. He turned in his seat and smiled. Philip watched him with a fond expression on his face.

"Are you done working?" Amory asked, keeping his voice level despite the warmth Philip's expression kindled.

"For now. I'll have more to do tomorrow. I sent everything back to the palace with the messenger." Philip strolled forward, stopping behind Amory's chair. "It's a beautiful drawing."

He glanced at it. Not bad, but not quite finished. "Thank you."

Philip leaned down, hanging over the back of Amory's chair and Amory's shoulders to get a closer look at the drawing, much as he had the first time he looked through Amory's sketches. It was becoming a habit, and Amory loved having Philip so close, feeling the warmth of his body, breathing in the scent of him. If Philip wanted to study all of his drawings that way, Amory had no objections.

Philip pressed a kiss to Amory's jaw, and nuzzled his face into Amory's neck. Or maybe Philip wasn't interested in looking at his drawings after all. Amory hummed a little in the shivery pleasure of the touch. He rubbed his cheek against Philip's soft hair, loving the happy almost-purr his action provoked.

Philip kissed his neck again. "Do you want to draw some more?"

He shivered at the feel of the whispered words against his skin. "Did you have something else in mind?"

"I thought we might go to bed."

Heat spread through his body. Still, he tried for light teasing. "It's the middle of the afternoon. Are you that tired after your paperwork?"

"I'm not tired at all." Philip continued his trail of light kisses along Amory's neck in between words. "Bed?"

He pulled back enough to look into Philip's eyes. What he saw there stole his breath. If they went to bed, it wouldn't be for more kisses and cuddles. It wouldn't even be for what they could do with their hands and mouths. If they went to bed, he and Philip would leave it lovers in truth. "Yes."

"You're certain?"

He cupped Philip's cheek and held his gaze. "Yes."

Those beautiful eyes blazed, and Philip drew him forward into a gentle kiss that quickly deepened and became more insistent. They were both breathing heavily when they parted. Philip straightened and held a hand out to Amory. He took it, allowing Philip to draw him to his feet, and walked into the house at Philip's side, his hand held securely in Philip's strong, warm clasp. They didn't speak as they walked through the corridors and up the wide front stairs. They didn't even look at each other. If they did, Amory doubted they would make it to their bedchamber before they started kissing and touching. And while he liked that Philip was freer with his affection, he didn't want to do this in a corridor. Certainly not for the first time.

Nervous anticipation hummed through him as they neared their bedchamber, but the nerves were less prominent than he would have expected. He was with Philip, and that made everything all right. Philip was the reason excitement was overcoming nerves, urging him to walk faster. He wanted Philip, wanted more than they'd done before. He wanted everything with Philip.

He was falling in love with Philip.

The realization hit him so unexpectedly and with such force, he had to stifle a gasp. He couldn't love Philip. They hadn't known each other long enough for love, surely. And falling in love with a prince was a bad idea anyway.

Before he could think too much about it, Philip tugged him into their bedchamber, and before Amory could blink, he had Amory's back against the closed door. Philip pressed against him, and kissed him. The kiss was deep and passionate, but also sweet and almost reverent. Philip's hands on his face felt cherishing, and the last of Amory's nerves were swept away.

Philip pulled back a little. "Amory."

"Yes," he gasped in response to the rough whisper.

They stumbled farther into the room, fingers fumbling with the fastenings of each other's clothing. Thankfully, they were dressed far less formally than they would have been at the palace. The simple clothes shed easier under Amory's suddenly clumsy fingers than the more formal ones would have. Then they were standing naked before each other for the first time.

Everything they'd done before had been under clothes and covers. Amory wasn't sure why, a bit of shyness perhaps on his part, maybe consideration on Philip's. But he could see all of Philip at that moment, and he looked at him greedily, drinking in the sight of all the pale golden skin covering sleek muscles and long limbs, the dusting of dark hair on his chest, the trail of it leading down…. He felt himself flush looking at the thick, hard flesh and thinking about it inside him. He wanted Philip inside, but his nerves didn't calm entirely with that desire.

Philip was studying him just as intently. He could feel his blush deepen at the scrutiny. Philip raised his gaze, and Amory's breath caught at the look in Philip's eyes—desire and deep affection and something like awe. The momentary resurgence of his nerves calmed under Philip's gaze. He was with Philip, and everything would be wonderful.

"You're beautiful, even more than I imagined."

He shook his head. No, he wasn't beautiful, but Philip was.

"You are." Before Amory could respond, Philip was kissing him again. Deep kisses that made him moan and ache for more.

They tumbled onto the big soft bed, rolling across the velvet coverlet in a tangle of limbs. Amory's hands were greedy as they stroked over Philip's smooth skin, greedy to map every inch of him. Philip's touch felt the same on Amory's body, but so very gentle too. Cherishing still, and Amory reveled in it, in every caress and grasping hand.

Suddenly, he found himself beneath Philip, stretched full length against him, skin to skin. Amory gasped into the kiss, Philip's body a welcome weight pressing him into the mattress. He never could have imagined it, never could have imagined anything, feeling so good. He wound his arms tightly around Philip, letting his fingers explore and clutch at the smooth expanse of Philip's broad back, and threw himself into the kiss. He could have drowned in the sweetness of it, but he didn't want that—he wanted to show Philip how much it meant to him. So he poured everything he had into kissing Philip. All of the desire, all of the new feeling that probably was love, all of the wonder that Philip would want this with him when he could have anyone.

Pulling back from the kiss, Philip smiled down at him tenderly, and that was beautiful and amazing too. Amory reached up and traced Philip's smile with his fingertips before curving his hand around the back of Philip's neck. He tugged Philip down into another kiss, and moaned as Philip's fingers swept down his chest, brushing over his nipples and curving around his waist. He pressed up into the kiss, hungry for much more.

After long moments, Philip broke away with a gasp. "Ready?"

"Please."

Philip stole a quick kiss before leaning over Amory and reaching for the nightstand. With the gorgeous expanse of that chest right in front of him, Amory couldn't resist. He ran his palms over its planes, tangled his fingers in the dark hair there, brushed Philip's nipples with his thumbs. Philip groaned and Amory grinned.

"You're going to kill me."

Amory's grin widened. "A good way to go?"

Philip moved, sliding back over Amory until they were face-to-face, the drag of Philip's body against his pulling a moan from Amory's throat. "The best."

He laughed. Yes, it was. And he wanted more of it. Philip must have realized it, because he opened the vial of oil he'd retrieved from the nightstand drawer. A pleasant faintly herbal scent perfumed the air as Philip coated his fingers in the pale gold oil.

Philip raised his gaze to Amory's, seeming to search for something, and he must have found it because he reached down between them, his fingers unerringly finding that small opening and stroking over it gently. Amory gasped. No one had ever touched him there, and he hadn't expected it to feel so good. Another stroke of Philip's fingers, and his legs fell farther open as he moaned.

Philip kissed him again. "Just relax and let me in, all right?"

He nodded and forced himself to relax as Philip pushed his finger inside. It felt odd, but not painful as he'd feared. Then Philip began to move his finger, and all he could do was moan. He felt utterly wanton, but Philip kissed him again, deep and slow. Philip kept kissing him as he moved that finger inside him, stroking in and out for the longest time before he added another finger and another. The stretch of the last finger wasn't comfortable, but Philip was gentle and slow, and then he brushed over a spot inside that made it feel like sparks were going off within Amory. Philip's smile took on a wicked edge, and he stroked that spot over and over again until Amory was writhing beneath him, the pleasure of it almost too much to bear.

"Please, Pip, please now."

"Yes," Philip answered, his voice ragged. Amory was gratified he wasn't the only one coming apart at the seams, but that only went so far.

He wanted Philip inside him. He needed Philip inside him.

Philip didn't seem inclined to argue. He swiped more oil on his hard member, and pressed it to Amory, pushing inside before Amory had a chance to think of becoming nervous again. Not altogether comfortable at first, but the feeling eased as Philip slid ever so slowly into Amory. His eyes fell shut. He was so full, because Philip was inside him, filling him. The thought was almost overwhelming.

When Amory opened his eyes, Philip was looking down at him, his expression achingly tender. He looked into Amory's eyes, searching, and something about that soothed. "You're all right?"

"Yes." He looked up into that beautiful, dear face. Philip would wait if Amory needed him to, Philip would even stop, putting his pleasure on hold for Amory's comfort. He knew that, and it made him love Philip more. "Move now?"

"Oh yes."

Philip moved slowly at first, then faster. And it was so good, so very good. Better than Amory imagined, and he knew the physical feeling wasn't the reason. It felt so right because he was with Philip and Philip was inside him, connected to him in a way he had never been connected to anyone before. He'd been right to wait, to wait for it to be Philip. The intimacy would have been wrong with anyone else.

Philip's gaze, intense and dark with passion and something else, something Amory couldn't quite name, held his the entire time they moved together. The intensity of that connection was almost too much, but just right too. He was so caught by Philip's gaze that his release caught him unaware, rising up and sweeping him away like a wave. He gasped out Philip's name and clutched at him, his eyes fluttering shut against his will. He wanted to keep them open, to keep looking at Philip.

A moment later, Philip stiffened and cried out Amory's name. He forced his eyes open and watched pleasure wash over Philip's face. Philip lowered himself to Amory, burying his face in Amory's neck, and Amory gathered him close. He could get used to having Philip so close, to feeling his weight. Far too soon, Philip moved off of him, but he didn't go far, sliding to his side and pulling Amory with him until they lay on their sides facing each other.

Philip looked concerned, but Amory couldn't quite find words. So he smiled and reached for Philip. The concern dissipated, replaced by a glow of happiness. Philip's lips met his softly, and they sank into lazy, sweet kisses, and that was so good too. He almost felt as if he was the one purring into the kisses as Philip's arms held him close.

When the kisses slowed and stopped, he nuzzled closer to Philip and closed his eyes with a happy sigh. He could feel Philip's chuckle vibrating in his chest as much as hear it. "I suppose a nap would be nice."

Somehow Philip managed to get them both under the rumpled blankets and sheets without dislodging Amory too much, leaving them tangled together under the blankets. Philip began combing his fingers through Amory's hair, and he hummed in pleasure at the sensation.

"You're all right?"

A glow of warmth spread through him at the care and concern in Philip's whispered question. He settled his head more firmly on Philip's shoulder and pressed a kiss to warm, bare skin. "Very much better than all right."

"Good." Philip kissed the top of his head. "Me too."

"Good. We have to do that again soon."

Philip's soft laughter followed him down into sleep.

SOON TURNED out to be as soon as they woke up from a long nap. Philip worried about hurting Amory by making love again so soon, but he gave in to Amory's reassurances. Maybe he gave in too fast, but the temptation was too much. He wanted to be with Amory again, craved it. The contact, the connection, the overwhelming pleasure, and all of it with Amory. It had been so much better with Amory than he'd dreamed. So much better than it ever was with Vasco.

They snuggled in bed after, exchanging more kisses and touching for the sake of touch, talking about nothing in whispers as afternoon wore into evening. He'd never had anything like it before. He and Vasco hadn't lingered after their trysts. They tumbled each other into bed, or onto a couch, and out again just as quickly, always concerned with keeping their secret. Even those rare opportunities when they could take their time, they'd never cuddled up together. They had never talked as freely as this either.

Vasco had been his friend, and he missed that, but Amory meant more to him than Vasco ever had. Amory was more to him, and he felt more for Amory than he had for anyone else in his life. He should be scared of that, of what he might feel and how fast it all was. But somehow he wasn't scared. He was happy, so happy to have Amory with him. He needed to figure out how to keep Amory with him always. Easier said than done, but he would find a way.

"Is everything all right?" Amory looked at him, dark eyes searching.

Some of his pensive feelings must have shown on his face. He did have to think, but not right then. He only wanted to savor being with Amory. He tugged Amory closer. "Everything is wonderful."

"Yeah?" Amory looked skeptical, holding himself far enough away so he could see Philip's face.

"Definitely," he said firmly. He dropped a kiss on Amory's lips and brushed mussed curls off his forehead. Then he kissed Amory's forehead, nose, lips.

Amory pulled back a bit and watched him closely, before a sweet smile dawned on his face. "Good."

They emerged from their cocoon of blankets sometime later, but only to clean up and wrap themselves in dressing gowns. Amory's was a soft emerald-green velvet that Philip had given him at his birthday, knowing the color would look beautiful against his ivory skin and auburn hair. And he'd been right. Amory seemed to glow in the rich color, and it was all Philip could do to keep from pulling him close and opening the dressing gown to see all that pale skin underneath. Knowing Amory was naked under the robe did nothing to help his self-control, but he held together what shreds of it he could.

They ate dinner sitting among the rumpled blankets and pillows of the large bed. Eating in bed was another thing he'd never done before, never even thought of doing with Vasco, but he liked the intimacy of it with Amory. And he had to stop comparing Amory and Vasco, even if there wasn't a comparison. It didn't seem fair to someone who had once been his friend.

The conversation rambled during dinner and provoked a lot of laughter. In between speaking, they fed themselves and each other bites of the simple meal. While eating a creamy custard, Amory launched into a story of some childhood mischief he and his friends had perpetrated. Even though the story included Amory's friend Tristan, about whom Philip wasn't sure how he felt, it still had Philip laughing almost uncontrollably imagining a much younger and more mischievous Amory.

Amory was talking and sipping his wine, happy and beautiful in the candlelight, and making Philip happy by being there and being him. He had made the right decision asking Amory to stay all those weeks ago. He was certain of that. He leaned close to kiss Amory's smiling lips. He kissed Amory slowly, thoroughly, and as gently as he could. Trying to express his thankfulness.

"Was that for anything in particular?"

"I can't kiss my lover when I feel like it?"

"You absolutely can." Amory leaned toward Philip this time, kissing him, an impish look on his face. "So can I."

"Yes, you can." And he would happily trade kisses with Amory for hours. "Let's take a bath."

"What—together?"

He chuckled quietly at Amory's shocked expression.

"Don't laugh at me."

"I wasn't." He took Amory's hand. "All right, I was. You looked so scandalized."

"I didn't realize grown men bathe together, that's all." A faint pink tint colored Amory's cheeks.

"Well, I've never done it, but the tub is more than large enough for both of us, and I like the idea of it." Hot water and Amory's slick skin against his—what wasn't to like? He brought Amory's hand to his lips. "Please? You must be sore. The hot water will help."

Amory's blush deepened. "A little. It's kind of a good sore, though."

He smiled and kissed Amory's fingers again. "Bath?"

They slipped together into the large tub, which Philip had started filling with steaming water scented with chamomile bath oil while they ate. The hot water felt good, and Amory leaning back against his chest felt better. They lounged there together without talking for a long time. Philip didn't feel the need to fill the silence. It was comfortable, as nice as the conversation had been earlier. Enough to be there together, exchanging the occasional caress or soft kiss.

After a while, he picked up the soap and a cloth and began to leisurely wash Amory. Amory looked up at him from where he rested against Philip's shoulder. "I can wash myself. I've been doing it for years."

"Congratulations," he teased. "Let me. I want to."

Amory sighed into the kiss Philip gave him, and nodded, allowing Philip to run the cloth over his body. He enjoyed the soft sounds Amory made, the little gasps and moans, as the cloth passed over sensitive spots. When he finished, Amory was more than a little aroused, but all he did was take the cloth from Philip's hand, a hint of mischief in his eyes.

"My turn."

Amory put him through the same glorious torture he'd perpetrated on Amory, but he hadn't realized it was torture at the time. Amory's hand guided the cloth slowly over Philip's body, over his chest and back, down his arms and legs. Amory didn't miss an inch of Philip's skin, and the result had him panting and letting out little moans of his own. Amory smiled, far too pleased with himself.

Philip pulled Amory into a kiss, and then stood to help Amory from the tub. They dried each other with the soft towels laid out for them, and Philip wrapped Amory in the velvet dressing gown. He shrugged into his own, and Amory smoothed the shoulders and tied the sash for him. He kissed Amory once more before they walked back into the bedchamber.

The room had been tidied, and the remains of their meal taken away while they bathed. The servants were well-trained, unobtrusive, and discreet, which was one of the things that made being at Alzata so relaxing. They did their jobs well and otherwise let Philip be.

He helped Amory out of the dressing gown before shedding his own. He draped both of them over a chair and followed Amory into bed. Amory turned to him as soon as he did, snuggling close. A flush of pure pleasure suffused Philip at the simple action. Wrapping his arms around Amory, Philip pulled him even closer. He tilted Amory's face up and kissed him. Amory responded eagerly, as he always did. They kissed for a long while, kissing for the sake of kissing, meant to go no further. It was as good as the rest, kissing Amory, getting to sleep with Amory in his arms. His last thought as he fell asleep tangled up with Amory was that he had just what he always wanted.

PHILIP WOKE early the next morning, realized where he was, and buried his head in the pillow. He gathered a still-sleeping Amory closer against his chest and closed his eyes again, slipping back into sleep. The next time he woke, bright sunlight was streaming in the windows, and Amory's eyes were open. His dark gaze was sleepy, but Amory smiled when Philip looked at him.

"I didn't wake you, did I?"

He shook his head and pulled Amory close for a kiss. Amory was warm and pliant with sleep, and he molded himself to Philip. When the kiss ended, he said, "Good morning."

"Good morning."

Their day followed the pattern set by the one before. They ate breakfast, Philip finding himself unusually hungry and Amory teasing him for it. Then they went for a ride, though a shorter one than the day before. Again, a messenger from the palace waited for them back at the house. He hated the interruption, but he knew it was necessary.

The hour was early enough that he decided to deal with the paperwork and correspondence before lunch. He settled at his desk in the small study, and Amory lounged in a chair near the window, reading a book he'd chosen from the library adjacent to the study. Philip said nothing, but he liked having Amory close. He glanced up from his papers every so often to look at Amory, sitting in the sunlight, absorbed in his book.

Amory waited patiently while Philip gave instructions to the messenger taking the paperwork back to the palace. When the messenger left, Amory asked, "Finished?"

"Yes, finished."

Amory came around the desk and held out a hand for his. He pulled Philip to his feet and kissed him. "Good."

They ate lunch on the terrace again. Amory retrieved his sketchbook after the meal, and they strolled hand in hand through the garden and over the lawn into the shade of the woods. After a little while, Amory wandered off the path, and Philip followed. He sat on the ground next to where Amory settled with his back against a tree, and watched as Amory opened his sketchbook to a fresh page.

Amory looked up at him. "You're sure you aren't going to be bored?"

"Definitely not," Philip replied. He laughed at the skepticism in Amory's eyes. "Draw, Amory."

With an eye roll, Amory turned away, back to looking at whatever had caught his eye in that part of the woods. Soon, he began to sketch, his long, graceful fingers making quick, careful strokes with the charcoal. No, Philip wouldn't get bored. Amory didn't realize how much Philip enjoyed watching him. He was awed at how Amory's art came into being under his hands. He was awed at a lot of things about Amory.

He watched for a long time as a sketch of the woods took shape. It was cool in the dappled sun under the trees, and the scents of earth and grass and wildflowers were heavy in the air. This place was quiet and peaceful, even more so than the rest of Alzata. And no one would bother them.

"Do you mind if I change?"

"Hmm? Change?" Amory asked, glancing up at Philip. Amory's eyes weren't quite focused, his tone a little absent.

He was almost surprised by the swell of affection he felt at seeing Amory that way. "Change into a cat for a while."

Comprehension dawned in Amory's eyes. "Oh, of course not."

By then, Philip had used his Talent more than once in front of Amory, and he no longer worried Amory would be scared of it. In fact, Amory seemed to enjoy watching him as a cat and to be comfortable petting and cuddling him. He would use it more, but Philip would much rather be with Amory when he had hands to touch him. He pulled up his magic without another thought, using it for the only thing it was good for, and changed into a large black cat.

He stretched and settled into his new shape. His Talent might be useless, but it was fun, and he didn't often get the chance to indulge in it, especially not outside. He couldn't exactly gambol about the palace gardens. He was far too large as a cat to be inconspicuous. His family had always kept their Talents a secret, and he saw no reason to change that through carelessness. But at Alzata, they had more privacy.

Amory was smiling. He reached out a hand to Philip, and Philip nuzzled his head into it. Amory smoothed those graceful fingers over Philip's fur for long moments, and Philip purred in pleasure at the gentle, caring touch. He would be happy curling up in Amory's lap for more of that, happy to laze there all afternoon, but Amory was drawing, and Philip didn't want to interrupt something Amory enjoyed. He moved closer and rubbed his head against Amory's cheek before stepping back.

"Draw." As usual, the word was a growling, rumbly mess, but Amory understood him.

"All right, for a while longer."

Amory turned back to his drawing, and after another moment watching, Philip turned away to wander the little clearing silently. He didn't talk much as a cat, not that he normally had anyone to talk to since so few people knew about his Talent. His family did, and he'd used his Talent around them when he was younger. His father had been proud Philip's Talent was strong, and some of his cousins had the same Talent, so they would practice together sometimes and play as cats, stalking each other through the woods. But they seldom spoke even then. Forming words was difficult, and they always came out garbled.

He had wondered before if speaking clearly was a matter of practicing. If he spent more time speaking as a cat, maybe it would get easier. But his cousins never seemed interested in trying when they were children. No one had told him explicitly, but it seemed to be assumed they didn't talk when they used their Talents. Since then, he had seldom changed in front of anyone and never in front of anyone he felt comfortable speaking to.

But he found he wanted to be able to talk with Amory when he used his Talent. Amory didn't laugh at the mangled words. Amory listened carefully so he could understand what Philip said. Amory would probably be willing to help Philip practice. He could admit to a certain amount of self-consciousness at his inability to speak clearly, but he trusted Amory enough to try.

He looked back. Amory was still sitting against the tree, absorbed in his drawing. So no cuddling up to him, and no talking. That was all right. Amory was captivating, absorbed in his work. Philip found a sunny spot, curling up on a soft, thick patch of grass. Part of him thought the action a little too catlike, but the rest found it far too comfortable for him to deny the impulse. He watched Amory for a while before slipping into a doze.

He woke to a gentle hand stroking over the fur on his back. Amory smiled down at him, sunlight making a nimbus of his auburn hair. "There you are."

He stretched, pushing into Amory's hand. "Amory. Done drawing?"

"Yes, for now anyway." Amory's gaze softened. "I shouldn't have woken you. You looked peaceful."

"I'm glad you did." He closed his eyes and let the magic in him rise up. The familiar tingling warmth washed over his body, and when he opened his eyes again, they were human eyes. "Because now I can do this."

He kissed Amory, loving how Amory leaned into him and made a little noise of surprise and pleasure. When Philip ended the kiss, Amory smiled. "I like that you can do that."

"Me too." He moved closer, sliding his arms around Amory's waist. "Why don't we—what's that?"

Amory looked around, confused, before his gaze followed Philip's to his sketchbook open on the grass. The page showing wasn't the sketch Amory had been working on last Philip saw. It was a new drawing, of the woods again but the focus was a sleek black cat.

Amory's smile faltered a little. "It's you."

"I didn't know you were drawing me." He carefully pulled the book closer and studied the drawing, amazed again how well Amory could capture light and shadow on the page. But it felt strange to see himself as a cat. Certainly, there were painted portraits of him at various ages hanging on the palace walls, but there were none of him as a cat. He wasn't quite sure what to say.

"I know I didn't ask, but you looked so peaceful there, so beautiful. I couldn't resist. I hope you don't mind." Amory looked worried as he said it, and Philip hastened to reassure him.

"I don't mind. It took me by surprise. No one has ever drawn me as a cat before." He looked down at the drawing again. "I love it."

Amory released his breath in a long exhale, surprising Philip with the depth of his relief. "I'm glad."

"I did say you could draw me if you liked." He bent his head and pressed kisses along Amory's jaw.

"You did." Amory drew in a swift breath when Philip nibbled at his earlobe. "But I'm pretty sure you didn't mean it to include when you were a cat."

"Mmm." He continued kissing down Amory's neck, smiling against his skin when Amory wrapped his arms around Philip's neck. "Only because I didn't think of it. You may draw me however you like."

Philip was pleased that Amory's voice was a little breathless when he next spoke. "Can I draw you nude?"

Shock flashed through him, leaving him blinking at Amory. Amory watched him, eyes full of mischief and heat but some seriousness too. Amory kept speaking. "Nude and rumpled and sprawled in the wreck of the bed, just the way we made it yesterday. I can still see you that way in my head."

By the time Amory was finished there was a slight flush to his cheeks that was utterly incongruous with his words, and so endearing because of it. "You've gotten bold, haven't you?"

Amory stole a quick kiss. "You love it."

"I do, yes." He stole a longer kiss, and then whispered into Amory's ear, "Draw me that way if you like."

Amory shivered. "So many possibilities."

He laughed, loving Amory's mischief, and kissed him hard. Amory was laughing too, as they tumbled over onto the grass, exchanging kisses.

CHAPTER 8

AMORY DIDN'T want to leave Alzata the next morning. He'd fallen in love with it, as Philip thought he would. He hoped they could take some of Alzata's tranquility back with them.

After the afternoon spent out on the grounds yesterday, they returned to the house and cleaned up. They ate dinner on the terrace, and once again curled together on the chaise to watch the stars before returning to their bedchamber and their bed. He blushed just thinking about what followed.

Philip interrupted his thoughts as they walked outside to their horses. "So do you like Alzata?"

He nodded. "Can we come back?"

"As soon as we can get away again." Philip took his hand. "Thank you for coming here with me. Everything… it can be a lot sometimes. Being here with you helps lighten the load."

Philip's simply stated words left Amory reeling. It took him a moment to find his voice. "I'm happy I can help. Anything I can do to make things easier for you…."

"You do." Philip smiled at him, and Amory resolved to do all he could to support Philip for as long as he had with him.

Back at the palace, Amory quickly missed the peace of Alzata. The university summer session began and with it Amory's classes. Classes were in the morning, so he left for the university after breakfast a few days each week, riding across town with the two royal guardsmen assigned to him. Having the guardsmen with him was strange, and garnered him more attention at the university than he cared for, but he understood why Philip insisted they accompany Amory outside of the palace. The guards were nice enough, so he did his best to ignore the stares of the other students.

After classes, he generally returned to the palace. When he had taken classes previously, he sometimes stayed around to see friends or spend time with Tristan, but Tristan wasn't taking classes that session. Last Amory heard, Tristan wasn't in Jumelle.

At the palace, he had art lessons and healing lessons to fill his time, and the court functions he attended with Philip. He liked that Philip wanted him there, even if he still thought it odd for it to be acceptable for the prince's lover to sit at his side the way a spouse would. He wasn't so naïve he couldn't see the jealousy or disapproval in some people, both women and men, veiled though it might be. Those who disapproved were as much present as those who were overly ingratiating, hoping to gain Philip's favor through Amory. Amory tried to ignore it because he liked his life at the palace despite the politicking. He would put up with a lot more to be with Philip.

He had just returned from the university by way of a stop at an orphanage in the city when he was informed his father was at the palace waiting to see him. Amory sighed. The visit he made to the orphanage, part of the charity work he'd taken on in the last few weeks, had put him in a good mood. He hadn't had any experience with children other than his siblings before his first visit to the orphanage, so he was surprised at how much he enjoyed his time with the children. He'd been looking forward to sharing stories of the children's antics with Philip over lunch. But it seemed he was going to have to speak with his father first. Or rather, let his father speak to him.

He forced himself not to drag his feet walking to the room where his father waited. It would have been perfectly acceptable to have his father brought to their suite, but he didn't want his father there, in his and Philip's private space, their home. He didn't want his father's criticism, whether veiled or overt, of his home.

The small gold sitting room was suitable for his father. The room had been decorated during the reign of some long ago prince who must have had extravagant taste no one dared rein in. The furniture was all heavy and ornate and the artwork ostentatious, and every surface that could have been covered in gold leaf had been. In his opinion, most of those surfaces shouldn't have been.

His father looked satisfied. Arnau always had seen rooms like that one as signs of nobility and wealth, regardless of taste. One of the servants had brought refreshments, which his father helped himself to already. Amory didn't care. Once he finished the conversation, he was going to eat lunch with Philip before afternoon audiences.

"Hello, Father."

"Amory." His father looked him over, but, not unexpectedly, didn't stand or move to greet Amory in any other way. "You look like you've done well for yourself."

Somehow Amory doubted the statement had anything to do with his looking happy. His father was more likely remarking upon the new clothes he wore, though they weren't all that different from the ones he'd brought to the palace with him. "And how are you, Father?"

"I would be better if you remembered your responsibility to your family."

Amory paused in the act of lowering himself into the chair across from his father's, but then continued the motion until he was sitting on the velvet cushion. "Excuse me?"

"I know you aren't that stupid, so don't play with me. You know how you got here, and you know why you're here."

He did know both of those things, but he doubted he and his father would agree on what they were. "Why don't you tell me why you think I'm here?"

His father's face flushed. "Don't you talk back to me, boy. I have given you every advantage a man in a family of our station could expect and more, and all to groom you to be a useful member of our family and our family's business. You have been useless and disappointing all your life, but you can and will be useful now in promoting our family's interests. That is why you are here."

"Is it? I thought I was here because I care for the prince," he said, his words careful, his tone even.

"Please. Don't be naïve. You may be young, but you know how these things work. Concubine, spouse, it doesn't matter. Liaisons among the nobility are not about affection." Arnau leaned forward in his chair, staring hard at Amory. "They are about power and politics. About improving the position of families. And that is what you are going to do for us now."

At one time, Amory would have been intimidated. Not anymore. "Our family owns the foremost glassworking business in Tournai. The royal family already patronizes our business more than any other. It seems to me that the family's position is excellent."

His father's words lashed out, "What did I say about talking back to me? Have some respect. I put you here. I can take you away from this."

"No, you can't. And even if you could, you wouldn't because removing me from the palace would hardly serve your purposes."

He shouldn't bait his father. The man's face was nearly purple with what had to be barely suppressed rage.

"You're hardly serving my purposes now. But you will. You will do what you're told, and you will use whatever influence you have to promote this family with the prince." His father's expression told Amory what he thought that influence was. "You will make this family the exclusive glassmaking business of the royal family. The nobility will follow, especially if you keep promoting it. Then we can talk about nudging the prince toward land grants, perhaps a title."

Amory gaped at his father. Was he serious? But obviously he was. Many marriages were for political and financial reasons more than love, and maybe Amory was somewhat naïve to think his own relationship with Philip was different. But he did love Philip, and he wasn't there to make sure his father was granted lands and a title. "It's time for you leave, Father."

"I'll leave when I'm ready. I haven't finished talking to you yet."

"You have. I've heard all I need to hear." He spoke quietly but firmly as he stood.

"You listen—"

"Amory?"

Amory turned to find Philip standing in the doorway, his face a polite mask, but his eyes filled with concern. He tried to convey as much reassurance as he could with his own eyes.

Amory's father got to his feet and bowed to Philip. "Your Highness. How good to see you. I trust you are well?"

"Very well, Master Arnau." Philip stepped forward until he was at Amory's side, his hand coming to rest at the small of Amory's back. The warmth of his hand was far more comforting than Amory could ever have imagined. "I didn't know you were expected at the palace today."

His father smiled ingratiatingly. "I came to visit my son. It has been months since we've seen him after all."

"Yes. It's unfortunate your visit will have to be so short."

"Short?" His father looked bewildered, then displeasure dawned as he realized he was being dismissed.

"Yes," Amory said. "I apologize, but the prince and I have a lunch engagement."

Amory found it almost amusing watching his father try to be pleasant to him. "I'm sure you won't be missed if you stay awhile with me, Amory. It has been a long time since we've talked, and I think we have much to talk about."

"I'm afraid he will be missed. Amory is a very important guest at this lunch," Philip replied. Amory bit back a laugh. Of course he would be missed. Lunch was to be him and Philip alone, something they hadn't managed in a week.

"If that's the case, I won't delay you, Your Highness. We'll have to visit another day."

"Another day, Father."

Amory sighed and let his shoulders slump as soon as the door closed behind his father. "Well, that was unpleasant."

"Are you all right?" Philip put his arms around him and drew him close.

"Yes, but apparently I'm to use my influence on you."

Philip grinned, the hint of wickedness making Amory's pulse kick. "You can use your influence whenever you like."

He laughed. "I'll remember that. But my father wants me to use it for his gain. Well, my family's gain. That's why I'm here, according to my father."

Philip's face darkened, and Amory shivered for another reason entirely, but Philip just ran his hands over Amory's back. Soothing. "That's not why you're here."

"I know."

"I know you do." Philip hugged Amory close again. "He's your father, so I have tried to exercise patience and show him as much favor as I can, but I won't let him overstep."

But that sounded like… "He's spoken to you before?"

"Yes, but he wasn't near as direct as it seems he was with you."

"When?"

"It doesn't matter."

"It does," Amory insisted, taking a step back. "You should have told me."

Philip sighed. "I didn't want to upset you."

"I don't need you to protect me. I do need to know what my father says to you." He wasn't so fragile that he needed Philip keeping anything unpleasant from him, and he hated that Philip thought he was. "I'm not weak."

"I never thought you were. I'm sorry," Philip said. "I should have told you."

"Thank you."

"I'll tell you if I hear from him again."

Amory laughed without any humor. "I'm sure you will, and I'm sure I will as well."

"You're probably right. He wants everything he can get." Philip kissed him gently. "He's your family, and I understand the importance of family. I will tolerate him, but only within reason. And I won't tolerate him upsetting you."

Warmth flooded through him at the evidence of Philip's care. "Thank you. But I'm not worried about me. I'm worried about Adeline and the others."

"I'm worried about you, but maybe we can do something for your siblings."

He looked up at Philip. "Do you think so?"

Philip nodded. "Have to think about what, but we can at least watch over them. You should invite Adeline to visit. You've been saying you want me to meet her, and maybe she would get along with Elodie. I'm sure your father would like it if his daughter was personal friends with a princess."

Amory laughed. "I'm sure he would, but Adeline wouldn't take advantage of that."

"From what you've told me, I trust she wouldn't, but if he thinks she is, then that can only be good for her."

He kissed Philip. "You're very smart."

"You think so?"

"Oh yes." He kissed Philip again, lingering. He was suddenly so very grateful for Philip and how Philip cared for him.

Adeline and Elodie did get along, eventually. Both young women were polite from the moment he and Philip introduced them not quite a week later. Adeline was a little overwhelmed on her first visit to the palace, and her first time meeting both Philip and Elodie. She looked calm, but Amory could tell from the tightness around her eyes and the way her hands gripped each other a little too tightly.

He knew Philip saw it too when he went out of his way to put her at ease from the first moment. Amory's heart warmed watching it, because Philip was doing it for him. Philip wanted to meet Adeline for him, and he was trying to calm her nerves for Amory too.

Elodie arrived at their suite slightly late, as usual. Elodie wasn't nervous meeting Adeline, but she was rather subdued and cautious, wary even. Or, perhaps better to say she acted more like a princess was expected to and less like Elodie normally did. But by the end of lunch, tensions had eased. Adeline's nerves had been calmed, and she was smiling. Elodie was chatting and happy once more, and the girls seemed to have forged the beginning of a friendly relationship.

After lunch, back in the sitting room, Elodie told them about the outdoor concert she was attending that afternoon, bubbling over with excitement about it for several minutes. Philip smiled indulgently through the whole recitation, long used to his sister's quirks. Amory wasn't quite as used to them yet, but he managed to sit, holding Philip's hand, and listen. What was difficult was not laughing at poor Adeline. He could practically see her mind spinning as she valiantly tried to keep up with Elodie's flood of words.

"It sounds lovely," Adeline said when Elodie finally quieted.

"Oh, why don't you come with us?" Elodie bounced in her seat. "I'm sure you would enjoy it."

"Oh, thank you, Your Highness, but I couldn't," Adeline said.

"Why not? We could get to know each other better." Elodie smiled, wheedling. "I won't let you refuse."

"Oh, well." Adeline glanced at Amory, a mildly panicked look in her eyes. "All right, if it isn't an imposition."

"Of course it isn't!"

Philip still looked indulgent, and Amory let himself smile. "I'll send a messenger to the house, so Mother and Father know where you'll be."

"Thank you, Amory."

A knock on the suite's door interrupted whatever would have been said next, and Lady Lilliale walked into the room at Philip's call. As always, Lady Lilliale was perfectly dressed, her hair impeccably done. She always reminded Amory of an elegant doll. Dipping into a curtsy, she smiled sweetly at Philip.

"Philip, I'm so sorry to interrupt, but Celeste said Elodie was here."

Adeline looked at Amory with a raised brow, but he shook his head at her, not sure what she was asking. Something about Lady Lilliale, but they would have to talk about it later.

"That's all right. I wouldn't want you ladies to be late for your concert. Elodie is looking forward to it," Philip said.

"As am I. Will you be coming with us, Philip?"

"No, I have audiences this afternoon, and Amory is accompanying me, but Adeline will be going with you."

"Adeline?" Lady Lilliale's brow creased delicately as she looked at Philip.

"Lady Lilliale, may I present my sister, Adeline?" Amory said. "Adeline, this is Lady Lilliale. She is a great friend of Elodie's."

Wide violet-blue eyes fixed on him and then Adeline for the first time since Lady Lilliale entered the room. "It's a pleasure to meet you."

Adeline dipped into a curtsy. "And you, my lady."

"You're coming with us this afternoon?"

"Yes, my lady. Princess Elodie was kind enough to invite me."

Elodie hurried to Adeline, startling her by taking her arm. "I thought it would be good for us to get to know each other, considering our brothers' relationship."

"Of course," Lady Lilliale said. "But we should leave so we aren't late."

"What would I do without you, Lil?" Elodie laughed and began to tow Adeline toward the door. Adeline managed to peck Amory on the cheek as she went by.

The door shut behind the chattering young ladies—well, it sounded like Elodie was doing most of the talking—and Amory and Philip looked at each other before starting to laugh. Philip drew him close and rested their foreheads together as they chuckled.

"That went well," Philip said after they calmed down.

He looped his arms around Philip's neck. "I suppose so. They seem to be getting along at least, but I wondered at the beginning."

"Yes, Elodie was a little slow to warm up, but she did ask Adeline to go with them today. That's good."

"It is." He bit his lip. "I worry about Adeline with them, though."

"She'll be fine. Some of Elodie's ladies are going, as well as Cathal, Vrai, and two of Lilliale's brothers. Another young lady too, I think."

"It's not that, or maybe it is. Adeline has never participated in this level of society. I hate to throw her into it with no warning or preparation."

"She'll be fine," Philip repeated. "Adeline seems to have a level head, much like her brother."

Amory arched into the little nipping kisses Philip was placing on his neck. Philip continued between kisses, "She acts more like a proper young noble lady than Elodie does. She's lovely, seems quite intelligent, and made charming conversation over lunch. She will be fine. In fact, she'll probably make quite a splash."

He was finding it difficult to think with Philip nibbling on that particular spot, but he managed a coherent sentence. "I'm not sure if that's reassuring."

"Cathal and Vrai will look after her. She may get a marriage proposal or two, but no one will bother her."

"Marriage proposals?" Amory laughed, and then moaned as the kisses traveled over his throat again.

"As I said, she's lovely. She's not from a noble family, but she is the daughter of a wealthy merchant family, and there are any number of sons of noble families who may be interested in her as a bride, especially taking into account your relationship with me." Philip pulled back and looked at him, grinning. "Do you think your father would consider it advancing your family's position if that happened?"

He groaned. "Please don't talk about my father while you're kissing me."

Philip chuckled. "Good point. We'll talk about it later. For now… we have some time before audiences and nowhere to be."

He put up no resistance as Philip pulled him into the bedchamber.

PHILIP LOUNGED in his throne on the dais, the chair next to him empty. He wished Amory was sitting there, but his lover looked like he was enjoying himself on the dance floor partnering Elodie. She had insisted he dance with her, and Amory couldn't refuse, though he didn't often dance. Philip wasn't sure why. Amory was graceful and as skilled as anyone else on the dance floor.

He liked watching Amory, but he missed having him by his side. For a long time after Amory first came to the palace, Philip kept him close at social events, worried Amory would be intimidated by the social aspect of court life. But, Amory had been required to attend the entertainments his father hosted, and he hadn't had much trouble adjusting to the difference in scale and intensity in court events. Amory could navigate court events well enough; Philip just liked having Amory close.

Having Amory next to him was unbelievable and thrilling, yet somehow entirely comfortable. Natural, as if it were meant to be. He no longer had a problem admitting that was exactly what he wanted. The months Amory had been with him were the best of his life, the happiest, and though it had only been months, he couldn't imagine life without Amory.

He hoped Amory felt the same. It seemed as if he did. They hadn't discussed it, but he believed Amory wanted to stay with him. But Uncle Umber had been pushing harder for Philip to marry. They'd had another argument that morning. His uncle pressed again the need to search for a wife. Someone from a good family or who brought a good alliance, who would be a suitable mother of his heirs.

"I've given everything to this country, Uncle," he finally snapped. "I do every day, and I have since I was old enough to understand what being a prince meant. I do it gladly, because I love Tournai. But I won't give that. I won't marry some woman for that. If I do, then there will be nothing left of me, of who I am."

"Then there will be nothing left of you except the prince of Tournai, which is who you are," Uncle Umber answered in his thundering voice. "Do your duty and be worthy of the title and all that comes along with it. Your father—"

"My father married for love. I don't see why I can't do the same."

His uncle had seen many reasons why he couldn't marry for love. Very few of them held any validity for Philip. In fact, Philip could see only one that had any true weight behind it, which was that any person Philip loved, being male, wouldn't be able to give him heirs, which seemed to be the most important of his uncle's reasons for him to marry.

He couldn't give that too. He hadn't lied when he said there would be nothing left of him. If he hadn't found Amory when he had, if Amory hadn't been just what he needed, he wasn't sure what he would have turned into. He was better with Amory, as a man and as a prince. And he knew, knew without asking, that Amory would stay beside him as his lover, even if Philip was forced to marry someone else. He watched Amory, smiling and happy as he led Elodie through the steps of the dance.

Amory looked up, and their eyes met. His smile softened into something intimate, for Philip. Amory would stay, but Philip wanted better for them than a relationship outside his eventual marriage.

"Your Highness."

Philip had been so absorbed in watching Amory and in his swirling thoughts that he hadn't noticed Vasco walk up to him. He hadn't known Vasco was back in the city. Vasco had spent most of the time since his marriage on his family's lands in northern Tournai. Philip didn't think he'd seen Vasco since the man's wedding. It felt odd seeing him.

"Your Grace." He nodded in return. He looked at the tall blond man in front of him. Vasco was undeniably handsome, but his expression was closed off. So different from when they were children, but was it so different from when they were lovers? Vasco hadn't been completely open then either. Philip's gaze was drawn back to Amory.

"He's acquitting himself quite well, considering."

He turned back to Vasco to find him studying Amory. "Considering?"

"Considering he wasn't raised to this. He's not a nobleman. He wouldn't have expected to end up dancing at parties at the palace, but he dances well for all that. And I've heard he has acclimated decently to living in our circle."

Philip had to force himself to relax and unclench his fists. Satisfying though it might be, punching Vasco would cause a scene he didn't need. Amory wouldn't want it either. But something needed to be said, even if the insult turned out to be unintentional. Philip didn't believe the implication of Vasco's words was unintentional.

"Amory acquits himself well for anyone. I've met any number of noblemen who can't navigate the waters of court half as well as he can. He may not have been born a nobleman, but he was raised a gentleman." It was about who Amory was, someone Philip was proud to have at his side.

"I meant no offense, Philip." Vasco flashed him an intimate smile that had Philip bristling. Vasco truly thought he could smile in such a way at him after everything?

"Don't call me Philip. It's inappropriate for you to do so."

Vasco's expression went blank with shock. "I've always called you by your name. We're friends."

"We were friends. We're not anymore. I tolerate it from Lilliale because she's like another sister, but not from you anymore."

"Yes, Your Highness. I apologize for presuming." Vasco fell silent. Philip looked back at the dance floor, feeling not a little awkward himself, but he didn't have any inclination to smooth over the situation. Finally, Vasco spoke again. "I'm surprised you aren't dancing. Lilliale always looks forward to a dance with you at these things. She was talking about it earlier."

"Perhaps I'll dance with her later." But he only wanted to dance with Amory. He'd successfully fended everyone else off so far. "She looks like she's enjoying herself dancing with Vrai."

"Yes, she does." Vasco studied the dancers. "Who is that dancing with the Earl of Calixto's son?"

"Amory's sister, Adeline."

Vasco's eyebrows shot up. "Really? I'm surprised you would invite your concubine's sister to a party."

Where was Vasco's attitude coming from? Was Vasco always so pretentious or had it developed after he inherited his title? "Don't ascribe your attitudes to me. Adeline is a lovely young woman. She's going to make an excellent marriage. Possibly with the earl's son. They've met several times, and they seem rather smitten with each other."

Vasco's expression portrayed frank astonishment for an instant before it cleared. "I'm still surprised. And I would think you would be more concerned with making an advantageous marriage for yourself rather than for your concubine's sister."

"I don't see how that is any of your concern." His voice lashed out, cold as ice, and he couldn't regret it. Who did Vasco think he was to say those things to Philip?

"The country needs heirs. You need to marry and sooner rather than later, Phi—Your Highness."

"I know best what I need, Your Grace, not you. And I'm happy as I am."

"What? With your commoner lover here in the palace?"

"Watch yourself." He pinned Vasco with a look he knew full well would set most trembling.

"I apologize. I shouldn't have said that." Vasco raised his hands in placation. "I just don't understand. It isn't like you to jump into something so quickly. You're not impulsive, not with something so serious."

"I am when it's right." And being with Amory was most definitely right.

Vasco looked taken aback at his vehemence. "This liaison of yours could affect your ability to contract a good marriage, especially since you're so open about it. I'm worried, of course."

"I don't see why you would be worried or even be thinking about it. It's none of your concern." Philip stood, tired of the conversation, and saddened too. "I'm going to dance."

"That's good. As I said, Lilliale has been talking about dancing with you all day."

"Perhaps later. I'm going to dance with Amory now."

Shock again, not as easily covered that time, but Vasco's voice held concern too. "Are you sure that's wise, Phi—Your Highness?"

"Quite sure."

Before he could say anything else, Amory's voice stopped him. "Philip?"

"Amory." He turned and smiled, beckoning Amory closer.

"I'm sorry to interrupt." Amory's eyes flicked between him and Vasco. His perceptive lover had noticed the tension.

"You weren't." He placed a hand on Amory's back, keeping him by his side. "Amory, this is Vasco, Duke of Marena."

Comprehension and wariness flooded Amory's eyes, but Amory was nothing but polite and pleasant, when he addressed Vasco. "Your Grace, it's a pleasure to meet you."

"And you, Master Amory." Vasco inclined his head in a nod that was correct for the situation and not one bit more than that.

Amory tensed at Vasco's cool tone, but he smiled kindly nonetheless. Philip pulled him a little closer. He didn't know what had gotten into Vasco, but he refused to let him upset Amory. Vasco made a low sound in his throat. Philip had no idea what that meant.

"Is your wife with you this evening?" he asked, realizing she wasn't with Vasco, which was odd. She should have greeted the prince.

"No, Bettina didn't accompany me tonight. She isn't feeling well."

"I'm sorry to hear that," Amory said. Philip knew the concern was sincere as well.

He added, "Yes. I hope it isn't anything serious."

"Not at all. It's nothing really," Vasco said. "Bettina is with child."

"Your first child. That's wonderful. You must be very happy."

"Yes, congratulations," Amory added.

Vasco barely flicked a glance at Amory. "Thank you. Yes. We're hoping for a boy."

"Of course." Philip wasn't surprised to hear that Vasco was hoping for an heir. An heir was the reason everyone was telling Philip to marry after all. But Philip tried to keep the bitterness from his voice. From Amory's expression of puzzled concern, he didn't do a very good job of it.

"Well, I hope Her Grace feels better soon," Amory said.

"Thank you." Vasco's words were almost grudging, and Philip bristled at the insult as he wondered again what had happened to the man who used to be his friend. "I'm sure she will."

Philip really was out of patience with the conversation. "We won't keep you any longer. I'm sure there are others you want to see after your long absence from court. Please give your wife our regards."

Another flash of surprise over Vasco's face. "Thank you, Your Highness."

After a brief bow, Vasco disappeared into the crowd, and Philip sighed. Amory turned to face him, resting his hand lightly on Philip's arm. "Are you all right?"

There was that gentle sweetness he loved about Amory, a soothing balm after too many confrontations. He shrugged. "He used to be my friend. I don't know what happened to him. I can't believe he was always like this and I never noticed. It's sad to think of how much everything has changed."

"I'm sorry."

"I'm not sad my affair with him is over," he whispered so only Amory heard. "If not, then I wouldn't have you."

Amory's smile was blinding. "I'm glad I'm here too."

He took Amory's hand and kissed it. "Good, and I will be all right."

"I know you will." Amory glanced away. "He doesn't like me."

He wanted to deny it, but he couldn't bring himself to do so. Philip wasn't sure why—class prejudice or improbable jealousy or something else entirely—but Vasco's dislike of Amory was obvious. Philip sighed. "I know. I'm sorry."

"It's not your fault."

"When you walked up, I was trying to take my leave of him and come find you."

"You were?"

"Yes. I wanted to dance." He threaded Amory's hand through the crook of his arm and began walking.

"You wanted to…"

"Dance. With you."

"But we never have before. Can we?" Amory looked charmingly befuddled with a hint of hope underneath. It banished the last dregs of upset from his conversation with Vasco.

"Yes. And I don't know why we haven't danced long before now." They had reached the dance floor by then, and he pulled Amory carefully into his arms, drawing him into the dance. It took a moment for them to get comfortable. He'd taken the lead role in the dance without any thought, which left Amory following in the traditionally female part. When Philip realized, he started to say something, but Amory smiled and shook his head. With some concentration, Amory adjusted, and they managed to move through the dance with a fair amount of grace.

"We should do this more often," he said in Amory's ear, taking pleasure in the shiver that ran through Amory. They should dance more often. Getting to hold each other that way, move together, was nicer than he ever thought it would be. Somehow intimate in a way he'd never realized dancing could be. But maybe he never had the right partner.

"I'd like that."

"Good." But he could feel tension creeping into Amory's frame. And he knew why. "Don't worry about them. Don't pay any attention."

"But they're watching."

"They're always watching. Let them." He looked into Amory's eyes. "Let them watch us dance. Let them see how much we feel for each other."

Amory's eyes were glowing. It looked as if he was going to say something, but he only nodded.

"Good. Now," he said, letting a little mischief into his voice, "What do you think of Adeline and Pierrick?"

Amory grinned, and they both looked to where the pair was still dancing. "They seem to be getting along very well."

"That's what I thought. I have a feeling a marriage offer may be coming."

Amory's eyes went wide. "Do you think so?"

"Yes. Why not?"

"Well, she's a commoner for one thing."

Philip hated that Amory thought that mattered for his sister, and probably for himself as well. "I don't think that's a problem. Pierrick and his family are progressive, and they would see being allied with a prosperous, important merchant family as a good thing. As for personally, he's a second son, so he has more freedom to marry as he chooses, and Adeline is a lovely girl. He would be insane to look elsewhere."

"Well, I think so, but she is my sister, so I may be biased."

"Your father will be happy."

Amory laughed. "Extremely happy. It's almost frightening to think about what this will do to him."

He laughed too, but however happy it would make Amory's father, Philip refused to push Adeline into a marriage she didn't want. "The important question is whether Adeline will be happy."

Amory sobered. "I think she will be. She cares for him already."

"Good, I'm glad. She should be able to marry someone she loves. Everyone should."

Amory's gaze was warm. "Many people wouldn't agree, both in your world and in mine."

He had a difficult time resisting the urge to kiss the sweet curve of Amory's lips. But then, he'd wanted to kiss Amory all night. "You're a part of my world now, you know. And my parents' marriage was a love match. I know it doesn't always happen, but I think everyone should have the chance to marry for love. Why do you think I haven't arranged a marriage for Elodie?"

"You want her to have that chance if she can."

He nodded.

"And you?" Amory asked, an indecipherable expression in his eyes.

"And me," he answered simply. Amory nodded and was quiet through the rest of the dance.

CHAPTER 9

AMORY AND Philip managed a much quieter evening a few days later. A fire crackled cheerfully in the sitting room hearth, dispelling the damp chill that had come with fall. Philip was reading in the corner of the couch, and Amory was curled at his side, reading his own book. Or trying to. Mostly he stared into the fire, wondering what was bothering Philip.

Philip had been quiet, pensive even, the last few days, and Amory was worried. With all the talk of marriage at that party, he wondered if Philip was considering marriage himself. Amory knew, had always known, that Philip would have to marry—with or without love. As much as Amory hated the idea of infidelity, he'd already decided he would stay as long as Philip wanted him. But what if Philip found someone he loved and wanted to marry? Philip wouldn't want Amory to stay with him then. Perhaps that was why Philip had been so quiet. None of this was a surprise, and thinking about it happening shouldn't hurt so much.

Maybe because it was so soon. They'd only had a few months together, and he'd expected more time—he *wanted* more time—with Philip.

Fingers gently combing through Amory's hair made him jump. "Are you all right?"

Amory moved just enough to see Philip while he answered the softly spoken question. "I'm fine. Why?"

"You've been quiet. I wondered if everything is all right."

"I've thought the same about you. You've been off since the party. I've been worried."

Philip's fingers paused but then resumed their gentle motion an instant later. "I'm sorry. I never meant for you to worry."

"What's wrong?" He often thought back over the day of the party, trying to figure out what could have upset Philip. "Was it seeing Vasco? Or something with Adeline? I appreciate all you've done for her, but you don't have to do any more."

"No, it's not that at all. I'm glad to help Adeline. I like her, and I love how happy it makes you." Philip leaned forward to kiss him lightly.

"Though I don't think she'll need much more help. Pierrick intends to ask for her hand. He wants to marry her."

Happiness for his sister filled him. Adeline talked about Pierrick often, and as contained a person as she was, that she mentioned him so much told Amory how she felt. "She's going to be so happy. She was telling me yesterday how much she hoped he might care for her."

"He cares for her a great deal. He asked for my permission to approach your father. He seemed worried I might refuse."

He laughed before he realized what Philip said. "Your permission?"

Philip nodded. "It's old-fashioned, but it has to with your being my lover, and therefore your sister being here under my care and sponsorship. I wouldn't have refused, not when I know how much they care for each other, of course, and Pierrick is a good man. I told him I would see your father with him."

"Thank you." Amory kissed Philip. "I appreciate all you're doing. Father will be better behaved if you're with him."

"I thought so. But it probably won't be enjoyable for me."

He kissed Philip again. "I'll make it up to you."

"I'll hold you to that." Philip pulled him closer and lingered over another kiss.

He forced himself to pull back when Philip would have continued the kisses. "What is it, then? If it's not Adeline. Did something happen when you were talking with Vasco that you didn't tell me about?"

He hated how jealous and insecure the question sounded, because, although the sight of Philip with the handsome, almost regal man the other night had caused a moment of doubt, he didn't think Philip wanted Vasco. He just wasn't sure what seeing Vasco would do to Philip.

"No, not really. He did say something to me, but it only echoed what Uncle Umber has been saying more and more." Philip looked weary just thinking about whatever his uncle and Vasco told him.

"What is it? Can I help?"

Philip shook his head and slumped back into the soft cushions. "They're pressuring me about finding a wife and producing heirs."

Amory had no idea what to say. It was what he feared. "What are you going to do?"

"I'm going to get married."

"Oh." A strange, yawning emptiness opened up inside him as he waited for Philip to tell him his fate.

Philip straightened in his seat and turned Amory to face him. He twined his fingers with Amory's. "Marry me."

He was so lost in his own sickening worries that it took him a moment to realize what Philip said, and then he couldn't believe he'd heard Philip correctly. "What?"

"Marry me, Amory," Philip repeated. He squeezed Amory's hands tighter. "Marry me. I want you to be my husband. I want to be yours."

Philip's words, so genuine, so filled with heartfelt emotion, melted Amory, and for a moment, he reveled in warmth and joy. But still. "I can't. We can't."

"Why not?" Philip's voice turned teasing. "Everyone wants me to get married. So we'll all be happy."

Amory was suddenly angry, angrier than he had ever been. He pulled his hands free and jumped to his feet. "Stop it. Don't joke, not about this."

Philip rose, his movements slow. "I'm not joking. Well, a little about that last part, but not about marrying you. Never about that."

"Everyone wants you to marry because you need a wife, a mother for your heirs. No one would be happy if you married me."

"I would." Philip stepped closer. "Because what I need is the man I love beside me, loving me, supporting me, as I do him, for the rest of our lives."

"You…." The shock hit him so hard the word came out breathless. "You love me?"

Philip cupped his cheek. "Yes, I love you. Do you love me?"

"Yes, of course I love you, but that doesn't mean we can marry." Amory's heart broke as he said it. He hadn't realized how painful it would be, but one of them needed to be sensible. "I'll be here, loving you, for as long as you want me. We don't need to marry for that to be true."

"I know. I know that. You'll stay with me no matter what, because that's the kind of man you are, but I want more for us." Philip's expression firmed, and Amory saw more than a little of the princely demeanor Philip adopted when sitting on his throne in it. "I want more than for you to be the lover outside of my marriage, whether it's acceptable or not. I even want more than what we have now for us. You are, in every way except one, already my husband, and I want that way too. I want everyone to recognize you as my husband, my consort."

"I don't need it." But his protest sounded weak to his own ears. Maybe he didn't need it, but he wanted the recognition, the assurance of his place at Philip's side.

"I do. I need it for us."

He could see that, could see Philip's need in the intensity of his eyes. "Philip, you're the prince. You need an heir."

The throne, along with noble titles in general, was required to pass to a bloodline heir. A titled nobleman who married another man effectively took himself out of the succession. The law was different for commoners. Laws allowed nonbloodline heirs for property not attached to a title, so two male commoners could marry and adopt a child to be their heir. Some of the wealthier commoners, like Amory's father, emulated the nobility in insisting on bloodline heirs, but that was mostly for show. For the first time, Amory wished fervently that Philip wasn't the prince. Because it was even more important for the prince to produce an heir himself, to show the strength of the throne and of Tournai.

"I'm also a man, and I need you. There wouldn't be a guarantee of an heir if I did marry a woman. And if I don't have a child of my own... well, Elodie is my heir now, and soon enough she'll marry and have children, and they can inherit. We'll have to make sure she marries a very steady man. And if by some strange event, she doesn't have children, I have cousins who could inherit the throne and pass it on to their children. There's Cathal, Vrai, Etan." Philip smiled. "Well, maybe not Etan. He'd have the same problem as I do, but he's not the oldest anyway."

He laughed despite himself. "Pip."

"I'm serious, I promise you. And if you insist I have a child of my own, well... maybe we can find a woman who wouldn't mind, and then I could acknowledge the child, make him my heir." Philip's forehead creased and he glanced away. "If I could manage it. I hate the idea."

"And if you did, I would love your child. But I would do that whether or not we were married."

"It would be our child," Philip interrupted. "If we do that, it would be our child, not my child or my heir. Our child to love and raise together."

"Our child." The phrase resonated through Amory. He had never thought about having a child of his own, and even in this discussion, he could easily forget the heir they spoke of was a child. He'd like to see Philip as a father. Philip would be a good father. Amory thought he might like to try himself, terrifying as the idea was. Their child.

"Yes. Our child, if we want. And our marriage. Please, Amory."

The vision of them married with a child tempted him so much, making him ache to reach out for it, to make it true, but he couldn't let Philip do that. "You're making everything far more difficult for yourself than it needs to be. No one would support this marriage—your uncle is going to hate the very idea of it. Please don't do this to yourself. I'm not going anywhere."

"I know you're not. I don't want you to, but that isn't why."

No, Philip had said it was because he wanted more for them. Because he loved Amory.

"I can't live my life for my uncle," Philip continued. "I already live it for this country, and now I'm living it for you too. I want to live my life with you."

"Philip." He stopped talking, because he wanted to say yes. He wanted to marry Philip, but they couldn't, could they?

"Amory." Philip took his hands and squeezed them. "Please don't let other people ruin this. Yes, there will be people who will be upset, but they will get over it. I will continue to rule this country the best way I know how, the way my father raised me to. And better, because you and I will be together, and having you with me makes me better."

"Being with you makes me better too. Stronger." He spoke quietly, but he knew Philip heard him because Philip's eyes shone at his words. "I do love you. Which is why I worry marrying me will hurt you too much. I don't want to be the cause of trouble for you."

"If there's trouble, we'll weather it together." Philip drew him closer and began feathering little kisses along his neck. "Marry me, Amory."

He shivered at the feel of the words breathed against his neck. "Not fair. I can't think when you do that."

"Good. I don't want you to think." Philip continued his pleasurable onslaught. "Marry me."

Amory moaned when Philip began nibbling at his earlobe. He closed his eyes and tried to hold on to his wits, tried to hold on to all the reasons Philip marrying him was a bad idea for Tournai. Doing so was difficult, when Philip's words of love and need ran through his mind over and over, and the idea of marriage to the man he loved took root inside him. He had been resigned to a position quite different from that of husband, or he'd been trying to resign himself to it. He wanted to be with Philip, the horrible feeling he got when he imagined what his life would be like without Philip told him so. But, he never thought to marry Philip.

But Philip thought of marriage. Philip, who Amory was still amazed actually wanted him at all. Philip, whom he loved more than anyone.

If he loved Philip, he needed to trust him.

"Yes," he blurted out. "Yes, I'll marry you."

Philip pulled back. His expression so shocked it was almost comical. "You will?"

"Yes, I will." Even though he still worried for what consequences might follow the decision. But he would stand by Philip no matter what came.

Joy flooded Philip's face, making him so beautiful it took Amory's breath away. That joy was all because of Amory, because Amory agreed to marry him, and it knocked him breathless to see it. Incredible to be able to make Philip so happy. Philip grabbed him and pulled him close. He wrapped his arms around Philip's waist and held on. Despite his lingering worries, joy began to bubble up inside him too, bright and clear, as he realized he and Philip were getting married. He would get to spend his life with this man, and no one could come between them.

He starting laughing, and Philip drew back enough to look at him. Philip's eyes were shining, and he was grinning like the lunatic he must be to think they could marry and it would all be all right. But Amory must be a lunatic too, because he'd agreed to it.

Then Philip kissed him, and Amory thought maybe he could actually taste Philip's happiness, his exhilaration, bright and sweet, on Philip's lips. He almost laughed at the fanciful thought, but he couldn't say it wasn't true. He sank into Philip, kissing him back for all he was worth and hoping Philip could feel his joy and love from his kiss too. He thought maybe Philip could from the way Philip pulled him closer, the way Philip's hands moved over his arms and back. So passionate but cherishing, almost reverent, too.

He yelped when Philip broke the kiss and swung Amory up in his arms all in one fluid motion. He grasped at Philip's shoulders, disconcerted at the feeling of being carried. "What are you doing? Put me down. I'm too heavy."

Philip grinned. Amory refused to acknowledge that he had screeched. "I'm carrying you to bed. And you are not too heavy for me to carry. Just stop squirming."

Amory froze. He did not want to be dropped. "Even if I'm not too heavy, I'm not a girl."

"I am quite aware that you're not a girl. But I don't see what that has to do with my carrying you."

"Pip—" He broke off when Philip tossed him onto the bed. He landed on the soft mattress amid the luxurious pillows and blankets with a bounce and was startled into laughter. Philip's grin turned into a full-blown laugh as he followed Amory down to the bed, stretching out on top of Amory and resuming his kisses. They kissed and loved that night with constant smiles and laughter.

PHILIP KNEW Amory was right. There were going to be any number of people who would not support his marriage to Amory for its perceived effect on the strength of the throne and Tournai. He had known that before he asked Amory to marry him, and he had pondered it, considered how it might affect him and Tournai. Because though he wanted to marry the man he loved, he couldn't allow himself to hurt the country he had been born and raised to rule. He would never forgive himself for that.

But he couldn't let go of the idea of marrying Amory either. He kept turning it over in his mind, as Uncle Umber pressured him to marry and produce an heir. He'd considered an arranged marriage, he really had, but he loved Amory. He couldn't bring himself to ask Amory to stay if he married someone else, nor did he want to marry anyone other than Amory. He hadn't expected it would take so much convincing to get Amory to agree, but he should have. Amory cared more about Philip than about anything Amory might want himself. Of course he would try to protect Philip. Philip loved him all the more for that.

But Amory agreed in the end, which was all that mattered.

Then they had to tell everyone else. Uncle Umber was predictably irate. Philip let him yell and rage for a while, hoping he might wear himself down and become more rational. But his uncle kept yelling, and Amory, sitting beside Philip, became more and more tense. Philip finally stopped his uncle's tirade when Amory's face went stark white. He would not let Uncle Umber hurt Amory or make Amory doubt his decision. Uncle Umber sputtered to a halt, drew himself up to his full height, and thundered that he would not set foot in the palace until Philip came to his senses.

They hadn't seen him since. It had only been a week, but as his uncle was normally at the palace every day, a week was a noticeable absence. Philip didn't like the rift with his uncle, hated that his uncle, his father's brother, had broken with him, but he refused to give up Amory to please Uncle Umber. Philip wondered what his father would think of his choice. He hoped his father would be happy for him, or at least understand.

The rest of his family's reactions were mixed. Shock with perhaps a bit of bewilderment was predominant, which Philip could understand, but he hoped that once the shock wore off they would be happy for him and Amory. Etan, though surprised, was entirely supportive and genuinely happy when Philip and Amory told him of their plans to marry. Philip might have even seen some small spark of hope in Etan's eyes at that moment.

Etan's wholehearted support went a ways to balance out Cathal's vociferous objections. He didn't yell the way Uncle Umber had, but Cathal made his opinion firmly and clearly known. Cathal believed the consequences of their marriage would be detrimental for Tournai, and while he didn't storm out of the palace, he did pull back from Philip. He had always been closest to Cathal out of all of his cousins, and to see him walk away... hurt. It hurt terribly, and he could see his pain reflected in Amory's eyes, even though he hadn't said anything to Amory about how he felt. He supposed he didn't have to. Amory always knew without being told.

Like everyone else, Amory's father was shocked. But he said nothing against them. Not surprising in the least, that reaction. If Amory married Philip, he would have a higher status than as Philip's lover, and Arnau could only see that as a good thing for himself and his family. Philip would have to keep watching that man. He would not be taken advantage of, and he would not see Amory hurt in his father's quest to improve their family's position.

However, Philip wasn't thinking about his own marriage at the moment, but someone else's. He spent a good portion of the morning with Arnau, Pierrick, and the Earl of Calixto negotiating Pierrick's marriage to Adeline. The negotiations were complicated somewhat by Arnau's bluster and the earl's reaction to it, but eventually they reached a consensus on dowries and settlements advantageous to both families. Pierrick himself didn't look much like he cared about those things.

As soon as they finished, Philip sent Arnau, Pierrick, and Pierrick's father out to the terrace where lunch would be served, and went to fetch Amory and Adeline. He could have sent a servant, but he needed a break from both fathers' posturing, and the errand was as good an excuse as any. If the other men looked at him oddly, he didn't really care.

He entered the suite through his study. There was work there waiting for him, but it would be there after lunch. Amory and Adeline's voices floated in through the open door to the sitting room, and he had no idea why, but he stopped at the door.

"How is everything really?" Adeline spoke, and he could hear concern in her voice.

"Good," Amory answered. "Well, Philip's family isn't happy with us, some of them anyway. It hurts him. I can tell even though he doesn't say much about it. They're his family and his closest friends. Cathal especially. And they've turned their backs on him."

"I can't imagine."

"I don't know if I can either, not completely, but I hurt for him. I keep hoping they'll change their minds." There was a pause, and then Amory spoke again, quietly, "I keep waiting for him to blame me."

"Why would he ever do that?" Adeline exclaimed.

"I don't know." Amory groaned. "It's just... it's my fault. If it weren't for me, none of this would be happening to him. He wouldn't have lost his family."

"And a lot of other good things wouldn't be happening to either one of you. Would they?" Another pause. "The prince chose to be with you. He chose to marry you. You didn't force him to do those things. He had to know what might happen."

"I know, I know. I do. Don't listen to me." Amory sighed. "I'm worried about him."

Philip closed his eyes. He should not be listening. It was wrong to eavesdrop on a private conversation. And yet he didn't move.

He heard a rustle of material he thought might be Adeline's skirts. "I know you are, Amory. I can see it. You love him, don't you?"

"Yes."

Even though Philip had heard it before, had heard Amory say it to him, hearing Amory tell his sister sent a thrill of warmth and happiness through him.

Meanwhile, Adeline was speaking again. "The prince loves you too?"

"Yes, he does." He could hear the smile in Amory's voice and could picture the pink that likely tinted his cheeks.

"Good. And he makes you happy?"

"So happy, Adeline. I never could have imagined being so happy. I want him to be happy too. I want to make everything better for him, to give him absolutely everything."

The breath clogged in Philip's throat at Amory's words. His Amory. He forced a breath in past the lump in his throat and pushed the door open. The brother and sister were hugging, but they let go as he entered the room.

"Philip." Amory smiled in welcome. Adeline smiled as well, a shyer one than her brother's, and stepped away from Amory to curtsy.

He smiled at them both, but he knew his smile was different when he looked at Amory. He didn't care, not anymore, that he wore his feelings for Amory so openly. He went to Amory and kissed him. As always, he had to force himself not to sink into the kiss, to deepen it and prolong it and follow it with many, many more. Kissing Amory was still his favorite pastime.

But Adeline was standing next to them, and others were waiting for them to eat lunch to celebrate the finalization of Adeline's betrothal to Pierrick. As much as he would rather pull Amory down onto the couch and keep kissing, he pulled away quickly, keeping a hand on Amory's hip, and turned to Adeline.

"Well, Adeline, it's official. You are betrothed to Pierrick." He grinned as her whole face lit up. Adeline's features were so similar to Amory's, but hers were softer, more feminine, and her auburn hair fell straight as rain to her waist while her brother's curled around his face. "My felicitations."

"Oh, thank you, Your Highness." She clasped her hands over her chest, and he got the impression she was trying to keep from waving them around. He almost laughed. Elodie would have been doing that and more. "For introducing me to Pierrick, and for everything."

"You're very welcome, Adeline. I'm happy to do it. You're going to be my sister soon."

Adeline beamed at him. "I'm going to like having you as my brother. I like seeing you and Amory together."

"I like it too," Amory said, leaning into his side a little. Enough so Philip could feel the warmth of Amory's slim body against his. It felt so right there.

"It all went well enough, considering both your father and Pierrick's are proud men."

Adeline snorted and then slapped a hand over her mouth, her face flushing bright red. Philip's eyebrows shot up. He had never seen Adeline do anything that wasn't perfectly ladylike, but Amory laughed.

She glared at Amory for a moment. "Hush, you. I'm so glad it went well, Your Highness."

"Me too," Philip said. "They're waiting for us now. We're all going to have lunch out on the terrace. It's warm enough today with the sun out."

"Is Elodie joining us?" Amory asked.

"No. She was going to visit Lilliale today. Apparently, Lilliale hasn't been feeling well."

Amory nodded, but there was a strange look on his face. "What?" Philip asked.

"Nothing really. It's just.... Lady Lilliale has always seemed a little infatuated with you. I was thinking she might be upset more than ill." Amory shook his head. "What do I know, though? I hope she feels better soon. It's good that Elodie went to visit."

"Yes," Philip said. Lilliale? Infatuated with him? He had always thought of her as a little sister. He hated that Lilliale might be upset over him, but he didn't know what to do about it. "We should get to lunch."

"Of course. I'll get my shawl." Adeline disappeared into the bedchamber Amory hadn't slept in for months.

Amory turned to him. "I'm sorry if I said something wrong."

"You didn't, not at all." He pulled Amory in for a kiss. "You do make me happy. So very happy, Amory."

Amory's eyes widened. "You heard us?"

"A little. I'm sorry for listening."

Amory shook his head. "It doesn't matter. I do want you to be happy. I think I would do anything to make you happy, to make you smile, Pip."

He looked at Amory, at a loss for what to say to something so heartfelt, so genuine. He had no doubt Amory would do anything for him. He traced a finger over Amory's lips. "Just be here with me, and keep smiling. I love to see you smile."

Lunch went surprisingly well. Arnau was so pleased with himself he wasn't particularly difficult, and Amory smoothed over any awkwardness. They toasted Pierrick and Adeline's betrothal, and his and Amory's was toasted in return. If the earl looked vaguely skeptical, he said nothing, and they all spoke of inconsequential things. Very little was said about the weddings except for a mention of timing. He and Amory planned to marry by Midwinter at the latest while Adeline's wedding wouldn't be until spring. Philip hoped he could convince Amory to marry him earlier than Midwinter. They were betrothed, and Philip didn't want to wait for them to be married.

Still, he was happy when lunch ended. He had work to see to, and he wanted it finished so he could spend the evening with Amory. After Cathal all but disappeared along with Uncle Umber, Etan had appeared in Philip's study and, with hardly a word, took up Cathal's duties. Once he figured out where everything was and what Cathal had been doing, Etan was a capable and intelligent help to Philip. He wondered if he could persuade Etan to stay when—if—Cathal returned.

He and Etan were working through a stack of papers preparing for a meeting when Elodie stormed into the study late that afternoon. Philip knew his expression must mirror Etan's look of surprise. Elodie usually made at least some nod to the proprieties, and she wasn't rude.

"Elodie?"

"Is it true?" Elodie asked, words sharp and accusatory, without greeting either him or Etan.

"Is what true?" He tried to remember anything that might have happened to upset Elodie, but he couldn't think of anything. He and Amory had told her of their betrothal before they told anyone else, and she had seemed happy for them, if surprised, so it couldn't be the betrothal.

"I can't believe you're playing dumb about this!" She folded her arms over her chest and glared at him. "Did you set up a marriage between Amory's sister and Lord Pierrick?"

He flicked another glance at Etan, but his cousin looked as confused as he felt. "Yes. We finalized it this morning. They're very happy."

Elodie flinched as if she'd been slapped. "I can't believe you would do that."

He didn't understand, and he found no help in Etan, who sat frozen in his chair. "Why are you upset? It's a good match for Adeline."

"Don't you take that reasonable tone with me, like I'm a stupid child. You know exactly why I'm upset."

He recognized the signs of an impending tantrum, despite her not having thrown one since she was a young child. She was moments away from stamping her feet, and he wasn't sure how to stop it from happening. When she was a child, there were stern lectures from their parents, nurses, or tutors and occasionally a bribe from him. He didn't think offering sweets would work anymore, not as it had when she was five years old. "I'm sorry. I don't know, El. Will you tell me?"

"I can't believe I have to!" There went her foot, stamping against the floor. The sound was muffled by the thick carpet, and the lack of effect seemed to only annoy her more. "You're my brother. You should know. No—you shouldn't have done it in the first place!"

"What did I do, Elodie?" He tried to force down his exasperation. His sister was a grown woman. She shouldn't be acting like a spoiled child.

"You set up a marriage between Lord Pierrick and that Adeline," she said, throwing her hands up.

"I did, but I don't know why you're upset. I thought you would be happy for her. I thought you and she got along."

"That isn't the point," Elodie snapped out, her voice almost shrill. "I'm your sister, not her. But you have Amory now, and you're doing things for his sister and acting like she's your sister. Only I should be more important, because I am your sister, and you should be thinking of me."

"Elodie. You can't be asking me to choose between Amory and you. Because I have a lot of people who don't like that I'm marrying him, and I didn't think you were one of them." Please let that not be, please. He didn't want to lose his sister too.

"No. It's not that." Elodie's fists clenched. "It's not Amory. I can see he makes you happy. But now you have him, and you've practically adopted his sister, so it's as if you have a new sister too. You negotiated an excellent marriage for her, but what about me?"

Hurt filled her eyes, and it baffled him. "But, Elodie—"

"What about me? Shouldn't you be making an excellent marriage for me? Your unmarried sister? Or did you not think of me at all because Amory asked you to help his sister? Do you like her better than me?"

Philip sighed. "I don't like her better than you. I offered to help her, because she needed it. I didn't set out to find her a husband, but it happened, and I'm glad she's happy."

"But still—"

He interrupted before she could get herself worked up again. Yes, she seemed hurt, but that didn't mean he would tolerate a tantrum. "And as for you, I haven't negotiated a marriage for you, because I'm hoping you'll be able to choose your own husband as I did."

His statement seemed to take the fight out of her. "Oh."

"And I know you have feelings for someone already. He's a good man. I like Faron." He bit back a laugh, amused by the surprise that blanked her features. Of course he'd seen it. She wasn't subtle. "I have no objections to a match between you and Faron if he feels the same."

But a marriage between Elodie and Faron seemed strange if he thought about his ruined friendship with Faron's older brother. He wondered what Vasco would think of the match.

"Oh," she said again and then stared at him, blinking. "I don't know if he feels the same."

"That's all right. There's no rush. If he does feel something for you, he'll let you know."

"Or he'll let you know." She smiled a little.

"Or that," he agreed. "But I think Faron would speak to you first."

She nodded, then looked down and fidgeted a little, shifting from foot to foot. "I'm sorry."

"Did you really think I would toss you aside for Adeline?" The storm seemed to have passed, leaving him shocked more than anything. Disappointed too. How could she think he would disregard his own sister and her welfare? "You're my sister, Elodie."

"I know, I know. I'm sorry. I don't know what got into me." She looked back up at him, her eyes damp. "I do like Amory. At first, because he made you happy, but then I got to know him, and now I like him for him too. I would never make you choose."

"Thank you."

"You'd probably choose him anyway."

"Elodie," he said, his voice full of reproach. He would choose Amory over anything, he already had, but he would never abandon Elodie.

"I'm sorry. I'm sorry. I didn't mean it. I shouldn't have said it. I don't know why I ever thought you would replace me. You wouldn't."

"Of course, I wouldn't. You're my sister, Elodie." He sighed. "I care about Adeline, but you are my sister, and I love you. If you want me to start looking for a husband for you—"

"No! Don't, not yet. Please?"

He choked back a laugh. He had expected that answer. "We'll wait, then."

"Thank you!" Her usual exuberance was back as she bounded over to throw her arms around him in a tight hug. She released him just as quickly and scampered for the door. "I'll let you get back to work."

He sat for a moment once the door closed behind Elodie, taking in the quiet, and then he looked at Etan. He was pretty sure Elodie hadn't noticed Etan, he had done such a good job of blending into the background. He looked the way Philip felt—wrung out. He wasn't certain where the tantrum came from. Normally, Elodie was... well, not calm. She was far too excited most of the time for calm to be a good description, but she was usually happy. He thought she outgrew the tantrums years ago.

"I love your sister. I do," Etan said, his voice tinged with something like shock.

"Yes, me too."

"But I do not understand her."

"You aren't alone in that either."

CHAPTER 10

"I GO away for a little while, and look what you get yourself into."

"I'm sorry?" Amory looked at Tristan, trying to see what he was thinking.

"No, you're not." Tristan's bright blue eyes were subdued, maybe a little sad, but he smiled at Amory.

"No, I'm not." He couldn't be sorry for everything that had changed in his life since he'd last seen Tristan.

They looked at each other for a moment, more awkward than they had ever been in their long friendship. Amory had thought getting caught with Tristan by Alban all those months ago might have ruined their friendship. He wondered if his betrothal to Philip was what would really finish it.

"Come inside." Amory pushed open the door to his and Philip's suite, and ushered Tristan through. If he was facing the end of his oldest friendship, he would rather do it in private.

Tristan stopped a few steps inside the door and looked around. "This is where you live? With the prince?"

"Yes." He walked farther into the room and settled on a chair by the fireplace. "This is home."

"It's not what I expected." Tristan must have seen something in his face, because he continued quickly while walking closer to Amory. "The rest of the palace is so formal and so... much. But this is nice, comfortable. Richer than anything I have ever seen, but it isn't too much. I can see how you could feel at home here."

"I do." He smiled a little, and Tristan sat near him.

"Good. That's good."

They fell silent again, and it stretched for long moments. Frustration made Amory want to scream. He didn't know what to do about it. Maybe if they'd talked sooner, but they hadn't seen each other since the disastrous day when Alban caught them in the garden. Well, disastrous perhaps for their friendship, not for everything else. If Alban hadn't caught them, then Amory wouldn't have met Philip, and he couldn't imagine his life without Philip in it.

Almost immediately after that day, Tristan's father had taken Tristan traveling out of the country, and they only just returned. Tristan found out Amory was marrying Philip, but this was the first time they'd seen each other. Amory wasn't surprised everything was awkward. He only wished it weren't.

"So you're really marrying the prince?" Tristan asked suddenly.

"Yes." He couldn't help the smile that spread over his face. He never could when he thought of Philip and how Philip wanted to marry him, despite Amory's worries.

"You love him, don't you?"

He couldn't decipher the expression on Tristan's face, which scared him considering how long he had known Tristan. He wouldn't lie to him, though. "Yes, very much."

Tristan nodded. "I thought so. It's all over your face."

"Is that—" He stopped, unsure how to ask what he needed to know. "Tris, are you… are you all right with me and Philip?"

"Am I all right with it?" Amusement flashed across Tristan's face.

"Don't. I don't know how to ask what I need to know. But you know what I mean."

Tristan smiled briefly, not quite his usual grin, but close. "I know what you mean. Would it matter if I weren't all right with your being in love with the prince?"

"Yes. You're my friend."

"But it wouldn't matter enough for you to give him up."

Amory's heart sank. "No, not enough for that."

"I would never ask you to, not if you love him."

"And us?" He almost didn't want to ask, but he couldn't ignore everything and hope it went away, that they could go back to normal. Especially when normal for them had been friendship and a lot of furtive kissing, which was no longer possible.

"You never loved me like that."

It wasn't a question, but he answered anyway. Even though he hated to hurt Tristan. "No. But I love you as my friend."

Tristan nodded. He didn't look surprised. "I don't think I love you like that either. I don't think I ever did."

"You don't?" An overwhelming flood of relief washed through him. He was glad he was sitting, it hit him so hard.

Tristan shook his head, sending a thick lock of hair falling over his eyes. He swiped it out of the way. "No. You're my best friend, and I love you that way. But it would have been so easy if we could have been in love with each other."

"I suppose." But he wasn't sure his answer was true. Yes, falling in love with his friend would have been nice, but he couldn't imagine himself and Tristan ever getting married.

Tristan looked at him as if he knew what Amory was thinking, and, well, he probably did. They'd known each other long enough. "The kissing was fun."

Surprised laughter burst out of Amory, but he had to agree. Kissing Tristan had been fun. "It was."

"Is it fun with the prince?" Mischief danced in Tristan's eyes, but seriousness lurked in their depths as well.

"Tristan."

"I didn't think you would tell me." Tristan studied him for a long moment, his gaze so intense Amory wanted to squirm. "It's because it's more than just fun, isn't it?"

Amory nodded.

Tristan sighed. "That's what I thought. I think I'm jealous."

He was surprised again, but also confused. "I don't understand. But I thought you said... of him? Or of me?"

"I don't know. Both of you?" Tristan shrugged and laughed at whatever look must have been on Amory's face. Amory couldn't imagine what he looked like at that moment. But just as quickly Tristan's face became thoughtful. "I think I'm envious of what you have together."

"I understand." He and Tristan had friendship and stolen kisses, but he and Philip... they had so much more. Philip was everything to him. He could understand Tristan wanting that for himself. "You'll find someone to have that with. It wasn't meant to be us, but there's someone out there who's meant for you."

"You're very naïve sometimes. The world doesn't work like that, not for people like us. But I would like to believe it."

"It worked like that for me. Against all the odds, it worked out for me. I found Philip, and we love each other, and now we're getting married. And it worked like that for Adeline too. She's marrying in the spring—an earl's son, and she really cares for him." He stared into Tristan's eyes, trying to will him to believe. "I'm living in the place where you would think every marriage would be arranged for maximum political and economic gain, and for me it's just the opposite. So I believe it can work."

"Maybe. It's wonderful about Adeline."

He gripped Tristan's hand, pulling his friend's attention out to him from where it had focused inward. "I want it to happen for you too. I want you to be happy, Tris."

"Thank you, Amory." Tristan gripped his hand back.

"So, still friends?"

"Always." Tristan pulled him up and into a hug. They held tight for long moments, Amory basking in relief that they were friends after everything that happened. Philip might have become his best friend as well as the man he loved sometime over the past months, but Amory wasn't sure what he would have done if he lost Tristan. So much history existed between them, so many shared experiences—not only their being each other's first kiss—that Tristan would always hold an important place in Amory's life.

The sound of a door opening and closing again broke into his thoughts. He pulled back from Tristan's hug, but he didn't let go, and peered around Tristan. Philip and Etan stood just inside the room. Etan's expression was blatant curiosity but Philip's was blank in a way Amory didn't like. He let his arms fall away from Tristan and held out a hand to Philip.

"Philip, come meet Tristan."

Philip's expression cleared a little, and he walked closer, taking Amory's hand. Tristan bowed, and he and Philip exchanged greetings.

"May I congratulate you on your betrothal, Your Highness?" Tristan said.

"Thank you, Master Tristan." Philip's demeanor was stiff, but his greeting was pleasant.

"I admit I was surprised when I heard, but I'm very happy for Amory and you." Tristan smiled. "The city was shocked, but there are a lot of people who are pleased as well. You are marrying one of their own after all."

Philip laughed. "I never thought about it like that, but I'm glad not everyone is opposed to the idea."

Amory squeezed Philip's hand. "Why don't we all sit down for a while? I was going to ask Tristan to tell me about his travels."

"Of course." Philip guided him to one of the couches and sat with him while Tristan took another. Etan still stood near the door.

"Etan? Are you joining us?" Amory asked, looking over at the man hovering as if he wasn't certain whether he should stay or go.

"Etan, yes, please join us," Philip said. "I'm sorry I didn't introduce you. Tristan, this is my cousin, Etan. Etan, this is Amory's friend Tristan. They grew up together."

"As we did." Etan walked forward.

Tristan had an odd look on his face as he stood again and bowed to Etan. "It is an honor to meet you, my lord."

"Etan, please, for a friend of Amory's. And it is a pleasure to meet you, Master Tristan."

Amory's eyebrows flew up at the near purr in Etan's voice and climbed farther as he took Tristan's hand. They couldn't go up any higher—not for lack of trying—as Tristan smiled a strange little smile, his eyes wary, but… interested?

"Then it's Tristan, please."

Amory glanced at Philip beside him, hoping Philip could tell him if he was seeing what he thought he was. Philip gave him a slightly bewildered, slightly incredulous look, enough for Amory to know he wasn't imagining things.

Tristan reclaimed his hand and sat again. Etan seated himself next to Tristan, not too close, but closer than necessary. Amory had no idea what to make of it. Perhaps best to let it go for the time being.

He settled closer to Philip, content when Philip rested his arm over Amory's shoulders, the warm weight of it feeling right. "Tristan, why don't you tell us about your travels?"

Tristan did so enthusiastically, describing the long trip he and his father took to Amaranta and Elleri. He painted a vivid picture of the places he had seen. Amory realized he was a bit jealous. He had never left Tournai and wasn't likely to. True, everything he wanted was right there with Philip, but the stories Tristan told made him wish a little that he could see some of those places.

The conversation wound around to events in Tournai while Tristan was gone, mostly the detailed story of how Amory had come to be at the palace and what he had been doing since. Tristan was gratifyingly irate at what Amory's father had tried to do all those months ago. Even Philip began to warm to Tristan as the visit went on, which made Amory happy. He wanted Philip and Tristan to like each other, and he hoped that wasn't asking too much of either of them.

"WHEN WE marry are you finally going to move in here?" Philip called from the dressing room as he changed for bed that night.

"Into your dressing room?" Amory responded with a laugh and turned back to the bedside table where he was sorting through a pile of books and papers, looking for his small sketchbook. He wasn't sure when so many of his things had migrated into Philip's bedchamber.

"Funny." Philip walked into the bedchamber, wrapped in his velvet dressing gown. "When are you going to move into this bedchamber with me?"

"You want me to?" He left off his search and straightened up.

"Yes. That's why I asked."

He plunked the books in his hands back on top of the others on the table. "Don't noble married couples keep separate bedchambers? Separate suites sometimes?"

"Many do. But many marriages aren't based on any feelings between the couple. Ours will be, and I would very much like you here, not all the way across the suite." Philip wound his arms around Amory's waist and pulled him close.

"You talk as if my bedchamber is across the country, not on the other side of the sitting room." He laughed and slid his arms up around Philip's neck. "We sleep together every night anyway."

"Yes, we do. Every night. So why not move in here with me?"

"Well, when you put it that way, it does seem silly not to." He grinned and kissed Philip. "All right, I will."

"You will? Good, we'll move your things tomorrow."

He laughed when Philip hugged him, arms squeezing until he almost couldn't breathe. "Eager? Why don't we move everything tonight?"

"You're joking, but be careful, I might take you seriously." Philip steered him toward the bed. "Tomorrow."

"All right."

He allowed himself to be coaxed into the big bed they did share every night, not that it took much coaxing. Philip stripped them both of their dressing gowns, and pulled the covers up over them. They snuggled down into the warmth of the blankets, cuddling up close to each other, tangling their limbs together and holding on. They did this often, whether in bed, on the couch, or on the soft rug in front of the fireplace. Once in a while, Philip changed into a cat and then sprawled against Amory, but often he didn't. They talked or stayed quiet, touched gently or stayed still and wrapped around each other. Sometimes it led to their making love, sometimes it came after, and sometimes all they did was sleep. Amory loved it whichever way, and he thought Philip needed it, that it fulfilled some need in him for touch and closeness.

That night they were quiet for a long time, lazily caressing each other's hair and skin. Amory thought about what moving into Philip's bedchamber would mean, but he gave up after a while. It didn't matter, because he was doing it. His thoughts drifted to Tristan's visit. All told, it had gone well. He was so relieved his friendship with Tristan wasn't ruined, and he hoped any lingering awkwardness would fade with time.

"Did you like Tristan?" he asked. "I know it was awkward for you to meet him."

"A little." Philip combed his fingers through Amory's hair.

"I'm sorry. Thank you for doing it, though. I wanted you to meet my oldest friend, and I appreciate it so much that you did."

"You're welcome." The slow movement of Philip's hand in Amory's hair continued, and after a while he spoke quietly. "I thought I would hate him. I think I wanted to, which is awful because you were so kind when you met Vasco."

Amory had been as kind as he could be, but he'd wanted to hurt Vasco, because Vasco hurt Philip. "It wasn't easy."

"Thank you for doing it." Philip kissed his forehead, and admitted, "I wanted to rip you away from him when I walked in that room and saw you hugging."

"Were you… jealous?" The idea was almost absurd, except it wasn't, and it gave Amory a secret little thrill that Philip would feel jealous about him. "You don't need to be. I don't feel anything other than friendship for Tristan. I don't even want to kiss him anymore."

"Well, that's a relief." Philip's smile was evident in his voice.

"Seriously, Pip, I don't want him that way. I only want him as my friend again."

"I know. I could see it. When you stepped away from him and held out your hand to me, I saw it."

"Good. I don't want you to think I want anyone except you." Because he hadn't from the moment he laid eyes on Philip. He was still amazed to think he was going to have Philip as his own for the rest of his life.

"I know you don't. I'm going to do my best to remember that when I see Tristan again. But I'm not sure Tristan feels the same about you."

Amory wasn't certain what Tristan felt himself. He hated to think he might have hurt Tristan. "I don't know. I think more than anything he wants someone of his own."

"As long as that someone isn't you."

He kissed Philip's chest, the only place he could reach without moving. He was far too comfortable to move. "Definitely not me. I'm yours."

"Yes, you are." Philip rolled so he was on top of Amory, and started kissing and nuzzling Amory's neck. "All mine."

Amory shivered, at the kisses, but mostly at the words. "Yes. And you? Are you mine?"

Philip lifted his head and looked down at Amory, his eyes blazing. "Yes. All yours."

Amory reached up and pulled him down into a scorching kiss.

WEDDING PLANS progressed as quickly as possible. Philip wanted them to marry soon, but he also wasn't going to stint on any part of the wedding. This would be a wedding on the scale of every other royal wedding if Philip had his way, and Amory didn't have the heart to argue. Well, he tried to tell Philip that such a large and formal wedding wasn't necessary. He did not call it a spectacle, however appropriate the word might be.

But Philip didn't agree. Amory understood that Philip thought their wedding needed to be the same as it would be if the prince were marrying a woman, even though Amory did hate the idea of that many people watching. He was thrilled to be marrying Philip. He was less than thrilled about being the focus of so much attention. Since he would be the prince's husband soon, he supposed he should get used to it. As the prince's lover, he should probably be used to it already.

Amory could only hope Philip's family attended the wedding. It wouldn't look good if the prince's uncle didn't attend his wedding, and more, Philip would feel awful. Amory didn't want Philip to feel anything but joy on their wedding day. He wanted Philip to be happy all the time.

Amory had briefly considered calling the whole thing off, or at least asking Philip to postpone the wedding for a while. Maybe with more time Philip's uncle would come to accept Philip's choice. He doubted some of the nobility ever would, from the snide comments he overheard and the derisive looks he received when Philip wasn't around. He was more worried about Philip than himself. He hated that his presence in Philip's life might cause difficulty for Philip as prince of Tournai. But Etan convinced Amory not to cancel the wedding.

"My cousin is a strong man and a good ruler, though the throne was thrust upon him far earlier than it should have been," Etan told Amory. "But before he found you, his duty was drowning him. He was drowning in responsibility and obligations and everyone's expectations of him. All of those things are still there, but they're not pulling him down like they were. That has to be because of you."

"And yet our betrothal only causes him more problems."

Etan shrugged. "Some people don't like it. Some people wouldn't like it if he married one woman instead of another. They'll get over it. Until then, he can weather it with you beside him. I think he can weather anything with you beside him. You ground him. So be happy, Amory, and make him happy too."

He wanted to make Philip happy, more than anything. Which was why he was in a little-used corner of the palace library hunting through large, dusty tomes that probably hadn't seen the light of day in decades. He had been studying healing magic for months, and though Jadis had been right in his initial determination—there wasn't all that much Amory could do—he found the magic and the theory behind it fascinating. He couldn't use much of it, but he read about it when he had the time.

Somewhere in all his reading, he remembered seeing a vague reference he thought might be useful. So he was digging through books of esoteric magic he didn't understand trying to find the origin of that reference. He was determined to do it too, but he hadn't told Philip yet. Partly because he wasn't certain he would succeed in finding what he thought might be there or that it would work if he did, and partly because the whole search felt a little desperate. He didn't want Philip to see that in him.

But ever since Philip had said "our child" Amory couldn't get the words out of his head. It wasn't only about Philip having the heir his duty required him to produce, and Amory not wanting him to have to find a woman with whom Philip could fulfill that duty. It was also, maybe more, about a child, a child of theirs. He wanted that, for the both of them. That having a child would help Philip as prince of Tournai was the secondary reason. But he hadn't found anything in all the days of searching, and he began to think he wouldn't.

"Amory?"

He jumped as the voice broke the silence of the library. Tristan walked over and perched on the table next to where Amory worked.

"Sorry. I didn't mean to startle you."

"It's all right. I didn't hear you come in." But he wasn't surprised to see Tristan. After his first visit to the palace a couple of weeks ago, he began appearing multiple times each week. Amory wasn't sure if Tristan wanted to see him or Etan on these visits. He and Philip watched with some amusement as Tristan and Etan circled each other. Philip lost a lot of his stiltedness around Tristan due to it, but Amory worried. He hoped Tristan and Etan could become friends, or more than friends. But he didn't want to see either of them hurt.

"Looks like you were engrossed in something, and I thought I was the studious one. What is all this?" Tristan peered at the books and papers spread out in front of Amory.

"Just a project I'm working on." He began closing books before Tristan got a good look at what he was reading, his so far unhelpful reading. "It's probably doomed to failure."

"Can I help?"

He shook his head. "No. Thank you. I'll muddle through and see if I can find what I'm looking for."

"What are you looking for?" Tristan was nothing if not persistent, but he would have no idea his curiosity was unwelcome at the moment.

"I don't even know if it exists."

"That would make looking for it more difficult. Are you being purposely evasive?" Tristan asked.

"Yes. I'm sorry."

Tristan studied him and then sighed. "You're very difficult, you know? Fine. Let me know if you need help."

"Thank you."

Tristan waited another moment, as if Amory might change his mind and tell him everything. But Amory wasn't ready to share this crazy idea, not with Tristan, not with anyone. He might never be. If he ever told anyone, he would tell Philip first, or only Philip. He didn't need everyone knowing how crazy he was if it didn't work out the way he hoped.

Another sigh from Tristan. "All right. Do you need to keep working on whatever this is? Or can you stop for a while?"

"I suppose I could." He wasn't making progress anyway. Maybe he was wasting his time. Not that he was going to stop, but he saw no harm in stepping away for the day. "What were you thinking?"

"It's a sunny day. I thought maybe we could go for a ride. We haven't done that since before I went away."

They used to go riding often, just the two of them or with other friends. Tristan had always shared Amory's enjoyment of riding and swimming and being outside. Philip enjoyed riding, and they went together often, but he wasn't as keen on swimming. Amory wondered if the dislike stemmed from what his Talent allowed him to become.

"I'd like that." He finished tidying away the books. No one minded him claiming a table in a corner of the library, but he didn't want anyone seeing what he was reading and wondering what he was doing. "Let's go."

They walked down to the stable together and waited out in the courtyard while their horses were saddled and one of the royal guard was summoned to accompany them. Tristan teased him about the guard, and Amory did his best to ignore it. The teasing, at least, was the same as always, even if the subject of it had changed.

Etan arrived as their horses were being brought out. His expression lightened considerably when he saw them, or maybe saw Tristan. Despite their friendship, Amory wasn't so deluded as to think he could cause so dramatic a change in Etan's demeanor.

"Hello, Etan."

"Hello, Amory. Tristan."

Amory didn't think he imagined Etan's eyes lingering on Tristan for a moment too long. He fought back a smirk.

"Where are you two off to today?" Etan asked them.

"Tristan thought it would be a good day for a ride," Amory told him.

Etan flashed a smile at Tristan. "It is that. Best to get as many in as you can now. The weather-workers are saying the rains will be starting soon."

The late autumn and winter rains made for dreary, chilly days, and a miserable time to be outdoors, but at least they seldom had snow as the lands farther north did. Amory offered, "If you aren't busy, you could come with us."

Etan looked startled at the invitation. They were friends, but he and Etan seldom did anything without Philip or some of Philip's other cousins present. Amory wasn't sure why not. Perhaps the opportunity had never presented itself. He enjoyed Etan's company, so it wouldn't be a hardship to spend time with him, even if he really invited Etan because of strange, never-before-realized matchmaking tendencies.

Tristan spoke when Etan hesitated. "Yes, please do join us."

Etan looked at Tristan, perhaps more startled than he had been at Amory's original invitation. But Amory thought he looked pleased too. "All right. I'd love to. Thank you."

They waited while Etan's horse was saddled, and then set out from the palace, the three of them with two guards trailing at a discreet but not too great distance behind. Amory couldn't imagine needing the guards, but Philip insisted, and he wouldn't worry Philip. Tristan headed for a popular trail to the north of the city that followed the river and then looped inland and back to Jumelle, making for a picturesque and convenient ride. They used to ride this trail often, so Amory wasn't surprised by Tristan's choice of direction.

Amory let Tristan lead them, grinning when Tristan let his horse have his head. Etan glanced at Amory with a grin of his own, and they both hurried to catch up. For a time they rode like that, enjoying the speed and the freedom, but after a while, they slowed and rode at a more leisurely pace, talking easily. But Amory's mind kept drifting, and Tristan and Etan became involved in a conversation of their own. When Amory noticed, he laughed to himself and dropped back to let them talk.

Soon, they approached the bend in the trail that would take them away from the river. He shivered as they took the turn and rode into the cool shade under the trees. There had been other riders on the trail along the river, but no one in the woods. Perhaps most people preferred the portion of the trail near the river on a late autumn day. It certainly was prettier, and warmer from being in the sun. The dense trees in the woods blocked most of the sunlight, leaving the trail in shade and noticeably chillier than the stretch along the river. The trail would eventually lead them back into the warmth of sunlight—out of the woods and to the city through some fields. In the spring and summer, the fields were filled with flowers and made for as pretty a ride as the river portion of the trail, but in the fall they were fairly barren. Etan and Tristan didn't seem to notice the change. They continued to talk as they rode ahead on the empty trail. Amory let his mind wander again and enjoyed the quiet in the small woods.

A rider on a large black horse seemed to explode out of the trees at the side of the trail, rushing at Amory, swerving only at the last second to avoid colliding with him. Amory's horse went crazy. He didn't see where the other horse and rider went as he tried to control Star and keep his seat. He managed to keep Star from bolting, but that didn't stop her from prancing and rearing and trying to toss him from her back.

He struggled with horse and reins, but he couldn't calm her, no matter what he did, and finally, he gave up the fight. What he managed was more of a controlled fall than an actual dismount, but it did the trick. He rolled when he hit the ground, coming to rest off the trail in a pile of leaves and twigs. He lay there, stunned and breathing hard, grateful Star hadn't trampled him and he hadn't rolled into a tree. Still, he would be bruised later.

He began paying attention to what was going on around him again when Tristan fell to his knees beside him. "Amory! Are you all right?"

"Fine. I'm fine." He struggled up to a sitting position, both Tristan and one of the guards, kneeling on his other side, putting hands out to help him. Etan was calming Star a little ways down the path. The other guard was missing. "What happened?"

"Did you hit your head? Do you not remember?" Tristan's voice whipped out, almost frantic with concern.

"I didn't hit my head. I remember what happened. I just don't understand what happened. Where is that rider?"

The guard answered. "He rode back into the woods. It looks like there's a smaller path that intersects this one here. Benno went after him."

"Crazy person," he muttered and moved to stand up. Tristan and the guard scrambled to help. Once he was on his feet, he took stock again. Yes, he was going hurt later. For the moment, he made sure he was steady and then brushed himself off. Tristan helped, pulling leaves from his hair. "Who rides so recklessly through a forest near a well-used trail where there are sure to be other people? Lunatic could get someone killed."

He looked up when the silence stretched too long. The three others exchanged speaking looks. Amory looked between the three of them. "What is it? Someone tell me what you all know that I don't."

"It's not that we know anything, Amory," Etan said. He had gotten Amory's horse calmed and stood near them, stroking Star's neck and watching Amory.

"Well, then, what do you think?"

"Sir, I saw the rider come out of the trees. He rode directly for you. He only turned away at the very last instant," the guard said.

For a moment, Amory didn't understand what the guard was trying to tell him. When it occurred to him, he wanted to laugh because the idea was so ridiculous. "You can't be serious. You can't possibly think he did it on purpose."

From the serious looks on the faces of all three men, they did indeed believe it. "Why would someone do that? It's stupid and too dangerous for a joke."

"We don't think it was a joke, Amory," Etan said.

"Then what...." He stared at Etan. "You think someone did this deliberately to try to hurt me."

"It looked deliberate," Tristan said, his musical voice more serious, and almost scared, than Amory had ever heard it. "You could have been killed."

Etan broke in while Amory was still shaking his head and preparing to speak. "You could have, Amory. If you hadn't managed to control your horse, you could have been thrown and killed or seriously injured."

The look in Etan's eyes, the tone of his voice, made Amory feel cold down to his bones. Was it possible Etan and Tristan were right? Had someone done it on purpose, to try to hurt him? "But why?"

Tristan shrugged helplessly, but Etan spoke. "I don't know for sure, Amory, but you're marrying the prince, and he has enemies. Whatever the reason, it happened, and now we need to be very careful."

"What we need to do is get you back to the palace," Tristan said, as Amory's mind reeled. Could someone really hate him or Philip enough to want to kill Amory?

"Yes, sir, it would be best if we returned to the palace now." The guard was focused on the woods around them, his gaze constantly moving. Looking for another threat.

Amory couldn't quite believe what had happened, but he nodded. The palace was where he wanted to be at that moment—the palace and Philip. "Yes, let's go home."

CHAPTER 11

AMORY BARELY remembered the trip home. Everything jumbled together in a blur of images and anxious thoughts. Etan, Tristan, and the guard surrounded him as closely as they could on the ride back. It was no leisurely ride this time, nor was it the carefree gallop that took them out of the city and along the river. Amory felt the contrast keenly. Just as he felt the worry and fear of his friends at his sides.

They thought someone had tried to kill him. He couldn't believe it, but at the same time, the idea was absolutely terrifying. Someone might have tried to kill him. His mind kept coming back to that one thought, and then shying away from it with an immediate denial. Because it couldn't be true. Why would anyone want to kill him?

Because he was the prince's lover, and someone wanted to hurt Philip. Because he was marrying the prince, and someone didn't want the marriage to take place.

He didn't want to think about those kinds of things either. Because what happened couldn't have been deliberate. He forced himself to hold on to that belief as he was hurried back to the palace. The guard pulled Amory from his horse and hustled him inside as soon as they pounded into the palace courtyard. The man didn't stop once they were indoors either. He kept moving, hurrying Amory along until they reached his and Philip's suite. The guard ushered him inside, Tristan followed, and then the guard closed the door behind them with himself in the corridor.

Moments passed in silence as he and Tristan stared at each other. Finally, Amory asked, "Where did Etan go?"

"To tell the prince what happened."

He nodded, and sighed, dropping down to sit on the edge of a chair. "He's going to be upset."

"The prince is going to be terrified."

Amory flinched at Tristan's blunt words. They were true, of course. Philip would be terrified as soon as he heard what happened, what Etan thought happened. "What is going on? I mean, this can't have been someone trying to kill me. It had to be some sort of crazy accident. No one would have tried to kill me."

Tristan looked more sober and serious than Amory had ever seen him. He sat across from Amory and looked at him for a moment. "We can't know that. It looked like he rode right for you. All four of us saw it. If he wasn't trying to kill you, then he was definitely trying to hurt you."

"I still can't believe it." Amory shook his head.

They fell silent. Amory leaned forward, propping his elbows on his knees. Letting his head fall forward, he ran his hands through his disheveled curls. This could not be happening, and he could not be sitting there doing nothing. But he couldn't figure out what else to do. He wanted Philip. He knew that much. Maybe they could make sense of it together, because he certainly couldn't alone.

He jumped to his feet. He would go find Philip. He had only taken one step when the door flew open, and Philip strode inside. Fear gave way to utter relief on Philip's face when his gaze landed on Amory. Philip crossed the room in a few long strides, pulled Amory into arms, against his chest, and held tight. Amory burrowed in, trying to get even closer.

"Amory," Philip whispered into Amory's hair, but said nothing more. Philip did keep holding him, which was all that was important to Amory. He was more shaken than he originally thought, which was disturbing in itself.

After a while, he realized the hands Philip ran over his back and arms and any other part of Amory he could reach weren't only soothing him. They were checking him over for injuries, making sure he wasn't hurt. And they were shaking.

"Pip," he whispered. "I'm all right. I'm not hurt, I promise."

"Etan said you were thrown."

"I wasn't thrown."

Philip pulled back far enough to glare at him.

"I wasn't exactly thrown. It was more a purposeful, not particularly graceful, fall." He put a hand to Philip's cheek. "The point is I'm not hurt. A few bruises maybe, but that's all."

"I want Jadis to have a look at you." Philip shook his head when Amory opened his mouth to disagree. "It would make me feel better. Please."

"What would make me feel better is a bath." He grumbled, but he had already given in, and Philip knew it. He couldn't refuse when Philip said please.

"I'll draw you a bath as soon as Jadis checks you over. You can soak as long as you like, I promise." Philip hugged him close again, and Amory winced. Philip's arm had tightened against a sore spot on his back, but at least Philip hadn't seen. He only would have worried.

A sharp rap on the door broke them apart but not by far. Amory didn't let go of Philip, and Philip wasn't letting go of him either. As Philip called out for whoever was at the door to enter, Amory looked around the room. Tristan was no longer on the couch, or anywhere else in the sitting room. He must have left while Amory and Philip were wrapped up in each other.

Jadis walked into the room with his bag in hand. Relief filled his eyes when his gaze fell on Amory. "Well, you don't look badly off."

"I'm not. But tell that to this one." He smiled at Philip to take the sting out of his words, a soft smile he filled with all his affection.

"Perhaps the prince will believe you if I examine you."

"Maybe then," Philip said and caressed Amory's cheek with gentle fingers.

"All right." He gave in, knowing full well he had no choice if he didn't want to make Philip worry more. Jadis was mercifully quick with his examination and gentle with the bruises and scratches decorating Amory's skin.

"Well," Jadis began, "just scratches and bruises. You'll be sore, but nothing more serious. Your Talent has already started to speed up the healing process on its own, but you'll heal faster if you use your Talent consciously as we practiced. I'll leave you with some salve to apply as well. It will soothe the pain and help with the healing."

"Thank you, Jadis," Amory said and accepted the jar of salve.

"Yes, thank you," Philip echoed. Amory stayed where he was while Philip walked Jadis to the door. Philip spoke with someone outside the suite before coming back in and closing the door.

"Can I have that bath now?" Amory hoped he didn't sound as pathetic as he thought. The bruises were already stiffening him up, and though the pain wasn't bad, he wasn't comfortable either.

Philip held a hand out to him. "Yes, you get your bath now."

True to his word, Philip prepared a steaming hot bath for him in the large tub, adding chamomile bath oil to the water. The scent alone relaxed Amory, or maybe he relaxed because he was alone with Philip. He began to take his clothes off, but Philip pushed his hands away gently and removed Amory's clothes piece by piece, every movement loving. Then Philip took his arm and helped him into the bath.

"Join me," he offered, but Philip shook his head.

"Not this time." Philip placed a soft kiss on his lips, and pulled a low stool over to the tub. Sitting, Philip took the soap and a cloth to wash Amory himself.

He wasn't injured enough to need so much care, but that didn't mean the care wasn't nice. In fact, the tenderness of Philip's actions was more than nice. It left Amory melting and warm inside. So he let Philip take care of him, reveled in it, allowing it to soothe both of them. Finally, he sank down into the water to his chin and closed his eyes. Philip's fingers trailed in the water and tangled with his, keeping them connected. Amory sighed, content with that simple action.

"Who were you talking to when Jadis left?" he asked after a while.

"The guard captain. The guard who chased the man who tried to hurt you, he hasn't been able to find him. The captain sent more guards to help."

Amory opened his eyes and focused on Philip. "You think it was on purpose. That someone tried to hurt me on purpose? Couldn't it have been an accident?"

He wanted it to be an accident because the alternative terrified him far too much to contemplate. That someone would try to kill him... no, it had to be an accident.

Philip's expression was serious, grave almost, and Amory knew what he was going to say. "From what everyone saw, it wasn't an accident."

"They could be wrong. It happened so quickly." Amory was grasping at possibilities, and he knew it. But he wasn't sure he could handle the idea of someone trying to kill him.

Philip shook his head and cupped his hand around Amory's cheek. His eyes filled with understanding and sympathy. "They weren't wrong. Etan, Tristan, and the guards all saw it. And the guard who went looking in the forest found what looks to be an area where the person may have waited until you were at the right part of the trail."

"It really wasn't an accident. He was trying to kill me."

Philip's hands tightened on him, an anchor as his world tilted and spun. "Yes, he was, but we're going to find him."

Amory stared at Philip for a long moment, and Philip held his gaze, confidence in what he said there for Amory to see. The thought of someone wanting to kill him gave him the chills. He shivered despite the warm water.

"Come on. Let's get you out of there." Philip retrieved a large, soft towel, and helped Amory out of the bath. Philip dried him and wrapped him in the warm velvet dressing gown Philip had given him months ago. He should feel pathetic about all the fuss Philip was taking with him. He hadn't been injured. But he couldn't stop shivering, and he knew he needed the care, the demonstration of how much Philip loved him.

Philip led him to their bed. Amory was grateful he'd moved into Philip's bedchamber with him. Without protest, he let Philip bundle him under the blankets although it wasn't even dinner time. Then he lay there and watched as Philip stripped off his own clothes, tossing each item haphazardly over a chair. Naked, he climbed into the bed beside Amory and pulled him close. Only then, with Philip's arms around him, did the shaking begin to ease.

But he had to ask. "Don't you have to go? I thought you had meetings this afternoon."

"Meetings can be rescheduled. I'm not going anywhere," Philip said.

"I'm fine. I wasn't hurt. We're making too much of this," he said, but he curled closer and rested his head on Philip's shoulder. "It was probably nothing."

"We're not, and it wasn't nothing. The guards are trained, and I trust their judgment. Someone tried to kill you today." Philip's voice went rough at the end, and Amory stroked a hand along Philip's side. Trying to soothe even though his own mind spun again.

"Why would someone try to kill me?" he asked after a while, his voice a whisper.

"Unless you have some dark secrets in your past I don't know about, because of me, love."

"This isn't your fault, Pip," he said firmly, suddenly realizing how Philip would blame himself, and he couldn't let him. "It isn't."

"Maybe not, but someone tried to hurt you because of me. Because you are my lover and my betrothed, and all they have to do to hurt me is hurt you."

Philip's low voice was harsh with pain and reproach, and Amory ached for him. He burrowed closer, snuggling into Philip. Hoping the closeness would help. "It still isn't your fault. It's theirs. I love you, Pip, and I choose to stand beside you. This changes nothing."

"I should send you away from me. To keep you safe."

Amory held on tighter. "I'm not going anywhere. I'm not so weak that I need to be sent away for my own good, so don't even think of it. I'm here with you. I'll always be here with you."

"You're not weak at all." Philip sighed and hugged him close. "I want you here with me."

"Good. So what do we do now?"

"We're going to find the man who tried to kill you, but until we do, we're going to be a lot more careful. We're going to give this person far fewer opportunities to get at you."

"Pip."

"I'm not going to lock you up or send you away, but we are going to take some sensible precautions until we figure out what's going on. More guards with you when you go out, for one. I love you, Amory, and I am not going to lose you if there is anything I can do to prevent it. Please don't argue."

There was that please again. And he really couldn't argue. Philip proposed taking sensible precautions. A little more caution, a little more thought as to what he did. There was nothing wrong with being careful. He had no desire to be killed and no desire to cause Philip more worry. Philip was scared enough for him.

"I won't argue. But you have to be careful too. If someone is trying to hurt you through me, they may decide to go after you directly. Please don't argue with me, Pip. I couldn't bear it if anything happened to you." He stared into Philip's eyes, willing him to see his determination.

"All right. We'll both be more careful." Philip kissed him, long and deep. "I couldn't bear to lose you either."

THE GUARDS scoured the small wood but didn't find the rider who had tried to harm Amory. Amory made no protests about the increased number of guards accompanying him on his outings from the palace, for which Philip was grateful. It eased his mind to know Amory was protected when he left the palace, and since he knew it eased Amory's mind as well, Philip didn't protest additional guards on his own outings.

But days passed and nothing happened. No more attacks. Philip hoped that meant the guards' presence acted as a deterrent. Maybe whoever was behind the attack would give up because he couldn't get at Amory. Amory, he knew, was more likely to doubt the original attempt had been anything other than an accident as time went by. Philip couldn't believe that. The action was far too deliberate to have been an accident, and whatever Amory wanted to believe, there were too many reasons someone might want to harm him.

Philip wished with all his heart it wasn't true. For someone to want to harm Amory because of Philip was horrible, wrong. But Amory's relationship with Philip was the only reason someone would have to do so. Amory possessed no enemies of his own that either of them could think of. Philip doubted Amory had any. There was such a gentle sweetness to him, such love in him—no one should want to harm Amory. And no one would if Amory hadn't agreed to marry him.

"Maybe he wasn't trying to kill you," Philip mused one day. Every time his mind was unoccupied or drifted away from whatever he was doing, he thought about what had happened to Amory, turning everything over and over.

Amory looked up from the papers he was reviewing while he slouched in a chair across from Philip's desk. "That's what I've been saying all along."

"No, I don't mean that. I don't think it was an accident." He tried to think of how to explain his sudden thought. "I think he rode at you deliberately, but maybe the aim wasn't to kill you. Maybe the goal was more about injuring and scaring you."

"Scaring me?"

"Yes, scaring you enough so you would leave."

"Leave you?" Amory repeated. "Nothing could scare me enough to make me leave you."

Warm pleasure flowed through him at Amory's words. "But he wouldn't know that. It's strange and far from foolproof as a method of murder. If this was about pushing you to break our betrothal and leave—"

"Because whoever this is doesn't want you to marry me."

He nodded. "Then injuring and scaring you could be what he wanted. Of course, if you were killed in the process, he probably wouldn't have been upset either."

Amory reached across the desk and took his hand, as if he could see how much saying that shook Philip. "No, I suppose he wouldn't have been. But it didn't happen. I suppose the theory makes sense. There are people who think this marriage is a bad idea, though I can't see most of them resorting to tactics like those."

Something in Amory's tone made Philip sit up straighter. "Amory, has someone said something to you?"

"No, not really. A veiled remark or two, some looks. I've heard some whispers at parties and so have Adeline and Etan." Amory tried to reassure him, knowing how upset Philip would be. "It's fine."

"It's not. Not at all." And how had he not known what Amory was dealing with? Knowing Amory, the situation was worse than he made it seem.

"It is, Pip." Amory held Philip's gaze, letting him see Amory's sincerity. "It doesn't matter what they say. It doesn't matter what anyone says. I'm not going anywhere."

"All right," he said after a moment. He raised Amory's hand to his lips. "I wish you'd told me. I wish you didn't have to hear anything like that, but all right."

Mischief sparked in Amory's eyes. "What might scare me away are all these lists."

Philip groaned and looked down at the papers he was supposed to be reviewing when he'd gotten bored and started thinking about the attack again. Lists, all of them. "Who knew getting married involved so many lists?"

"Not me. Guests, food, decorations...." Others were compiling everything for them, but he and Amory needed to approve everything.

"All the parties leading up to it. And fittings for all the clothes we'll need for the parties and the wedding."

"Then scheduling the events on the day of the wedding." Amory waved more papers. "Did you know there's going to be a parade we have to ride in?"

He almost laughed at the look on Amory's face. "Yes, but I'd like to take that off the schedule. It sounds needlessly risky to have you in the open."

"Surely there will be guards around us at the parade."

"Yes, but I'm still not sure I like the idea." He hated the idea of Amory so exposed. "And…."

"And?"

Philip sighed. Amory was going to tease him. "The security issues are my main concern, but also… it's going to be nearly Midwinter so it's going to be cold out there."

Amory's lips were twitching and his eyes dancing, but he didn't laugh. "You are such a cat."

"Hmph. Do you have any desire to be out in the cold in an open carriage for that long?"

Amory's expression slipped into something Philip could only call affectionate indulgence. It should have annoyed him, yet somehow it didn't. "Not at all. So why didn't you eliminate the parade from the beginning?"

He sighed. "It's tradition. For a hundred years at least, the newly married royal couple has been paraded around the city so they can be seen by everyone. I've been told people come in from the surrounding countryside for a glimpse. People would be very upset if we didn't make ourselves seen. I thought maybe we could go out on one of the balconies or the palace walls and wave, but I'm not sure it would work."

Amory nodded. "We'll do whatever you think is best."

Of course Amory understood. Philip needed his subjects to see their marriage as any other royal marriage, so he needed it to be traditional in all the little ways. And part of him wanted the trappings of it for Amory, illogical as that was, since Amory would have been happy with something much simpler. Philip probably would have been happy with the same thing.

"Thank you."

Amory smiled the sweet smile Philip loved so much. "You're welcome. Now, should we go through the rest of these lists?"

He sighed again.

Neither he nor Amory was good at planning a wedding. As days went by, the details, the lists, the intricate protocol began to make them both crazy. Philip wished they had someone to push some of the planning over to, but they didn't. Elodie was too young and flighty for them to rely on her. Philip's aunts might have been able to help, but his uncles still weren't coming anywhere near the palace so his aunts hadn't either.

They muddled through, relying heavily on the palace staff. They fit in time to go over lists and requests, for meetings about protocol and planning, all around other duties and responsibilities, and in Amory's case, studies. Philip would never have imagined Amory would spend so much time reading and studying when he'd seemed so reluctant to take classes in the first place. Philip admired his dedication.

However, as dedicated as they both were, the constant activity began to wear on them. Philip felt it, and he could see it in Amory's eyes as well. When, a little over a week before their wedding, Philip woke to a bright sunny day, he called a halt to meetings and planning, to everything for a while. He and Amory needed some time to themselves. While he would prefer that time be spent in bed all day, he knew someone would only interrupt them. But they could take advantage of the weather instead and go for a long ride. They would be surrounded by guards for security, but they would be out of the palace, together and away from everything.

Amory agreed eagerly, so eagerly that Philip laughed. But that didn't stop them from changing into riding clothes and hurrying out of their suite before someone could catch them with something they needed to see to right at that moment. They were holding hands and laughing like children by the time they reached the courtyard in front of the stables. Philip was suddenly reminded of their time at Alzata. They hadn't managed more than one other visit in the months since their first trip, which Philip regretted. He wished they could go there, but so close to the wedding a trip to Alzata was impossible. After the wedding, they would visit for a few days as a sort of wedding trip, as much of one as they could ever take.

It couldn't come soon enough for him.

Less than a month until they would be at Alzata again. And married. The thought of them married was enough to make him smile. Amory looked at him and smiled in return. Philip wanted to kiss him right there, but stable hands brought their horses out. Maybe after their ride they would have time to go back to bed.

Amory's eyes widened as if he could see the thought in Philip's eyes, and maybe he could. Amory knew him so well, it was almost frightening. Amory nodded and turned to the horses. "Ready?"

"Let's go." Philip went to his horse, aware that Amory was walking to his own, and as he was about to mount up, everything went mad.

Star shrieked, and Amory shouted. Philip whirled around in time to see Amory, just settled into the saddle, fly off the horse's back as she reared up. For an instant, Philip froze in shock and terror, his whole body going cold as Amory flew up and then crashed down onto the cobbles of the courtyard.

"Amory!"

He scrambled over to where Amory lay, so still, and dropped to his knees beside him. He was afraid to touch Amory, afraid to check... but then Amory drew in a shuddering breath and groaned.

"Amory." The first word was a whisper, but then he shouted over his shoulder, "Get a healer!"

He didn't hear the reply as he turned back to Amory, whose dark eyes were fluttering open. It was the most beautiful thing Philip had ever seen, those eyes opening. "Amory, love, don't try to move."

"Wasn't planning to." Amory tried for a smile, but it came out closer to a grimace.

"Well, if you can be sarcastic, it can't be too bad." He managed a smile for Amory, despite wanting to weep when he heard Amory's pain-filled whisper, seeing him lying on the cobbles.

Amory started to laugh, but it turned into a whimper, and Philip hushed him gently. "Shh. The healer will be here soon, love. Everything is going to be fine, I promise. I'm here."

He gave in and gently brushed Amory's curls off his forehead before cupping his cheek with careful fingers. He probably shouldn't touch Amory, but he thought they both needed the contact, and it seemed he was right. Amory let out a long shuddering breath at Philip's touch, his face relaxing the smallest amount. Philip hoped that meant having him near was helping.

A moment later, Jadis and two other healers arrived at a run. Jadis dropped to his knees on Amory's other side. Not sparing a glance for Philip, Jadis laid his hands on Amory's chest and closed his eyes. Philip waited as patiently as he could, stroking Amory's cheek, looking down into Amory's pain-glazed eyes. He was trying his best to keep his terror from showing on his face. He didn't want Amory to see his fear. Amory needed to stay calm.

Finally, Jadis opened his eyes. He looked up at Philip. "It isn't anywhere near as bad as I feared."

Relief crept into the edges of Philip's consciousness but couldn't completely replace fear.

Jadis looked down at Amory. "Amory, I know it doesn't feel like it now, but you were very lucky. I'm going to help you with the pain, and then we're going to take you inside and get to work healing you, all right?"

Amory looked like he was about to nod but thought better of it. "Yes."

"Good. Here we go." Jadis laid his hands on Amory again and closed his eyes. Philip watched Amory and was rewarded by the easing of some of the tension in Amory's features. When Jadis opened his eyes, he motioned for the other two healers to help him load Amory on the stretcher. Philip was forced to let go of Amory while they did, even though he wanted to cling to him, willing him to be all right.

Once Amory was on the stretcher, he bent and brushed his lips over Amory's forehead. "Everything is going to be fine. Jadis is going to take good care of you."

"Love you," Amory said.

"I love you too."

He watched as the healers carried Amory away and tried to pull himself together, to function through the sick fear choking his breath and freezing his limbs. He didn't think he would ever get the image of Amory flying through the air, the sickening sound of him hitting the ground, out of his head. But Jadis said Amory's condition wasn't too bad. Amory would be all right. He had to be all right.

"Cousin. Philip." Etan was at his side, his hand on Philip's arm steadying. Philip hadn't noticed him arrive, but he was grateful for Etan's presence.

"Etan." He couldn't go on, couldn't force any other words out. He was supposed to be enjoying a leisurely ride in the countryside with Amory before taking him to bed, not waiting to see if Amory survived and in what condition.

Etan gripped Philip's arm more firmly. "It's going to be all right. Amory was awake and talking to you. That's good."

"Yes."

"The palace healers are the best in Tournai. They'll take good care of him."

"I know." He took a deep breath. "I know."

"Let's go inside. I'll wait with you."

He nodded. "I don't understand what happened. Amory is an accomplished rider, and his horse is well-behaved."

"Your Highness, my lord." The voice came from behind him and Etan and belonged to one of the more senior stable hands, Philip saw when he and Etan turned. The man continued speaking when Philip nodded. "I think I know why the horse acted that way. I was unsaddling Star, and I found a few of these under her saddle blanket. There are some deep scratches there."

Philip took the object the stable hand held out to him without thought, hardly noticing the pinpricks of pain where it touched his fingers. It was a small seed pod, bluish in color with sharp spines. The tree that produced these pods was indigenous to Tournai and common on the palace grounds. He stared down at it as his mind slowly turned over the implications of finding such a thing under the saddle of Amory's horse. Where it would cause Star pain enough to make the usually well-behaved horse shake her rider from her back.

"Someone did this deliberately." Etan gave voice to the thought that was surfacing through the fog of fear and anxiety in Philip's mind. "It couldn't have been an accident."

"No, it couldn't. Someone tried to hurt Amory, again." More than hurt him. He saw Amory flying through the air again but blinked the image away. "Who saddled the horse?"

"I don't know, Your Highness," the stable hand said. "With preparations for your wedding and the upcoming holiday, there have been more people in and out of the palace and the stables. I saddled Your Highness's horse myself, but I don't know which hand saddled Master Amory's."

Rising frustration and rage brought an almost welcome relief from gripping fear. "How can you not know—"

Etan's hand on his shoulder stopped him from shouting at the cringing stable hand. "We'll find out who saddled Amory's horse. In fact, we'll find out everyone who was near Amory's horse today. Someone must have seen something, if nothing else."

Philip nodded, and spoke to the stable hand. "All the stable hands are to stay here until they're spoken to. In fact, no one leaves the palace grounds."

"Yes, Your Highness." With a bow, the man disappeared into the stables.

"Let Captain Loriot speak to them," Etan said, anticipating Philip's desire to talk to everyone himself. "It's what he's here for, and you are in no shape for it."

He wanted to argue. He wanted to do it himself. But Etan was right. He was too volatile to undertake that kind of questioning. "Fine. See to it, but I want to know what he finds immediately."

"Of course." Etan turned to the guard captain who had arrived at some point, again without Philip noticing. He didn't stay to listen. He strode across the courtyard toward the closest door into the palace, but he hesitated a step across the threshold. He wanted to be near Amory, but prince or not, he doubted the healers would let him in while they were working. He stood in the corridor, debating, when a hand landed on his arm again.

"Come on. Let's go wait in your suite." Etan's face held compassion and worry. "You'd only get in their way if you went to Amory. They'll know where to find you when you can see him."

Philip nodded, knowing Etan was right even if Philip wished he weren't. He walked with Etan through the palace corridors, sunk into his own thoughts, but aware enough to notice the unnatural silence. News of what happened to Amory must have spread through the palace already.

Etan sank into a chair in the sitting room as soon as they arrived, but Philip couldn't settle. He tried to sit, but he only popped up a moment later and began pacing the room. Etan gave up trying to get him to sit after a few moments and let him pace, but he didn't leave Philip alone, even though he snapped at Etan repeatedly. Philip didn't want to admit how grateful he was for Etan's patient presence.

The wait felt like days but was only hours. Long hours. Donatien came in, and Philip realized he had duties he should be attending to, but he couldn't, not when he wasn't sure what was happening to Amory. Etan and Donatien held a whispered conversation, presumably about how to rearrange Philip's responsibilities that day, while Philip paced patterns into the thick carpet. Donatien disappeared as quietly as he'd appeared. Philip would have to remember to express his gratitude to both of them when he could think again. He wouldn't be able to allow himself to feel, to worry for Amory so much, to make Amory his entire focus, if he didn't have Etan and Donatien.

Time passed, and Philip continued to pace. Servants brought food, but he only managed to choke down a few bites of something before he was up and moving again. Etan didn't push him to eat, probably afraid Philip would take a swipe at him. Elodie burst into the room after the meal, her eyes wide and frightened. She threw herself at Philip, giving him little choice but to catch her.

"Where's Amory? Is he all right? What happened? I was out with Lilliale, and when we got back, they told us he was thrown from his horse, but he always seemed like such a good rider, so I can't believe it could have happened. Did he really get thrown?"

The flood of words was too much for Philip to deal with at that moment. "Elodie, slow down."

"Not until you tell me, because I can't understand why people are saying these things. They're talking like he's badly injured. What happened to Amory?" It was a demand more than a question, and Philip couldn't handle demands.

"Someone tried to kill Amory. That's what happened to him," he snapped. Elodie jumped back, looking like a kicked puppy. At some point, he would feel terrible for upsetting his sister, but not right then. "Someone purposely caused a situation that would make his horse rear and throw him. Yes, he is injured. The healers have been working on him since this morning, and I don't know anything. I don't know if he's all right."

Elodie stared at Philip, opening and closing her mouth several times without saying anything. Yes, he was going to feel bad about it later, once there was room in him to feel anything except fear.

Etan walked up to her and placed an arm around her shoulders. "El, why don't you go back to your suite with Lady Lilliale for now? I'll let you know when we hear anything about Amory. Go on."

Etan gave her a little nudge, and she nodded. She turned and went to the door where Lilliale waited for her in silence. Philip hadn't noticed her there in the flurry of Elodie's arrival. Lilliale was wide-eyed and still, staring at him, but she moved when Elodie drew even with her, turning and following Elodie out the door, which Etan closed behind them.

"Thank you," he said.

"You're welcome. She was worried when she heard something happened to Amory, but you can't handle how excitable she gets right now."

"Still." He sighed.

"She'll be fine. She'll go back to her rooms, and Lady Lilliale will calm her down." Etan resumed his seat. "Once she knows Amory will be fine, everything will be forgiven."

"Once I know Amory will be fine... Amory has to be fine." Philip looked up at Etan. "We're to be married in a matter of days, Etan."

"I know. You will."

He tried to be reassured by the calm confidence of Etan's voice, but he wasn't quite. "Has anyone told Amory's family?"

"Not yet."

"Adeline should know, at least, and Tristan. You should let them know."

Etan nodded. "Once the healers let us know how he is, I'll tell them."

"All right." They didn't know anything at the moment anyway. He rubbed his hands over his face. He needed to know how Amory was. He wanted to send Etan to the healers to demand information—he wanted to go himself—but he knew it wasn't a good idea. Even if waiting did make him crazy. He kept pacing.

He had no idea how much longer he paced while Etan slouched in a chair and stared at nothing. Long enough for the sun to begin to sink and dusk to fall. He was staring out the window at the coming twilight when the knock on the door came. He whipped around to look at the door, and Etan sat up straight. "Enter."

Jadis, looking so exhausted Philip wasn't sure how he was upright, walked into the sitting room and managed a bow. "Your Highness."

"Jadis, please, how is he?"

"He's all right, Your Highness. He'll be fine."

Philip sank into the nearest chair, relief turning his knees to water. He gestured Jadis to a chair as well, worried the man would fall over. "Tell me."

"He was very lucky, Your Highness," Jadis said as he lowered himself into the chair, his movements slow and careful. "Minor internal damage and only a minor head injury. There were several broken bones— wrist, ankle, ribs—and a dislocated shoulder."

Philip could feel himself going pale at the thought of Amory injured so severely.

The healer continued, "We fixed the internal injury immediately. Normally, we would heal the breaks over time. It's easier on both healer and patient. However, I didn't believe that was the best course of action in this case."

"What do you mean?"

"We healed all of Amory's injuries today. That's why we were working on him for so long."

"But you said it's best to heal them over time."

"I felt it best to heal his broken bones all at once. He wants to be on his feet for his wedding." Jadis smiled faintly.

"We could have postponed the wedding if it was better for Amory." Stubborn, wonderful Amory.

"I know. But that wasn't my sole consideration, just one of many. Not the least of which is that leaving him injured and immobile would leave Amory vulnerable."

He could see from Jadis's expression that the healer knew Amory's fall was no accident. Philip closed his eyes and nodded. "All right. So he's healed now?"

"He is. However, healing on this scale has costs. We had to draw on Amory's own Talent for healing himself to increase our own powers and heal him completely."

"What does that mean for him?" he asked, fear clawing its way up inside him again. He was grateful for Etan's silent presence at his side.

"It means he's going to be extremely tired for some time, Your Highness. So I don't want you to worry if he sleeps for quite a while. Also, he's going to experience some soreness, tenderness to the injured areas, and perhaps some weakness as the healing really sets in. It shouldn't last more than a few days."

"All right." That didn't sound too bad. Not pleasant for Amory, but so much better than the alternative. He would make sure Amory rested until he was well again. Perhaps he would lock Amory in the bedchamber and post guards at the door—keep Amory resting and safe at the same time. "What now?"

"I'm having Amory brought back here. He doesn't need to be monitored constantly, and he'll be more comfortable in his own bed than in the infirmary. I'll check on him in the morning."

"Thank you, Jadis."

Jadis must have heard the fervent relief and gratitude in Philip's voice, because his expression softened. "You're welcome, Your Highness."

Additional healers arrived then, escorting servants bearing Amory on a stretcher. Philip jumped to his feet and rushed to Amory, but he stopped himself from flinging himself at Amory with so many people in the room. Instead, he directed the stretcher bearers to the bedchamber he shared with Amory and watched while they transferred Amory to the bed. The healers fussed over Amory for a moment, getting him settled under the blankets, before filing out of the room.

Jadis paused next to Philip. "Send for me if you need me, but you shouldn't. I'll see you in the morning, Your Highness."

Etan was next. "Now we know he's all right, I'll go tell Elodie and then Adeline and Tristan."

"Please tell them not to come yet. He won't be able to have visitors if he's sleeping." And he wanted some time with Amory before other people descended upon them, despite Amory sleeping during that time.

Etan nodded. "I'll be back in the morning too, but send for me if you need anything."

"Thank you, Etan." He meant it not only in gratitude for his offer, but for everything Etan had done for him that day.

Etan reached out and pulled Philip into a tight hug. "You're welcome. I'll see you in the morning."

Then Philip was finally alone with Amory. For a while, he stood in the bedchamber doorway, staring at the sleeping figure in the large bed. After a day spent wishing he could rush to Amory's side, he was oddly hesitant. He could have lost Amory. Slowly, he walked until he was standing at the bedside looking down at the man he loved.

Amory's skin, always ivory pale, was nearly translucent, and purple smudges darkened the delicate skin under his eyes. He looked exhausted even in sleep, but he was alive and well, and Philip couldn't ask for more.

He didn't want to disturb Amory. Even without Jadis's warning, he could see Amory needed sleep. But Philip had to touch him, had to prove Amory was real and not the figment of his terrified mind. He brushed Amory's tousled curls from his forehead, smoothing them back. Giving in to temptation, he trailed his fingers gently over Amory's face, tracing the beloved features. He froze when Amory's nose scrunched up. He found it adorable, but he didn't want to wake Amory.

"Pip?" The word came out a whisper, low and slurred, barely understandable.

"I'm here." He sat on the edge of the bed at Amory's side, careful not to jostle him. "I'm right here."

Amory struggled to open his eyes and focused slowly on Philip. He could have wept at the weariness in Amory's face, greater since he was awake, or maybe wept in relief that Amory was looking at him with those big, dark eyes. He smiled instead, answering the sweet smile that curved Amory's lips.

"Glad you're here." Amory's eyes closed but then opened again with what looked like an extreme force of will. "Sorry. So tired."

He bent and kissed Amory's forehead, his hand stroking Amory's hair. "That's all right. You sleep, rest, so you can feel better. I'll be here when you wake up."

Amory nodded sleepily and reached up toward Philip. "Kiss me first? A real kiss."

Philip grinned, blinking back tears. His Amory would be fine. "Of course."

He leaned forward and slipped his arms under Amory's body, holding him lightly, carefully, while he placed an almost chaste kiss to Amory's lips. He meant it to be fast, so Amory could sleep, but once he had Amory in his arms he couldn't let go. It hit him, all over again, what could have happened, and he clung to Amory as if he would never let go. He never wanted to let go. He realized he'd straightened up, pulling Amory with him, only when arms wrapped around him and a heavy head came to rest on his shoulder.

He should let Amory go and tuck him up in bed where he could sleep in peace, but Philip couldn't make himself. Amory didn't seem to mind. In fact, he seemed content where he was, resting against Philip. His eyes stung again with impending tears. He might have lost Amory. He blinked against the burning in his eyes and pressed a kiss to Amory's temple. "I love you."

"Love you too," Amory murmured against his neck. Philip could tell Amory was close to sleep, but he kept holding him. Amory could sleep against him for a little while, long enough for Philip to believe Amory was all right.

CHAPTER 12

NEARLY FOUR days later, Amory was going out of his mind. He'd slept a full day after the healing, waking in time to eat dinner and then dozing off again to sleep through that night. He had slept on and off for the whole second day as well, waking only for meals and short conversations with Philip. On the third day, he managed to stay awake more but was still confined to bed, and he hadn't been inclined to argue. Fatigue dragged at him, and his whole body hurt. So he dozed and read the day away.

As Philip promised, though Amory only remembered the promise in a vague, fuzzy way, Philip had been there when Amory woke the first evening, and Philip was there, it seemed, each time Amory woke after that. Philip often sat on the bed next to him, stroking his hair while Philip worked, reading the vast amount of paper that crossed his desk and carrying on whispered conversations with Donatien or Etan. It warmed Amory to know Philip wanted to be close to him, that Philip was so concerned for him, and during the first couple of days, when Amory felt so horribly weak and tired, Philip's presence comforted like nothing else could. Nothing would happen to him with Philip there.

It was the fourth day. He didn't hurt as much, the soreness dulled down to a minor ache in his wrist and ankle. And he wasn't as tired anymore either, except tired of being in bed. But Jadis thought another day of rest would be a good idea, just to be safe, and when Amory would have ignored him, Philip asked him to do as the healer said. Philip had done his best to hide how scared he'd been, but Amory had seen it, and he couldn't refuse Philip.

That didn't stop him from being less than pleased to be stuck in bed, and not for any pleasant reason. He finally persuaded Philip to go about his day as he normally would. He missed Philip's company, but he didn't want to pull Philip away from his responsibilities for longer than necessary.

Tristan and Adeline arrived together in time to eat lunch with him and Philip and then visit with him when Philip went back to his office. This visit was the first time he had seen either of them since the incident.

If they visited the first, or even the second day, he wouldn't have known it. He had vague memories of Etan and Elodie during that time, in addition to Philip and Jadis. Elodie had been very sweet during her brief visit, but he hadn't been awake enough to keep up with her.

Tristan and Adeline sat at Amory's bedside and talked about nothing of particular consequence for a while after Philip left them, trying to keep Amory entertained, but his part in the conversation tended to lag.

"Amory, you are very grumpy today," Adeline said suddenly.

"Excuse me?"

"You know I'm happy you're all right. So happy and so relieved. I can't tell you how scared I was when Lord Etan told us what happened. But you're being very grumpy."

"She's right. You really are," Tristan said, ignoring Amory's glare. "Any particular reason you're doing your best to make us dislike you so much? Did you want us to leave?"

Amory nearly growled. "Let me think why I might be grumpy. I'm stuck in bed, bored to tears after days of doing nothing more than lying around tired and sore, because someone is trying to kill me. In the most inept way possible."

Adeline went pale, and he regretted his outburst immediately. It wasn't like him to let his frustrations get the better of him to where he hurt someone else.

"Why inept?" Tristan asked before Amory could apologize to Adeline.

Amory sighed. "Because there are better ways to kill someone. There was no guarantee either of the accidents they set up for me would actually kill me. Unless they are trying to scare me off. Philip and I thought maybe they want to make me leave him because they don't want me to marry him."

"They might have killed you even if they didn't mean to."

Another shiver of fear coursed through Amory, and he wrapped annoyance around himself like a blanket. He didn't want Tristan and Adeline, especially Adeline, to see how scared it made him to think about someone trying to kill him, and how close that someone had come. The healers were good, but if he had landed differently, they might not have been able to do anything. He might have died a few days ago. Philip knew how afraid that made him, but he knew how terrified Philip was as well. Without Philip's saying anything, Amory knew, from how tightly

Philip held him and the tremors running through his body sometimes. But Amory didn't want to be anything but strong for Adeline.

"Yes. They might have."

"That's one way to get you to leave the prince," Tristan finished for him. Adeline looked horrified when Amory nodded.

Adeline grabbed his hand with both of hers. He bit back a wince as the ache in his wrist intensified at her tight hold. "You have to be careful, Amory. Please, you have to."

"Of course I'll be careful, Adeline. I have no desire for anything bad to happen to me and neither does Philip. I'm as safe as I can be right here, surrounded by palace guards." Ignoring the slight twinge in his ribs as he moved, more stiffness at the moment than anything else, he stroked her hair, pinned up in elegant coils, with his other hand.

"You were in the palace when this happened," she whispered.

That was another reason he was so scared. "But now we're being even more careful. Philip has more guards on duty all the time, and everyone is being vigilant. I promise I'll be so careful."

"But you won't leave the prince."

He pulled back, shocked she would suggest it. "No, I won't leave him."

Her eyes were wet with tears. "But if you left him, you would be safe. If they only want you to not marry the prince, then if you left him and came home, they wouldn't try to hurt you anymore."

"I can't, Adeline."

"Why?" Her question was desperate, almost a wail, and like nothing he had ever heard from her. Tristan put his hand on her shoulder, but he met Amory's eyes, and Amory could tell Tristan understood. Adeline probably did too, but she was too scared to accept it.

"Because I love him. And I won't leave him, not for anything. Philip and I are going to have a life together. I won't let whoever this is take that away from us."

PHILIP WAS in his office, but he wasn't especially productive. His thoughts kept drifting to Amory, to worry for Amory. He'd had to force himself from their bedchamber, even though Amory said he could go. He half feared it might be a dream, that if he let Amory out of his sight,

Philip might return to find he'd imagined the last few days and Amory was gone. The fear wasn't rational, but it plagued him anyway.

Captain Loriot reported to Philip again that morning, but he had no new information. Philip wasn't sure how it was possible, how no one had seen someone tamper with Amory's horse. Philip wanted to hit something, to beat someone bloody.

Whoever did it... it terrified him how close they'd gotten. To be in the palace stables with no one noticing or thinking them out of place. After finding out Philip and Amory were going out riding, they'd acted immediately, so they must have been waiting for an opportunity. He and Amory were going to have to take further precautions, or he was going to keep Amory locked in their bedchamber for the rest of their lives. And while the idea did have its intriguing aspects, more so if he could manage to lock himself in with Amory, Philip didn't think Amory would accept it.

So he had to think of some other way of protecting Amory, of catching the person who wanted him dead.

He was worrying over that while he should have been going over proposed revisions to a trade agreement when Cathal appeared in his office. Philip managed to keep his shock, and hope, from showing on his face, keeping his expression impassive through will and long experience.

"Cathal."

"Good afternoon, Your Highness," Cathal said with a bow.

"What are you doing here?"

Cathal seemed mildly surprised, uncomfortable even, but he rallied and smiled in his charming way. "I thought you might need me. Things do tend to fall apart when I'm not here."

"Things are fine. Etan is more than capable. In fact, I'm hoping he'll stay on permanently."

"Oh. Well. That's good. I'm glad my absence didn't cause any undue problems for you." Cathal seemed to fumble for what to say. "I know I haven't been here in quite a while. It ended my affair with Celeste. She got tired of not seeing me."

"Understandable." He didn't blame the woman. He also didn't care.

"Yes, well. It's going to be uncomfortable seeing her for a while. I was wondering if you could help me—"

"No," Philip interrupted.

"What?"

"No. I'm not going to help you to not see her. I'm not going to ask Elodie to get rid of Lady Celeste when she seems to be working out for my sister. No more. Clean up your own mess this time."

"But—"

"I said no, and I meant it, Cathal." He was not doing that for Cathal. For one, Lady Celeste was a steadying influence in Elodie's household, but he also didn't feel inclined to do his cousin any favors at the moment. It might be uncharitable of him, but Cathal had abandoned him and Amory. Philip needed some time before he would trust or want to help Cathal again. "I'm not getting rid of her. You'll just have to be an adult about it when you see her."

"Of course, I... all right." Cathal floundered for a moment. "I heard about Amory's accident. There are rumors the fall wasn't an accident. Is he all right?"

"Yes, Amory is going to be fine. Thanks to some luck and some very good healers." He kept his voice steady, his face impassive, refusing to let Cathal see what he felt.

"That's good. I'm glad Amory's all right."

"Are you?"

"Yes. Why wouldn't I be?" Cathal's dark brows pulled together, as they did whenever he was perplexed.

"Because the rumors are true. Amory's fall wasn't an accident, Cathal. Someone wants Amory dead or at the very least injured and away from me." If it were an enemy of Philip's, he could have just as easily gotten to Philip's own horse as well. Philip pushed down rising terror again at the certainty of the gut feeling that Amory was the target.

"Someone is trying to kill Amory?" Cathal went blank with shock, but Philip couldn't help the skepticism he felt, and he hated feeling it. Cathal was his cousin, his friend. Only Cathal had turned away from him and Amory.

"Yes." He studied Cathal, but Cathal displayed nothing but shock.

"But why?"

"Why do you think? Someone doesn't want me to marry him, quite a bit apparently since they're willing to kill him to keep it from happening." He paused, but Cathal stared at him, saying nothing. "You and your father—a lot of our family—don't want me to marry him."

"I have my concerns, and yes, Father is against the match, but his reasons are understandable—wait." The shock swirled with betrayal and anger. "You think we had something to do with this?"

"I don't know what to think. I don't want to think it, but I wonder. You're so against this marriage, Cathal. Your father is so against this marriage. Then this happens to Amory. What am I supposed to think?"

"That you know us well enough to know we wouldn't do something like this." Cathal's voice was tightly controlled as he fought to hold on to his temper. "You and I, Philip, we're not only family, we're friends."

"I thought I did know you, but then you abandoned me because of my choice of betrothed. Your father issued ultimatums before he walked out the door—he wouldn't come back until Amory was gone. I thought I knew you all, but I never expected that from any of you. I thought you would stand by your family and your prince."

"My father is worried about you and Tournai. He can't understand what you're doing. You're the prince. That means you have responsibilities, and one of them is to ensure the continuity of the succession. You must produce an heir. What will neighboring kingdoms think of Tournai if its prince won't do that most fundamental thing?" Cathal's voice got louder as he spoke, losing the battle for calm.

Anger stirred inside Philip. He'd thought long and hard about his responsibilities to his country, to himself and to Amory, and he'd made his choice. He didn't regret it, and he wouldn't change it. And to imply he had thoughtlessly put himself ahead of the duties he'd sworn to perform, the duties he had prepared for and lived up to his entire life... oh, yes, that made him angry.

Before he could open his mouth to tell Cathal exactly what he thought of Cathal's accusations, a hand came down on his shoulder. Etan stood at his side, glaring at Cathal.

"Cousin," Etan said to Philip, "you have some time before audiences. Why don't you go see Amory? He's getting restless confined to bed." Despite talking to Philip, his eyes remained on Cathal.

"I have some business left to attend to here." Philip looked at Cathal as well.

"Let me handle my brother, please. Go see Amory."

He struggled between his desire to stay there and deal with Cathal and his desire to see Amory. "Are his sister and Tristan still here?"

"They just left. Amory is bored," Etan told him. "You should take him with you to audiences today."

"Jadis said he should rest another day. I don't want him tiring himself and setting back his recovery."

"Right now he's in more danger of setting back his recovery through sheer frustration. Audiences won't be strenuous, and getting out of bed and leaving that room will probably help his mood. Take him with you."

Amory had seemed irritated. Maybe getting out of their bedchamber would help. "All right, I'll go see him. You'll take care of things here."

"Of course."

Cathal looked murderous at being handed off to his younger brother, but perhaps that was good, after Cathal's harsh words. Philip stood and nodded at Etan. Let Etan deal with his brother. Philip would take the more pleasant option of spending time with Amory.

Or perhaps not so pleasant.

He stepped into the bedchamber as Amory snapped a book closed and flung it toward the foot of the bed. It bounced once and settled among the tangled blankets. Amory looked up at him and frowned.

"Did the book do something to offend you?" Philip walked into the room and retrieved it, setting it on the bedside table.

"I'm tired of being in this bed."

"I thought you liked being in our bed." He tried for a leer, but he wasn't sure he managed it.

Amory's lips quirked. "Pip, you know what I mean."

"I do, and I understand." He climbed onto the bed next to Amory. "Is that all that's bothering you?"

"No," Amory said after a moment. He paused again and when he finally spoke, his voice was small and quiet, and Philip hated hearing it. "I'm scared."

He put his arm around Amory and pulled him close. "I'm scared too. Terrified. But I'm not going to lose you. We're going to keep you safe, and we're going to find out who is trying to hurt you, and…"

"And we're going to get married." Amory looked up at him from where his head rested on Philip's shoulder.

"Yes, we are." He kissed Amory's forehead. "Would it help your boredom to get out of bed for a little while?"

"You're going to let me out of bed?" Amory grinned, his eyes taking on some sparkle. "That shouldn't be a good thing, should it?"

He laughed, relieved Amory could tease. "Not at all. But don't worry, I'll get you right back in bed later."

"Good." Amory kissed him quickly, then again. "You're really going to let me up for a while?"

"Yes. You can come to audiences with me if you like. I can't guarantee how interesting it will be, but I know I'd like your company."

"I'd like that." Amory's brow furrowed. "Do I have time for a bath first?"

He chuckled at Amory's plaintive question. "Yes."

He insisted on helping Amory out of bed, even though he knew he was being overprotective. Amory grumbled but let Philip help him. Maybe Amory liked having Philip's arm around his waist as much as Philip liked putting it there. Amory was a bit stiff and slow climbing into the bath, and Philip reached out to steady him.

As he sank back into the hot water, Amory must have seen something in Philip's face because his smile turned reassuring. "I really am all right. Still a little sore, but much better. The hot water will help."

Philip nodded, but the knot of worry remained inside him.

"Maybe you could help me bathe?" Philip loved the gleam that came into Amory's eyes. It was far more reassuring than anything Amory could have said. Philip began stripping out of his clothes. "What are you doing?"

He laughed at the expression of surprise on Amory's face and stepped into the bath, settling in behind Amory. "I thought it would be easier to help you from in here."

"Easier, hmm?" Amory asked, leaning back against Philip's chest.

He hummed a little at the contact, reveling in the feel of Amory's leanly muscled body against his own. "Oh yes, much easier."

Amory chuckled, and Philip took up soap and a cloth to wash him. He ran the soapy cloth gently over Amory's skin. Washing, yes, but more than that, caressing, cherishing. He could have lost Amory, but he hadn't, and he wanted to touch, to show Amory he was loved. To prove to himself Amory was still there.

As he stroked cloth and hands over Amory's skin, Amory relaxed further and further until, by the time Philip set the cloth aside, Amory was boneless against him. He wrapped his arms around Amory and held him close. Amory hummed, a sound of pure contentment, and turned his head enough to press a kiss to Philip's neck. Amory nuzzled his face there and stayed. Philip smiled and closed his eyes. Yes, content.

Amory murmured, "I think I could be persuaded to go back to bed."

He chuckled. "I wish I could take you back to bed. It's been too long since we've touched this way."

"Yes."

"But we have to go to audiences now." He laughed at Amory's grumble, despite feeling much the same way. "Later, though."

Amory sighed. "That better be a promise."

"It is."

He liked having Amory with him in audiences. He assumed Amory liked attending them as well, since he'd accompanied Philip to most since the first time, but Philip couldn't understand why. Audiences could be long and tedious. But having Amory there made it better. Sometimes just his company, his presence, made the task easier, but sometimes his witty comments, whispered so no one except Philip would hear, did it. They'd gotten into the habit of discussing the more interesting occurrences and petitions afterward, and he found himself seeking Amory's opinion.

Amory was becoming a partner for him in that area of his life as well, something Philip hadn't expected or realized he wanted until he had it. For the first time in his life, Philip felt like he had someone with whom to share the duties and burdens of his position, of ruling, even if Amory wasn't actually his co-ruler. Wasn't yet, and might never be. But Amory was someone who would stand beside him, would do everything he could to lighten the load, as he would for Amory. Was it any wonder he wanted to spend the rest of his life with the man?

After audiences, Lord Tangi stopped him in the corridor and drew him away from Amory and Etan, then proceeded to drone on for far too long about nothing important. Philip kept Amory in sight the whole time, paying as much attention to Amory as to the man talking to him, despite knowing Amory wouldn't thank him for his anxiety. Amory was standing with Etan in full view of four royal guardsmen. Amory was safe.

But Philip didn't trust that what should be true actually was. He wasn't sure he trusted anything or anyone with Amory's safety, not after seeing Amory crumble to the cobblestones a few days ago.

The interminable conversation finally ended, perhaps too dismissively on Philip's part, but he wanted to get Amory back to their suite where he would be safe, and where he could rest. Because despite

Amory's protests to the contrary, he was still uncomfortable after his injuries and their rapid healing.

Amory came along without protest, taking Philip's arm when he offered it. Etan stayed behind, but the guards trailed after them. Until whoever had tried to kill Amory was caught, guards would follow them everywhere and security would be far tighter.

Amory kept darting little sidelong looks at him. Perplexed, almost incredulous looks.

"Is something wrong?" he asked as they walked into the suite.

"No." Amory sat on the couch in the sitting room, obviously not ready to go back to bed whatever he'd said before audiences. "Did you ask your cousin if he tried to kill me?"

"Which cousin?" he asked with a grin, but Amory's expression made it perfectly clear he wasn't going to allow Philip to joke. Philip sighed. "Who told you?"

"Etan. You accused Cathal of trying to kill me. I can't believe it."

Philip slumped onto the couch next to Amory, sighing in relief and pleasure when Amory's fingers found their way into his hair. "I didn't accuse, so much as ask."

"You asked him if he tried to kill me?"

He glanced at Amory, who looked as if he wasn't sure if he should be amused or horrified. "I asked if he or his father knew anything about what happened to you. Whether they tried to kill you was more implied than anything else."

"Be serious, Pip."

He sighed again. "I am being serious. I hate thinking my family might have had something to do with this, but I don't know what else to think right now."

"Pip."

He took Amory's hand and squeezed. "Someone is trying to kill you. Maybe... most likely to keep us from marrying. My family, my uncle especially, does not want me to marry you."

"But they're your family. And you and your cousins... you're all so close." The emotion in Amory's eyes was painful to see, as if he himself could feel all of Philip's pain at the thought of a betrayal of that magnitude from his own family. He didn't want Amory to feel any of what he felt, not when he felt as he did right then.

"I know. I don't want it to be them, any of them."

"So who else could it be?" Amory asked. "We don't know your family did this. There has to be someone else."

"I don't know. It's not anyone in your family." He tried to make the absurd suggestion in a teasing tone, but it didn't quite work.

Amory gave a short laugh, but there wasn't much humor in it. "No. My father would have to be stupid to kill me now, and my father is many things, but he isn't stupid."

"That he isn't, especially when it comes to situations that could benefit him." Philip ran a hand over his face. "I'm sorry. I shouldn't have said that."

"Why? It's true." Amory peeled Philip's hand from his face and kissed his forehead. "My father is an expert at using everything to his own advantage."

He lifted Amory's hand to his lips. "Sorry."

"Don't be sorry about him. He's always been that way."

"Nevertheless. I hate when things hurt you, love." And what Amory's father did, and had done, continued to hurt Amory, despite his professed resignation to it.

"And I hate when things hurt you." Amory's dark eyes were filled with the pain he felt on Philip's behalf. "It can't be your family, Pip. It can't. There has to be someone else."

"Because you don't want me to be hurt?"

"Yes," Amory said. There was amusement in his eyes at the absurdity of his own assertion. Nevertheless, Philip knew if Amory could make it so Philip wouldn't have to feel that betrayal, he would. Philip hadn't thought he could love Amory any more than he already did, but in that moment, love swamped him.

He pulled Amory to him and held him, burying his face in Amory's curls, breathing in Amory's scent. He whispered, "Thank you."

"For what?" Amory whispered back. But he held on just as tightly and let Philip snuggle in as close as he needed.

"For being you." Only Amory could love so much, so completely, and Philip was grateful for it. After a second's pause, he laughed a little. "That was horribly sentimental."

"Yes, it was." Amory said in a whisper, "But I liked it anyway."

"Just don't tell anyone."

"Your secret is safe with me." Amory resumed stroking his fingers through Philip's hair in the way Philip liked. "We're going to find out who did this, and whoever it is, we'll get through it together."

They would. He had someone, someone standing with him. And they would find whoever was trying to hurt Amory, and they would get married, and they would live their lives together.

THE NEXT day, Amory felt well enough to spend the whole day out of bed, which was a good thing, since he and Philip were getting married in three days. Three days. He couldn't quite believe it. Despite the weeks spent planning, the wedding hadn't felt quite real. He supposed the distraction of attempted murder hadn't helped him settle into the idea either. But the wedding was suddenly quite real. And the biggest thing he felt was joy. Oh, there were nerves too, both for the day itself, and for what came after—marriage to a prince and all it entailed—but those nerves were overshadowed by the utter joy that he was going to marry Philip. The rest… he meant what he said to Philip. They would get through it together.

Not everything about their wedding was the way tradition dictated, or the way they planned. The second attempt on Amory's life changed everything. His recovery, even hastened by the healers, meant a few of the parties and events leading up to the wedding had to be canceled. Except for missing the winter fair in the city, he wasn't disappointed by the cancellations, and many other events were going forward as planned. He didn't tell Philip how he felt, but he had a feeling Philip knew. Philip always seemed to know. Most of the time Amory liked it.

He hoped Philip wasn't getting suspicious of all the time Amory spent in the palace libraries. He didn't want to tell Philip what he was looking for until he knew if there was something to be found, until he knew if it could work. With the wedding so soon and parties and gatherings every day, he didn't have much time for research, but he stole time in the libraries again when he could despite beginning to think there was nothing to be found, that he had wasted a lot of time and gotten his hopes up for nothing.

Which, of course, was when he found something.

The day before the wedding, he snuck off for a little time in the library while Philip was in a meeting. He flipped pages, resigned to the fact that he wasn't going to find anything, but unable to keep from looking through one more book. One last book. That one was a thick, dusty old tome that looked as if it hadn't been taken from the out-of-the-way shelf in decades. And there it was, what Amory had been looking for all along. A spell, a potion, perhaps a way to give Philip something amazing. If it worked. The spell was complex magic, sorcery as well as healing, and far beyond his own limited knowledge and capabilities. He would have to consult Jadis and a sorcerer to see if it might be possible.

He sat back and stared at the words on the page, black ink only slightly faded by time. Just letters, words. So innocuous, and yet they could change his life. The rush of triumph, of excitement, was tempered by worry. He never imagined doing anything like what he was considering, never could have imagined it, but he was considering it. Could he do it?

"Yes." He stopped and took a breath. Yes, he could do it. Not only for Philip, but for himself too, he could. His decision was only whether to go to Jadis or to Philip first. He didn't want to get Philip's hopes up if it couldn't be done. But he also wanted to discuss it with Philip first, because they should decide together from the start. Philip should know before Amory talked to anyone else.

He wouldn't talk with Philip that day. On the afternoon before their wedding, they didn't have the time the discussion deserved. And maybe he wasn't quite ready to talk about it. He needed to keep it to himself a little longer, to let it settle into his mind as a real possibility. It killed him to keep anything from Philip. It felt... wrong. But he needed to wait a little longer.

If Philip noticed how jittery Amory was, he must have attributed it to nerves over how public their wedding was going to be. But Amory couldn't argue with how Philip chose to soothe him. He would never argue with that.

Then, the next day, they got married. The simple statement encompassed so much. The utter joy of marrying and starting a life with Philip made him almost giddy. Philip couldn't seem to stop grinning as they dressed that morning either. Amory knew as soon as he woke it would be the best of his life.

Their wedding day was also possibly the longest day of Amory's life. Every moment seemed to be spent in motion, from the moment he woke beside Philip. They'd chosen not to sleep separately the night before. They were lovers and had been lovers for quite some time, and everyone knew they were lovers. Sleeping apart would be a flimsy pretense that would make neither of them happy. It seemed more important to wake up happy on their wedding day.

They stole a few moments of quiet while eating breakfast together in the suite as they always did, and then they helped each other dress in clothes specially made for their wedding ceremony. Both sets of clothes were made of white silk and velvet, embroidered and trimmed in gold, the workmanship impeccable. The color and style were traditional for wedding clothes in Tournai, only the quality of the materials distinguishing them from wedding clothes of the lower classes. They had been tailored to fit his and Philip's frames, but that didn't make Amory comfortable in them. He was sure they didn't look quite right on him. Philip, however, looked amazing. The clothes accentuated his broad shoulders and slim waist, and he looked as if he'd been born wearing the ornate gold circlet that rested on his dark hair.

"You look incredible," Philip said. Amory had been so enthralled with Philip's appearance he hadn't noticed Philip's attention.

He shook his head. "No, I don't. You do."

"Yes, you do," Philip replied, his voice low and husky, his gaze heated. Amory shivered. Maybe he didn't look so bad, if Philip was looking at him that way. Philip reached for him and pulled him close, kissing him long and slow. "Now. Let's get married."

The ceremony was held in the palace, the large throne room crowded with guests, despite whom Philip was marrying. Seeing the crowd alleviated some of Amory's fears. He wouldn't have cared if he and Philip exchanged vows in private, but for Philip's sake, he wanted everyone to attend. He recognized many faces in the crowd, nobles he met during the months he had lived in the palace. Jadis was there, toward the back of the crowd, as were Vasco and his wife and siblings. Amory almost felt sorry for Lady Lilliale, sitting silently among her brothers. Her childhood infatuation was ending. Vasco's presence made Amory feel awkward. Philip's former lover had not warmed up to Amory in the time since they'd first met, and he was Philip's former lover, but they couldn't exclude a high-ranking family from the invitations.

His own family was there, his father puffed up with pride and satisfaction, his older brother looking somewhat sour. But the rest of his family—his mother, Adeline, his other siblings—all looked happy. Tristan was there too, a bright grin lighting his face and a thread of wistfulness in his eyes. Tristan would be his witness in the ceremony. To Amory's surprise, Philip had been comfortable with his choice when Amory broached the subject before asking Tristan.

Etan was Philip's witness. Amory had a feeling that before Philip had been abandoned by much of his family, Philip might have chosen Cathal, but Cathal had walked away, even if he did try to come back, and Etan had been there. Philip and Etan were closer and probably always would be.

The real surprise was that the rest of Philip's family chose to attend. Amory knew Elodie would be there and he was pretty sure Cathal would attend after his tentative overture a few days ago, but he hadn't known what the rest of Philip's family would do. It would have been a horrible insult if they hadn't attended, but Amory hadn't been sure that would stop them. He spent so much time worrying about what it would do to Philip if they didn't attend the ceremony, both personally and as prince. The relief at seeing them there, aunts, uncles, and cousins, even if they didn't all look as joyful as the occasion called for, swept through him, threatening to weaken his knees.

His mind chose that moment to remind him of Philip's suspicions, and tension stiffened his muscles again. What if Philip's family really had tried to kill Amory? Their presence at the wedding didn't mean they hadn't. A lot of people in the crowd were probably keeping up appearances and currying royal favor. But he was disconcerted to think someone who might have tried to harm him was there watching him marry Philip. He didn't want to think of it, not on their wedding day. He only wanted to get married.

Everything blurred into a sea of faces and finery as he stood at the front of the room with Philip, only Philip's dear face clear to him. The ceremony wasn't short, the vows and pledges long, complicated, and very traditional, but the depth of joy and love in Philip's eyes made it all right, would make anything all right. He had to blink back tears when they exchanged rings, gold bands worked in a complicated pattern representing love and loyalty. He stared at their joined hands adorned with matching gold rings before looking up. Philip's eyes were damp too, but he was smiling hugely.

They were married. Amory's whole world changed in that moment.

He would have liked to bask in that joy, but after the marriage ceremony came the part Amory was far less certain of—the coronation. He was marrying the prince, which came with new responsibilities, with a whole other public life attached to it that was more than a little daunting, but he would do it for Philip. He would do more than that for Philip.

He reminded himself of that as he made his oath, as a gold circlet was placed on his head. The crown was simpler in design than the one Philip wore, but it weighed heavily on Amory's head. He wasn't sure if that heaviness was more literal or metaphorical, but either way, he felt it. Panic fluttered in his stomach. He wasn't sure how he was supposed to be Philip's consort. But then Philip was there in front of him, his gaze warm and radiating love and confidence in him. Philip believed in Amory, and he refused to let Philip down. So he stood tall next to Philip when with fanfare, they were announced as "Prince Philip Alexander Stefan Mael and his consort, Prince Amory."

Amory's head didn't stop spinning for the rest of the day. After the ceremony, there was a short reception with light food and drink, but Amory and Philip managed to eat only a little. The guests all did their best to congratulate them before the end of the reception, even though most of the guests would be back later for a formal dinner and a ball to celebrate the marriage.

Neither he nor Philip was looking forward to the next part of the day—the parade through the city. Philip had eventually given in to the pressure of tradition to schedule it. They considered canceling it after the second attempt on Amory's life, but that action had the potential to draw far more attention than they wanted. Philip ordered more guards and shortened the parade route. That last could have been for another reason. Philip was not looking forward to a long open carriage ride on a winter day.

The weather cooperated as much as it could at least. The day was chilly, but the sun was shining brilliantly in the icy blue sky. They bundled themselves into the white velvet cloaks that matched their wedding clothes, which hopefully would keep off the worst of the chill, and climbed into the carriage.

Philip crowded close to him as soon as they were both seated. He probably did it to share warmth, but Amory enjoyed the closeness. Having Philip pressed against his side helped as they passed through the palace gates and the crowds lining the streets began to cheer. He wanted to shrink in on himself but forced himself to sit straight and smile. Philip's hand found his between them and held it tight. He smiled at Amory, his expression once again filled with confidence and encouragement.

"I love you," Philip whispered in his ear.

"I love you too." Amory took a deep breath. He could do it.

Philip nodded, and they turned to the cheering crowd. They spent the rest of the parade waving and throwing coins and sweets to the children in the crowd, another long-standing tradition. The carriage, a well-kept antique, was only used for parades at coronations and royal weddings. Servants in the stables had worked on it in the days leading up to the wedding, polishing the metal and touching up the white paint and gold leaf that covered the outside. The cushions had been replaced before Philip's coronation, so they were marginally comfortable as the carriage rattled along the cobbles of the city's main street. Well, they would have been comfortable if it weren't so cold.

The people in the crowd didn't seem to notice the cold. Waving and cheering, they filled both sides of the street, pressed together from the front of the buildings to the edge of the cobbles, which was as close as the guards surrounding the carriage would let them get. A few people jeered and yelled insults, but they were by far the minority and were swallowed up by the crowd. Still, Amory could feel the tension in Philip's body pressed against his. He was as stricken hearing those yells, but they couldn't let their reactions show, couldn't let the crowd see they were affected. He squeezed Philip's hand, hoping for comfort, for himself and for Philip.

With the press of people in the streets and the noise of their cheers and yells, Amory felt far too exposed in the carriage. He forced himself to push his shoulders straight because he kept hunching them. Frustration, along with a bit of anger, helped him in the battle. Because he wanted to run back to their palace suite where no one could hurt him, and that was… unacceptable. It was his wedding day. He should be happy, but he was scared and tense and worried. And he hated it.

"All right?" Philip asked him quietly, the smile still in place, but concern filling his gaze. He knew Amory far too well.

"Yes, of course." He didn't want Philip worried for him on their wedding day. Philip didn't look convinced, but he said nothing more. Philip pressed closer to his side. Amory would never argue about being closer to Philip for any reason.

CHAPTER 13

BY THE time Philip and Amory reached the dinner and ball that night, Philip was heartily tired of wedding festivities and crowds and guards. He hadn't had a moment alone with Amory since they dressed that morning, and time with Amory was all he wanted. Just a little time alone with Amory—poor Amory who was practically drooping next to him when they returned to the palace—to absorb that they were married and to bask in the joy of it for a little while. He didn't get it.

Dinner seemed to go on forever with numerous toasts and various entertainments—musicians, acrobats, a sorcerer producing enchantments to impress their guests. He lost count of the number of courses as ever-more-lavish dishes produced by the palace's cooks were placed before them. Perhaps he should have taken a larger role in designing and approving the menu, but the palace employed people to plan menus for large court dinners, and they were far more experienced than he. Everything was delicious, of course, but there was so much of it, more than he had ever seen at a court function. By the time the extravagantly decorated cake appeared, he didn't think he could eat another bite.

After dinner, the entire party moved to the largest ballroom, which was decorated with greenery and hothouse flowers. He and Amory led the first dance under the glow of hundreds of candles and the eyes of the hushed guests. One was far more romantic than the other, but Philip made the best of it, enjoying the closeness. Especially when Amory relaxed into the dance and Philip's arms despite the people watching.

Afterward, they retired to the dais, where a second throne replaced the chair Amory usually occupied next to Philip's. Amory gave Philip a rueful smile, but he sat without comment. Philip took Amory's hand and tangled their fingers together, as they sat back to watch the dancers and to accept the well-wishes of yet more guests. He refused to let go of Amory's hand. The hand clasp was the most contact they would have until the ball was over, unless he could convince Amory to dance with him again, and he was going to make the most of it.

Amory didn't object. He curled his fingers into Philip's, brushing the back of Philip's hand with his thumb. Philip tried to hold back a shiver at the sensation, but Amory knew. Philip could tell from the little knowing smirk on Amory's face.

They did dance again, more than once, to Philip's surprise. Amory wasn't always comfortable dancing with him in front of so many people. He wondered if Amory felt more assured of his place at Philip's side and in Philip's life because of their wedding. He hoped so, though his position hadn't ever been in doubt, not to Philip.

For once, tradition worked for them, dictating that a newly wedded couple not be separated at their own wedding festivities, requiring them to stay within reach of each other at all times, to dance only with each other. Philip was quite satisfied with that. He was also quite satisfied to realize he would never have to dance with another young lady who was determined to marry him and become a princess. He'd found a man who loved him for him, not his title.

"What are you thinking?" Amory asked.

"That I'm very lucky."

Amory shook his head, his eyes filled with affection. "I'm the lucky one."

The ball would continue long into the night, but Philip and Amory didn't stay and celebrate with their guests. As soon as custom deemed it acceptable for them to retire from the party, Philip made sure they did. Let everyone enjoy themselves there. He looked forward to spending the rest of the night alone with Amory.

Philip and Amory had been firm that no one was to follow them to their suite to cheer or whatnot, as was often what happened when the prince married. So the crowd saw them off from the ballroom. Amory was blushing at the clapping and cheering. Philip couldn't imagine how red Amory's face would have been if they had been escorted to their bedchamber.

The sounds of music and merrymaking faded the farther they got from the ballroom, leaving him and Amory walking through empty corridors alone. Amory let out a quiet sigh and moved closer to him, brushing their fingers together before taking Philip's hand. They encountered no one except silent guards on their walk to the other side of the palace and their suite. He wasn't surprised—all of their guests were in the ballroom and the servants were discreet enough to make sure they weren't seen.

He ushered Amory into the privacy of their suite and closed the door behind them, shutting out the world for the rest of the night. Servants had been in to light the candles and the fires. If they'd done as he requested, which they always did, wine and some of Amory's favorite sweet pastries would have been left in the bedchamber.

Amory turned to him with the genuine, sweet smile he seemed to reserve for Philip. There was fatigue in his chocolate-dark eyes, but a glow of happiness too. Philip reached out and brushed at Amory's hair before cupping his cheek. Amory closed his eyes and nuzzled into Philip's palm.

"It's our wedding night."

"Yes." Amory opened his eyes to look up at Philip.

"Long day." He swept his thumb over Amory's cheekbone, back and forth.

"But the best day." No doubt of Amory's sincerity, and Philip was surprised to find himself a little relieved. So much had happened recently, and so much went along with marrying the prince without everything else that happened, he wouldn't have blamed Amory for having doubts.

"The very best." He brushed a kiss over Amory's lips. "You look tired."

"You do too."

"Too tired?"

"To consummate our marriage? Never too tired for that."

"Come to bed?"

"Oh, yes."

They walked into their bedchamber together, and yes, the wine and pastries were there. The bed had also been invitingly turned down. Amory smiled again as his gaze took in the room, but he just turned to Philip for another kiss, longer and deeper than the last. He loved kissing Amory, had from the very first. They could probably spend their whole wedding night kissing, and he wouldn't be disappointed.

Well, he would be disappointed, but only because he had plans. He got nervous thinking about them, but his nerves were equaled, if not overshadowed, by anticipation. He figured that meant he was right about doing what he planned, so he would be disappointed if they did nothing but kiss that night. Some other night they could kiss for hours.

They undressed each other, hands fumbling with the fastenings of the fine wedding clothes, because they didn't want to leave off kissing long enough to undress properly, but they finally managed it and collapsed on the bed in a tangle of limbs and bare skin and breathless laughter. For a long time, they lay together, kissing and touching. Philip reveled in it, letting it evolve naturally despite nerves and desire screaming at him to get on with things. But he always wanted Amory. He couldn't believe sometimes that their passion continued to be so explosive, so consuming, but he also never wanted that to change.

Amory's hands glided over his skin, grasping, caressing, passionate but gentle as only Amory could be. Philip let him take control of their kisses as they became more intense and held on, moving his hands over Amory's skin and pulling him closer. He needed to feel Amory against him, smooth skin and lithe body and silky curling hair. Amory moaned, the sound sending shivers coursing through Philip.

"Pip, please," Amory whispered against Philip's lips.

"Yes," he answered and stole another kiss before Amory rolled away to rummage in the nightstand. Amory was back an instant later, pressing a little bottle of oil into Philip's hand, but Philip shook his head and gave it back.

"Pip?" Amory's eyes were passion-dazed and puzzled.

"I want you to have me tonight." Saying the words sent a rush along his nerves. He'd never done it before, never imagined doing it. He wasn't sure why. He didn't think his reluctance was about his being prince and his station. But more that he had never imagined having someone he trusted enough, which may have been because he was the prince and there weren't many he could trust implicitly. But he had Amory. And Amory loved him more than Philip thought possible. Philip could feel that love every day, and Amory was everything to him. It felt right to share the experience with Amory.

Amory's eyes widened almost comically. "You do?"

"Yes."

"We've never done that before."

"I know." He ran his fingers through Amory's hair, slowly, soothingly.

Amory nibbled on his lip. "I've never done that before."

Amory's nerves somehow calmed his own. "I know, love. I haven't either."

"You haven't? You and...."

Philip was grateful Amory stopped speaking before he said the name of Philip's former lover. He didn't want anyone in their bed except the two of them.

"No, we didn't. I never wanted to before now." He kept stroking Amory's hair, seeing the motion was calming Amory and enjoying the slide of Amory's soft hair between his fingers.

"But you want to now?"

"Yes, I do. I want you inside me, Amory. I want to feel that, to have it with you. Only with you."

Amory's smile bloomed. Philip really did love that smile. He couldn't resist kissing it.

"Do you want to, Amory?" He hadn't considered it could be something Amory might not want to do when he realized what he wanted, but suddenly he worried he was pushing Amory.

Amory looked at him as if he were crazy. "Yes, of course, if you want to."

He traced his fingers over Amory's cheek. "So much. You're nervous?"

Amory laughed a little. "Yes. I don't want to do something wrong or hurt you."

"You won't. I know you won't." He kissed Amory. "It's going to be wonderful, just as our first time together was. Please, love."

"Yes." Amory bent to kiss Philip. The kiss lengthened, went on and on, rebuilding passion the pause for conversation had banked. Amory's hands began their caresses again, exploring every inch of Philip's skin with those long, graceful fingers. Amory finally pulled his lips from Philip's, but only to begin to trace the same path his fingers had taken. Amory kissed and nipped his way down Philip's throat and over his chest, teasing at his nipples along the way, sending sparks through Philip's body with every touch. He writhed under Amory's touch, wanting more, wanting everything.

"Now, love, please," he gasped as Amory sucked at one of his nipples.

Amory murmured an assent and retrieved the bottle of oil amid the blankets. A moment later slick fingers teased their way between his legs, stroking and pressing. Amory kissed him deeply as he pressed a finger inside. Philip gasped and moaned into the kiss, the intrusion strange but good. Wonderful too, because it was Amory inside him.

That thought echoed through his head as Amory replaced fingers with hard member. Philip expected discomfort, maybe even pain, whatever he'd told Amory, but there wasn't any. He thought he would feel invaded, but he didn't. He was vulnerable, yes, more so than he'd imagined, but he knew Amory wouldn't take advantage of that. He felt connected to Amory, intimate in a whole new way. Their bodies linked, their gazes held, their hands clasped. The pleasure of the connection was as great as the purely physical sensation, and the pleasure only built and spiraled as Amory moved inside him until it burst within him like showers of stars. Amory followed, calling out Philip's name in almost stunned pleasure.

Afterward, they curled together. Philip managed to snag the blankets and pull them over him and Amory, who lay half on top of him, and then contemplated never moving again. Never moving sounded perfect. He was comfortable with Amory warm and sleepy against him. Yes, perfect just as they were.

After a while, Amory hummed a little and snuggled closer. "That was incredible. Thank you."

"It was, so thank you." He tightened his arms around Amory and nuzzled into his auburn curls. "We'll have to do it again."

"I'd enjoy that."

"But not tonight."

"Oh? Have something else in mind?" Amory lifted his head enough to look into Philip's eyes.

"Well, we have to finish consummating the marriage." He said it seriously, but mischief tried to curve his lips.

"Didn't we do that?"

"We have to consummate it the other way around too, don't we?"

Amory stared at him and then laughed. "Oh, that's the rule, is it?"

He grinned. "Definitely."

"Well, if it's a rule...." Amory shifted to kiss Philip. "Then I suppose we have to."

He chuckled and kissed Amory again before pulling him back down to lie against Philip's chest. "In a little while."

THEY LEFT the next morning for a few days at Alzata. Even if Philip couldn't be completely out of reach of the palace and his duties, Amory was happy to have the time alone with him as something of a wedding trip. Philip seemed far more disgruntled with their inability to take more time away.

A cold rain fell in sheets the morning after their wedding, so they chose to make the short trip by carriage instead of horseback. Amory had no desire to ride in such weather, and Philip was even less enthusiastic. At least the rain hadn't come yesterday, while they were being paraded around the city.

The carriage ride was surprisingly pleasant. They cuddled close together under a blanket for warmth. Amory chuckled as Philip leaned back against him, blatantly making himself comfortable with Amory as his pillow, but he didn't argue or tease Philip about it. A long day yesterday, after several busy weeks, and a night—though incredible—involving very little sleep left him exhausted. He curled his arms around Philip and sank into the pleasure and warmth of holding Philip close, letting himself doze while Philip read.

Rain still poured down when they arrived at Alzata, and they were soaked in the short dash into the house. Philip's whole demeanor radiated misery as he dripped on the marble floor. Amory steadfastly held back laughter, even though the task became difficult when Philip glared at him. Taking pity, he shuffled Philip into their bathing room and a steaming hot bath. Which he then followed Philip into, since he looked so inviting.

They emerged from the bathing room a long while later, wrapped in their dressing gowns, warm, smiling, and flushed, shoulders bumping and fingers brushing. A tureen of hearty soup and a loaf of freshly baked bread waited for them in their bedchamber. They ate a leisurely meal and sipped their wine as a maid slipped in to collect the dishes. Amory glanced out the windows. The downpour hadn't slowed. He shivered looking at the icy rain, so he shut all the curtains, leaving them snug and warm. Philip rose from his chair. He carried their glasses to the bedside table and set them down.

Amory followed Philip into the big bed. Grinning, Philip pulled Amory in to curl at his side and tugged the covers up over both of them. Amory hummed happily and settled closer. Cozy and warm and comfortable, they sipped their wine and cuddled in the glow of the crackling fire. Philip stroked his fingers absently through Amory's hair. Amory had absolutely no desire to move from that spot, maybe ever.

The rain continued unabated the entire time they were at Alzata, so they didn't have to pretend to want to go outside and do something. Instead, they indulged themselves and stayed in bed or lounged about on the comfortable chairs in the sitting room next to their bedchamber. They read a little, and Amory did some sketching while Philip did the work he couldn't put off. But mostly they stayed in bed, curled up like cats, lying together, kissing and touching. They made love often—in their bed, in the bath, on piles of blankets and pillows in front of the fire. The servants didn't bat an eye when he and Philip directed their meals to be brought to their bedchamber.

They were decadent and lazy and wonderful, those days they snatched together. Reality and duty would intrude soon enough, but until then they enjoyed their time alone. No responsibilities, no worries, no fear for Amory's safety. The entire world shrunk down to them. He knew it was impossible, but Amory sort of wished it could stay that way.

"Is something wrong?" Philip asked him as they lay cocooned in bed together on their last night before returning to the palace.

"No," he replied just as quietly. "Nothing's wrong."

"Well, something is bothering you. You look worried." Philip took Amory's hand and twined their fingers together between them.

"I'm not looking forward to leaving tomorrow."

Philip kissed Amory's fingers. "I'm not looking forward to it either. These few days have been wonderful."

He smiled. "They have."

"We'll come back as soon as we can." Philip kissed his hand once more before giving it a squeeze. "Is that all that's bothering you?"

He hesitated, thinking of what he needed to discuss with Philip. It hadn't plagued him as much the past few days. Philip was wonderfully distracting. Amory must have hesitated too long, because Philip's brow furrowed. "Something else is worrying you. What is it?"

"It's not that something is worrying me, not really. I just… there's something I want to talk to you about." He stopped and laughed a little. "I guess I have been worrying over it."

"Just tell me. You can tell me anything." But Philip looked to be bracing himself for whatever Amory was going to say next.

"It's not anything bad, I promise," he hastened to reassure Philip. "Just something I wanted to talk about."

"All right," Philip said, his expression easing somewhat, but he was still far more tense than he had been a moment before. Amory felt terrible. Philip needed the relaxing time before their return to the palace. Perhaps he shouldn't have brought it up, but Philip had asked, and Amory was tired of thinking about it all on his own.

"Remember when you asked me to marry you—"

"I couldn't forget that." Philip's whole face changed with the memory, softening with affection.

"Neither could I." The memory relaxed him despite his nerves, and he kissed Philip briefly, pulling back before he could get carried away. "We talked about your needing an heir, then."

"And I told you not to worry about it."

"I know."

"I should be quiet and let you finish what you want to say, shouldn't I?"

"Thank you. We talked about an heir, but we never talked about children, about whether we want a child separate from whether you need an heir. But you said something then, about how if you had a child, it would be our child, and I started thinking. Leaving aside the issue of an heir, do you want children, Pip?"

For a moment, Philip stared at him blankly. "That is not what I expected you to ask."

Amory laughed a little. "What did you expect?"

"I'm not sure. I was just hoping you didn't regret the wedding." Philip continued before Amory could gather his wits and reply to that ridiculous statement. "All my life, it was something that was expected of me—I would produce heirs. No one talks about it in any other way except as a duty, a responsibility to provide for the future. I would love any child I had, but I don't think I ever thought about it any other way."

"All right."

"Is it… something you want? I said we could find someone who wouldn't mind having a child for us. I'm sure there are women who would, knowing their child would be heir to the throne, though we would have to think about how to go about it."

And Philip would do it, Amory knew, if Amory wanted a child, even though the expression on Philip's face, the tension in his body, screamed he was uncomfortable with the idea of actually doing what he suggested. Amory loved him for it, that he would do something solely to make Amory happy. But Amory would never let him do something he didn't want. "I think it might be something I want, if you do. Not only because I worry about your not having an heir, but because when you said the words 'our child' that day, I couldn't get them out of my head. I realized that having a child together might be wonderful."

"So you do want us to find someone." Philip's discomfort hadn't lessened, but Amory doubted he realized it showed. Amory didn't much care for the idea either for any number of reasons, the fact that he didn't want to share Philip only one of them.

"No. I have another idea." He took a deep breath—no going back once he told Philip. If Philip wanted it too, Amory was committed. He wasn't completely comfortable with the idea, but, well, their child. "There was something in a book I read while I was studying with Jadis, a vague reference, but I remembered after that night. So I went looking to see if there was something to it, if it's actually possible."

Philip brushed Amory's curls off his forehead, waiting patiently through Amory's convoluted rambling. "If what is possible?"

"There's a spell. It's beyond me—I'm no sorcerer and barely a healer of any kind—so I'm not certain what it entails or if it would work, but if it did, it would allow a man to carry a child." He stopped, biting his lip, and waited for Philip's reaction. He couldn't guess what it would be.

Philip stared at him. He opened his mouth to speak, closed it, blinked several times, and then stared some more. Amory was about to ask if he was all right when Philip finally spoke. "You found a spell that would make it possible for a man to carry a child?"

"I believe so, yes."

"That's not possible."

"It may be, but I don't think it's easy. I found the spell in a very dusty old book I don't think anyone has read in a very long time."

Philip still looked incredulous. "Or perhaps it's dangerous or few men wanted to carry children."

He shrugged. "Maybe. Who knows why it isn't performed more often?"

"Amory, what are you saying?"

He took another deep breath. "I'm saying if we want to have a child, with this spell we wouldn't need anyone else. I could carry our child."

"I thought that was what you were saying." Philip shook his head as if to clear it. "You would want to do that? I can't imagine...."

"I couldn't either. I still can't really. This isn't something I ever imagined, let alone wanted to do."

"But you do now?"

He put a hand to Philip's face, looking into his dear eyes, so bewildered at that moment. "I've thought a lot about it, and frankly, it still seems strange when I think about it too much. But it's a way we can have a child if we want one, and for that, for you, I'd do it. I love you, Pip."

"I love you too." Philip sighed. "You never thought I should do it, instead of you."

He shook his head. "I don't think a pregnant crown prince would go over well with the people of Tournai. But I can do this for us."

"You want to?"

Did he? He was arguing strenuously when he wasn't sure carrying a child was something he could physically do, but the more he argued, the more he convinced himself he did want to do it for Philip. He nodded.

"Have you spoken to anyone else about it? Someone who would know more about the spell?" Philip asked after a moment.

"No. I wanted to talk with you first."

"I'm glad you did." Philip brushed a kiss over Amory's knuckles again and then paused, thinking. "We can talk to Jadis when we get back. After we hear what he says, we can discuss it more."

"All right." He smiled and squeezed Philip's hand.

Philip smiled too, but his eyes were serious. "Even if this spell won't work for us, we can have a child if you want to."

"Only if you want to as well, and only if we're both comfortable with how." He looked into Philip's eyes, hoping Philip could see his sincerity. "I want everything for you, Pip, and for us. I want to make you happy and give you everything I can. But I don't need anything except you to make me happy."

Philip's gaze went soft and a bit grateful, and he nodded, seeming to be at a loss for words. He kissed Amory, slow and deep, and then pulled him in, cuddling him close to Philip's body. Amory held on tight and rested his head on Philip's chest, savoring that closeness. As long as he had that, he was happy. He wanted Philip to be happy too.

THE RAIN chose to stop on the morning they had to leave Alzata. Normally, Philip would be annoyed, since he and Amory enjoyed rambling around the grounds there, but he was perfectly happy to have spent the whole time indoors this trip, and almost the whole time in bed. He didn't think Amory minded either, but they both laughed at the sun streaming through the windows that morning.

They decided to travel back to the palace on horseback instead of in the carriage, taking advantage of the sunny, if not particularly warm, weather to cut down on the travel time. The carriage left with their bags while they breakfasted, and later he and Amory set out at a brisk pace, eager for an invigorating ride. Philip kept glancing over at Amory, riding at his side, enjoying Amory's delighted laughter.

After a while, they slowed, still surrounded by the squadron of guards that rode with them and had kept up easily. The ride took on a leisurely air then, as they talked about nothing serious. They would be back at the palace soon, and serious would find them then. They pointedly didn't talk about what Amory had brought up the night before. Philip couldn't quite believe they actually had the conversation in the first place.

He tried not to think about it, but the memory was never far from his thoughts despite his efforts. Amory's revelation that he'd been thinking about ways for them to have a child of their own had shocked him, not only because of what Amory found, but because he had no idea Amory was thinking of children. They'd talked about an heir, everyone talked about his needing to produce an heir, but few people ever spoke of an heir as a child. A child to love and care for and not a necessity for a healthy, strong Tournai.

Long before he asked Amory to marry him, Philip had made his peace with not producing an heir himself. Others wouldn't, didn't, see it the same way. But Amory wasn't talking about an heir, though if what he proposed was possible and they did it, Philip would have one. No, Amory was talking about their having a child, and that was something he hadn't considered.

He would have to consider it. They both would. If what Amory found was possible, they would have the ability to have a child of their own if they wanted, if it would make them happy. And the very fact that Amory was willing to do what he proposed, to carry their child, was mind-boggling and awe-inspiring. What Amory would do for him, the lengths he would go…. Philip was without words. He felt a certain measure of guilt that he couldn't ever do the same, couldn't imagine himself doing the same either to be honest. Not because he didn't want to give Amory everything. He did.

But that was all to be considered another day. They needed to know if what Amory proposed was possible before they discussed it anymore. He understood what Amory meant about the words "our child" staying with him. They echoed in Philip's mind as well and provoked all manner of feelings he couldn't quite put names to. He shied away from trying.

Instead, he focused on Amory, how the sun made his hair glow red, how his cheeks were pink from the bite of the winter wind, how his eyes sparkled. But there was strength too under that beauty, such strength. He had married that man. He'd gotten so lucky when Arnau brought Amory to the palace all those months ago.

"Maybe we should have taken the carriage," he said.

Amory glanced at him, his expression quizzical. "I thought you wanted to take advantage of the sunshine. Aren't you enjoying yourself?"

"I am, but I realized we could be enjoying ourselves quite a bit more alone in the carriage."

Amory stared at him and then laughed, even as a faint blush tinted his cheeks a rosier shade of pink. "You're terrible."

"You love it. And this is our wedding trip, for a while longer anyway. We should make the most of it." He let his smile become wicked and winked at Amory.

Amory shook his head fondly. "I think that's what we've been doing since our wedding night, but I suppose we could slow down and wait for the carriage. We didn't pass it that long ago. There might be enough time to—"

Amory broke off with a shout and a jerk of his shoulder.

"Amory? What—"

Star made a high sound that could only have been caused by pain and reared, dumping Amory, who had been struggling one-handed with the reins, onto the road. Fear coursed through Philip, turning his insides to ice, when Amory fell from his horse, and that was before the arrow hit the road next to Amory.

"Amory!" Without thinking about it, he was reaching down to Amory, who to his relief was conscious and moving. As soon as Amory gripped his arm, Philip hauled him up onto the horse behind Philip. Amory wrapped his arms around Philip's waist. The guards closed in around him and Amory, shielding them with their own bodies and horses.

"Your Highness, we have to get out of this area," the head of their guard contingent called to him. At Philip's nod, they were moving, galloping along the road through the forest.

"Are you all right?" he asked Amory.

"Fine." But there was something in Amory's voice.

"Amory. Tell me the truth."

A pause lasting several breaths and then, "I really am fine. Don't worry about me."

"What am I not worrying about?"

"One of the arrows grazed my arm, but I'm fine. I'm more concerned about the number of times I've been dumped off that horse lately."

The laugh, short and strangled, was forced from Philip. "How bad is it?"

"Well, it's embarrassing. Falling from one's horse displays a complete lack of dignity the prince's husband should possess."

He appreciated Amory's attempt at humor. He did. But still. "Amory."

"It's just a graze. It's bleeding, and I won't lie and say that it doesn't hurt, but it isn't bad."

He had to take Amory's word for it, for the moment at least, because he couldn't stop to check. They had to get away from the attack, from under cover of the trees. He assumed their guards were getting them out of the woods as quickly as possible. Getting back to the palace would be better, and once they got there, he was sorely tempted to lock his husband in their bedchamber until Philip found out who was trying to kill him.

Amory's arms squeezed his middle tighter, the strength of his hold reassuring. He wished they weren't running for their lives right then, because having Amory pressed so close against him would be very enjoyable otherwise.

They burst out of the woods what was probably moments, but felt like hours, later. The change of landscape alleviated his fear marginally.

There could be an army of men hiding in those woods, waiting for them. Outside the woods, the trees lining the road thinned, giving way to fields, which would be the predominant landscape until they reached the city. Philip felt more exposed and vulnerable in the open, but it would protect them that day. The archer or archers used the trees for cover. Much less cover out of the woods.

But more people were on the road, which made their speed more perilous. Philip was sure any number of curses and grumbles followed them as they passed, but he couldn't think of it then. They needed to get Amory safe.

The guards began to slow them down as they came to a busy crossroads. They stopped at the side of the road, and the head of their guard dismounted and came to Philip and Amory. "Are you all right, Your Highness?"

Philip nodded shortly, more worried about Amory than himself in any case.

The guardsman looked at Amory. "And you, Your Highness?"

He felt Amory's body jerk against his and twisted to look at him, the fear that Amory was hurt worse than he admitted slicing through Philip. But Philip's heart slowed when he saw Amory's face. He almost laughed—Amory wasn't used to his new title.

"I'm fine. Thank you."

"Let's take a look at your arm if we're stopping."

Amory sighed and managed to dismount without help. Philip followed him to the ground, and they stood in the circle of guards and horses while Amory pushed back his cloak. Philip bit back a gasp at the blood staining what had once been a pristine pale green sleeve.

"It's not bad," Amory said firmly and gripped Philip's arm with the hand of his uninjured arm, obviously sensing the terror coursing through Philip at the sight of the blood.

"Let me see." The day was too cold for Amory to remove clothing at the side of the road, so they widened the slice the arrow made in Amory's sleeve. Philip wiped at the blood on Amory's arm with his handkerchief and examined the wound. It was bleeding, but slowly, and the cut looked angry but not deep. "All right, it's not bad."

Amory huffed out a breath. "Like I said."

"Are you healing it?"

"Some. I was trying to stop the bleeding and make it sting less." Amory shrugged and winced. "I couldn't concentrate for anything more."

"You did well doing this much. Let's bandage it for now, and we'll let the healers finish it when we get back." He rigged a bandage out of clean handkerchiefs and tied it securely around Amory's arm despite how Amory's face tightened in pain. Done, he couldn't stop himself from leaning forward and resting his forehead against Amory's. "I'm sorry for hurting you."

"It's all right," Amory whispered and kissed Philip, lingering long enough to reassure. "What now?"

Philip forced himself to step back from Amory, but he kept a hand on Amory's waist. "We get back to the palace. Benno?"

"Yes, Your Highness. We could leave now, but I would like to wait for the carriage to catch up and have Your Highness and Prince Amory travel the rest of the way by carriage. It shouldn't be long in arriving."

"Fine. Did anyone get a look at who did this?" Philip asked.

"No, Your Highness. They were well hidden, and I didn't want to spare anyone to search the woods when our priority is protecting you and His Highness."

Philip tried to stamp down frustration and anger. He understood the guard's position, despite Philip's preference for someone going into the woods and catching the person behind the attempt. He wanted them caught and punished, and he wanted the situation over.

"Has anyone seen my horse?" Amory asked suddenly, and Philip choked on a laugh.

"She's smart. She probably ran for home when she was spooked. We'll find her."

Amory nodded and said nothing else. He didn't move out of Philip's hold either.

The carriage arrived several tense minutes later. The guards checked it over briskly but thoroughly and ushered Philip and Amory inside. Philip had barely sat when the carriage began moving. Amory hadn't quite settled himself, and he lurched sideways into Philip. Philip helped Amory right himself and then slid his arm around him.

Amory pressed into Philip's side and tilted his head to rest on Philip's shoulder. "I don't think I'm in the mood for what we were talking about doing in the carriage before."

It took him a moment to realize what Amory was talking about. That conversation seemed like years ago. He laughed a little, as he was sure Amory intended. "I'm not in the mood either, I'm afraid. Just stay right here, all right?"

Amory nodded, moving closer. He didn't complain. He wanted Amory as close as possible, and he kept Amory there through the rest of the trip back to the palace.

CHAPTER 14

PHILIP WOULDN'T let Amory go when they arrived and were hurried inside. He might have felt strange about it, but Amory made no move to pull away. Too close. It had been too close.

As much as he wanted to take Amory directly back to their suite and hide him away where he would be safe, Philip needed to find out who was trying to kill Amory more, so they went to Philip's office instead. He considered sending Amory back to the suite on his own, but he didn't want Amory out of his sight, and Amory was a grown man—he deserved to be a part of the discussion, even if Philip wished he could protect Amory from everyone and everything that could hurt him.

Before they reached the office, Philip was yelling for people he needed. He was sending the entire palace into an uproar, but he couldn't begin to care. Once in the office, he divested Amory and himself of their cloaks and got Amory seated on the couch. Amory was shaking his head and giving him a look that could only be described as fond exasperation. At least it was fond.

"You didn't need to demand a healer quite so forcefully. I really am all right," Amory said gently. But he winced when Philip helped him out of his sleeve.

"Imagine yourself in my position. You could have died, Amory. Today and a few days ago." His voice broke, and he swallowed hard against the lump in his throat. "Right in front of me. I saw it both times, and now you were hit by an arrow and you're cut and bleeding. If you were me, what would you be doing?"

Amory leaned forward and kissed him. "Exactly the same thing."

"So you're not going to argue with me? You're going to let the healers take care of you?"

"I haven't argued yet, have I?" Amory shook his head when Philip stared at him. "No, I won't argue. I'll let the healer treat my arm."

"Good."

"It frightened me too, you know. It still frightens me. Someone is trying to kill me. Could have killed both of us today." Amory's voice was low, his eyes holding an almost lost quality. "What are we going to do?"

"We're going to catch them." He took Amory's hand again and lifted it to his lips. He kept hold of Amory's hand as Jadis arrived and began to examine the wound on Amory's arm. Amory didn't need his hand held while a healer examined him, but Philip wasn't ready to let go. Amory didn't pull away, so maybe he wasn't either.

"It's not bad," Jadis pronounced. "You've been healing it?"

"A little." Amory winced as Jadis moved his arm.

"Good work." Jadis rummaged through his bag. "I'm going to clean it and apply a salve, then bandage it again. At the rate you heal, it should be completely healed in a day or two. I doubt it will even scar."

"Thank you, Jadis," Amory said and then turned to Philip. "See? Nothing to worry about."

"No, nothing except how you were injured in the first place."

"Well, yes, there is that."

Jadis set to work, and Philip watched in concern as Amory tried to suppress any indication he was in pain. Captain Loriot arrived, along with his second-in-command. Neither of them batted an eye at the sight of the newly crowned Prince Amory sitting shirtless in Philip's office while a healer prodded at his arm.

"You know what happened?" Philip asked them.

"Yes, Your Highness. Your guards informed me of the incident," Captain Loriot replied. "I've already sent men to search the woods and the surrounding area."

"Good. I want whoever this is found." Philip thought a moment. "Get a sorcerer to work with you. See if he can find anything. I'm tired of there being no trace found."

"Yes, Your Highness. Master Savarin returned to the city two days ago."

"Fine. Send word to him that I need him to work with you in the search." Savarin was the most powerful sorcerer in Tournai. It was a stroke of luck he'd returned from his travels.

"Yes, Your Highness."

"And we need to increase security here at the palace, and for Prince Amory himself as well," Philip said. "I know we already talked about this, and I've seen your reports, but it's far too easy to get into the palace and close to Amory."

"Yes, Your Highness. We've already put into place the measures I detailed in my report, but I agree to the need for further measures, especially in Prince Amory's personal security," Captain Loriot said.

"Philip," Amory said quietly.

Philip looked at Amory, sitting next to him while Jadis bandaged his arm. "Please don't argue about this, Amory."

"I won't, and I'll take every precaution Captain Loriot says I should, but I want you to increase your own security as well." Amory shook his head before Philip could begin arguing. "Yes, every attack has been directed at me, but today those arrows were fired at us while we were together. I don't see any reason for you not to take precautions as well."

Captain Loriot spoke before Philip could. "I agree with Prince Amory, Your Highness. We don't know who is behind this or why they're doing it. We don't know they won't attack you directly. An increase in your personal security would be prudent."

He looked from Captain Loriot to Amory, but the look in Amory's dark eyes persuaded him. "All right. I'll take whatever precautions you advise as well."

"Thank you, Your Highness. I'm going to increase guard presence in the palace further. I want guards with both of you in and outside the palace. I would also like Savarin to bolster the magical protections on your suite. I'll draw up a guard schedule and have other recommendations for you shortly."

"Fine. Let me know as soon as you find anything in the woods."

"Yes, Your Highness."

Philip slumped back into the couch after the guards bowed and left the room. Amory lifted Philip's hand to his mouth and kissed it gently. He didn't tell Philip everything would be all right, for which Philip was grateful. He wanted to be hopeful, but they had no idea who was trying to kill Amory. And their enemy had gotten too close already.

Philip wouldn't give up the search. He couldn't. They had to find out who was trying to kill Amory. Because he and Amory only just began their life together, and he refused to let someone cut it short. So he said it. "It's going to be all right."

Amory looked into Philip's eyes for a long moment and then nodded. "Yes. It will."

"I'm all done with Prince Amory," Jadis said. "Were you injured, Your Highness?"

"No, I wasn't."

"Excellent, then I'll leave you, Your Highness," Jadis said, turning to repack his supplies in his bag.

"Thank you, Jadis," Amory said.

Philip echoed his thanks and then stopped and thought. He wasn't convinced of Amory's idea about them having a child, but he had promised Amory they would discuss it with a healer before making any decisions. Whether they could have a child wasn't the most important consideration at the moment, but then again, maybe it was.

"If you have a moment, Jadis, there's something else we'd like to discuss with you."

Amory looked at him, curious and a little worried. Philip squeezed his hand in reassurance.

"Of course." Jadis put his bag down and turned his attention fully to Philip and Amory.

"Amory did some research recently into something about which we could use your opinion."

Philip watched comprehension dawn on Amory's face. At Amory's nod, Philip told Jadis what Amory found, Amory elaborating some points along the way. Jadis said little at first, but his eyebrows began a steady climb toward his hairline. He asked for clarification once or twice before Philip and Amory finished.

After a brief silence, Jadis seemed to shake himself. "Well, this is not something I've ever heard of anyone doing."

"You've heard of the spell, though?" Amory asked.

"Only in the vaguest terms. I read references to it during my training, but I don't think it's been used in recent memory. You're considering this?" Jadis asked.

"Possibly," Philip answered. "We need more information about what it entails, what the dangers are. More information in general."

Jadis nodded. "If I could have Prince Amory's notes, it would be helpful. I'll do some research and study the spell. If it has a component of sorcery and not only healing, which I assume it does, I'll need a sorcerer's opinion as well. I don't have those powers or that knowledge, Your Highness."

"Certainly. Ask Savarin. And keep this confidential," Philip said. They did not need it becoming public knowledge.

"Of course. You didn't need to ask, Your Highness. I'll let you know what I find."

"Thank you, Jadis. I'll get my notes to you today," Amory said.

A moment later, the healer was gone, leaving Philip alone with Amory, who immediately turned to him "I didn't think you would speak to him so soon, especially with everything that happened today."

Philip shrugged. He surprised himself too, but he'd promised Amory, and he wouldn't lie. The idea of a child of their own was intriguing. "I said we would."

"But right this minute?"

"After everything that happened today… yes, right this minute. We're going to be careful, more than careful, and we're going to find who is trying to hurt you. And our life will go on, and this may be a part of it. So we'll see what Jadis and Savarin have to say."

There was so much in Amory's eyes, but he smiled and nodded. "All right."

WHOEVER TRIED to kill Amory on the road was long gone by the time the search began. Philip was frustrated on a level Amory had never seen before, and that worried him despite understanding the feeling. He was frustrated himself, and he was afraid too, which made the frustration all the worse.

The guardsmen conducting the search found signs of someone hiding in the trees along the road and probably someone on the ground. Perhaps an archer in a tree with a lookout below. Amory could see Philip biting back what would have been a cutting remark or a curse, his fists clenched. He didn't blame Philip. The guards weren't telling them anything they couldn't have surmised from what happened.

The sorcerer wasn't much more help. It was the first time Amory met Savarin, but Philip told him Savarin often accepted assignments from the palace. A tall man with broad shoulders and bright blond hair, he had the air of sophistication that came from travel and a sharp look in his eyes. He towered over Amory, and though he was quite handsome, Amory found him more intimidating than attractive.

"I found no indication they were using magic at all, except for this." The sorcerer passed something across the desk to Philip.

Amory looked at what Savarin handed Philip as Philip turned it over in his hands. It didn't look like much—a twist of silvery metal on a frayed black cord—but Amory knew next to nothing about sorcery. He assumed the object wasn't dangerous since Savarin let Philip handle it.

"What is this?" Philip asked Savarin, and Amory didn't feel quite so ignorant anymore.

"A charm spelled to make the wearer unnoticeable, or less noticeable really."

"What does that mean?" Amory asked, hoping he wasn't asking something obvious. Philip's hand came up to cover Amory's where it rested on Philip's shoulder. Amory stood at Philip's side as he sat behind the large desk, but he allowed Philip to draw Amory down to perch on the arm of his chair. Neither of them was moving far from the other if they could help it.

"It means that when someone wears the charm it would be very difficult, if not impossible, for them to be seen, Your Highness. It's not that they are invisible. If you collided with someone wearing the charm, you would see them, or if you expected them to be where they were, or you were actually looking for them. There are also spells to counteract these charms. For instance, the palace's protection spells prevent these charms from working on the palace grounds. But without counterspells, it would be as if the wearer wasn't there."

Well, that was... interesting. He and Philip were silent for a moment. If Amory knew Philip, he knew his husband was taking in the implications of what they'd been told.

"And you believe the men in the woods were wearing these?" Philip asked.

"I do, Your Highness. It would ensure you and your guards saw nothing before and during the attack."

Philip nodded, accepting the answer he had clearly anticipated. "So where would they get these? Do they have a sorcerer working for them? You said you didn't believe they were doing magic themselves."

"No, I don't. There isn't a sorcerer in this group, or at least there wasn't in the forest." Savarin reached across the desk and took the charm from Philip, studying it for another moment. "They could have a sorcerer working with them who made this, but it's as likely they bought it. Good ones like this are expensive, and their sale is regulated, but I believe they're sold at more than one shop in the city. Sometimes legally, sometimes not."

"Is there any chance of figuring out where they were purchased and who purchased them?" Amory asked.

"Possibly. If I can figure out who made it." Savarin stared at the charm. "And if I recognize who made it. If they didn't buy it here in Tournai, I doubt I'll be able to, but I'll try."

"Good. Let us know what you find," Philip said.

"Yes, Your Highness." The sorcerer rose and bowed to Philip and Amory. "Your Highness."

After the sorcerer strode from the room, Amory looked down at Philip. Philip's face was tight with frustration and anger, the extent of which he hadn't allowed to show in front of Savarin. "Nothing again. Always nothing."

Amory sighed. It was mostly true, but he hated seeing Philip so frustrated. He hated feeling it himself. "The charm is something."

"I suppose."

"If he can find out who made it, he may be able to find out who purchased it. It's something."

"Yes, though little enough," Philip grumbled.

A wave of something desperate and scared built inside Amory, and he couldn't keep it from spilling out. "It's something, Pip. I need it to be something, because otherwise I begin to think we're never going to find out who's trying to kill me. And if we never find them, how long is it going to take them to succeed? They're not going to give up."

Philip's face went blank with shock an instant before pain rippled across it, and Amory wished he could take those words back. "Amory."

"I'm sorry, I'm sorry. I'm fine, really."

"You're not." Philip pulled Amory into his lap. "Neither am I. But we're going to find out who's doing this, and we're going to stop them. Yes, the charm is something. It's the first thing we have, so that's good."

Philip's arms wound around Amory, pulling him against Philip's chest. Amory let him, let Philip soothe him after his embarrassing outburst and the constant fear that followed him. He rested his head on Philip's shoulder, holding on to Philip as well, and hoped it helped Philip too.

In the following days, Amory stayed close to the palace, and to Philip, as much as possible. It felt a little cowardly, as if he was hiding, but keeping close to the palace was also safer. He was surrounded by guards when he did leave, but he was far more secure in the palace. The guards clearly believed so as well. No one went so far as to restrict his movements, but restrictions were probably coming, the longer the danger continued, and perversely, they might annoy him then, but Amory was happy enough for the moment to restrict his own movements.

That there was so much for him to do at the palace helped. Well, what helped most was how reassured Philip was when Amory was close by, but having plenty to do as he adjusted to his role of consort helped to keep him from going crazy. Palace security had been increased beyond anything Amory could have imagined. There were more guards in the corridors, on the walls, and at every gate, and everyone going in was searched. If they could get in—the guards adhered far more to lists of permitted visitors and appointments than they ever had in the past.

Somehow Amory still didn't feel safe.

They had been unable to keep knowledge of the latest attempt quiet, so the whole city knew someone was trying to kill him, which was probably for the best. The new security measures would only cause talk and fear otherwise. Tristan and Adeline brought stories of an air of horror in the city with them when they visited. If there was any other reaction, no one gave voice to it anywhere Tristan or Adeline could hear.

Adeline was almost as worried about Amory as Philip, as was Tristan, but he handled it better. Adeline could only be distracted with questions about her wedding plans, and then only sometimes. Tristan was quieter, watchful and concerned, but Etan could usually tempt him into conversation. Amory liked watching Tristan and Etan together, getting to know each other, becoming friends. It provided a distraction for Amory, but only a fleeting one.

Despite everything in the palace to occupy his time and mind, despite the love of his friends, Amory couldn't escape the anxiety plaguing him. It made his chest tight and his whole body tense. Absolutely the only thing that helped was Philip. When he was with Philip, he found some measure of calm, and Philip did as well. When they closed themselves into their suite at night and lay close together, Amory could breathe again. He could feel the tension seep out of Philip's body, his own muscles relaxing the same way.

They escaped to Alzata more than once during those weeks. Elodie wanted to go with them every time they went, but they couldn't bring her. Bringing Elodie meant bringing Elodie's ladies, her maids, and possibly her friends, because she was a very social creature, and her natural inclinations to surround herself with people were opposed to what they were trying to do by visiting Alzata. They tried to make her understand, but Amory wasn't sure she did. How could she? She was young and carefree. She worried about him and Philip, but she wasn't living with the constant fear. No one had tried to hurt her, and though her security was increased as a precaution, it didn't hamper her movements or dampen her spirits.

Amory felt safer with Philip at Alzata. The estate was isolated and well-protected by walls, guards, and strong protection spells, and with few people having any reason to go there, Alzata was easier to keep secure. Traveling there in a closed carriage surrounded by a veritable army of guards cut the risk during travel, but Amory sometimes wished they could stay at the estate, just the two of them, until whoever was trying to kill him was found. Unfortunately, they couldn't stay there, hidden away together, for longer than a few days at a time. Those few days probably saved both his and Philip's sanity.

And through those long weeks, there were no further attempts on Amory's life. It should have made him feel better, but it didn't.

"I FOUND out who produced the charm found in the woods," Savarin said with little preamble. Philip liked that about him; he could get straight to the point.

The scene in Philip's office was very similar to the one when Savarin first brought them the charm. Savarin was in the chair across the desk from Philip. Amory was beside Philip again, but he perched on the edge of Philip's desk, twisted to face Savarin.

"And?"

"He makes his living making charms of various types but mostly protection charms. He's extremely skilled at it. His charms are in demand."

"Do we know who bought this one from him?" Amory asked.

"No, Your Highness. He doesn't sell directly to customers," Savarin said. "He supplies two high-end shops in the city with a variety of charms, including a very limited number of the type of charm we found in the woods. We have records of customers and items purchased from one of the shops."

"And the other?" Philip asked.

"The records from the other shop are not as detailed or complete, certainly not as detailed as the law requires with regard to sales of this charm. We were able to obtain a list of customers and lists of items sold, which include when the items were sold. However, they are not matched up with the customers who purchased them." Savarin shook his head in something that might have been disbelief or disgust or both. "Captain Loriot is working through the lists we received to find who purchased these charms."

"Which we won't be able to do with regard to the second shop," Amory said. Philip could hear the frustration mounting in his husband's voice, and he laid a hand on Amory's thigh, hoping to keep Amory calm. Frustration and disappointment dragged at Philip too. He'd hoped the charm would finally provide them with something to point them in the right direction. Something that might end their ordeal.

"No, Your Highness, we won't. However, Captain Loriot will question all of the shop's customers. "

"For whatever that's worth," Philip muttered, but he knew Amory heard him, and Philip thought Savarin did too.

"The other complication, Your Highness, is that the charm may have been purchased from someone who bought the charm legitimately or stolen. There are shops in certain parts of Jumelle dealing in such stolen merchandise. We're looking into those as well."

"Thank you, Savarin."

"You're welcome, Your Highness. I'm sorry I don't have better news. I will continue to help in the investigation in any way I can."

Philip nodded. He was about to dismiss the sorcerer when the man spoke again.

"I do have something to report on the other matter you asked Jadis and me to look into, Your Highnesses. I would like to bring Jadis in as well, if I may."

It took Philip a moment to realize what Savarin was talking about, his mind was so focused on the investigation. He got it as he felt Amory's leg tense under his hand. Philip gave Savarin his assent almost absently and looked up at Amory as the sorcerer walked to the door.

If Savarin was going to get Jadis, it must mean the strange idea of Amory's might work. If the answer was no, Savarin could have told them himself. He could see the same realization in Amory's eyes in a swirling mix of hope and nervousness. Philip had mixed feelings himself. The idea of a child of their own was incredible. But he wasn't sure of it, if it would work, if the risks of it were worth what could come of it. He wasn't certain he wanted it to be possible, despite the powerful allure of a child.

Jadis must have been waiting outside in the corridor, because he followed Savarin back into the room immediately, giving Philip no time to prepare himself for whatever the discussion would bring. Jadis bowed to him and Amory and then took one of the chairs across the desk as Savarin settled back into the chair he'd recently occupied.

"So what do you have to tell us?" Philip asked.

Jadis and Savarin glanced at each other and then turned back to Philip and Amory. It was Savarin who spoke. "We have both studied what Prince Amory found, and we believe the spell could work."

Philip looked up at Amory again, but there was so much in Amory's eyes Philip couldn't decipher it in one glance. He turned back to Jadis and Savarin. "Tell us."

"I'll save you most of the details of the spell, Your Highness. Trust me when I tell you it is extremely complicated and takes real power to cast properly. I can cast the spell. At the same time, Prince Amory— we've been assuming Prince Amory would be the one to carry the child."

"Yes," Amory said. "It would be me."

Savarin nodded. "All right, good. I would perform the spell, and at that time Prince Amory would drink a potion Jadis and I would brew together."

"Like the spell, the potion is complicated. The most complex I've ever seen," Jadis added. "It involves impeccable timing and more ingredients than I've ever heard of in a potion, but we do have access to all of them."

"The spell and potion take two days to work. After that, Prince Amory would be capable of carrying a child. Whenever you choose to try to conceive, Prince Amory will have to drink another potion that will activate the magic of the original spell in his body," Savarin explained.

Philip took a moment to sort through everything Jadis and Savarin had said. He thought about asking for more details of the spell and the potions, but he wasn't a sorcerer. His education in using his odd, and not particularly useful, Talent gave him no context for understanding most sorcery, let alone a spell of what seemed to be abnormal complexity. Instead, he focused on something else.

"You said you assumed Amory would be the one. Does which of us would be the one carrying the child make a difference to the spell?" And didn't it feel odd to talk about one of them carrying a child?

Jadis and Savarin glanced at each other before Jadis answered. "Yes, it does. Amory's healing Talent is the key."

"I barely have a healing Talent," Amory said, but the protest had little heat to it.

"But what you do have is a strong Talent for healing yourself. This is a delicate, complicated spell attempting to do something that does not occur naturally for you. It's changing your body, Amory," the healer explained, his expression serious. "Your Talent for healing yourself makes this possible. It allows the spell to work and ensures your body adapts and remains healthy while the baby is growing. Without that Talent, the spell wouldn't have a chance of success."

Amory nodded, but in the way that said he was thinking about Jadis's words more than agreeing. He was probably trying to filter them through what healing training he had, but Philip was thinking of something else.

"If Amory's healing Talent is important to the spell, does that mean there are substantial risks to him we should know about?" he asked.

"There are risks, of course. There's even a risk the spell won't work, but I don't believe that will be the case," Savarin said.

"If the spell does work and Amory does become with child, there are risks to Amory, as there would be with any pregnancy, but more so with this one," Jadis added. "Any pregnancy can be dangerous to mother and child, but the male body wasn't designed for childbearing so this one could be more difficult or uncomfortable, even painful, than average for Amory as his body accommodates the growing child. There may be some additional fatigue or symptoms because of it, but I believe Amory's healing Talent will keep him healthy while he carries the child."

Philip didn't like the sound of any of that. Jadis might believe Amory's Talent would keep him safe, but the healer didn't know. And Philip couldn't risk Amory. He was about to say so when Amory spoke.

"What about the, uh, birth?"

A good question, one Philip hadn't begun to think about and wasn't sure he wanted to. He was too busy worrying over the risks of the entire endeavor.

"Well, you can't exactly give birth the usual way," Jadis said, but he didn't joke further, probably seeing that Philip, at least, couldn't handle it. "More magic, both sorcery and some healing combined. Aside from the pains letting you know it's time for the birth, the whole thing will be painless."

"Sounds as if I'd have it a lot better than women giving birth then," Amory said, trying for the same teasing tone Jadis used. He smiled down at Philip, inviting him to share the joke, but Philip couldn't.

"I want to discuss the risks Amory would face," he said to the two men across the desk.

Some time and much discussion later, Amory closed the door behind Jadis and Savarin and came back to Philip. Amory perched on the edge of the desk in front of Philip. Amory held out a hand, and Philip slipped his into it, letting the connection ground him.

"So," Amory said, looking into Philip's eyes. "What are you thinking?"

"I'm thinking…." What was he thinking? So many things, but mostly that he couldn't bear to lose Amory. "I don't think we should do this."

"You don't?" Amory looked disappointed? Hurt? "You don't want a child after all?"

"I didn't say that. And I've told you I don't need a direct heir."

"And I thought we were talking about more than an heir. A child." Amory's brow furrowed. "Am I wrong about that?"

He let out a frustrated breath and shoved a hand through his hair. "No, you're not. Of course this is about more than an heir. And it's not that I don't want a child."

"Then what's wrong? Why don't you want to do this?"

"I don't want to do this because I don't want anything to happen to you. Did you hear what they said? This could be dangerous for you."

Amory's face softened. "Pip."

"You could be hurt. You could die. And I can't lose you, love." His grip tightened on Amory's hand. "I can't, not for this, not for anything."

"You won't." Amory cupped Philip's cheek with the hand Philip didn't hold. "You won't lose me. Yes, there are risks, but you heard Jadis. He believes I'll be fine."

"But he doesn't know, and you can't either. No one has done this before, or at least not for so long no one remembers it. Whatever they think, both Jadis and Savarin admit this could be dangerous for you, and I don't want you hurt." He continued before Amory had a chance to do more than open his mouth to reply, "Is it so terrible?"

Amory blinked, thrown off from whatever he'd been about to say. "Is what so terrible?"

"Us. Is it so bad with just us? Would it be so bad if it were just the two of us always?" he asked quietly, almost afraid of what answer he would hear.

Amory stared at him for a moment, his face utterly blank with surprise, then flooded with emotion and aching tenderness. "Of course not, Pip. If I get to spend the rest of my life with you, only with you, it would be more than I could have ever dreamed of having. I love you."

The relief he felt at hearing those words was shocking. He hadn't realized he was so worried until Amory told him there was no need for him to be. "I love you too, so much. You're everything to me. I don't need anything else but you, by my side, forever."

Amory smiled at his words, which even Philip knew were overly sentimental, and leaned forward to kiss Philip gently. After a lingering kiss, Amory sat back and regarded Philip seriously. "I asked you once, but you said you hadn't thought about it, and I'm wondering if you've thought about it since then. Do you want children, Pip? It's all right if you don't. I won't be angry."

He had no doubt Amory wouldn't be angry with him, but Amory might be disappointed if he wanted children himself. It didn't change the answer either way. "It's not that, love. I have thought about it—I could hardly not think about it after our conversation—and the idea of a child with you is an appealing one. But it doesn't negate the very real risks to you. Aren't you worried at all?"

"I am. I heard everything Jadis and Savarin said, and yes, I worry about the risks." Amory bit his lip. "And beyond them, I'm scared at the very thought of what I'm proposing I do. The idea is strange and… and not quite right, but I want to do it."

"Why?"

"Because it would be our child, Philip, together. Not your heir, but our child, and I think you would be such a good father."

It almost hurt seeing the love and belief in Amory's eyes. "I think you would too. But that doesn't change how dangerous this is for you."

"Jadis and Savarin are the best there are, and they believe I'll be fine. You trust them."

"I don't trust anyone when it comes to your life. I've nearly lost you more than once recently, love." The thought sent pain lancing through him, something of which must have shown.

"Oh, Pip." Amory leaned close and kissed him again, then rested his forehead against Philip's. "Do you trust me?"

"Yes, of course."

"Then trust that I do not want to leave you, and I wouldn't do anything I believed would lead to your losing me. There are risks when women have babies. Perhaps they're greater for a man, but I trust Jadis when he tells me my healing Talent will keep me healthy while I carry our child." An odd look came over Amory's face. "It sounds strange to say it."

"It sounds strange hearing it too." He studied Amory. "You really want to do this?"

"I do. And not only because you do need an heir, whatever you say about it. I never expected to want anything like this. I never thought about children before you, but I would like a child with you. Our child." Amory's eyes were serious, but a soft, gentle smile curved his lips. "But only if you want to. We don't have to have a child, or we can wait a while if you're not sure or not ready. You have to want it too, if we're going to do this."

He looked at Amory, waiting so patiently for Philip's answer, whatever it turned out to be. And if Philip didn't give Amory the answer he hoped for, Philip knew it would be all right. In that moment, he loved

Amory even more than he had before, something he hadn't thought possible.

He'd never thought of children either, not as anything more than the heir he was duty-bound to produce. But he could suddenly see a child with Amory's eyes and dark curls flopping over his forehead and Amory's sweet smile. He could see their child running through the gardens of Alzata and laughing while he and Amory watched. Maybe while Amory sketched. A stunning picture.

Staring into Amory's eyes, Philip felt a smile spread across his face.

AMORY HAD assumed that even if Philip wanted a child, he would want them to wait. Perhaps he thought so because of Philip's initial reluctance and concerns about the spell or perhaps because of the danger to Amory from the attempts on his life. Whatever the reason, he never expected Philip to agree he wanted their child and then want the spell performed as soon as possible. Yet Philip did exactly that.

Amory could tell just looking at his husband that Philip was still worried, and he resolved not to pressure Philip about trying to have a child. Savarin and Jadis would perform the spell, but it would need a few days to take effect. Afterward Philip and Amory could try to get Amory with child whenever they liked, but they didn't have to do it immediately. The spell was permanent so they could wait as long as they liked.

The potion had taken Jadis and Savarin five days to brew. Which gave him five days to worry and think, even though he knew worrying made no sense. He didn't regret the decision to go forward with the spell, and he trusted Savarin and Jadis. The spell wasn't even the potentially dangerous part. And still anxiety made his whole body tense.

Amory stood in the center of Savarin's workroom while Savarin wove the spell, trying not to fidget. He'd been told to stay still, whether for the actual spell or for Savarin's concentration, he didn't know, but he supposed it didn't matter. Philip had insisted on coming with him, and he leaned against one of the unadorned walls of the workroom, out of the way but very much present. Philip's gaze never wavered from Amory, and Amory was so grateful for it. Ignoring whatever Savarin was chanting, Amory held Philip's gaze, letting the love and support he saw there soothe him through the spell.

The magic was so powerful even Amory with his limited Talent could feel it buzzing in the air around him. The intensity of the magic increased with each passing moment, more and more, higher and higher. Suddenly, the hairs on the back of his neck stood up straight. The magic swept through him in a cold rush, swamping his entire body and leaving odd, tingling sensations in its wake. His eyes widened, and he drew in a sharp breath, but he forced himself to stay still otherwise. Philip stood straighter, concern flooding his face, but Amory stared at him, trying to convey that he was all right. Philip couldn't interrupt. Amory didn't need him to; the sensations weren't painful, just uncomfortable. He almost expected pain with a spell that would have such a monumental effect on him. He wasn't upset to be wrong.

After what felt like a very long time, the sorcerer fell silent. The cold tingles raced through Amory's body, crawling over his skin, but he did his best not to react, hoping not to scare Philip further. Jadis stepped forward and offered Amory a cup.

"Drink all of this straight down."

The potion was a deep shade of blue and seemed viscous. He wondered what was in it, but it was probably best he not know. He looked back up at Philip and downed the contents of the cup in one go.

He managed to swallow without gagging, but it took some effort. "That is vile."

A wave of dread swept through him in the wake of his thoughtless pronouncement. He worried he had ruined the entire spellcasting by disrupting Savarin's concentration, but Jadis laughed.

"I know, but there's nothing to be done about it," Jadis said. "Give it a moment, and then you can have some water."

Philip bit his lip, amusement crinkling the corners of his eyes. Amory aimed a sour look in his direction, which didn't help Philip's efforts to keep from laughing any, but he couldn't hold on to the disgruntled expression for long. He loved seeing Philip that way, smiling and mischievous, even if the reaction came at Amory's expense. Philip grinned at him.

He was so distracted by Philip and his brilliant smile it took him a moment to realize the tingles were beginning to subside. Gradually, the strange sensations lessened and faded away. Savarin peered at him intensely for a few moments and nodded, plainly satisfied by whatever he saw. Jadis handed Amory a glass of water, which he drank with gratitude.

Jadis and Savarin stepped back as Philip came to Amory and took him in his arms. Amory melted into the embrace, overwhelmed. The experience hadn't been painful, but it had shaken him nonetheless. He'd never experienced anything like what he just went through, and the spell marked the beginning of something he could hardly imagine doing even after long consideration.

"All right?" Philip asked.

He pulled back enough to look into Philip's eyes, to see the unconditional love and support there again. "Yes."

"Good." Philip pressed a gentle, chaste kiss to his lips.

When they separated, though not by much, Jadis and Savarin came forward again. Jadis handed Amory a stoppered glass bottle filled with pale green liquid. "Your other potion."

The one he would have to drink if he and Philip wanted to try for a child. The thought created a flutter of nerves in his stomach, but he didn't want Jadis or Savarin to see his reaction. "Does it taste as bad as the last one?"

Jadis shook his head in admonishment as Philip laughed. "Well, it's not going to taste like sweets, Your Highness, but it should be better than the other."

"That's a relief, but I'm not sure anything could be worse than that last potion." He turned to a grinning Philip. "It really was awful."

CHAPTER 15

"You—you really want to? Now?"

"Yes."

Amory hadn't looked away from the glass bottle and its pale green contents since Philip walked back into the room and set it on the table next to him. Amory was frozen staring at it, so different from his relaxed posture while they'd been sipping wine in front of the fire a moment before. Philip began to wonder if he had done something wrong by suggesting they try to conceive that night.

Finally, Amory looked at him, his eyes large and bewildered. "I didn't think you would want to do this so soon. You didn't want to at all not long ago."

He sat next to Amory on the couch. "It's not that I didn't want to, that I didn't want a child with you. I was scared something would happen to you. I'm still scared, love, but you're willing to take this risk for us, and you believe it's going to be all right. And I trust you."

"All right. But even so, I'd think you would want to wait until we find whoever is… whoever is trying to kill me."

Philip hurt hearing the slight tremble in Amory's voice. Amory was so strong, but Philip knew he was scared. Philip was too. He slid an arm around Amory and pulled him close against Philip's side. "I thought about it, and we can wait if you want. But I'm not going to let him get close to you again. I'm not going to let him hurt you. And we can't let him keep us from living our lives."

Amory was quiet for a long while, just looking at him, and Philip wondered again if he had done the wrong thing. Maybe with the threats to Amory's life trying to have a child was too much. Maybe he should have waited.

Just as Philip's worries began to get the better of him, Amory leaned forward, bridging the small amount of space separating them, and brushed a gentle kiss over Philip's lips. Then Amory pulled out of Philip's arms. Philip's relief at the kiss drained away, and he opened his mouth to take back the idea altogether.

But Amory pulled away only far enough to turn to the bottle on the table. He unstoppered it and poured a dose into his empty wine glass, his hands trembling slightly. Turning back to Philip, Amory gulped down the pale green liquid.

Philip almost laughed at the way Amory wrinkled his nose. "How does it taste?"

Amory frowned, looking as if he was seriously considering the question. "Bitter, but not quite as bad as the first one."

"Well, I suppose that's good."

"I guess so." Amory smiled. "We're really doing this."

He cupped Amory's cheek. "Only if you want to."

"I do." Amory kissed him again, lingering before pulling back and laughing. "I'm nervous. I don't know why. I shouldn't be."

He stroked his thumb across Amory's cheek, back and forth. "I am too, but it's all right."

Amory nodded. "Bed, then?"

They walked into the bedchamber together and turned to each other when they reached the side of the bed. Neither of them moved for a long moment. Amory looked almost helpless when he met Philip's eyes, and Philip was shocked at how awkward they were. It had never been awkward between them, not even at the beginning.

"This is so strange. I don't know what to do. I didn't feel this way when I really didn't know what to do."

Philip laughed at that, and Amory did too, a real laugh. Hearing it loosened something inside Philip he hadn't realized had tightened up. "All right, here's what we're going to do."

Amory nodded, both expectant and trusting.

"We're going to forget there's anything different about tonight." He shook his head when Amory opened his mouth. "Trust me. Let everything else go. It's you and me together. Nothing else matters."

He kissed Amory, long and deep, before he could reply, and when he broke the kiss, his tense muscles were beginning to relax and so were Amory's. He ran his fingers through Amory's soft curling hair. "Bed?"

"Yes."

They undressed each other slowly and climbed into their bed, slipping beneath the blankets because of the chill in the air. Philip pulled Amory close, savoring the feel of Amory's body against his own, of his soft skin under Philip's hands. He forced himself to forget what the result of the night could be and to let himself be consumed by all that was Amory. They kissed for a long time, drowning in those kisses, as they used to at the beginning when kissing was all they did. Only there would be more than kissing tonight.

Amory explored him with lingering caresses of his long-fingered artist's hands, sending shivering heat through Philip's body. It made him want more and everything and now. He eagerly returned the touches, the kisses, delighting in Amory's every moan and sigh.

After a while, the gentle explorations weren't enough, and Amory reached for the oil they kept at the bedside. He pressed it into Philip's hands and urged Philip over him. But, as much as he wanted more, as much as he wanted to be inside Amory, Philip wasn't quite ready for it to be over. Amory was laid out before him and so beautiful. Philip had to spend more time kissing and touching him, loving him with hands and mouth. How had he gotten so lucky to find someone like Amory, someone who loved him so much, who gladly took on his burdens? Someone who did everything for Philip's happiness, including finding a way to give him a child. And how he wanted to make Amory happy, happier than he had ever been. If his gaze became filled with something like awe, if his hands moved over Amory in a way that could only be described as reverent, well, Amory deserved to be worshipped.

After a while, he used the oil to slick his fingers and slid one slowly into Amory, enjoying the sweet little whimper he made. For the longest time, he moved that one finger, forcing himself to go slow, arousing without urgency. And loving how Amory writhed beneath him. But it couldn't go on forever. Their awkwardness might have melted away in leisurely kisses and touches, but urgency reared up to take its place.

When he finally pushed into Amory, they both moaned. After a moment to savor the feeling of being tightly held inside Amory, Philip began to move, spurred on by Amory's gasps and moans and the way Amory wrapped himself around Philip and held on with all he had. But Philip wanted more and closer. As much as he'd said they should forget there was anything different about that night, there was something different, something special that could come from it.

He pulled out of Amory and sat back.

"Pip, what—" Amory's question turned into a gasp as Philip flipped him over onto his stomach and pushed back inside slowly. He draped himself over Amory's back, tucking his chin over Amory's shoulder.

"Yes," Amory whispered and took Philip's hands, tangling their fingers together, connecting them even further. Philip murmured his agreement and began to move in long, slow strokes that took them spiraling into pleasure.

Later, they snuggled together under the covers, drowsy and sated. Amory nestled his head into the curve of Philip's neck, making him smile. How had he ever slept without Amory's warmth pressed against him?

"Do you think it worked?" Amory asked, his voice sleepy.

"I don't know." But even if it hadn't, the night had been perfect.

TWO DAYS later, they found out it had, in fact, worked. Jadis could tell with a simple use of his Talent that Amory was with child. It only took a moment or two, and he left Amory and Philip as soon as he delivered the news.

Philip looked as stunned as Amory felt at the healer's pronouncement. He'd wondered over the last couple of days if he could use his own Talent to find out if he was with child, but he hadn't tried. Maybe he'd been a little afraid to know either way.

He and Philip stared at each other in silence for long moments. Emotion tangled and tumbled in Amory, a jumble of too many feelings. Surprise, yes, a little fear, something odd and unnameable at the idea that he was carrying a child inside of him. And an almost overwhelming joy.

The same joy lit Philip's eyes, and they grinned, falling into each other's arms. Then they were laughing and kissing, and it was only when he tasted salt that he realized he was crying, but he didn't care, because Philip was crying too. After the tears stopped, they clung together. Amory let the joy and fear wash through him as he buried his face in Philip's neck, inhaling Philip's comforting, familiar scent. They were having a child.

The last weeks of winter passed almost mundanely into spring after that momentous event. No one knew of the baby except him, Philip, Jadis, and Savarin. Amory and Philip discussed it at length and decided they would wait to tell anyone Amory was with child. With a threat hanging over Amory's head, with not knowing how to tell everyone, waiting was best. And even though neither of them spoke of it, Amory knew they were both worried about the risks of Amory carrying a child.

The calendar filled with social engagements in late winter and early spring. Elodie was in her element at each and every one, glowing all the more because she was often attended by Vasco's brother, Faron. Vasco and the rest of his family were usually present, as were some of Philip's cousins. Cathal's attitude seemed to be softening, but he was still a little cool toward Amory. He thought Cathal's embarrassment over his previous behavior caused him to keep his distance, but Amory remained most comfortable with Etan out of Philip's cousins. Adeline's wedding ushered in the spring. Amory found it laughable how puffed up Arnau was throughout the ceremony, but Adeline was happy, which was all Amory wanted.

Through it all, he became all the happier with their decision not to tell anyone about the baby. He was still learning to accept his own condition. Jadis hadn't lied about the potential physical discomfort. Fatigue dragged at him. Minor nausea plagued him in the mornings during the first couple of months, and there were strange aches and soreness in his muscles as his body came to accommodate the growing baby inside him. But the mental discomfort bothered him the most. There were times he could not understand how he was a man who was with child. Even though the idea had been his, it seemed wrong. But when those thoughts surfaced, or when the physical discomfort increased, he reminded himself what he was going through it for—their child, his and Philip's, and he wanted that child.

Philip wanted the child too, which became more apparent each day. Philip worried about Amory, but he was plainly happy, smiling a small, secretive smile and brushing his fingers over Amory's stomach often. Gentle and filled with wonder. Amory found it odd at first, but it was nice, that little touch. Different, really, because the gesture wasn't about Amory as Philip's other touches were, but about the child inside him as well.

Not that there was any outward indication of the child, not for months anyway, until there suddenly was. While dressing one morning, he realized there was a slight curve to what had once been his flat abdomen. He stopped, shirt dangling from the fingers of one hand as he rested his other on the small bump. He examined his reflection in the large mirror in their dressing room, surprised by the change. He shouldn't have been. Intellectually, he knew the change was coming, and yet... he hadn't expected it, not truly. And he wasn't sure how he felt about it. Part of him recoiled at the sight, but part was elated at the tangible sign his child was healthy and growing, making the fatigue and pain worth it. The turmoil kept him paralyzed in front of the mirror.

Philip appeared behind him. Amory watched in the mirror as Philip studied Amory's reflection and then placed his hand over Amory's. The warm weight of Philip's palm over his was reassuring in ways Amory almost couldn't comprehend.

"Are you all right?" Philip asked, perceptive as always.

"Yes." He would be.

Philip kissed Amory's temple. "I suppose we'll have to think about new clothes soon."

That was something he wasn't quite ready for. He pulled on his shirt and tunic and tied the cloth belt looser around his waist. "We'll have to think about telling people."

Philip's expression became thoughtful. "Do you think we should? Tell people?"

Even though he'd said it, Amory didn't know how to answer Philip. "I—I don't think I'm ready for everyone to know."

"Not everyone. Maybe a few people close to us to start." Philip pulled Amory against him, his hands rubbing up and down Amory's back in a way that instantly soothed.

They should. Elodie and Adeline certainly, Etan and Tristan too. It was time, even if Amory didn't feel ready. He sighed and nodded.

He and Philip decided to tell them together, all at once, but as they stood in front of their friends and family, Amory wasn't certain they'd made the right decision. Perhaps they should have told them each on their own. When Philip finished speaking, the group stared. Amory would have laughed at the blank shock on their faces if he weren't so worried about what they would say once the shock wore off. Philip held Amory's hand tightly—Amory wasn't sure if it was for Philip's comfort or his own, but he took it either way.

"You're not joking, are you?" Etan asked, breaking the silence after what felt like an eternity.

"No, we're not." Philip glanced at Amory and back to Etan.

"I didn't think so, not with a story like that." Etan smiled, but he still looked more than a little dazed. "You're having a child. Unbelievable."

Tristan shook his head. "The things you get yourself into, Amory. I can't even imagine."

"It's amazing." Adeline's laugh was surprised but delighted, and she jumped up from her seat beside Elodie to hug Amory. He wrapped his free arm around her, so grateful tears came to his eyes. He blinked them away before anyone saw.

"It really is. But I still can't imagine it," Tristan said.

Etan nodded. "I can't either, but I'm very happy for you both."

Tristan and Etan gathered around and there were more hugs, and Amory felt the knot of fear and anxiety loosening inside him. It might be all right. Until Philip looked back toward the couch.

"Elodie?"

She'd risen but hadn't moved farther than that, her hands clenched in front of her. "You didn't tell me."

"We're telling you now," Philip said.

"But you didn't tell me before. It's been months, and I had no idea." Elodie stamped her foot, and Amory braced himself. He knew the signs of Elodie winding herself up into one of her occasional tantrums. She was a sweet girl, but the tantrums came at the oddest moments for the strangest reasons. "I'm your sister."

"Yes, and Adeline is Amory's sister, and we're telling you both now." Philip's voice was calm and patient, but Amory could feel the tension in his frame just standing next to him.

"But you should have told me before. You should have told me when you made the decision. I had no idea you were thinking about this. I didn't know it was possible. You should have told me."

Amory tried not to wince as Elodie's voice became increasingly shrill. He couldn't understand why she was so angry. As much as he loved Elodie, she had no part of their decision to have a child.

"Elodie, calm down. Now." Philip's firm tone was overly patient, which showed how little patience he had left. "There was no reason to tell you then. It was our decision, mine and Amory's alone. We've told you now we know that Amory and the baby are well, and we hope you'll be happy for us."

Elodie stared at Philip for a long moment. The rest of them were silent as well, Etan, Tristan, and Adeline standing awkwardly by. Amory couldn't blame them. He wished he weren't there. Elodie's angry expression melted into a pout.

"Of course I'm happy for you," she said, her tone a bit grudging, but knowing Elodie, she would calm down and be enthusiastic by tomorrow.

Amory supposed it could have gone worse.

THERE HAD been no attempts on Amory's life in the months since their return from their wedding trip. Far from calming Philip's anxiety, the waiting and lack of information only made it worse, especially given Amory was with child. He assumed the new security measures were helping, that their unknown enemy was having trouble getting to Amory. The thought gave him some satisfaction but no comfort. He couldn't believe whoever wanted to kill Amory would give up.

He was almost relieved when they received information through Savarin that someone was trying to hire a sorcerer to kill Amory, presumably having little luck getting close to Amory any other way. Philip had hoped the information would lead them to their enemy, but it seemed he found out somehow and went to ground. Philip was enraged, but he tried to calm himself for Amory's sake. Amory was frustrated and angry and despairing in a way that scared Philip, and Amory needed to stay calm, or as calm as possible, for his health and the health of the child.

At least they thwarted their enemy's search. If they wanted a sorcerer of any skill and power, they would have to go outside Tournai. Not impossible, but much more difficult. Savarin was discreetly contacting sorcerers he knew outside Tournai to warn them, hoping to make it even more difficult.

But they went on, as if they weren't worrying constantly, as if Philip wasn't scared all the worrying would affect Amory and the child he carried. At times he wondered if they should have waited until Amory was safe again to have a child. He'd thought it best to continue their lives as normally as possible. But seeing the strain on Amory sometimes... he wondered.

Not that Amory let the strain show, at least not to anyone except Philip. That night, at Elodie's birthday ball, he was the epitome of a gracious prince, socializing and dancing with Philip. Amory had to be tired and anxious, but he didn't look it. He glowed, the most beautiful thing Philip had ever seen. Philip couldn't keep himself from touching Amory, holding his hand, resting a hand low on his back, or even putting an arm around him. He managed somehow not to touch the slight curve to Amory's abdomen, hidden under cleverly worn clothes, but he fought the temptation to do so all the time. He was drawn to it, the physical evidence of their child.

"Sit for a while?" he asked Amory as he led him off the dance floor.

Amory gave him a look that said he knew perfectly well what Philip was doing, trying to get Amory off his feet. But he didn't protest, which told Philip he was correct about Amory feeling tired, maybe sore. "For a little while. And maybe something to drink."

Somehow they both acquired glasses of wine punch as they made their way back to their thrones through the crowd. Another dance began behind them, and Philip smiled to hear Elodie's laughter. She was enjoying herself. He didn't delude himself into thinking her happiness didn't have something to do with Faron's attention, but he knew it didn't stem entirely from that.

Etan was standing near the thrones with Tristan, the two in some sort of conversation to the exclusion of everyone around them, which they broke off to greet Philip and Amory. Philip caught the mischief in Amory's eyes when he looked at the other two men, but Amory hid what would probably have been a smirk behind his glass.

"Ugh." Amory jerked the cup away from his face.

Philip moved closer in concern. "Amory?"

"The smell of something in here is making me sick."

Philip saw the signs—the slight green tinge to Amory's skin, the rapid breaths through his mouth. He'd seen it before, often early in Amory's pregnancy. Then, there had been little chance of Amory keeping the nausea at bay, and Philip could do nothing but hold Amory and try to soothe him, feeling helpless. He had been as relieved as Amory when the nausea began to subside. These days, Amory was seldom sick. When he was, the illness came mostly in response to some sort of smell. The smell of mushrooms made Amory ill every time, so Philip banned their preparation in the palace. Apparently the wine punch was another.

"Here, give it to me," Etan said, stepping forward and taking the glass from Amory as Philip sniffed at his own glass. Wine, spices, fruit. "I'll drink it."

"Thank you." Amory leaned back in his chair, fighting not only to get the nausea under control, but to not look ill in the middle of a ball.

Philip set his own glass aside, away from Amory, and took his hand. "Are you all right? Do you need to leave? Lie down for a while?"

Amory shook his head but continued to take slow breaths. "I'll be all right in a moment. I don't—"

The sound of glass shattering interrupted Amory. They both turned in time to see Etan fall to his knees, gagging and coughing, his hands clutching at his throat.

"Etan?" Tristan dropped to the ground next to Etan. "Etan?"

Philip and Amory scrambled down to Etan's other side as the man began to convulse. Amory laid a hand on Etan's chest and gasped sharply. "He's been poisoned. Someone get Jadis." He shouted the last sentence to be heard over the music and voices.

Philip glanced at the broken glass and the deep red liquid spreading over the marble floor. Etan had drunk from that glass, Amory's glass. Philip's whole body turned to ice as he looked at Amory. He saw the same knowledge in Amory's eyes, but Amory resolutely turned back to Etan, laying his hands on Etan's chest. It took a moment for Philip to realize what Amory was doing, but then he grabbed for Amory's arms.

"Pip, stop."

"No. You can't do this. You could hurt yourself. You could hurt—you know what could happen if you use your Talent right now, in your condition." He kept his voice low, especially for those last few words, but made it no less forceful for that. He couldn't let Amory use his Talent and put himself and their child in jeopardy.

"I have to. He's been poisoned. I don't know what with, but it's strong." Amory looked at him, his eyes wide and frightened but determined too. "If I don't do something, I don't think he'll live long enough for Jadis to get here."

A bolt of fear for his cousin shot through Philip, and he hesitated, but his fear for Amory was equally as great. "And if you kill yourself?"

"That poison was meant for me."

Philip knew it, but he didn't want to examine the knowledge too closely yet. "That doesn't mean you should kill yourself. This isn't your fault."

Amory stubbornly shook his head and focused on Etan, ignoring Philip's continuing pleas. Philip watched as color leached from Amory's face, as his hands began to tremble. When pain tightened Amory's face, Philip decided pulling Amory away from Etan was what he would have to do. He wrapped his arms around Amory, and careful of the baby, began to gently tug Amory back.

"No, don't—"

"Amory, stop now and move away." Jadis dropped to the floor on the other side of Etan, another healer following him. "I can take care of Lord Etan."

Amory allowed Philip to pull him away and collapsed into Philip's lap, his head coming to rest on Philip's shoulder, his eyes fluttering shut.

"Amory?" He could hear the fear in his own voice. Amory's mumbled reply did little to calm him, especially since Amory didn't open his eyes. He cradled Amory in his arms, one hand resting protectively over Amory's stomach, over the child growing there. "Jadis?"

"Yes, Your Highness." Jadis gestured for the other healer to continue treating Etan, and reached forward to lay a hand on Amory's forehead. Jadis's expression fell into disapproving lines, and he left his hand on Amory's head for a few moments before sitting back. "He overextended himself. Used too much of his Talent."

"Will he be all right?" Philip asked.

"Yes. He's lucky. Let's get him to bed." Jadis looked to the other healer who was working under Tristan's hovering presence. "Elio?"

The man glanced up. "We can move him."

"Good."

Philip refused help and lifted his husband into his arms. Amory would be mortified when he found out. As he straightened with his precious burden, he realized the guards had moved the crowd back and away from the small group on the floor, for which he was grateful. He hadn't thought to order it. He instructed several to stay behind to wait for Captain Loriot while the rest accompanied him and Amory back to their suite. His orders were more terse than usual, but he couldn't begin to care. He swept from the room with Amory in his arms.

By the time he'd laid Amory carefully on their bed, his mind was whirling. He loosened Amory's clothing and removed his shoes with gentle hands. Jadis came up beside him. "Your Highness, why don't you step out of the room for a moment? I'm going to examine Amory more thoroughly and then do what I can to bolster his strength and the power of his healing Talent until he can rebuild it himself."

"I don't want to leave him."

"For a moment, please, Your Highness."

He hesitated, torn. Jadis needed space to work, but everything in Philip rebelled at the idea of leaving Amory right now, of leaving him alone and unprotected. He nodded. "For a moment."

"Thank you."

He left the bedchamber reluctantly and crossed the sitting room to the bedchamber that once belonged to Amory, where Etan had been brought at Philip's orders. Etan lay pale and still in the bed, his face damp with sweat, as the healer mixed something in a cup on the bedside table. Tristan sat in a chair near the window, well out of the way, but everything about him yearned for the bed and the man in it. Despite his worry for Amory, Philip crossed the room and laid a hand on Tristan's shoulder. A shudder went through Tristan's body.

"The healer was able to halt the progression of the poison," Tristan said, his eyes never leaving Etan. "He's mixing an antidote now."

"It's a complicated one," Elio said absently as he worked. "The poison is very rare. If I hadn't made a study of poisons and their antidotes, I never would have recognized it."

"So the average healer wouldn't have been able to save Etan?" Wouldn't have been able to save Amory, but Philip didn't say that.

"Possibly not. Probably not. I don't want to sound arrogant, but most people wouldn't have been able to identify the poison, let alone treat the victim."

Tristan tore his gaze away from Etan to look up at Philip. "Your Highness?"

He realized his fingers were digging into Tristan's shoulder. "I'm sorry, Tristan."

"It doesn't matter, Your Highness. The poison… it was meant for Amory."

He nodded. Hearing the words spoken so starkly in the silent room froze everything in Philip. Oh, he knew what Tristan said was true, had known from the moment Etan was poisoned, but hearing it so plainly stated was almost too much. He couldn't remember who had handed them the glasses of punch. Had his own drink been poisoned as well? No way of knowing, but Amory's had been poisoned and Etan was paying the price. He was silent for long moments, feeling Tristan's concerned gaze on him but unable to respond as he tried to pull himself together.

"Yes," he finally said. "I'm going back to Amory."

"I…."

He took pity on Tristan, who couldn't admit how much he wanted to be there, maybe even to himself. "Why don't you stay here with Etan? Let me know if you or he need anything."

"Thank you, Your Highness."

Philip strode from the room and back across the sitting room. He stepped into his bedchamber in time to hear Jadis lecturing Amory. "You cannot do this, Amory. Your Talent is being used now to keep you healthy while you carry this child, to keep your body from being harmed while the child grows, and to sustain the womb your child is growing in. Your Talent is the only thing making it possible for you to carry a healthy child to term. If you use it for other things, your powers are depleted and can no longer keep you healthy. Do you understand me?"

"Yes." Amory's reply was so low Philip almost didn't hear it.

Jadis sighed. "Amory, I know you wanted to help Lord Etan, and you did, but you need to think about the consequences for you and your child when you act. You cannot use your Talent for anything else until this child is born."

Philip stepped into the room. "Please, listen to him, Amory."

Amory looked at him from where he lay against the pillows. Philip was happy to see a little color in his cheeks, but Amory was still far too pale and drawn. "I will."

"Good." He went to the bed and sat next to Amory. "You terrified me."

"I'm sorry."

"Please don't do it again." He leaned down and brushed a kiss over Amory's lips. He straightened after but kept an arm around Amory, holding him close. Amory didn't object, snuggling in against Philip's side. He must have been exhausted to do that so easily with another person in the room. "How is Amory?"

Jadis didn't pretend he hadn't been listening to them. "He's going to be fine, but I'm insisting he stay in bed for at least a few days, possibly as long as a week, depending how quickly his energy returns. I can't say for certain because I've never had a patient in his condition before."

"He stays in bed for as long as you deem necessary," Philip said before Amory could argue. He choked back a laugh when Amory huffed beside him.

"Etan?" Amory asked.

"The healer is preparing the antidote now." He looked at Jadis. "He said it's a very rare poison, one that most wouldn't know the antidote for."

Jadis nodded. "I'm not surprised. Using something common and easily counteracted wouldn't be smart."

"No," Philip agreed, his voice even, despite the fear coursing through him in waves. He tightened his arm around Amory.

"Might I suggest you both begin using tasters, Your Highness?" Jadis asked. "Somehow this person got into the palace and managed to poison a drink meant for one of you. It might be safer to have someone tasting your food from now on."

Amory stiffened beside him. He could imagine Amory's horror at the suggestion. In many ways, he shared it, which was why he didn't use tasters, but with Amory's safety in the balance, he was tempted to change his policy. But he might have a better idea.

After Jadis left the room to check on Etan, Philip slid farther down on the bed, and despite the blankets tangled between them, Amory turned and curled into Philip's body. He buried his face in Amory's hair, breathing in his scent, reassuring himself that Amory and their child were all right.

"I really am sorry," Amory whispered.

"I know. And I know why you did it, but please don't scare me again."

"I'll try."

They didn't talk for a long time after. Philip let himself relax, Amory warm and safe in his arms in the dim room. He ran his hands up and down Amory's back, tracing his spine and sweeping over firm muscles. At first, Amory made pleased little noises, but after a while he fell silent, and Philip began to think he'd fallen asleep, probably the best thing for him. He was startled when Amory spoke, his voice low and scared.

"What are we going to do?"

"We're going to Alzata."

CHAPTER 16

CONTRARY TO their hopes, almost two weeks passed before they left for Alzata. Amory was confined to his bed for a week recovering. Philip expected him to begin complaining around the third day, but Amory didn't. He slept much of the first few days and took his orders to continue to rest in bed for the remainder of the week gracefully. Philip would have been terrified at such out-of-character behavior if Jadis hadn't told him Amory was improving. Nevertheless, Jadis advised them to wait before making the short trip to Alzata.

The delay wasn't wasted time. Philip had affairs to put in order before he left, because this trip wasn't going to be a short one. He and Amory would stay there until whoever was trying to kill Amory was caught. The security was better at Alzata than at the palace, so Amory would be safer, especially after the security increases Philip ordered. Captain Loriot and Savarin collaborated to make sure Alzata's physical and magical defenses were as strong as they could be before Amory took up residence.

Philip also spent a lot of time coordinating how he was going to rule the country from Alzata without moving anyone else from his government there. He and Amory trusted few people outside their close circle of friends. Etan would be able to help when he was well again, able to stand in for Philip for many things at the palace and trusted to come to Alzata with matters Philip needed to see to, but Philip would have to make the trip back and forth from Alzata often. He would take on the additional travel because he could not send Amory away alone.

He could have used Etan's help with the preparations, but Etan was confined to bed, weak but recovering well under Tristan's watchful eye. The man had hardly left Etan's side since the poisoning, but Philip was beginning to wonder if they would ever admit to feelings other than friendship for each other. Cathal arrived back at the palace, both to see his brother and to again offer his services to Philip. That Amory was with child was no longer a secret, and while Philip's family was shocked, many of them were also awed at what Amory was doing for Philip and Tournai.

Their attitudes seemed to be softening somewhat at the imminent arrival of an heir, but Philip wasn't ready to trust them again, even Cathal. He accepted Cathal's help in the palace, but he wouldn't be inviting him out to Alzata yet.

Living at Alzata was an adjustment for both Philip and Amory, but also a welcome change. The constant threat, the uncertainty when or where their enemy might strike next, had worn on both of them these past months. While the move seemed at first like one more disruption, it turned out to be a relief. Amory felt safer at Alzata, and Philip worried a little less with them there.

He also enjoyed—loved—the time alone with Amory while he carried their child. As weeks passed and the pregnancy become more obvious, Philip found it almost impossible to be away from Amory for too long or to keep from touching him and his stomach. They couldn't spend their entire lives hiding away from the rest of the world there, and he knew Amory only agreed to stay because of the baby. But Savarin and Captain Loriot continued to investigate, and Philip believed they would succeed in hunting down their quarry. Until they did, he chose to look at the nearly uninterrupted time with Amory as a gift.

Because any time spent with Amory was a gift.

He leaned in the doorway to the bathing room, watching Amory lying in bed shirtless, one hand resting on the bump of his stomach. Amory's eyes were closed, but Philip could tell he wasn't sleeping. Philip wondered if the baby was moving. He wanted to lay his hand over Amory's, but he also wanted to keep watching.

"Looking at me?" Amory asked, his eyes still closed.

"I am."

"And liking what you see?" The words were flirtatious, but the vulnerability beneath the teasing tone was obvious. Amory had a difficult time believing Philip found him attractive with his body changing in ways he never thought it could or would. Philip wanted to soothe away his uncertainty more than anything.

"Always have."

Amory's lips curved in a smile, and he opened his eyes to look at Philip. "Come show me?"

He went to the bed, sliding in next to Amory. Reaching for Amory, filling his hands with smooth warm skin, as he covered Amory's smiling lips with his own.

"YOU'RE GOING back to Alzata to be with Amory tonight, aren't you?" Elodie asked.

"Yes, as soon as I finish up what I need to do here." Which couldn't happen quickly enough. He hadn't wanted to leave Amory at all that morning, and he wouldn't have if it weren't for a meeting with the ambassadors from Amaranta and Elleri that shouldn't be rescheduled. And still, he'd considered sending a messenger to cancel the meetings. Amory had been so tired that day, their continuing inability to figure out who wanted Amory killed taking its toll on his husband in conjunction with the strain on his body.

"Can I go to Alzata with you?" Elodie asked eagerly. "I can be packed and ready to leave when you are."

Philip stifled a sigh. He hated to refuse his sister, but what she proposed wasn't a good idea. "I'm sorry, but not this time, El."

"Why not? I want to see Amory, and the weather has been so nice. It would be fun to spend some time in the garden there."

"Spend some time in the garden here. It's bigger, and you always said you liked it better than the one at Alzata."

"No, I didn't. I like it fine there, and you and Amory are there." Her face was set in stubborn lines, but at least she didn't stamp her foot.

"Amory hasn't been feeling well. He isn't up to visitors right now." He kept talking before she could protest. "I'm sorry, Elodie, but it isn't a good idea. I'll take you to visit another time. Besides, weren't you talking about a couple of parties this week? You don't want to miss those. You were excited."

"I was, but…."

"And Faron is right over there. In fact, he's walking toward us right now."

Elodie's eyes widened, and then a bright smile spread over her face. Philip let relief wash through him. When he walked away a few moments later, Elodie and Faron were deep in conversation. Conversation with Faron would distract Elodie nicely.

AMORY WAS puzzled. He strode down the hallway, or he sort of did. He could feel the way he walked and balanced changing as the small bump of his stomach became more obvious, and it felt decidedly odd. He wouldn't have thought such a change would happen so soon. But that wasn't causing his confusion at the moment. He was puzzled because he'd been informed that Elodie had arrived at Alzata.

When he came to the stairs leading down into the large entrance hall, she was walking through the front door, surrounded by her ladies and Lady Lilliale, a flurry of curls and spring-colored gowns. He wanted to droop just looking at them. He was tempted to turn back around and go hide. He walked down the stairs instead.

"Hello, Amory," Elodie called out as soon as she saw him, with a delighted laugh and a clap of her hands.

"Hello, Elodie. What are you doing here? Where's Philip?" He looked around as he descended the last few steps, but his husband wasn't in sight.

"I came to visit you, silly. Philip was still at the palace when we left, but I'm sure he'll be along later."

"You came alone?" Amory was shocked nearly speechless. "Does he know?"

"No. I wanted to surprise you, and he didn't want to bring me." Elodie shook her head. "And I didn't come alone, so no need to worry. Lilliale is here, and three of her brothers escorted us."

He wasn't sure how to respond to Elodie's pronouncement. He wasn't happy. He could have accepted Elodie's presence if she'd come alone, but he wasn't all right with her bringing so many people with her. And the people she brought. He had no desire to socialize with Lady Lilliale and her brothers, especially Vasco who barely tolerated Amory, when he wasn't feeling his best. He hoped Vasco wasn't one of the brothers who accompanied them.

And he didn't want them to see him when he felt disheveled and vulnerable, with his stomach becoming so much more prominent. Philip kept telling him he was beautiful, but Amory wasn't comfortable looking so different. He could come to terms with it, and he would, because the changes in his appearance were all for a very good reason, and the baby chose that moment to move around as if to emphasize his thought, but it didn't mean he wanted Vasco and his siblings to see him when he was feeling so vulnerable.

But that wasn't his biggest problem with the surprise visit. No one was supposed to come to Alzata. They were keeping Alzata closed and secure so no one could get to Amory, and Elodie brought so many people with her. The only reason they weren't turned away at the gate was because she was Philip's sister, and she was on a list of permitted visitors. Elodie and her friends might not be security risks, but Alzata was his retreat. His and Philip's, his with Philip. He didn't want a disdainful Vasco spoiling his feeling of comfort and safety.

Elodie was a sweet girl, but sometimes she didn't think.

He sighed. "It was nice of you to think of me, but you shouldn't have done this. You should have waited for Philip."

Elodie's face darkened with annoyance. "Why? I wanted to cheer you up since my brother said you weren't feeling well. Besides, this is my family's house, and I can be here whenever I like. I don't need Philip's permission."

Her tone was half-petulant, half-angry, and Amory was truly weary. "Actually, this is my house. Philip owned it, and he gave it to me."

Elodie looked as if he'd slapped her. Her mouth opened, but no words came out. Meanwhile, Vasco, Faron, and Rayan filed in the front door behind the ladies. They joined their sister in staring at Amory's stomach, which apparently was more noticeable than he'd thought in his loose shirt.

Weariness dragged at him so much that continuing the conversation seemed like far too much work. Anything more he said would come out harsher than it should, or maybe not. He couldn't think about it. Let Philip handle his sister. "It was nice of you to want to visit, Elodie, but I'm afraid I'm far too tired today for the type of party you seem to have in mind. I'm going to nap. Why don't you all enjoy the grounds, and I'll see you at dinner after my husband returns?"

He didn't wait for an answer, which he knew was rude, but he didn't care about his manners at the moment. It was rude, too, to leave his houseguests unattended, but Elodie and her traveling companions had invaded his home uninvited, perhaps against Philip's express wishes. Amory might own the estate, but Alzata was Philip's home as much as it was his. It didn't seem a response was forthcoming anyway. Elodie was stunned silent, something he didn't think he had ever seen happen to the loquacious princess.

He escaped back up the stairs and to his bedchamber, telling a servant on the way that he didn't want to be disturbed. Before uninvited guests had descended upon him, he hadn't planned on taking a nap. He'd been thinking about spending the afternoon on the terrace, sketching or reading, mostly basking in the warmth and the sunshine until Philip returned. He supposed he might have ended up lulled into a nap out there. But his whole plan had changed. If he went out on the terrace, or almost anywhere else in the house, he would be obligated to be a gracious host.

He refused to play host to a bunch of guests he didn't want. And he didn't much care how childish that made him.

His bedchamber was the only place he would be safe. No polite person would burst in on him there. As soon as the door was closed and locked behind him, he let out a breath of relief. He knew he was probably being cowardly, but he was going to let Philip deal with their unwanted guests. Philip would have words with Elodie anyway, which was Philip's responsibility not his. Amory tried to treat her like a sister, but if she'd gone against something Philip specifically told her, Philip needed to discuss it with her.

With little else to do, Amory went to the bed and lay down. Both his book and his sketchbook were in other parts of the house. He could have gone to retrieve them or sent a servant for them so he didn't have to leave the room. But suddenly he didn't want to talk to anyone at all, and the idea of a nap was tempting. He closed his eyes and let sleep claim him.

He didn't think he slept long, but he did sleep well, and he felt revived when he woke, more confident that he could handle the sudden influx of people in his house. People who were even then prowling somewhere around the estate, he was sure, with Elodie, who was probably pouting still. Enough annoyance remained that he wasn't quite ready to go out and face them. First, he called for a servant and asked for food to be brought up to him, reiterating his wishes to be left undisturbed after they brought it, and then he closed himself into the bathing room.

He soaked in the large tub for a while, letting the hot water and herbal bath oil soothe his aches. His body really wasn't made for childbearing and it didn't take easily to it. The baby moved again, quick flutters that never failed to fill him with awe. His baby, his and Philip's. No, he didn't regret anything. He wished Philip was with him. Ever since the first time they'd bathed together in the huge tub, he had preferred sharing it with Philip. Perhaps tomorrow Amory could coax Philip into the tub with him. He smiled. Probably wouldn't take much convincing. He tipped his head back and relaxed into the water.

His mind wandered, musing over why Vasco was there. Amory understood Elodie wanting to come even without Philip's permission. He understood her bringing all of her ladies and Lady Lilliale. He could see Faron escorting Elodie and Lady Lilliale, since he was Lady Lilliale's brother and he seemed to care for Elodie. Amory didn't know the other brother, but it made no sense for Vasco to show up. He had thrown Philip over and ended their friendship, and he didn't care for Amory at all. Was it to save face in some way or to hide the circumstances of his previous relationship with Philip? Amory would find out sooner or later. After Philip spoke with Vasco, which would probably be right after Philip spoke with Elodie.

Amory let those concerns go for the moment. He didn't need to borrow trouble. He should have told them to leave as soon as they arrived, but the way he'd been feeling, he hadn't wanted the unpleasant confrontation. Elodie was behind the visit, and alienating his husband's sister was a bad idea, even if she did need to learn to think before she acted. Best for Philip to tell her, not Amory.

He lingered in the bath until the water went cold and then dried himself with one of the soft towels laid out near the tub. He would have to dress more formally than he would have if he and Philip didn't have guests for the evening. Formal dress would be a challenge—much of his clothing was getting snug. He would have to do some searching to look presentable. He was mostly annoyed to have the quiet evening with Philip he'd planned snatched out of his hands.

He pulled on his dressing gown and bypassed the dressing room for the moment. The maid should have left his snack in the bedchamber while he was bathing. He would eat and then see what his wardrobe held. He was halfway into the bedchamber before he realized he wasn't alone.

"What are you doing here?" he snapped out, outraged that Rayan would be so bold as to come into Amory's bedchamber uninvited.

Then he saw the wicked-looking knife in Rayan's hand.

PHILIP WAS happy to ride back through the gates of Alzata late in the afternoon. He felt as if he'd been gone for days instead of hours, but he was actually returning earlier than planned. He wasn't ashamed to admit he missed Amory. He was so used to having Amory with him all the time, talking with him, touching him. Simply having Amory's presence at his side. It was startling how necessary Amory had become to his life.

He dismounted at the front steps, still surrounded by guards on horseback, and handed his horse off to a waiting servant. Jadis dismounted beside him.

"If it's all right, I'm going to clean up before I see Amory, Your Highness," Jadis said as they climbed the steps to the front door. Jadis had accompanied Philip back to Alzata for Amory's weekly examination. With the pregnancy such an unknown and risky proposition, Jadis had been checking on Amory regularly after their move to Alzata despite the presence of a healer at the estate. The regular examinations eased Philip's mind. He was still worried for Amory despite the pregnancy going smoothly so far.

"The bedchamber you used last time you visited should have been prepared for you. I'll let Amory know you're here," he said.

"Thank you, Your Highness. I'll be with you both shortly." Jadis disappeared up the stairs while Philip stopped in the entry hall, as the housekeeper bustled up to him.

"Welcome back, Your Highness," she said and curtsied.

"Thank you. Do you know where Prince Amory is?"

"Yes, Your Highness. Prince Amory is in his bedchamber. One of the maids brought food up to him. He asked not to be disturbed so I've ordered the staff out of that wing to give him some quiet," the housekeeper said. "Princess Elodie, her guests, and her ladies are out exploring the grounds. They said they would be back by dinner."

Distracted by worry about why Amory had closed himself in their bedchamber—Was he feeling worse?—he almost missed the rest of what the housekeeper said. "That's fi—wait. My sister is here?"

The housekeeper looked startled when he snapped the question out. She stammered slightly when she spoke again. "Yes, Your Highness. Princess Elodie arrived this afternoon with her guests and her ladies."

He bit back a vicious curse. He told Elodie she couldn't visit, but she'd defied him and come anyway. Unbelievable. He was going to have quite a talk with his sister. He was tempted to track her down immediately, but he wanted to make certain Amory was all right more than he wanted to have that discussion with Elodie.

"Thank you." He dismissed the housekeeper with a nod and took the stairs two at a time. He would see Amory to reassure himself he was well, and frankly because he had missed Amory that day. Then he would handle Elodie.

The upstairs corridor was quiet and empty, and Philip strode down it without encountering anyone else. But the servants were well-trained and would obey the housekeeper's orders. He wondered if Amory was sleeping, if he really was unwell or if he'd gone to their bedchamber to escape their unexpected guests. Hiding wasn't like Amory, but Philip wouldn't blame him if he had. There were any number of perfectly valid reasons why Amory wouldn't want guests at the moment. Philip didn't even know who was with his sister.

He heard Amory's voice as he approached the door to their bedchamber, but he couldn't make out the words. His spirits rose knowing Amory was awake. How much he wanted to talk with Amory all the time, to lay out all the annoyances of his meetings knowing Amory would help him work through them, still shocked Philip. With a smile on his face, Philip pushed open the door to the bedchamber.

"—don't want to do this," Amory was saying as the door opened. It took Philip endless seconds to realize what he was seeing. His mind lagged behind his body, which was moving as he took in the scene in the room. Amory backed up toward the bed with one hand out, warding off or trying to reassure, and the other splayed over his stomach in a protective gesture, and Rayan advancing on him with a large knife ready in his hand.

Philip leaped into the room, his only thought to protect Amory. Midleap, he was calling on his Talent, using it to change himself into the powerful cat, and giving himself the advantage of teeth and claws against the knife. The magic rushed through him in a flood, and faster than ever before, he was a cat.

He collided with Rayan, the force carrying them both to the floor. He felt a burning slice of pain in his left side, but he didn't let it distract him. He heard Amory yell, but he couldn't concern himself with that either. He had to keep Amory safe.

Rayan hit the ground hard and the knife flew out of his hand, skittering across the wood floor. Philip didn't see where it went and didn't care. The man struggled beneath Philip, bucking and heaving, pushing, hitting, but Philip had claws and teeth and the leverage and strength of his sleek cat body. He wasn't going to let him up. He wasn't going to let him live. Rayan dared to try to kill Amory, to kill his unborn child with him. Tried to kill the people Philip loved most. He understood what it meant to see red as a mist descended over his vision. He growled. No, the man wasn't walking out of there alive.

He grappled with the struggling man. Rayan managed to keep Philip from landing a bite, but he swiped at him with claws, sinking them in when he could as Rayan bucked and rolled. Rayan managed to get a kick in with his heavy riding boots and Philip hissed, loosening his grip enough for Rayan to jerk back, but the movement only snapped the back of his head into a table leg. Rayan went slack, and Philip prepared to pounce again, to make certain Rayan would never hurt his family again, but a voice made itself heard, dimly over the rush of blood in his ears and the thundering of rage through his head. He almost didn't recognize it; then all at once, it resolved itself into Amory's beloved voice, calling for him.

"Pip! He's unconscious now. He can't hurt us. Pip, please come away now."

He didn't want to listen. Rayan had tried to kill Amory. He deserved to die. He deserved to have his throat ripped out.

"Please leave him and come to me. Please."

The desperation in Amory's voice broke through, and Philip lifted his head. Amory was kneeling on the floor nearby, gripping the knife that had flown from Rayan's grasp in a steady hand. Amory let out a long breath and put the knife aside when Philip met his eyes. Slowly, Philip moved off of Rayan, leaving the man sprawled on the floor. He was using the magic to change himself back as he walked toward Amory. He studied Amory, searching for injury as Amory's intense gaze did the same thing to him.

Amory's eyes widened at the same instant Philip staggered, a sudden pain blooming in his side and with it a wave of weakness. He stumbled into Amory's arms. Amory's face was a mask of fear and panic as he urged Philip down to the floor.

"Pip. You're bleeding. He cut you." Amory fumbled with the blood-soaked clothes at Philip's side, and Philip hissed at the pain. He hadn't felt the pain when he was fighting with Rayan. "Let me see how bad it is."

"It's fine. I'm fine." But his voice didn't have the strength he would have liked, certainly not the strength needed to convince Amory. He hissed when Amory's hands came down on top of the wound.

"I'm sorry, but this is deep. I have to get this bleeding stopped."

"Wait," Philip gasped out. "Jadis is here. Get him."

"I'm not leaving you here bleeding." Turning his head toward the open door, Amory shouted for Jadis, but he kept his hands pressing hard against the wound in Philip's side. It hurt, worse than anything Philip had ever felt. And he was starting to feel lightheaded, his vision graying at the edges. He tried to focus on Amory. He hated the fear and worry in Amory's eyes.

"Where is he?" Amory asked, but Philip was pretty sure the question was rhetorical, and pressed harder against Philip's side. Philip forced himself not to flinch away. Amory bent and kissed Philip's forehead before straightening and shouting for Jadis again.

"I'll be fine." Philip tried to reassure Amory. "Are you all right?"

Amory let out a laugh with no humor in it. "I'm not hurt. You're the one who's bleeding, and you'll be fine, yes, as soon as I get this bleeding stopped. Then Jadis can fix you up, and you will be fine."

He managed to concentrate on Amory despite his spinning head, and a jolt of fear went through him at the look on Amory's face. He knew what Amory was thinking, and it terrified him. "You can't. You can't use magic."

"I have to, a little, to slow the bleeding until Jadis gets here to help you." Amory looked fierce. "I won't lose you."

"You'll hurt yourself and the baby. You can't."

"Just a little to slow the bleeding. It won't hurt me."

Philip tried to move away, but Amory was easily able to grab him and catch him close again. It didn't help Philip that he didn't want to struggle too much and risk hurting the baby. Or, worryingly, that he didn't have the strength to struggle. Amory pressed his hand firmly against Philip's side again, and Philip felt the tingle of magic.

"No. Don't."

Amory shook his head, his expression a mask of concentration nearly covering his fear. Cold terror raced through Philip at that look, at Amory's stubbornness. Because it could get Amory and their child hurt, maybe killed. Amory needed all of his healing Talent to take care of himself.

"Don't do this, please."

Amory didn't answer but kept at his task, his face going paler.

"Please, Amory."

"Amory, stop." Jadis's voice cut sharply through the air and broke into Amory's concentration. The tingle of magic ceased when Amory startled, and relief made Philip even weaker. Jadis dropped to his knees beside them and gently pulled Amory away. Amory didn't protest. He also didn't move far, getting out of Jadis's way but staying near Philip. Amory looked down at him, staring into his eyes and running his fingers through Philip's hair as the healer began his work. The fatigue in Amory's beloved face and the slight tremble in his fingers were not reassuring. But Jadis was there, and he would take care of Amory too. They would both be all right. It was Philip's last thought before the darkness claimed him.

CHAPTER 17

PHILIP DIDN'T know how much time had passed when he came back to himself. He realized before trying to open his eyes he wasn't on the floor any longer, so someone must have moved him after he passed out. To a bed from the soft mattress beneath him, and from the scent of Amory on the pillows, his own. Amory. Fear gave him the ability to force his eyes open.

Amory was next to him on the bed, sleeping and so still. Philip turned to look at him, to make sure he was only sleeping, that he was all right, and gasped at the painful pull in his side. Hands on his shoulders urged him back against the pillows.

"I healed the wound," Jadis said. "But it's going to be tender for a day or two, so no sudden movements and lots of rest, Your Highness."

"And Amory? The baby?" Philip's voice was a rasp, but he thought the words were understandable.

Jadis turned to the bedside table and poured water into a glass from a pitcher. "He's going to be fine and so is the baby, but he has to stop trying to use his Talent on others. A lesson I thought he would have learned already."

He drank deeply from the glass Jadis handed him. "Apparently my husband is a slow learner."

Jadis flicked a glance at Amory's sleeping form. "And a deep sleeper, or I imagine you'd be in trouble for that remark, Your Highness."

"Probably." But he planned on a serious conversation with Amory when his husband woke up. Philip could not take more terror of the kind he'd felt that day. "Is he supposed to be sleeping?"

"Yes, he needs rest to recover his strength. I bolstered it as much as I could, and used my own magic to keep both him and the baby healthy, but his own is what's needed. He must stop using his Talent for anything else."

"I couldn't let Philip die." The statement was made in a whisper, but Philip's heart leaped to hear Amory speaking.

"Amory." Ignoring the pull in his side, Philip turned to face his husband. Amory's eyes were closed, but as Philip watched, his eyelids with their long lashes fluttered and finally opened. Amory's face was far too pale for Philip's liking, but his eyes were clear. He reached out and cupped Amory's cheek, brushing his thumb back and forth over Amory's cheekbone.

"Are you all right?"

Philip choked on a laugh, cutting it off before it could turn into a sob. "I should be asking you."

"You're the one who was stabbed."

"And you're the one who nearly killed himself using his Talent when he shouldn't have."

"I wasn't going to lose you, Philip. You saved me, I save you." Amory covered Philip's hand with his own. "That's how it works."

"But if you kill yourself doing it, then it doesn't work. Promise me you'll take more care, love. I can't lose you." He glanced down at Amory's rounded stomach. "Either of you, now."

"I promise. If you don't nearly get yourself killed again."

"Deal." He bent and kissed Amory. A brief kiss but one flooded with his relief and love. "Now, how are you feeling?"

"Tired, but all right otherwise. And you?"

"Fine. A little sore, but Jadis healed the wound." It was only then, saying the man's name, that Philip remembered they weren't alone. He looked back, over his shoulder. The healer was standing in the same spot, doing his best not to stare at them. Philip pushed away embarrassment at being seen in such an intimate moment with Amory.

"Well, now you're awake, let's have a look." Jadis bustled around to Amory's side of the bed and spent a few moments checking Amory over. Philip and Amory were quiet until Jadis lifted his hands from Amory's forehead and stomach. "You and the baby are fine, but you need rest. A lot of rest to recover the strength you lost and to give your Talent the time it needs to get back to full strength. I know you'll hate the idea, Amory, but I'm insisting on bed rest until you recover your strength."

Both Philip and Amory let out sighs of relief at Jadis's first words. Amory's face fell when Jadis mentioned staying in bed, then his eyes narrowed. Philip would support Jadis, but he was reassured to see that Amory might argue. The impulse told him more than anything that Amory would be fine.

Finally Amory nodded. "All right, just to be sure."

Philip held back another relieved sigh. Despite Jadis's presence, he leaned down and kissed Amory again. "Thank you."

Amory smiled wryly, fondness in his eyes.

A few moments later, after Jadis got Amory comfortably propped up against some pillows, Philip asked what happened after he passed out. Rayan was no longer in the room, but blood was soaked into the rug and smeared on the polished wood of the floor.

"Rayan is dead."

Amory took Philip's hand in the moment of silence after Jadis's statement, but Philip didn't feel anything for Rayan, certainly not remorse. Taking a life would weigh on him, but he had done what he had to do to save Amory and their child. He would make his peace with his actions. He gestured for Jadis to continue.

"He sustained severe blood loss and a head injury. I wasn't able to get to him in time." Jadis stared at Philip. "I won't ask why he looks as if he was mauled."

"Best not to."

Jadis nodded. "The guards took his body away. They arrived shortly after I did on what I understand was their scheduled patrol of the house."

Managing to miss Rayan's attack on Amory by moments. Dumb luck on Rayan's part or had he gotten the information out of someone in the house? Philip wouldn't have thought the servants at Alzata would let information as important as guard schedules slip, but he would have to check.

"Since we didn't know exactly what happened or who was involved, only that Rayan tried to kill Amory, we confined all of your guests under guard," Jadis continued. "Captain Loriot is waiting to speak with you."

"And my sister?" Philip asked. He could only imagine what Elodie would have done when all of her guests were hauled away by royal guards. "What has she been told?"

"Very little. The princess has been asked to stay in one of the bedchambers with her ladies. Her Highness... isn't pleased," Jadis finished delicately.

"No, she wouldn't be. But I'll have to talk to her later." And he was looking forward to the discussion even less than he was before. "I have to deal with our... guests first."

He sent Jadis to fetch Captain Loriot while Philip slipped from the bed and dressed in clean clothes. His side pulled while he dressed but wasn't terribly painful, and he was finished dressing by the time Captain Loriot arrived. Philip perched on the edge of the bed next to Amory while the captain reported on how Vasco, Faron, and Lilliale were being held in one of the upstairs sitting rooms and protesting their confinement vociferously.

Philip forced back all of his feelings—betrayal, disbelief, rage—at the thought of his childhood friends trying to murder his husband and listened to Amory explain what had happened before Philip arrived. He took Amory's hand and held tight, fear coursing through him again when he thought of what could have happened, what almost happened. Amory could defend himself, but alone, without weapons, and unable to do as much for fear of harming their child, against a man with a knife....

"I'm all right," Amory said, loud enough for Philip alone to hear him. "And no one is going to try to hurt me anymore. We know who it is now."

"Yes." Knowing was a relief the likes of which Philip had never felt before, even if the knowledge of who had been trying to kill Amory hurt.

Amory's expression softened, and he squeezed Philip's hand. Amory understood. Which was why Amory insisted on going with him to talk to their guests. Their prisoners.

"You're supposed to stay in bed. Rest."

"I know, and I'll come right back to bed afterwards. I'll sit on a comfortable chair while we're with them, but I'm not letting you do it alone. I know this isn't going to be easy, love, and I want to be there with you."

"I'll be all right. I don't want you to hurt yourself."

"I won't. I want to be there for you, and for me too. They've been trying to kill me, Pip, and I want to know why. I need to do this." Amory's face was set, but not from stubbornness. In Philip's worry over Amory, he had become so protective that sometimes he forgot how strong Amory was himself. Because he was so strong, and the force of his love for Philip was even stronger.

Philip nodded. "We need to do it together."

AMORY AND Philip walked into the room where Vasco and his siblings were being kept accompanied by Captain Loriot and six royal guards. Captain Loriot wouldn't allow them into the room otherwise. Amory had no desire to argue, and Philip said nothing. Neither of them was stupid or reckless. Philip might disagree about that assessment with regard to

Amory's actions, but Amory couldn't let Philip bleed to death in front of him.

Inside the sitting room, a stony-faced Vasco leaned against the mantle while Faron paced the room in agitated patterns. Lady Lilliale sat on a couch near Vasco, perching on the edge of a cushion, her pretty face bewildered. All three watched as Amory and Philip walked in with their guards. Vasco and Faron bowed, but Lady Lilliale jumped to her feet and let out a flood of words without so much as a brief curtsy. "Philip? What's going on? Why are we here? We were with Elodie and the guards came and dragged us away. Elodie was so upset, and I didn't know what was happening. They scared me."

"You'll forgive me, Lilliale, but that isn't a concern of mine," Philip said. His words were sharp, but the arm he wrapped around Amory's waist was careful. Philip led him to another couch on the other side of the room and helped him sit. Amory would have been more annoyed with Philip's coddling if he weren't so tired and if it weren't so nice. He warmed when Philip rested a hand on his shoulder, uniting them.

Lady Lilliale flinched. "I—I don't understand."

"Don't you?" Philip's gaze landed on each of the siblings in turn. "Your brothers understand. It's why you're all here."

"What do you mean?" Lilliale's face was a study in confusion, her eyes wide and blinking as she glanced from Philip to each of her brothers. "Elodie invited us to come with her. It's supposed to be a party."

"Ah, yes, and I'll be having a conversation with Elodie, because she wasn't supposed to come here today. Let alone bring anyone here." He had to pause to make sure he could keep his voice even as he continued. Just the thought of how close he'd come to losing Amory.... "And I'll bet it was your brother, Faron, who convinced her it would be a good idea to come, and to bring you all along with her."

"I don't understand, Philip," she repeated. She looked over her shoulder to Faron and back to Philip. "Why would he? And what does it matter if he did? It's a visit, just for fun."

"Lilliale, I'm afraid it's far more than that." Philip had known Lilliale for a long time, but he couldn't tell if she was as confused as she professed to be. He hated that it had come to the point where he had to be suspicious of her, his sister's friend. But they were all taught to hide their feelings to survive at court.

"Then what is it?"

"Your visit was an excuse for your brother to attempt to kill Amory."

"What? No." Lilliale dropped back down into her seat as the color drained from her face. "No. They wouldn't. They couldn't. Where's Rayan?"

"Rayan is dead. He was killed while trying to stab my husband and consort to death today." He studied the siblings, watching their reactions. Lilliale swayed in her seat, and Faron placed a hand on her shoulder, his other hand clenched at his side. Vasco's only reaction was to close his eyes. "I know Rayan tried to kill Amory today. He's tried to kill Amory before, multiple times. What I want to know is why, and who else was involved."

Silence stretched out for long moments.

"I will find out. One way or another, I will find out. But it will be far easier if you tell me now." Philip fixed each of them with an intense stare. More silence. "I don't believe Rayan planned and executed all of this on his own. It's obvious he didn't as Faron convinced Elodie to bring you out here today. I can also assume the reason you all came here was to divert suspicion from Rayan. I think you're all involved."

"Lilliale had nothing to do with this," Faron said.

"Faron," Vasco snapped out. "Quiet."

"No," Philip said. "He's going to talk. You all are going to talk."

He stared at Vasco, standing near the mantle, the man's posture proud. Pain sliced into Philip's heart, perhaps worse than the knife wound to his side. These men had once been his friends; Vasco had been more than a friend. Lilliale was Elodie's best friend and like a sister to him. Philip would have let Faron marry Elodie. He never expected a betrayal from them. Amory's hand covered his on Amory's shoulder and squeezed, linking them. Anchoring him.

"Now." His voice lashed out, making Lilliale jump, but he didn't care. "Tell me why, now."

"Why do you think?" Faron's words broke the silence, nearly at a yell. The guards shifted, ready to protect Amory and Philip, at the outburst and the naked anger on the man's face. Vasco tried to quiet his brother again, but Faron ignored him. Faron had always been hotheaded, likely to jump to attack or defend when the situation involved something he cared about. Philip had thought he'd grown out of some of those impulses. Apparently not. "You hurt our sister. Betrayed her with this farce of a marriage you entered into. Did you think we could let such an insult pass?"

Philip didn't know what he expected to hear, but that wasn't it. "Excuse me?"

"Don't deny it. You know what I mean." Faron was furious, yelling and gesturing wildly, and very obviously unrepentant. He seemed to have forgotten he was speaking to the prince. Or perhaps he didn't care. "You were supposed to marry our sister. Everyone knew you were to marry Lilliale. Do you know what it did to her, and to our family, when you turned from her and married him? She was devastated. She deserves to be princess, and we were going to give that to her."

Only Amory's hand on his allowed Philip to hold on to his composure at the venom in Faron's voice. The pressure of Amory's hand was calming, restraining, even though Amory's shoulder was tense under Philip's hand. Amory wasn't as calm as he appeared. He was either too exhausted to get visibly upset, which was worrying, or he was keeping himself calm for Philip.

"I was never going to marry Lilliale. Nothing was agreed upon— the possibility of a marriage wasn't even discussed. I have never done anything to make you believe otherwise. Anything more was something you hoped for, but that's all."

"You were never going to marry me?" Lilliale asked, her voice small and plaintive. "But I thought you cared about me. Elodie always talked about how we would be sisters. I would make such a good wife to you, a good princess for the country."

"I never planned to marry you, Lilliale. I'm quite sure you would make someone a good wife, but not me." On any other day, he would have felt bad for crushing Lilliale's hopes, for the tears spilling down her cheeks.

"But—but I love you! We're supposed to get married. That's always been what's supposed to happen." She looked at her brothers. "They told me it would. I was going to marry you."

"Did they?" Philip asked as Vasco closed his eyes in what looked like resignation. "They told you we were going to marry even after I was already married to Amory. And you didn't think what they told you was strange? Especially when attempts were being made on Amory's life?"

"I thought you would realize you made a mistake. That being married to me would be better for you and Tournai than being married to a man. That's all." Her eyes were wet, and more tears spilled over and drenched her cheeks. Shock and grief and hurt swirled through her eyes, made her face a mask of pain, but there was something more in her eyes. A dawning of knowledge and dread. Lilliale wasn't a stupid woman. She had to have sensed something more was happening even if she willfully ignored it.

Philip turned his attention back to her brothers. "So, because your sister was disappointed she couldn't marry me, because you wanted her to marry me, you decided to kill my husband?"

The silence seethed with anger and frustration. Vasco and Faron were not men who regretted their actions, except perhaps getting caught. If they'd had their way, Amory would be dead, Lilliale would be Philip's wife, and no one would ever know the crimes they committed.

"And perhaps you wanted to punish me too."

"You deserve it," Faron said, the words vicious. "For leading her on and then hurting her. You deserve to be punished."

"Faron, stop talking," Vasco said, speaking for the first time in several moments.

Philip looked to him, studying his former lover, his former friend. Unlike Faron who wore his emotions plainly on his face, Vasco remained stoic. "I've heard enough." He turned to Captain Loriot. "Take them into custody and transport them back to the city. Have the rest of their family taken into custody and questioned as well."

Faron yelled, demanding his family be left alone, and struggled as he was forcibly removed from the room by two guards. A guard came for Lilliale, taking her arm and leading her out. He was gentle with her but firm, keeping her moving when she tried to turn her teary, bewildered gaze back on Philip and Vasco. Before a guard could reach him, Vasco turned to Philip. "Philip—Your Highness, may I speak with you? In private?"

Philip didn't want to hear anything Vasco had to say, but that was an emotional reaction, one he couldn't afford. He nodded and looked to Captain Loriot. With a gesture and a few words, Captain Loriot dismissed the remaining guards to the corridor outside the door, leaving Philip, Amory, Vasco, and Captain Loriot the only occupants of the room.

"I wanted to speak in private."

"I don't care," Philip answered. "You can talk with Amory and Captain Loriot present or not at all."

Vasco was silent before he nodded. "Lilliale had nothing to do with it. Neither did my mother or my wife, or anyone else in the family."

"I think you can understand why I might not take your word for it. The rest of your family will be questioned."

"They had nothing to do with this, Your Highness. Please don't punish them for something they weren't a part of, something they knew nothing about. Spare them, I beg you." Vasco's stoic façade cracked enough for Philip to see the very real fear for his family. Philip almost told Vasco he should have thought of them before he and his brothers embarked on an assassination plot, but he wasn't that cruel.

"You know me well enough to know I won't harm an innocent person, or you should. If, as you say, they weren't involved, they'll be released." He considered the man standing in front of him. "And you? How involved are you?"

Amory's fingers moved in small, soothing motions over his. Amory knew him far too well.

"I knew what they were doing," Vasco said, his voice strong. "I didn't stop them. I helped them."

Philip had expected it, but he'd hoped to be wrong, hoped his old friend hadn't had a part in trying to kill Amory, hoped Vasco was the type of man who wouldn't. But Philip wasn't wrong, and hearing the confirmation was like a blow to his chest.

"Why?" Amory asked, speaking for the first time. Perhaps he knew Philip couldn't speak, despite wanting to ask that very question.

There was disdain in Vasco's eyes when he looked at Amory, and the unimaginable level of gall it took to look at Amory in that fashion rekindled an anger in Philip that burned away some of the hurt. "Why do you think? I would do anything for my sister, for her happiness and her well-being. I would do anything for my family." Vasco paused, and if anything, his eyes got harder. "I couldn't believe what you did, Philip. Marrying this—this—him. You shouldn't have done it. You shouldn't have been able to do it. It's not something men like us can do. We get married to women of good families. We produce heirs. We have a duty and a responsibility to carry on the legacies of our families and our titles."

Philip found his voice again. "I've never found that loving Amory has interfered with my duties and responsibilities. He eases the burdens of them."

"I had to marry, Philip, a woman who would give me heirs and be a proper duchess. You should have done the same, and it should have been Lilliale. She would have made a perfect princess."

"Not with me. I was never going to marry her, Vasco. I wasn't going to marry a woman at all." Looking back, he could see it, that he never would have. And after meeting Amory, Philip never could have married anyone except him.

"You're a fool, Philip. Marrying a man and a commoner."

He stared at Vasco. "You didn't expect to pick back up again with me, did you? You can't be jealous. You never loved me. You couldn't have left me as easily as you did if you had."

"I cared for you, which is why I know you've made a mistake. But I wouldn't have married you." Vasco looked Amory up and down. "I would never have done what he's doing if I could."

"But you chose to punish me for marrying the man I love anyway." Philip shook his head. "We're done here. Get him out of my sight."

He forced himself to stand straight as Vasco was hustled from the room, but he couldn't stop his shoulders from slumping as soon as the door closed behind Vasco and Captain Loriot. He would have to be strong again, but he needed a moment.

"Pip."

Amory's voice was soft, so full of love and concern it made Philip's chest ache. His eyes brimmed with the same love and concern, along with understanding and the echo of the horror and sadness filling Philip. Amory said nothing more but opened his arms. With a shudder, Philip dropped down to his knees and fell into Amory's arms, letting Amory hold him, hold him together in the face of betrayal by those who used to be friends.

"IT'S OVER. It's finally over."

Amory and Philip clung to each other for long moments after Vasco was taken from the room. Amory could almost feel Philip's hurt and betrayal radiating off him, and Amory hurt for him. His only desire was to soothe it all away, to comfort Philip, to protect him from everything bad in the world and everyone who might hurt him.

Then Philip murmured that it was over and kissed Amory. He'd been so concerned for Philip he hadn't thought of what the confrontation meant. A wave of stunning relief hit Amory so hard he might have fallen if he hadn't already been sitting. He didn't have to be afraid anymore. He and Philip could live without the constant fear and anxiety of the threat to Amory's life hanging over them. They could anticipate the birth of their child. They could just love each other. And with that amazing realization, he clung to Philip for a different reason.

But it wasn't over, not entirely. And the aftermath of what Vasco and his brothers did would be painful for far too many people.

Despite the fatigue dragging at him and making him wish for his bed, Amory insisted on accompanying Philip to speak with Elodie, knowing the conversation would be a difficult one. He wasn't wrong—in fact, it might have been more unpleasant than he anticipated. Philip spared his sister no details, explaining to her how Faron, Rayan, and Vasco had come to Alzata to kill Amory. She reacted as he expected her to. First with shock and disbelief, then a healthy amount of denial. And Amory couldn't blame her. She loved Faron—how could she believe he would plot to carry out a murder? Unfortunately, she then acted as she often did when faced with something she didn't want to hear. She fell into a tantrum.

But apparently the day had been too much for Philip, and Amory couldn't blame him either.

"Enough," Philip snapped out. Elodie stopped and stared at her brother with wide, startled eyes. When Philip continued speaking, his voice was firm but not unkind. "I know this is a shock, and I know it hurts, but it is true. You're going to have to accept it. Mourn for what could have been, but accept what is. It's time to grow up, Elodie."

Mourning was perhaps the best word Philip could have used. Over the weeks that followed, Elodie did mourn for the future she thought she would have with Faron. While Elodie needed to grow up, Amory wished she could have had a less painful way of doing it. He wished often those weeks could have been less painful for all of them. Vasco's entire family was questioned and investigated. His mother, Lilliale, and his youngest siblings and wife were released and left the city, but Vasco, Faron, and one of their other brothers were put on trial for treason and attempted murder. And if the trials weren't difficult enough, then came the punishments—imprisonments and executions and stripping Vasco's family of their titles and land.

Amory stood beside Philip through every moment of it, doing what he could to make it easier and wishing he could do more. In those long days, Alzata was their refuge again, not from a killer but from the difficult decisions to be made and consequences to be faced. Amory refused to let the place be tainted by what happened there. Their first time back was strange for both of them, but the awkwardness soon passed, through stubbornness and a love of the estate. Even as the situation in Jumelle began to ease, they went, enjoying the quiet and the privacy to love each other and to prepare for the birth of their child.

As time passed, the flutters of movement Amory felt from their child became strong kicks Philip was delighted and excited to feel. Philip spent more time with his hands on Amory's growing belly, which Amory indulged him in, even when it seemed their child was playing by kicking at his father's hands. A few more aches seemed a small price to see Philip so happy. Philip's happiness, their child's health, they made everything better for Amory whenever he began to feel uncomfortable in his changing body.

And every moment of physical pain and mental discomfort was worth it the first moment Amory held his child. Of course, the baby decided to arrive at the most inconvenient time. Pain ripping through his abdomen woke him from a sleep he had only just managed to settle into despite the late hour. Philip called for Jadis and then held Amory, arms wrapping tight around him. Philip's voice and hands were soothing and calm, but his eyes were panicked and afraid, and somehow Philip putting aside his own fear to calm Amory's made Amory love him more. He tried to stifle his groans, seeing the reflection of his pain in Philip's eyes, how the fear there flared at every sound Amory made, and to concentrate only on the feel of Philip holding him so securely.

Jadis and Savarin arrived without delay, pulled from their own beds in the palace where they'd been staying since the time of the birth grew near, but looking composed and confident. Their calm competence soothed Amory's nerves further. Because he was nervous, afraid really for what was to come, and the burning pain didn't help. Jadis and Savarin pushed Philip from the room, despite Philip's protests. Amory had to force himself not to reach out for Philip and beg him to stay, to hold his hand through the pain and fear.

"I'm going to make you sleep now, Amory," Jadis said. "When you wake up, the procedure will be done and your child will be here. Relax now."

How could he relax? What a ridiculous thing to say. He was about to tell Jadis so, but Jadis laid a hand on his forehead, and everything went black.

When he woke again, his abdomen was slightly sore, and he was groggy, fuzzy. His eyelids were far too heavy to try opening them, and he wondered why he should bother. He should go back to sleep. Jadis murmured for him to wake up, and a baby was crying.

His eyes snapped open. Jadis's face came into focus above him. "Everything went perfectly. You may be a little tender and tired from the healing for a day or so, but you'll be fine. Let's get you sitting up so you can meet your son."

"Son?" Jadis helped him to sit and propped pillows behind his back, but Amory wasn't paying attention to him. His gaze flew around the room, searching, until it settled upon Philip, holding a small bundle in his arms. "Philip."

Jadis stepped out of the way, and Philip was there. Amory didn't realize he'd held out his arms until Philip settled the precious blanket-wrapped bundle in them, handling the baby as if he were the most breakable glass. The baby's cries quieted, and he snuffled a little as he seemed to snuggle into Amory's arms. He couldn't sort out all the emotions rushing and swirling through him at his first sight of his son's sweet face. Happiness that he had taken the chance. Awe that such a perfect, beautiful child came from him and Philip. Utter joy and complete fascination with the tiny baby he held in his arms. And the most profound love. He never could have imagined the day his father brought him to the palace with such despicable motives how his life would turn out, but he was so happy it had.

He didn't want to let the baby go. He didn't want to look away. But Philip was beside him on the bed, one arm around his shoulders holding him close, the other sliding beneath Amory's so they held their child together. Tearing his eyes away from the baby, he looked up at Philip. Philip seemed to feel Amory's eyes on him, even though he stared at their child with every bit of the awe Amory felt written across his face, and he turned to look at Amory.

Philip's eyes held such joy, such love and adoration, it nearly took Amory's breath. They looked at each other for long moments, their child held in their arms. Amory couldn't find the words to express the love, the joy, the gratitude filling him to overflowing, but they didn't need any. He saw everything he needed in Philip's eyes, and he hoped Philip could do the same. After a long while, Philip smiled and kissed him, gentle and lingering, as their son slept in their arms.

Keep reading for an exclusive excerpt from

The Artist's Masquerade

By Antonia Aquilante

As the first-born son of the Duke of Tournai and cousin to the prince, Cathal has always tried to fulfill his duty to family and country, including following through with an arranged marriage to Velia, cousin to the emperor of Ardunn. But it's Velia's companion, Flavia, who fascinates Cathal. Cathal doesn't know that Flavia is really Flavian, a man masquerading as a woman to escape Ardunn, a restrictive place in which Flavian's preference for men is forbidden.

Even when Cathal discovers Flavian's true gender, he cannot fight his attraction to him. Flavian is intrigued by Cathal, but Cathal is still betrothed to Velia, and Flavian worries Cathal is more taken with his feminine illusion than the man beneath it. While both men battle their longings for each other, spies from Ardunn infiltrate the capital, attempting to uncover Tournai's weaknesses. They are also searching for Flavian, who possesses a magical Talent that allows him to see the truth of a person just by painting their portrait—a skill invaluable to Ardunn's emperor.

Coming soon to
www.dreamspinnerpress.com

CHAPTER 1

"IT'S TIME you took a wife."

Cathal managed to keep his surprise hidden with some difficulty. That blunt statement was not what he'd expected when he received the summons to his father's office. A discussion of family business, perhaps, or questions about happenings at the palace—even a diatribe about one of his cousin's choices, since Father seemed to hate every one since the prince's marriage to Amory—was what usually precipitated a call to his father's presence.

He'd never imagined Father would bring marriage up today. Cathal had seen no indication that Father was even thinking in this direction. Father said plenty as he pushed the prince to marry, and plenty more when Philip married a man instead of the woman Umber would have chosen, but he'd never said a word about his own sons' need to marry.

Cathal probably shouldn't have been so surprised. He was twenty-five years old and his father's heir, and Umber was a royal duke and dynastically-minded. Producing an heir for the dukedom was Cathal's duty, despite the existence of his younger brothers. He'd always known it, and he would never think of shirking that duty.

"Of course, Father." He wasn't interested in any woman in particular, but there were plenty of women who would make him a suitable wife. He was certain he could find someone who wouldn't make the duty a chore. "I will begin looking for a wife immediately."

"No need. It's all arranged." Father returned his attention to the papers on his desk, as if what he said was of no particular consequence. As if he hadn't just told Cathal his entire life was about to change and taken Cathal's last bit of choice away at the same time.

Cathal snapped his mouth shut when he realized it was hanging open. "It is?"

"Of course."

Of course it was. Cathal should have expected this as well. Umber would never leave such an important choice—a family alliance, a mother for future dukes—up to Cathal. Father should have, or at least he should have asked for Cathal's opinion. He was of age and had proven himself trustworthy time and again, or he thought he had. It left a sour taste in his mouth to think that Father respected him so little.

"May I ask whom I will be marrying?" He immediately regretted his tone as Father arched a single brow.

Father let out a huff that expressed his disappointment more eloquently than a hundred words would have, but he answered anyway. "She's a cousin of the emperor of Ardunn. Velia is her name. Beautiful, by all accounts, and accomplished, but the connections are the important part."

Cathal hardly heard anything after Ardunn. Cousin to the emperor of Ardunn? What was his father thinking? And how had he even managed it?

Father looked up again, and this time his huff held more than a little annoyance. "Why are you looking at me like that?"

Cathal didn't know how he was looking at his father. Usually he had more control, but incredulity seemed to have obliterated it. "Ardunn, Father? I don't understand. Why—"

"Don't be stupid. If your cousin isn't going to do his duty and marry for the good of this country, then it falls to you to take up where Prince Philip failed."

That made even less sense. "But, Father, you negotiated a marriage contract with the emperor of Ardunn? Does Philip know?"

His cousin couldn't know. Cathal had damaged their relationship and weakened the trust Philip had in him—he knew that—but Philip wasn't vindictive enough to keep something so big from Cathal, especially considering the prince's hatred of arranged marriages. Though how a prince came by such a view Cathal would never know. Nevertheless, Philip would have said something, which meant Father had been negotiating with someone in Ardunn without Philip's knowledge or consent.

Umber scoffed. "He'll know soon enough."

"But, Father, negotiating with Ardunn…. What did you—"

"Are you questioning my ability to negotiate a marriage for my son?"

"Of course not, sir." Just the prudence of doing so with a powerful foreign emperor without the knowledge of their own ruler. "But—"

"This is the marriage your cousin should have negotiated for himself, but since he wouldn't do his duty, we have to do it for him. For the good of Tournai and this family."

"But, Father—"

"No more." Father slapped a hand down on the wooden surface of the desk. "It's done, and when she arrives next month, you will marry this woman. We're finished discussing it."

Cathal gritted his teeth against further protests and gave a sharp nod.

A few moments later, dismissed by his father, Cathal dragged in a lungful of crisp air. Spring was taking hold, but the mornings were still cool. Right now, he was thankful for that gulp of bracing air.

The meeting had not gone as he'd anticipated.

He shook his head and strode down the steps into the garden. This house, where Cathal grew up, was probably the largest home in the city. Constructed generations ago of pale gray stone, the house had three stories surrounding this inner courtyard and the garden it contained. He'd played here as a child with his brothers and cousin, chasing each other, hiding among the statuary and bushes. As he grew older, he'd come here when he needed a moment of peace. Now he spent most of his time at the palace, and the garden was the domain of his mother and younger sisters, who often sat on the benches near the central fountain to do their needlework.

He didn't linger, couldn't if he wanted to. He couldn't even go up to the palace and inform Philip of the betrothal, because Cathal was due at the harbor to inspect improvements to the harbor defenses. He strode through the garden, taking the most direct route from Father's office to the front of the house. He ducked inside again and made for the entrance hall without slowing.

His sister's melodic laugh and the quiet murmur of his mother's voice floated back to him. He smiled as he stepped from the corridor into the grand room. At his first step onto the red marble floor, both women looked up from where they were arranging early spring flowers in a large vase on the polished table in the center of the room. They smiled at him, identical smiles of welcome. His youngest sister looked remarkably like Mother, though Meriall was only fourteen. She was the only one of them to inherit Mother's golden brown hair and not Father's much darker locks.

It surprised him each time he saw Meriall how grown up she was becoming. It seemed just yesterday she was trailing after their brother Etan, getting into scrapes, and jumping on her brothers whenever she saw them. Now she was a young lady. The oldest of his three younger sisters was married, and his second sister was nearly seventeen. Cathal might have expected, if he'd thought of it at all, Father to be negotiating a marriage for her, not for Cathal.

Meriall and Mother were still smiling at him, and they left off fussing with the flowers and greenery as he approached. When she was younger, Meriall would have flung herself at him. She'd learned more appropriate behavior since then, but a part of him missed her enthusiasm. Then again, she would probably still throw herself at Etan. They'd always been closer.

"Cathal." Mother held out her hands to him and tilted her head for his kiss to her cheek. "I didn't know you were here."

He brushed a kiss over Meriall's cheek as well. "Father wanted to meet with me."

Because he was watching, he saw the flash of concern in his mother's warm brown eyes. Did she know her husband's plans for Cathal? "Is everything all right?"

No, he didn't think she knew. He doubted Father would have consulted her anyway. He flicked his glance at his sister, wondering if he should speak in front of her, but everyone would know soon enough. "Father wants me to marry."

Mother blinked, once, twice, the only sign of surprise on her serene face. "I didn't realize, but you are getting to be that age. There are many lovely girls you could meet and consider. Perhaps we can have a party and invite some of them."

"Actually, Father has it all arranged already."

"Oh. Well. I didn't realize you and your father had chosen someone. I wish you'd told me." The statement wasn't much of a rebuke, not the way she said it, but from his gentle mother, it was still censure.

"I wish he'd told me. I only just found out myself, Mother." He bit back impatience. His ignorance of his father's actions wasn't Mother's doing. "She arrives in a month. I assume we'll all meet her then."

"Arrives? From where? Who is she?"

He didn't blame his mother for her bewilderment. "Father says her name is Velia. I only know that she's a cousin to the emperor of Ardunn."

"The emperor? Does His Highness know?" Mother had been the wife of a royal duke for nearly thirty years. She could see the implications as well as he could.

"It doesn't appear so." He glanced from Mother, who was admirably controlling her surprise and concern, to his sister, who was watching with avid, undisguised curiosity. Well, he shouldn't be talking about Philip's lack of knowledge of his father's actions anyway. "You'll have to ask Father for more information. I don't know anything else."

Mother frowned. "Will you tell your cousin?"

"I can't now. I'm due at the port, and I may be tied up there for most of the day." And he didn't want to put this information in a note. Still, someone needed to tell Philip, and Cathal wasn't sure when Father would. "I'll tell him when I return to the palace later."

She nodded. "I'll speak with your father. We'll see you soon?"

"Of course." He took his leave of his mother and sister and strode out through the large front doors into the morning sunlight again. A servant appeared immediately with his horse. He mounted up and guided the horse out through the imposing gate, open now in anticipation of his departure. He needed to hurry if he wasn't going to be late for his appointment, and he refused to be late. He would sort out the rest later, including informing the prince.

Philip was not going to be pleased.

"YOU'LL NEVER guess what Uncle Umber has done now."

Amory turned at the sound of Philip's voice. Philip walked into the nursery still dressed for the court function they'd attended earlier, and looking every inch the prince. But he was always Pip to Amory. Philip's voice was pitched low, in deference to Amory's efforts to coax their six-month-old son to sleep, but incredulity and frustration came through despite the pitch. A sinking sensation went through Amory's midsection. Pure dread. "What now?"

Despite whatever had happened, Philip smiled when he looked at Amory and the child in his arms. Philip came closer and kissed Amory softly, resting one hand on Amory's shoulder and the other gently on their son's back. Amory leaned up into the kiss, lingering, savoring. Nearly two years together and he still couldn't get enough of kissing Philip.

When Philip finally drew back, he was still smiling. The baby blinked up at Philip owlishly from where his head rested on Amory's shoulder. Amory was still awed every time he looked at their son. Even when the baby didn't want to sleep.

"He giving you trouble?"

Amory smiled, fond despite a slight frustration. "Stubborn baby is tired but won't sleep."

"Let me try." With the ease of long practice, they transferred the baby from Amory's arms to Philip's, though Amory hated to relinquish the warm weight. Silly, he knew.

Philip settled the baby against his own shoulder and began rocking smoothly side to side. He often had better luck getting their stubborn son to sleep than Amory did. Amory liked to think it was because the stubbornness came from Philip.

"So what has Umber done now?" Knowing Umber, it could be anything.

"He's arranged a marriage for Cathal," Philip answered in the same near whisper Amory used.

Amory didn't bother to hide his surprise, though he wondered why he was so surprised in the first place. Umber's concern was always for Tournai and its royal dynasty. "We should've expected it. He's never going to let his children make their own choices about whom to marry."

Philip sighed. "I know you're right. Love and happiness aren't relevant concerns to my uncle."

Amory knew that well. "And Cathal? He's well past the age of majority. He could refuse."

"He'll go along with it."

Of course Cathal would. Duty was Cathal's one watchword. "Have you spoken with him?"

"Not yet. He was delayed at the port—he's been there all day. But I will talk to him."

Amory was not at all surprised by Philip wanting to help Cathal. Philip hated the idea of arranged marriages, and he loved Cathal, despite their recent difficulties. He would want Cathal to have the best chance at happiness.

"Cathal, of everyone, needs to find someone to love, someone to balance him," Philip added.

Amory nodded. "Do you know who Umber is considering for a bride?"

"Forget considering. He's decided and arranged the thing. Contracts have already been signed."

"What?" He barely managed to keep his voice down. Cathal was first cousin to the crown prince. By all rights, Umber should have consulted Philip first, and with how important Umber held tradition to be, it was shocking and insulting—and frankly, suspicious—that he hadn't. "Why?"

"I assume he didn't want me to interfere while he negotiated a marriage between Cathal and a cousin of the emperor of Ardunn."

Amory opened his mouth, but no words came out. A woman from Ardunn? A cousin to the emperor?

Philip must have seen enough in his expression. "Exactly."

Amory found his voice. "What is he doing?"

"That's the question." Philip craned his neck to look down at their son's face. "He's asleep."

Amory shook his head, exasperated but unable to be truly annoyed at Philip. "I don't know how you do it."

Philip flashed him a grin. "It's a gift."

He shook his head again as Philip carefully laid the baby in his cradle. But he smiled when Philip took his hand. "You're ridiculous."

"You love me anyway." Philip walked with him from the room and closed the nursery door quietly behind them.

"I do." He tried to make his voice sound long-suffering, but the laughter he couldn't quite suppress rippled through his words. If anything, Philip's grin widened. They walked hand-in-hand to their own bedchamber.

As Philip closed the door behind them, Amory returned the conversation to a more serious topic. "What do you think your uncle is up to?" He hated to bring it up, but the question needed to be asked. While Umber had been less vocal in his displeasure since the baby's birth, he certainly hadn't changed.

"Who knows?" Philip looked weary saying it, and Amory stepped forward, wanting to soothe that weariness away. He brushed Philip's hands aside and took over unbuttoning Philip's shirt. "It's obvious he wants to show his power. You know I would never interfere if he was just choosing a bride for Cathal here."

"Well, you would talk to Cathal."

"Yes." Philip sighed. "I know most marriages are arranged. That doesn't mean I'm ever going to like it. But if Cathal told me he agreed, if he at least liked the girl… I wouldn't have said anything more, and I wouldn't have disputed the choice. But Uncle Umber negotiated a marriage with an Ardunnian imperial cousin. And I can't undo it without provoking serious consequences."

And the consequences really were the issue. Amory helped Philip out of his shirt and tossed it over a chair. Before he could start on Philip's breeches, Philip reached for the fastenings to Amory's upper garments. "Why do you think he did it?"

"I don't know. Power? I just don't understand why the emperor agreed. Uncle Umber has no authority to guarantee to anything, to even negotiate anything on behalf of Tournai. What could he have promised?"

"I don't understand either." The brush of Philip's fingers over Amory's skin as he pulled off Amory's shirt made him shiver. Amory forced himself to focus. "What will you do?"

"Talk to Cathal. Find out as much as we can about this betrothal." Philip trailed his fingertips down Amory's chest. "Tomorrow."

Amory let out a long sigh. "Yes, tomorrow. For now, come to bed."

ANTONIA AQUILANTE has been making up stories for as long as she can remember and, at the age of twelve, decided she would be a writer when she grew up. After many years and a few career detours, she has returned to that original plan. Her stories have changed over the years, but one thing has remained consistent—they all end in happily ever after.

She has a fondness for travel (and a long list of places she wants to visit and revisit), taking photos, family history, fabulous shoes, baking treats that she shares with friends and family, and of course reading. She usually has at least two books started at once and never goes anywhere without her Kindle. Though she is a convert to eBooks, she still loves paper books the best, and there are a couple thousand of them residing in her home with her.

Born and raised in New Jersey, she is living there again after years in Washington, DC, and North Carolina for school and work. She enjoys being back in the Garden State but admits to being tempted every so often to run away from home and live in Italy.

Twitter: @antoniaquilante

Facebook: www.facebook.com/AntoniaAquilanteAuthor

E-mail: antonia.aquilante@gmail.com

Website: www.antoniaaquilante.com

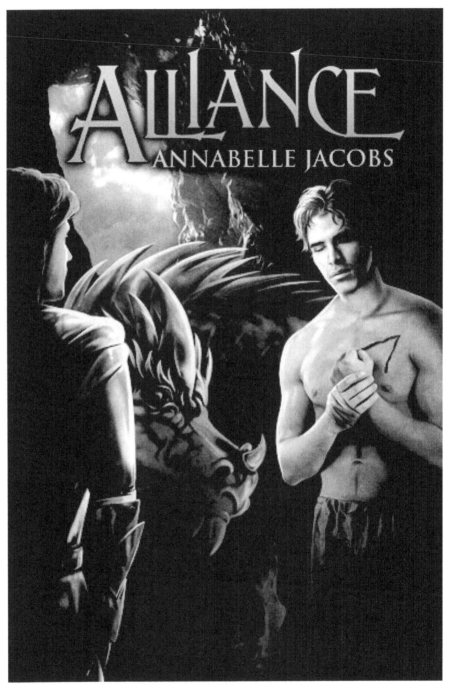

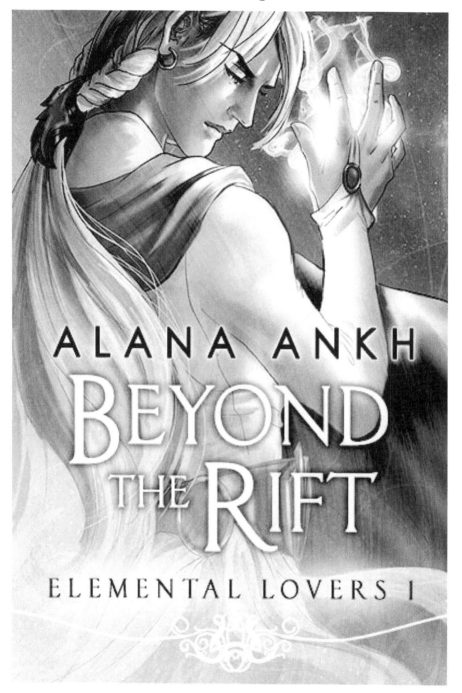

ALANA ANKH

BEYOND
THE RIFT

ELEMENTAL LOVERS 1

Also from Dreamspinner Press

www.dreamspinnerpress.com

Also from Dreamspinner Press

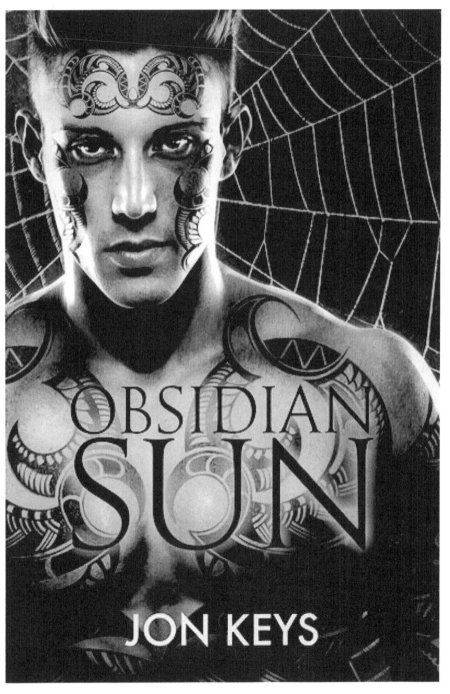

OBSIDIAN SUN

JON KEYS

www.dreamspinnerpress.com

Also from Dreamspinner Press

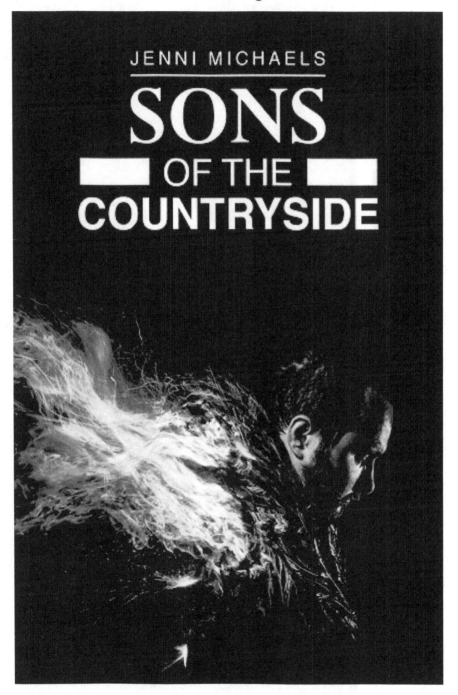

Lightning Source UK Ltd.
Milton Keynes UK
UKOW06f0618101215

264414UK00001B/169/P